KEPT

KEPT

A Victorian Mystery

D. J. Taylor

Chatto & Windus

LONDON

Published by Chatto & Windus 2006

2 4 6 8 10 9 7 5 3

Copyright © D. J. Taylor 2006

D. J. Taylor has asserted his right under the Copyright, Designs
and Patents Act 1988 to be identified as the author of this work

First published in Great Britain in 2006 by
Chatto & Windus
Random House, 20 Vauxhall Bridge Road,
London SW1V 2SA

Random House Australia (Pty) Limited
20 Alfred Street, Milsons Point, Sydney,
New South Wales 2061, Australia

Random House New Zealand Limited
18 Poland Road, Glenfield,
Auckland 10, New Zealand

Random House (Pty) Limited
Isle of Houghton, Corner of Boundary Road & Carse O'Gowrie,
Houghton, 2198, South Africa

The Random House Group Limited Reg. No. 954009
www.randomhouse.co.uk

A CIP catalogue record for this book
is available from the British Library

Hardback ISBN 0 7011 7895 7
ISBN 9780701178957 (from Jan 2007)
Trade paperback ISBN 0 7011 8036 6
ISBN 9780701180366 (from Jan 2007)

Papers used by Random House are natural,
recyclable products made from wood grown in sustainable forests;
the manufacturing processes conform to the environmental
regulations of the country of origin

Typeset by Palimpsest Book Production Limited, Polmont, Stirlingshire

Printed and bound in Great Britain by
Clays Ltd, St Ives plc

TO MY MOTHER

Contents

Please to remember that I am a Victorian, and that the Victorian tree cannot but be expected to bear Victorian fruit.

M. R. James

Beneath the signs there lay something of a different kind.

A la recherche du temps perdu

MR HENRY IRELAND

We regret to inform our readers of the death of a gentleman long known and respected in this locality. Mr Henry Ireland, who had lately returned to his estate at Theberton after some years spent in the metropolis, was found stunned by the roadside in the vicinity of Wenhaston this Thursday last, the wound sustained to his head sufficient as to altogether forestall any hope of recovery. In the opinion of Sergeant Morgan of the Suffolk constabulary, who attended the case, Mr Ireland was the victim of a tragic misadventure, his horse running away with him and precipitating him upon the hard surface of the road. The coroner's court, meeting at Woodbridge, confirmed this judgement. Mr Ireland, who had recently passed his two-and-thirtieth year, will be remembered as an enlightened landlord, a fond husband and the charitable benefactor of his parish, fully deserving of the regard in which he was held by tenant and peer alike. In token of this esteem a large and genteel congregation assembled at St Wedekind's, Theberton to witness his passing, including the Lord High Sheriff, Sir Jeremy Teazle, His Honour Judge Beeves, currently presiding at Ipswich Court, and not a few gentlemen whose names are known beyond the county in which their work is done . . . [*continues*]

Woodbridge Chronicle and Intelligencer, August 1863

DREADFUL INCIDENT AT EASTON

Police from the Watton station attending at Easton Hall this Friday last were the witnesses to a most melancholy scene. Constables Lambert and Farrer had been summoned to the property, the seat of Mr James Dixey, by Captain McTurk of the metropolitan force, who had called at the house on a private matter. The premises were at first supposed to be empty. A search of the grounds having been ordered, however, an awful discovery was made on land adjacent to the back parts of the house. Here, dreadful to remark, lay the body of an elderly man, his clothing very much disordered and his throat torn out with such savagery as to suggest the agency of a wild animal. The deceased was later identified as Mr Dixey. Constable Lambert, who said that he had seen nothing like it, confirmed that the deceased was found in the lea of a high thorn hedge and that a quantity of animal tracks, doubtless those of the beast that brought about his terrible end, could be observed in the wet earth. Further piquancy was added to this unfortunate event by the discovery of a young woman, insensible but alive, in an upper room of the house. . . . As for an explanation of this deplorable crime, none is yet forthcoming, although Captain McTurk, in a confidential communication, has assured us that the best efforts of his officers are being directed to a speedy resolution. Let us hope [&c., &c.] [*continues*]

West Norfolk Gazette, December 1866

Part One

And always there is the land.

Twenty miles to Norwich, where there is a market and a great guildhall, and the houses of the Manchester men, and all manner of manufactures and marvels. Twenty miles again to Lynn, where there are high-masted ships in the harbour and a sight of the grey North Sea. Twenty-five to Ely, set on an island in the fens. Ten to the market towns of Swaffham and Wymondham. To the East a low, flat pasture of cows and sheep, for this was wool country once, where each shearing meant a fresh stone in the church tower. To the North the lea of the Wash, where only the curlews and the sandpipers tread, and all is mud and samphire. To the West the rampart of the fen, with its dykes and causeways, which the people call cansers *and* cockeys. *To the South the fatlands, sown with corn and barley. The wind blows down from Jutland and there is nothing to stand in its way. What lies beneath it? Scrollwork of fern and lattice of ivy, and pools of sedge, great draughty halls where the wind rattles the panes like a forest of tapping hands, cottages gathered together against the lifting air. A land of winding backroads and creaking carts and windmills, a land of flood, and eels and elvers and all that comes from water, a land of silence and subterfuge, of things not said but only whispered, where much is kept secret which would be better laid open to scrutiny, of sermons preached in damp churches where scarcely a few may hear, gnarled green timber gone a-moulder and shadows winding into dark. A land of endless horizons, of grass grown up six feet high by the beaten track, of the cries of the birds, and human voices, who found it so when they came, and will leave it thus behind them when they depart.*

I

Eggmen

I will happily declare that there is no sight so harmonious to the eye
or suggestive to the spirit as Highland scenery. A man who sits on
the Metropolitan Railway to Marylebone may be comforted by what
he sees, but I do not think he will be inspired. A ziggurat raised by
some bold industrialist for the purposes of his manufacture is an
edifying spectacle, no doubt, but a mountain is moral. Philosophy
quails before it, science grows mutely respectful, and literature is both
exalted and cast down. The traveller who desires a sense of his own
insignificance will discover it here on some descending slope, down
in the shadow of some mighty summit, there beneath some rill that
has run since the dawn of time. God walks in the mountains, but it
is the mountains that will drive Him out, with their granite secrets
and the truth that lies concealed in their stone, and mankind be
reduced to an ant-like insubstantiality beside them. Or so we are told.

It was late in the afternoon of an April day in the year of Our
Lord 186–, on a steam-engine moving slowly forward – impossibly
slowly – along the Highland line through Inverness-shire, a line so
lately instituted that everything about it had an air of novelty. The
uniforms of the officials shone as if they had only that morning
arrived in bandboxes from the seamstress, the engine appeared to
have been polished up overnight, and even the passengers – subdued
Highland folk, for the most part, with their baggage piled at their
feet – seemed to have donned their best clothes for the occasion. All
this Dunbar observed from his seat in the corner of the third-class
carriage, and though grateful for the mechanised wonder that drew
him nearer his destination, he thought that he did not like it. Outside
the window the sky was darkening, so that the distant peaks and the

valley through which they ran turned red and purple, and for a moment he bent his eye on what lay beyond him rather than things nearer at hand. A herd of Highland cattle grazing the sloping moor; a woman and her child waiting patiently at a wayside crossing; a flock of birds – he knew about birds, for in a certain sense they were his profession – wheeling away to the north: all these Dunbar saw and brought together in his mind to feed his sense of dissatisfaction.

'Of course,' he said at length, 'it's not as if they're civilised folk in these parts.'

The words brought Dewar, who lay sprawled next to him on the double seat of the compartment, one arm thrown over the square teak box they had brought from Edinburgh that morning, out of his half-slumber.

'Ain't they though?'

'Surely not! Why it's not more than a century since Cumberland smoked them out and made them pay. My grandfather's father fought at Culloden. Saw a man stick a babby with a bayonet. Said it would stay with him till his dying day.'

Dewar drew himself up from his slouch and began to dust down his shirt-front with a spotted handkerchief that he took from the pocket of his coat.

'Why would a man stick a babby with a bayonet? It seems an uncommon devilish thing to do?'

A fellow-passenger, moving along the train's corridor, had that traveller peered in through the compartment window, would have seen an odd assortment of persons and their gear. Dunbar, a tall, gaunt man of perhaps fifty years of age, wore a green sporting jacket and a pair of corduroy trousers, which combination made him look not unlike a gamekeeper. Dewar, shorter and rather younger, was the more ill-favoured of the two, fat and somewhat unhealthy-looking, his costume completed by a shabby frock-coat of which the braid was beginning to part company with the lapels. Rolled up in bundles on luggage racks, or strewn about on the floor, lay a variety of miscellaneous items, each of which posed some question as to the object of their journey: a pair of heavy walking boots, two cork life jackets, a woollen scarf and a coiled length of rope. Dewar's gaze, which had fallen for a moment or two on the square teak box, widened to take in this further cargo.

'We seem to have brought a deal of stuff with us. How are we to carry it all, I should like to know?'

Something in the set of Dunbar's eye perhaps disclosed that he did not regard his associate with complete confidence. 'I can see you're new to this game, my boy. Green you are indeed. Why, when we get to the other end there'll be a gig to meet us. Take us right to where we want to go as well, I shouldn't wonder.'

There was an unspoken question in this statement which the younger man either did not appreciate or chose not to answer. But his companion persisted.

'What line of trade was you in before Bob Grace pushed you my way?'

'Grocer.'

Something in this spoke of ruinous mischance, of hope denied, tragedy even. Another man would have given up the pursuit, but Dunbar continued easily.

'General or green stuff?'

'General.'

'Any reason for giving it up?'

Dewar stared before him at the cork life jackets draped over the opposing seat. 'Wife took bad and I had to nurse her. It's hard on a fellow when that happens.'

'Harder still when she dies. Very hard. Here, have a fill of this and you'll feel better.'

They smoked Dunbar's tobacco companionably for a while, nodding at the people who wandered along the corridor and resting their feet on their bundles. It was now perhaps half past four in the afternoon and the light was growing grey. Outside the land continued to rise, and there were shadows creeping down among the granite escarpments of the hills. The day was drawing in. Dunbar was not an imaginative man – a rock to him was a rock which might have to be scaled, a mountain stream the hazard of wet feet – but nonetheless something of the bleakness of the prospect communicated itself to him and he clasped his hands together against a cold that he could not yet feel but knew would come.

'D——t! This ain't Piccadilly Circus, by George! Did you ever see such a place?'

Dewar, less impressionable even than his mentor, stared vaguely beyond the window. 'They say Highland air's very bracing. I believe that's the case. Will it snow, do you reckon?'

'I shouldn't wonder. I took an eagle's nest in a blizzard once, twenty miles south of here at Loch Garten, and had three fingers bitten by the frost. No trains in those days. Nor a path for a pony either. Why, the fellow I was with, he and I had to haul our boat over the hills to reach the river.'

The words seemed to waken in Dewar a curiosity that had previously been lacking in him. Rubbing his small eyes with the flat of one hand and knocking his pipe out on the iron casing of the carriage window with the other, he cleared his throat once or twice, looked as if he were about to speak and then thought better of it.

'You look as if you wanted to say something,' Dunbar chided him. 'Why don't you let it out?'

'You're a professional man. You'll only laugh at me like as not. But never mind, I will say it. Why would a man pay good money for you to bring him eggs?'

Dunbar beat his hand sharply on his knees. 'Why, there are any number of queer trades. There are fellows in London who collect up slop pails and sell what's in them for fertiliser. You'll have seen them about their business. I knew a man that traded in dolls' eyes – blue, brown and green, only the green ones was a farthing a dozen dearer. Why shouldn't a man take ospreys' eggs, or eagles', if he's a mind?'

'He can't eat them.'

'I daresay he can't. But he can look at them. Haven't you got anything that you sits and looks at?'

Dewar thought. 'My wife had a fancy for china dogs once. As much as a shilling she'd pay for a china dog at Hoxton market. But there isn't no china dogs now.'

'There you are. China dogs. Waterloo medals – look at the market there is for them. Why, I was at the sea once, Devon way, and there was a dozen folk out under the cliff looking for those rarey stones that are made so much of. Fossils, they call them. But what we're after, there's few enough of them to be had now. Take these ospreys, that the people here call eagle fishers. They don't come to Loch an Eilein crag no more. It's six years since I've taken from Loch Morlich. There may be nests at Loch Arkaig, I don't know. But think of it! These might be the last of them in all England. That's worth a ten pound note if ever a thing was.'

'And what if there aren't no more?' Dewar wondered.

'What about if there aren't? I had a gentleman come to me the other day – a clergyman he was, many of them's from the clergy – enquiring of auks' eggs. Now there hasn't been an auk seen in these parts for a century. On St Kilda's perhaps, or Shetland, but not here. There are some that would have given him guillemot with a touch of dye, but I'm not one of that kind, which is perhaps a weakness in me.'

He lapsed into silence, perhaps imagining that he had said too much. Dewar thought regretfully of the china dogs that had once processed over the mantelpiece in Hoxton and now, like certain other things, were gone from his life.

'We shall be there soon, I suppose?' he ventured.

'Yes, we shall be there soon. You had better help me pick up these things.'

Together, swaying a little against the rhythm of the engine, they began to reduce the mass of luggage to some kind of order. This task accomplished, Dunbar selected a thick great-coat from the topmost sack and placed it over his shoulders. Beyond the window he saw that twilight was falling. A furious tawny sun hung low over the further-most crags so that their sharply descending slopes seemed livid in its shadow. Skeins of birds flew north above their heads, following the train's course for a moment and then veering away into invisibility. Dewar looked up.

'What kind of birds is they?'

'Black-backed gulls. Petrels. Nothing there for us.' He resumed his position at the window. 'Put on your coat, man. There'll be an end to trains before too long.'

Doing as he was bidden – his own coat was a threadbare affair from which the buttons hung by solitary threads – Dewar sensed that the train had begun to reduce its speed. A great black hedge shot up suddenly to the left of them, so near that he could have reached out from the window and plucked at the trees. In the distance there was a glimmer of water. Then, in what seemed only an instant of time, the darkness receded and the tawny light illumined their surround-ings once more. They were travelling – rolling – gently descending – at ever decreasing speed and with a great shudder of brakes through a country of flat fields and broken stones, at whose outer edge a spur of dark forest could be seen approaching from higher ground to the north.

'This is the place,' Dunbar announced. 'I recollect it.' He saw Dewar's face, somehow mournful in the gloaming as he bent to retrieve his kit. 'Come now. There are worse trades for a man to follow.'

5

'It's not work that I'm used to,' Dewar volunteered. For a moment Dunbar thought that he could see him in his grocery, obsequious behind the counter, hands dusty with flour, meal sticking in his sparse hair. Near stationary now, the train shook convulsively once or twice and then came to a halt. 'But I hope I shall give satisfaction.'

Dunbar did not answer, but seized the first of their bags and began to heave it to the door. It was no more than a halt – a long, low platform with a granite slab for a seat, a single lantern, a pair of stone outhouses at the further end and a solitary attendant gaping at them from behind a muffler. Beyond the clump of buildings a narrow road descended through the fields. Here a pony and trap waited in the gathering dusk. Dunbar saw it and sniffed.

'I don't doubt Mackay to be the most punctual man in Strathspey. Here, see if the place runs to a handcart.'

His voice was lost in the noise of the engine's wheels as they began once more to revolve. A cloud of steam, blown back on the wind, enveloped them both in dense white vapour. The station attendant said something in a broad Scots accent that Dewar could not interpret. There was no handcart. He began miserably to arrange the baggage in a kind of pyramid upon the granite seat, while Dunbar went to greet a tall figure with a mastiff dog at his heels who now loomed into view at the further end of the platform.

'Mackay,' Dunbar said on their return. He seemed strangely exhilarated, poking at a strip of his shirt-collar levered up by the wind. 'Invaluable factotum to the gentry. The laird's right-hand man, forbye. Whose own great-grandfather brought the Prince over from Skye in a row-boat, or so they say. Is that not right, Mackay?'

'I'll thank you to hold your tongue, Dunbar,' said the laird's right-hand man. Dewar could not tell if he was amused or made angry by this familiarity. 'That's a deal of clutter ye've brought with ye.'

'But you'll carry it for us, Mackay. Is that not right?'

'There's snow coming, I have no doubt. I can take you to the boat-house. And maybe return in the morning. But no further, mind.'

'Suit yourself, old party.' Again Dewar caught the lilt in his companion's voice. 'Suit yourself.'

Silently they began to load their belongings onto the cart. It was quite noiseless now, except for the rumble of the train as it descended into the valley beyond them, altogether dark save for the sparks flying up along the track which danced for a moment in the air above the engine stack and then fell back into nothingness. Dunbar stopped in his loading to watch its progress, murmured something unintelligible under his breath and then resumed his labours. Presently, illumined by the pale light of Mackay's lantern, the cart bore them away down the hill, past thickets of pine trees, a mass of undergrowth in which something unseen moved briefly for a second and then was gone out of the lantern's range.

'There's no wolves, are there, in these parts?' Dewar wondered cravenly.

Dunbar laughed. 'No, no wolves. Not for a hundred years and more. That was a fox, most like. Or a marten. But no wolves.'

It was by now quite dark, and with an absence of moon that, Dunbar calculated, boded ill for the night's activity. Something of the place's immensity now communicated itself to him – a silence that, he acknowledged, proceeded from the entire absence of man – and he fell quiet, recalling similar excursions: walking twenty miles from Grantown once in the middle of a snowstorm; a journey into the upper reaches of Norway where in the few hours of daylight the sun seemed to hang on the rim of the horizon like the yolk of an egg. At the same time his eye began to accustom itself to the terrain and its distinctive character: the cracked stone on the path that glittered in the lantern light; dense banks of fir heralding the innermost parts of the glen; what his memory told him was the smell of water borne back over the tree-tops. The mastiff dog, huddled up at his master's feet, caught some second scent and moved its muzzle restlessly. They were nearing their destination.

'Stop the cart!' Dewar cried suddenly. His face, caught in the lantern glare, was unnaturally white: submerged, Dunbar thought, like the underside of a fish thrown breathless upon the river bank. 'Stop the cart, sir, I beg you.'

Mackay jerked on the reins. 'Why, what ails you?'

Dewar took in a gulp of air. A fish, Dunbar thought again: the belly of a trout turned up from the Wensum or the Yare. 'I must . . . That is . . . A man has to relieve himself occasionally,' he protested. 'I've had no opportunity since Edinburgh.'

'A nervous creature, that,' Mackay remarked, as a series of violent detonations marked Dewar's progress into the undergrowth.

'He'll do,' Dunbar said. 'It's little enough he's getting. And at least he'll stay dry.'

'He may not, for all that.'

Shamefacedly, Dewar returned to the cart. The warm aroma of excrement trailed behind him. So woebegone did he appear that Dunbar, conscious of the hours that stretched before them, determined to lighten the younger man's spirits.

'Come, Dewar, this will never do. We must take you out of yourself, indeed we must. Look, this is where our journey takes us. Did you ever see such a spot?'

The sight towards which he now extended his hand, as the cart came suddenly out of the forest's edge and onto the fresh turf, was certainly a magnificent one, whether seen by day or night. Illumined now by faint streaks of moonlight, the loch stretched for perhaps a mile beyond them, falling away at its uttermost extremity into impenetrable borders of trees grown right up to the water's edge. Cold and depthless the water seemed, black in the moonlight, its surface ruffled here and there by the tremor of the wind but otherwise undisturbed. In the very midst of it, so centrally placed that it seemed to accord to some geometrical plan, lay a small island topped by a cairn of rock. This, closer inspection revealed to be a ruin some twelve or fifteen feet high, the topmost ramparts altogether crumbled and fallen away. As they watched, a dark shape moved off the surface of the water a quarter of a mile distant, soared briefly into the night sky beyond the tree wall and then was gone.

'There's our tenant,' Dunbar remarked. 'What will he say when he finds the bailiffs have called, I wonder?'

A little way along the loch's surround, at a point where an inlet dipped into the forest, they found a boathouse, very blear and empty in the darkness, with a couple of canoes hung on hooks from the wall and a nest of field mice that scurried away at the approach of Mackay's lantern. Dunbar stood by the glassless window, clapping his hands together against the cold, as between them Dewar and Mackay unloaded the baggage. In his mind he was calculating shrewdly, but the nature of the calculation was lost on the other men, both of whom now regarded him expectantly as the great mastiff dog loped around the hut poking its nose into the empty nest and worrying out an abandoned straw hat from beneath the table.

'You'd best be off, Mackay,' he said. 'You have business to attend to, no doubt. Back after the dawn, mind. You can leave the lamp.' The Scotsman gave a nod and moved off into the darkness, the dog

8

following at his heels. 'Now,' he went on, 'we've work to do. Attend to me, if you please.' As Dewar watched uncertainly, he slipped out of his great-coat and began to tug open the buttons of his green jacket.

'What's that you're doing?'

'What does it look like that I'm doing? However else do you suppose a man could reach the rock?'

'I thought we might . . .' Dewar gestured at the two canoes.

'Both in need of caulking and not a paddle in sight. No, I'll not drown in an upturned coracle. Not while I can swim. Here, take this.'

Standing in his underthings, as he strapped the cork life jacket around his chest, Dunbar indicated a bundle of rope that he had taken from a sack. 'Now, tie the end to this loop here. A good strong knot.' Wondering, Dewar did as he was bid. 'This is our means of contact, d'you see?' Dunbar went on. 'A single tug and you're to draw me in. Two pulls and there's danger.'

'What am I to do then?'

'Do? Why, pull on the other jacket and swim out to find me! Come, let's be off.'

They moved out once again into the silence of the loch, two tiny figures swallowed up in space and silence. Dewar felt something light yet piercing strike against his forehead. It was a snowflake. He clutched at it and felt it melt between his fingers.

'It's cold enough,' he muttered.

'And you haven't even to swim. Take the rope!' They were at the water's edge now. Dewar felt his feet sink into mud. Without turning Dunbar slid into the water, like an otter, immersing himself limb by limb until only his head and shoulders remained above the surface. 'Here's luck!' he called back. Then with a powerful overarm stroke he launched himself out into the moving blackness.

Alone on the bank, Dewar tried at first to keep his eye fixed on his companion's bobbing head. Within fifty yards, however, it had vanished altogether. After that he bent his mind on the noise of Dunbar splashing, but after a moment or two even this passed out of earshot. He looked vainly at the rope, which lay coiled in his hand, and wondered what he would do if there came two tugs on it. It was certainly very cold. Narrowing the range of his vision, he strained to glimpse the outcrop to which his friend was headed, but found only shadow, vague shapes of nothing in the dark air. He was quite alone, he realised, altogether thrown upon his own resources. A sudden thrill of terror struck through his body. Was that a twitch on the rope? No, he assured himself, it was merely the coil playing out as Dunbar swam on. A moment or two passed: Dewar had no means of knowing how long. Then, from far off, from some place he could not see, high over the lake, there came a shriek of something – human or animal, he could not determine – which sent him into a paroxysm of fear. The rope, he observed, had ceased to play out. Despairing, he pulled on it himself but there was no response. It hung slack in the water, disappearing from sight only a yard or two from his feet.

What was to be done? There was a box of sulphur matches in his pocket and remembering them he pulled one forth and struck it on the heel of his boot, but the wind caught it and extinguished it almost from the moment of its striking. What was to be done, he asked himself again. He resolved to fetch the lantern from the boathouse, and then told himself that this would be the action of a fool. There was more snow falling now, gently descending on his scalp, on his shoulders, on the coil of rope that still lay in his hand, and he watched it with a kind of benevolent detachment. Surely it was too cold for a man to swim out there in the frozen lake? What should he do if his companion failed to return? He was conscious that, apart from believing that he had been set down in Inverness-shire, he barely knew where he was, that he possessed no return railway ticket – this was in Dunbar's care – nor the means of purchasing one. All these thoughts tumbled about his head and oppressed him in a way that was immeasurably increased by the solitariness of the place and the lateness of the hour. A man could die out here, he thought, could perish under a rowan bush or out on the open moor and not be found. What if he were to be that man? He had a sudden vision of himself dancing helplessly through driven snow, falling to his knees as the drifts piled up above his head.

Almost without apprehending that the thing was upon him, he became aware of a disturbance away to his left, out in what seemed to be the darkest part of the lake: a shout – undoubtedly a human voice – and a splashing of water. The rope jerked so violently in his hand that for a second it fell from his grasp into the mud. Seizing it he began to pull with what seemed to him superhuman industry, staring all the while into the blackness before him. 'Dunbar,' he called into the raw air. 'Where are you? Answer me.' But there was no more shouting, only the slow, steady noise of someone beating a path through the water towards him and a black lump that, through some mysterious agency of the light, suddenly declared itself to be a human figure swimming on its back.

'Gracious heavens, Dunbar, is that you?'

Teeth chattering, water cascading from the extremities of his body, Dunbar made his way through the shallows. He seemed in excellent spirits.

'Who the devil did you think it was? And why didn't you pull the first time I tugged on the rope, eh? But never mind, it's all well that ends well – look here!' He extended his hands, palms upwards, and Dewar saw that in each lay a small ruddy-brown egg. 'Quick, man, to the boathouse, and the whisky, or I shall perish of cold.'

Later Dewar would remember the strangeness of the scene: the snow continuing to fall over the silent lake; himself on his knees in the doorway of the hut attempting to light a fire out of brushwood and old paper; an owl calling out in the trees and contending with Dunbar's voice as, towelling himself with a piece of rough cloth, he recounted his exploits.

'I got over quite safe – it was a distance of a quarter mile, perhaps, no further – and tied the rope to a stone. The cock bird flew off before I reached the island. After I had climbed up to the top of the ruin and was just on the nest I put out my hand to catch the hen, but when she felt me she gave a scream and shied away also. Anyway, I took two eggs and was thankful for them. The question was: how to carry them, for in my haste I had forgotten my cap. I tried putting one egg in my mouth but I could not breathe with it. There was nothing to do, I decided, but to swim ashore on my back with an egg in each hand. Which is how you found me. Still, I have had worse journeys. Now, be a good fellow. Step outside and fetch me a reed from the shore.'

'A reed, did you say?'

'Naturally. How else am I to blow the eggs?'

'Blow them, you say?'

Dewar went shivering out into the night and stumbled to the shore. The reed fetched, Dunbar trimmed it with his knife until he had fashioned a tiny straw three or four inches in length and pointed at one end. Then, craning towards the lamplight with the first egg in his palm he made a tiny mark in the shell with the tip of his knife. This done, he inserted the straw and placed the blunt end between his lips. 'You suck away, see, and then discharge the yolk' – he spat suddenly and a gob of white, viscous slime spattered onto the floor – 'thus. There is no art to it. Then rinse the inside with a little of this whisky, line your travelling case with some moss, and we are done.'

And so they laboured on for half an hour or so, as the fire burned down to its embers and the snowflakes fell hissing onto the hot coals, so that a passer-by chancing to peer through the boathouse window might have thought Dunbar's gaunt, bony face that of an old wizard instructing his protégé in the magical arts and the eggs some rare treasure sprung from their devisings.

Dunbar whistled as he worked, or sang snatches of the Skye Boat Song. He seemed in the highest spirits still, his manner ever more confidential and mysterious.

'You see, we are getting on famously,' he remarked at one point. 'You must come and look me up in London, indeed you must. 18 Watling Street, above the chandler's, will find me when I'm not at my business.'

Then something else struck him and he said:

'That was a bad business in Suffolk, to be sure.'

'What business was that?' Dewar wondered.

'You don't know? Or perhaps you are a cleverer fellow than I take you to be and pretend not to know?'

'I know nothing.'

'At any rate it was a secret that should have been kept and has not been. But let us say no more about it.'

And so the lamplight flickered, the snow fell desultorily over the loch, the mice came scurrying back beneath the boathouse door and nothing more was said about it.

II

Mr Henry Ireland
and his Leavings

At the time at which our story commences, Mr Henry Ireland of
Theberton in the county of Suffolk had been dead a year. It is perhaps
necessary to say of this gentleman only that he was subject to the
gravest misfortune. Black care had waylaid him and flung him from
his horse, and though he had struggled to regain his seat and continued
on his way it was to find his assailant ever grinning from the saddle
behind him. And yet there was a singularity about Mr Ireland's tribu-
lations sufficient to imbue them with a terrible pathos. Who does not
know the man who is ruined in an instant, so to speak, who break-
fasts very heartily with his wife and children, only to arrive at his
counting house to find the blinds still drawn, the funds fallen and the
clerks whispering among themselves? Such men, if they possess forti-
tude and friends, can generally salvage something from the wreck.
Rothschild was a bankrupt once, they say, and Lord Palmerston's
stamped paper the delight of the bill-discounters.

On the contrary, Mr Ireland's misfortunes had crept up on him
by stealth, so gradually in fact that he barely glimpsed their approach.
At the age of twenty-five, on the death of his father, he had come
into his property. The enthusiasm with which the young man set up
as squire would have touched the heart of the stoniest philosopher.
He proposed to make a study of agriculture, to import breeding cattle
from the continent, to build model cottages, even, for his tenants.
There was nothing, in fact, that might not have been done, could the
payment have been received in good intentions rather than ready
money. But then it was discovered that Mr Ireland senior had encumbered the estate with debt and that there was, in addition, an entail

that no man, and certainly no lawyer, could break. After this Mr Ireland junior gave up his schemes of marsh drainage and tenants' cottages and retired to London to live off his rents.

All this, however, would have counted as nothing to the young man – would have mattered to him as little as the fine Suffolk rain – had he succeeded in his chief ambition. This, it may be flatly stated, was the gaining of a wife whose hand would be worth the winning, whom he could love and be loved by in return, and whose affection would be the lasting glory of his days. Such paragons are not easily found, and yet Mr Ireland, in the weeks before his marriage, had dared to hope that he had secured one. He was at this time a man of thirty: soft-voiced and even-tempered, well-disposed towards his fellow men, conscious of the failure of his agricultural schemes, but resolved that, as a husband and a father, he would conquer the world anew. Many men have made such resolves, and many have wished that they could make them. Alas, it was here – here in the hour of his nuptial triumph, as the very orange blossoms descended on his hymeneal carriage – that Mr Ireland's troubles began.

At the time of his marriage, which took place at St George's, Hanover Square, and was reported in the fashionable newspapers (for Mr Ireland wanted the world to know of the grand prize he had brought down), Miss Isabel Brotherton was a young woman of three- or four-and-twenty: of medium height, graceful in her carriage and with abundant auburn hair of which it was said that Titian might have painted it. Her father, now dead, had been a literary man, it is true, but of an altogether superior kind. Dickens had called at his house, and duchesses pressed him to attend their parties. Mr Thackeray himself had stood pall-bearer at his funeral, and a royal prince subscribed five guineas to his memorial edition. And so Mr Ireland felt that in the matter of station, though he might have done worse, he could not have done better.

Of all the things in the world, perhaps, a marriage is the most perplexing to write of. Who can tell whether Mr Brief, of Her Majesty's Northern Circuit, the proud father of three bouncing girls and the proud owner of an elegant stucco house in Kensington Square, is a happy man, and whether his Drusilla, formerly Miss Bates of Cheam, is all to him that she should be? By the same token who knows whether, on the days when her lord and master quits her for the Northern Circuit, Mrs Brief does not creep away into her bedroom and weep bitter tears for the hardness of her life? At any rate Mr Ireland, seeing his wife as she stood before him, felt that he was a happy man and the friends to whom he opened his doors said that he was a lucky fellow and that Mrs Ireland was a woman of spirit. For myself, I am inclined to agree with them. There are, heaven knows, some women to whom the duty of hospitality is merely that, who bid you to their table with the same air that they rattle florins in the church collection plate, but Mrs Ireland was not among their number. Though she spoke little herself, she had a way of listening to those who did that mingled the highest seriousness and the richest mirth, and the gentlemen who snuffed up her husband's beefsteaks and sampled his claret went away convinced that they had eaten a very agreeable dinner. As to their wives, well, I am not certain that Mrs Ireland was altogether a great favourite among ladies. She had a habit, in a soft, feminine way, of poking fun, of saying sharp little words that were remembered long after her smiles and her solicitations were forgotten.

'As to having nobility in the house, I am sure I should make some dreadful blunder,' she once exclaimed to Mrs Desmond de Lacey, 'serve up peas out of season or forget which was a Liberal and which was a Conservative.' Mrs Desmond de Lacey, whose husband was the younger son of a cousin of the Marquis of Lothian, laughed, but I do not think she liked it. Happily there were enough people who did like it to make an invitation to Mrs Ireland's drawing room worth the having for a while, and Mr Ireland, as I have said, watching his wife among the tea cups, or telling Lord Fawkes that he was the wickedest old man alive, thought that he was happy. There was a child, and the child died, but though Mr Ireland mourned sincerely he did not allow this mischance to prey upon his mind. There would be other children, nurseries full of them, the gardens of Eccleston Square would ring with their voices. And yet it seemed to him in the months after the infant's death that a change had come over his wife. She grew melancholy, no longer smiled at her dinner guests or told Lord Fawkes, to his lordship's great delight, that he was the naughtiest old sinner in Christendom. Her sharp words grew sharper, her gaze less placid. A judge's wife went away in tears from the house in Eccleston Square and her friends said that Mrs Ireland was deranged with grief.

All this Mr Ireland observed with the most painful unease. It seemed to him that it behoved him to speak to his wife, without having the least idea of what he ought to say, that soft words were needed, but of a subtlety that was altogether beyond his power to frame. Finally, one afternoon in February when the square lay invisible in the fog, having spent the morning brooding over his dilemma, he approached a drawing room on an upper floor of the house in which it was his wife's custom to spend her leisure hours. She was seated in a small armchair with her hands clasped in her lap, and though her eyes were open it seemed to him that she scarcely saw him and that his very presence in the room was painful to her. But he was a courageous man in his fashion and he determined to speak the sentences he had come to say.

'My dear,' he said, 'it seems to me that you are very unhappy.'

'You are right,' she said, not looking up from her chair. 'I am very unhappy. And yet if I am it is my responsibility, and mine to bear.'

There was something so dreadful in these words that he was quite nonplussed. It seemed to him that, in these circumstances, nothing he could say would have any effect. And yet, however savage might be his reception, he knew that he had a tougher skin than the judge's lady and that to say nothing were simple cowardice.

'My dear,' he began again. 'Isabel. You are labouring under a great grief.'

Again she did not look up, but continued to stare fixedly at her lap. 'That is so. It is a great grief. I had hoped it was a shared one. If that were so, it would be easier to bear.'

He understood that this was a reproach, and the words were torture to him. But he could think of nothing to say, was merely conscious of a faint terror of things unseen, things altogether beyond him but capable of reaching out to strike him a mortal blow. Standing thus in this irresolute state, not knowing whether to stay or go, he found his attention drawn to his wife's hands, which were turning ceaselessly, as it seemed to him, over a twist of some pale material held in her lap. This motion of her fingers, though disagreeable to him, was somehow fascinating, and he studied it for a full half-minute before enquiring:

'Isabel. What is it that you have there?'

She looked up at him, but blindly, so that even now he fancied that she did not see him. 'It is a lock of the child's hair, cut from his head on the morning that he died. Surely you must remember that?'

He did remember it – remembered it as if it had happened but a moment ago – but there was something in her attitude, some secret steeliness, that he feared to provoke. Her face, seen in the shadow of the room, seemed very white. Outside the lamps were being lit, one by one, in the square. At length he said:

'I would not give you further pain for all the world. There are people coming tonight. It cannot be helped. Shall I have them turned away? You have only to speak and it shall be done.'

'No, do not send them away.' She rose suddenly to her feet, and the twist of hair fell fluttering to the Turkey carpet. 'I have been weak. But I shall be strong. You had better go now, Henry, if you would be so kind.'

That evening she dashed a wineglass over the tablecloth, shrieked that her husband meant to murder her and was led away in hysterics. After this people ceased to say that Mrs Ireland was a woman of spirit and she retired altogether from polite society.

What was to be done? Mr Ireland, in his distracted state, was of the opinion that doctors were needed. Let doctors be summoned! Let the house in Eccleston Square be turned into a sanatorium if it would stop his wife from swearing that he meant to kill her and crooning over a twist of a child's hair in her lap! The doctors who examined her were cautious. There was no sign of organic disease, they assured Mr Ireland, but perhaps his wife might benefit from a change of air. A sea voyage, a tour around the Swiss lakes, a month or two at the continental spas sampling the waters – all these were proposed by the deferential gentlemen who stood in Mr Ireland's drawing room as a cure for his wife's lowness of spirits. And meanwhile perhaps it might be best to keep Mrs Ireland from company, late nights and associations that might be – distressing to her.

Mr Ireland received this advice with the gravest misgivings. And yet, he assured himself, all was not lost. His wife was estranged from him, but it might be possible, if care were exercised, to win her back. To this end, and mindful of certain ancient connections of his family, he arranged a journey to the country with which he shared his name. Even in the pit of his anxieties, the thought was pleasant to him. An inn or a castle or hilltop where he and his wife could be to one another as they had been in the early days of their marriage – all this, surely, would supply a balm beyond the realm of medicine? And so a passage was booked on the Bristol to Cork ferry for the last day of April and, in a closed carriage, accompanied by a single servant, the Irelands set off. It was a fortnight since Easter and the flowers were out in the Wiltshire lanes as they rolled by. What occurred during the three weeks they were away I am not at liberty to say – Mr Ireland would not speak of it even to his closest friends – but there were no inns, or castles, or hilltops. And from the day of their return there was no more talk of lowness of spirits. The deferential gentlemen who had advised sea voyages and Swiss lakes and the pump room at Baden Baden were all thrown over, and the celebrated Dr Conolly, of whom the world knows, was summoned to give an opinion. Like those he had supplanted, Dr Conolly was a prudent man. He would not say that his patient was – mad. But perhaps it might be better if Mrs Ireland were to be removed from Eccleston Square and to a place where care might be taken that she should not – injure herself. Throughout these proceedings Mrs Ireland was confined to her room, and the door of the room was locked with an iron bolt.

Not the least of our misfortunes is their mockery of bygone hopes. A month after his return to England, Mr Ireland discovered a parcel thrown amongst the discarded trifles of his dressing room. It contained a copy of Mr Thackeray's *Irish Sketchbook*, which Mr Ireland had thought it well to carry with him while he surveyed the castles and the hilltops, and a nosegay of flowers presented to his wife on a bright morning in Cork before certain dreadful events of which he could not bring himself to speak. And it seemed to Mr Ireland, examining these items as he stood in his dressing room with the sun streaming in through the casement window, that his life was ruined and that the book and the flowers were far more a testimony to his wretchedness than the woman in the next room. Failure lay all around him. He had inherited a property, and the property had crumbled to ashes in his hands. He had married a wife, and Dr Conolly would say only that extreme caution and tender ministrations might yet produce a favourable result. At any rate, Mr Ireland assured himself, there should be no more pretence, whether as regarded himself or the world at large. The house in Eccleston Square was shut and the servants paid off, the gardens where he had been wont to walk on summer afternoons given up to nursemaids and their charges, and Mr and Mrs Ireland departed to Suffolk and fell altogether out of the life they had known.

It may be wondered whether there is anything more instructive than the person who disappears in this way. A man pursues his professional calling in a certain street, let us say, for twenty years, eats his dinner in a certain chop-house, talks with certain cronies, and then, mysteriously, is gone. Who notices his passing or remembers him? The agent's board is up above his chambers for a fortnight until a new tenant engages them, the waiter at the chop-house regrets his patron for a day or so – that is all. So it was with the Irelands. Such of their friends as wrote letters received courteous but unforthcoming replies. A pertinacious gentleman who proposed a visit was told roundly that the state of Mrs Ireland's health would not permit it. And thus the Irelands slipped altogether out of view, so that they might have died or followed the emigrant trail to Oregon for all that anyone knew. For there are some mysteries that are always hidden, and some secrets that are for ever kept.

*

GEORGE ELIOT'S JOURNAL

22 March 1862

A bright day of radiant sunshine, not the least inclemency. George engrossed in literary tasks, articles for the *Cornhill*, writing to Mr Martin anent his translations &c. I, having no other occupation, spent the afternoon in reverie, reading Mr Hutton in the *Spectator* – at least I supposed it were Mr Hutton – on Arnold's last words on translating Homer. Thence to dine with the Irelands at their house in Eccleston Square. This I was interested to see: a pleasant, commodious residence, the rooms all crammed with dull, old furniture, scarlet draperies. A profusion of mirrors, many portraits of old gentlemen in periwigs. A dozen of us sat down: a sucking barrister from Lincoln's Inn, Mr Masson who writes for the magazines and a silent wife, a literary man whom George recalled from some endeavour lost in time. With Mr Ireland I was, of course, familiar. A conventional kind of a man, I should suppose: tall, ruddy-faced, soft-spoken, talking a little of his property in Suffolk (it is embarrassed, George says, and a source of shame to him) and equestrian pleasures, solicitous of his wife. I acknowledge freely that it was she to whom my eye turned the more often: a slight, sorrowful woman with exquisite (there is no other word) red hair – I would have run my hands through it, negotiated to buy it at six shillings the yard like some Russian huckster – in whom deep reservoirs of feeling contended with the topics of the day. In short, a decidedly unusual representative of the female species, and yet some deep unhappiness so manifest in her that it pained the heart to see. Thus, on my asking would she and her husband go away this season, she replied with great emphasis: *Go away? Why, I have been drifting rudderless for too long.* This seemed such a singular expression that I enquired: what did she mean by it? She replied with perfect politeness and yet, it seemed to me, great private misgivings that there were times when she *felt like a boat rowing on the ebb tide and could not for the life of her steer herself to safety.* Mr Ireland, I saw, was watching her closely and here interjected, 'My wife has peculiar fancies, Miss Evans.' Although there was suavity in the words I fancy they were troublesome to pronounce.

Meanwhile the dinner was proceeding around us – soup, cutlets, a beefsteak, none of which was sufficient to distract the eye from the curious intelligence at my side. As the meal continued, Mrs Ireland's behaviour became more singular still. While the servants were clearing the savoury from the table I observed her carefully decant the contents of a salt cellar upon the tablecloth. This task accomplished, she availed herself of a half-empty glass that lay nearby and, with infinite care and solicitude, began to drip claret wine upon the salt. All this with a look of such stealth – cunning, rapt introspection – as to suggest an animal bent on evading capture. Fascinated, and somehow liking her for this absorption, I enquired again: what was she doing. *To be sure*, she replied, *was it not well known that salt was a sovereign remedy for spilled wine? And would not the servants thank her for it in the morning?*

I had hoped for further converse but, on retiring with the other ladies, I noticed that she was gone. Indeed we had not been a moment over our negus before Mr Ireland appeared to announce that his wife was indisposed and had been conducted to bed by her maid &c. I will confess that I missed her presence in that little room – talk all of the Queen, the Duchess of A——'s ball – would have liked her there, if only to drip claret onto the tablecloth, and that the rest of the evening had no pleasure for me. Reflecting on these incidents I felt that I had observed a rare and generous spirit, yet struggling to convey some great distress of which it was perhaps only partly aware: the effect disturbing to the mind, a life wreathed in shadow breaking out now and again in hard, bitter laughter. George, to whom I explained something of this, *unhappy*: said that Mrs Ireland's afflictions were well known, her husband near beside himself with anxiety. All this, I found, worked on me very curiously – the silent woman in her house of dull old furniture and serried mirrors – to the point where, the following day, I determined to call, neglected an article I had promised to Mr Chapman and took an omnibus to the further end of the Buckingham Palace Road. Alas, it was a fool's errand. The house seemed quiet, the blinds drawn down, with only a little servant girl in a creased mob cap to tell me that 'Master and Missus' had gone away that morning to the country, although the number of coats, hats, etc., upon the hallway hooks suggested that, if this were the case, they had taken very little of their clothing with them. And so I took my leave and walked for a while in the Square's gardens, past the nursery maids and their carriages and the small boys with their hoops, musing on the peculiar circumstances to which I had been witness, casting an occasional glance at the house, from whose upper window, I am tolerably certain at one point, a woman's face stared balefully down . . .

*

Jas Dixey, Esq.
Easton Hall
Near Watton
Norfolk

My dear Dixey,
    Although our acquaintance is not so very intimate, yet you are the man that my father always said that he respected most and have ever been a friend to me. Be assured, then, that I should not have cared to burden you with this letter were it not for the extremity in which I have been plunged. In truth I have been so sorely tested this last month and more that I have not known which way to turn. You will perhaps more fully comprehend the pain of these afflictions if I say at the outset that not one particle of what follows is exaggerated, coloured or in any way distorted in the telling.
    You will have heard – who has not? – of our troubles. It was ever the case that when a man stands well before the world, the world is silent, yet, should adversity strike, the air is filled with clamorous voices. Thinking that sea and country air might be beneficial, I proposed a tour of the southern counties of Ireland (we had property there once, in Roscommon, though, alas, the

estate is fallen into ruin). To this, in a lucid moment, Isabel heartily
assented. Indeed, prior to our departure she seemed better, almost
– less languid, more sensible of her condition, *sorrowful* even, that
her state was so.

Alas that the hopes I had entertained of her recovery should
be so cruelly dashed! We had set out on our journey by carriage,
stopping at London and Devizes, were a day out from Bristol in
the packet, seated on deck in the morning sun, when Brodie our
servant came to me from below in a state of much anxiety to say
that her mistress could not be found. Needless to relate, I straightaway instituted a thorough search of the ship, but could discover
nothing. Our cabin was empty, the keepsake at which I had left her
reading discarded on the bed. Near out of my mind at what this
might portend, I rushed hither and thither about the deck peering
beneath the canvases of the row-boats, even turning up the very
coils of rope in an effort to find some clue. On the instant a
gentleman who had been amusing himself by looking out across
the stern of the vessel came rushing up to declare that he had seen
a large object floating in the waves, resembling, as he put it, a
giant water beetle resting on its back. At my urgent solicitation the
ship's boat put out, and in half an hour retrieved my darling from
the sea. It appears now that she concealed herself in a water closet
to the rear of the ship and by this means flung herself from its
window, would have drowned had not the air become trapped in
her skirts. When found she was paddling in a feeble way and was
pulled out quite demented . . .

Of the hours that followed – we were then two days' journey from
Cork – I can scarcely bring myself to speak. So fearful was I that she
would once more seek to destroy herself that in the night I lay beside
her chained at the waist by a piece of ribbon, so that I should know
if she stirred. Happily the ship's cabinet contained a supply of
laudanum and this, freely administered, was sufficient to pacify her
until such time as we put into harbour. What was to be done?
Knowing too well what would be the likely outcome, I could not
immediately propose that we return to England. There was no one to
whom I might apply. In the end I secured rooms for us in the city,
representing my wife as excessively fatigued by the voyage, &c. . . .

We were a fortnight at Cork. You cannot conceive the horror of
it. The dull, *hopeless* look on her face, as if she knew full well the

22

secret of her malady but could not bring herself to gainsay it. Of Irish doctors I think nothing. One prescribed brandy and milk, another walks by the shore – this when the poor creature could scarcely stir from her bed! – a third hot baths and chafing. Finally there came a little man – a Mr Fitzpatrick – who did, I think, do her some good: ordered that she should not be disturbed, but her mind kept occupied, &c. She remarked once that her head 'ran away with her like a carriage that would not stop', which both he and I thought significant. And yet even here, when given rest and occupation, it was clear that her intellect was forcing her back upon a particular course, viz. when read to out of one of Mr Smith's novels, in fact a humorous piece about a tipsy labourer and his family, she burst out in a passion, talking of the poor children, and how should they have clean shirts, and what could be done, as if these were real infants living in some shanty a furlong distant.

Come the end of the first week she was, if not recovered, then a dozen times better than she had been. Indeed she read to me, as we sat in our lodgings, a comical piece from *Punch* about a servant girl who mislaid her mistress's things, and swore it was the cat, and was found drinking porter with the boots over a pair of pawn tickets, over which we both laughed much. I remember it above all, a Sunday morning with the bells ringing and the folk hurrying to service in the street below our window (there is no Protestant church else we should have joined them). She ate a good dinner, drank a glass of 'clar't' that Dr Fitzgerald had prescribed for her – he is a Sligo man with the most uncouth brogue you ever heard – and seemed content, but for certain remarks that betrayed to me the febrile tenor of her mind. Thus, at one juncture, picking up a newspaper – this was after the *Punch* reading – she observed that the print *swam* before her, made it impossible for her to contemplate, that there were shapes she saw between the adjacent columns as clear as day to her tho' perhaps not discernible to all . . .

Still, the afternoon waxing fine and there being no other occupation available to us, I determined to take her walking upon the sands. Indeed, she seemed to relish it, took off her stockings even – they are very free and easy here, the gentlemen march about the shore in their shirt-sleeves – and paddled in the rock pools in such a droll way that I could not forbear to laugh. There was a little black-haired tinker girl playing nearby – I could see the family's wagon drawn up on the shale and an old father smoking a pipe on its seat – and Isabel befriended her, searched with her among the rocks for crabs, walked with her to the sea's edge and looked for ships, &c. All this was very poignant to me, a circumstance that I would have prolonged to its utmost limit, were it not that suddenly there came a terrible shriek from the water. Looking up from this reverie I saw to my horror – you will scarcely credit it, but it is true nonetheless – that she had picked the child up in both arms, as one might seize a bolster, and dashed her into the waves. What was to be done? In an instant a crowd had gathered around us – the old father hastened across the sands yelling 'Murther!' – and it was all I could do, having ascertained that the child was unhurt, to spirit Isabel away. The people looked at us very strangely as I half-pushed, half-pulled her along the street. Yet once taken to our lodgings she grew tractable, did as I bade her, but sat in a chair by the window wearing the most desolate expression I have ever seen on a human countenance and pray that I shall not see again. Dr Fitzgerald, who presently arrived in answer to my summons, looked very grave and vowed that he could do nothing, in fact insisted on our immediate return . . .

Since that time it has gone very hard with us. There is no pattern to her madness, which manifests itself first as a fury of self-reproach, then as stark dolorousness, then again as a curious silent melancholy. On our return I of course consulted Mr Procter, formerly Her Majesty's Commissioner – you will perhaps know him by his other name, Cornwall. Procter's opinion was that an institution might suit, and to this end he conducted me around what he termed his 'favourite place'. This, I freely confess, I feel quite sick to think of even now – a great grim house out in the wilds of Herefordshire, with bars on every window and wild-eyed women roaming the gardens. Procter shook his head about other places . . .

Lately she has been at Camberwell with Mrs Baxter, a most respectable person, with experience of these cases, &c. Here she is humoured, has a parlour to herself, is kept clean and seems well enough. And yet I am filled with the gravest foreboding. Visiting her this Whit Monday past, thinking to take her to Peckham Fair or on some other jaunt, I found, to my disquiet, that she did not know me, merely stared up interestedly from beneath her bonnet, enquired of her keeper who was that man, why had he come, & so forth. On my asking her at one point if she would take a turn in the garden, she replied only, 'Alas, sir, I had better not,' following this with some rigmarole about the Queen, the Houses of Parliament, like fragments of the morning's *Times*, almost, picked up from the floor. The sadness is that in all other respects she is unchanged, the gracefulness of her form and gesture just as I remember. Half a dozen times indeed I found myself regarding her in the absolute confidence that her next utterance would make perfect sense, that the events of the past months had been no more than a ghastly nightmare. Alas, this was a delusion as grave as that which has afflicted her . . .

This has been an infernally long preface, my dear Dixey, to what is a simple request, but there was much that you should know and much to tell about our life since last you saw us. Rest assured that if you can find it in your heart to accommodate that which I now propose, I shall be eternally grateful, as indeed would Isabel, could she but grasp the nature of what I ask . . .

*

And then, quite unexpectedly, Mr Ireland died. According to the *Gentleman's Magazine*, which furnished a synopsis of the affair, he fell from his horse out riding in the Suffolk back lanes, was brought home with half his skull stove in and never spoke again. It was said also, though not in the *Gentleman's Magazine*, that his wife, when the news was brought to her by the village clergyman, gave a solitary shriek of laughter and then resumed her embroidery. It was said, lastly, that at his funeral, during the singing of the final hymn, when the coffin was about to be removed to its accustomed resting place, a woman dressed all in black with a veil over her face appeared as from nowhere in the church porch only to vanish before anyone could address her, and that this woman was Mrs Ireland.

The will was read and – proved. Are not wills always proved? It is only in novels that mysterious strangers arrive to frighten the lawyers and codicils are discovered under the deceased's bedstead. The property, being entailed, passed to a cousin of Mr Ireland's, the Fellow of an Oxford college, who, arriving to inspect his inheritance, pronounced it inconveniently rural and returned to his lecture rooms having left his benefactor's two dozen fields and water meadows in the hands of a bailiff. Mr Ireland's money, such as it was, was reserved for the upkeep of his wife, the capital sum to be placed in a fund administered by certain trustees and released at so much per annum. All this was reported, and embellished, in that highly respectable Suffolk journal, the *Woodbridge Chronicle and Intelligencer*. Beyond that, however, lay much that those who took an interest in Mr Ireland's leavings professed to be unsatisfactory. Where, for example, was Mrs Ireland, the beneficiary of this testament, of whom nothing had been seen since the day of her husband's death? Certainly not at the late Mr Ireland's house, which was shut up and administered by an old housekeeper. But if not there, then where? Why, answered the lawyers to whom this question was put, Mrs Ireland had been placed in the care of a relative, expressly selected by her husband in the event of his early decease. Beyond this, Messrs Crabbe & Enderby of Lincoln's Inn did not care to elaborate. There were rumours about the lady's situation, about an earlier bequest, about her condition – only rumours, to be sure, but there is many an established fact that begins life as a rumour.

All this, in fact, had the makings of a singular mystery. An evening newspaper that had once employed old Mr Brotherton produced a very severe leading article baldly enquiring what had become of his daughter. A celebrated literary gentleman wrote a satirical essay in *All The Year Round*, 'Lost, Stolen or Strayed: On a Vanished Young Lady',[*] in which not a little fun was had at the expense of Messrs Crabbe & Enderby and mention was made of the duties of the Lunacy Commissioners. And in this manner Mrs Ireland's whereabouts became, in a small way, a matter of public remark. She was supposed to have been seen variously at Brighton and at Edinburgh, in a hotel at Paris and on a steamer cruising the Rhine. A gentleman who had known her husband swore that he had glimpsed her on the platform of a metropolitan railway station in the company of a group of nuns, and for a week a rumour went round London that Mrs Ireland was the victim of a popish abduction. To all these representations Messrs Crabbe & Enderby replied in their blandest manner. They had followed their late client's instructions; they were answerable only to his trustees. Of Mrs Ireland's lodgement, health, condition of mind and so forth, nothing could be said without prejudice to that high degree of confidentiality on which her late husband had insisted. So, at any rate, said Mr Crabbe of Crabbe & Enderby when the matter was put to him.

[*] See Appendix I

Now Mr Crabbe was the most persuasive old lawyer who ever presented his petition at the King's Bench, but it was thought that in the business of Mr Henry Ireland's will he was – not lying, for no lawyer ever lies – but not saying as much as he might have said. It was at this time, furthermore, that mention began to be made – nobody knew where the tales came from, but ever so many people believed them – of a certain Mr James Dixey, of whom it was said that he knew everything about the case that was to be known. As to his connection with the Irelands, no one was exactly sure, but those people who made it their business to be cognisant of their fellow men, soon discovered that they knew all about Mr Dixey: that he was an elderly man, somewhere between sixty and seventy, who lived in great seclusion at Watton in the county of Norfolk, occupying his time in correspondence with learned societies, and that he had once presented a pair of stuffed lions – acquired nobody quite knew where – to the Norwich museum. This was Mr Dixey, of whom it came to be asserted that he was Mr Ireland's second cousin on his mother's side, and the person to whom the care of his wife had been assigned.

When these facts became known – or rather when these speculations became prevalent – a body of opinion grew up whose aim was direct action. Let Mr Dixey be addressed, this body proposed, let representations be made to him concerning Mrs Ireland's well-being, either by letter or in person, and then the mystery – and practically everyone had now assured themselves that there *was* a mystery – could be solved. But Mr Dixey lived in West Norfolk, from which fastness he could rarely be enticed: letters sent to him came back unopened, for there is, alas, no law requiring a gentleman to answer his correspondence. At this, certain elements of the Ireland party waxed wrathful. Hot-tempered old ladies demanded that deputations should be sent to Watton, that raiding parties, even, should be encouraged to break down Mr Dixey's door for the purposes of confronting him. Needless to relate, no such steps were ever taken. Norfolk, to be sure, is a long way distant. Gentlemen, too, have their business to attend to. Further, it was felt that however uncertain the legal provisions surrounding his ward, when it came to outright trespass on his property Mr Dixey might be supposed to have the law on his side.

*

'Upon my word, John, I think something ought to be done!'

'Done! I don't doubt that something should be done. The question is: who is to do it?'

The participants in this exchange were a mother and her son, the former a stout, grey-haired lady of perhaps sixty years, the latter a tall, bearded gentleman, clad in the latest metropolitan fashion, of about half that age. The scene of their conversation was a small back parlour in a house in the vicinity of Marylebone High Street and the time about ten of the clock on a bright morning in early March.

'Really, John! I sometimes think you are the worst person in the world for putting yourself forward. There is that young man from Oxford that is to have the property who never set eyes on poor Henry Ireland but once in his life . . .'

'Mother, the estate was entailed, as you very well know. I could no sooner have inherited it than could Lord John or the bench of bishops.'

'And then poor Isabel disappearing off the face of the earth and being forced to live with a dreadful old man in the country. And you that used to be so fond of her.'

'As to that, Mother, it's all gammon. I don't suppose I ever saw her since she was twelve years old. And though I never did care for Ireland I think we can take it that he knew what he was about when he made a will.'

'Even so, John.'

Mrs Carstairs, as she stood regarding her son, was conscious that their conversation was not proceeding in quite the way that she had intended. She was aware, too, that much of what she had said was, to a degree, disingenuous. No doubt the property that Mr Ireland had bequeathed to his distant cousin from Oxford was entailed. No doubt, too, a young gentleman of thirty can scarcely be induced to intervene on grounds of sentiment in the affairs of a young lady whom he last met when she was in short frocks. Nonetheless, despite this admission Mrs Carstairs imagined herself to be rightfully aggrieved.

The connection between the Carstairs and the Brothertons – Mrs Carstairs was a widow, John her eldest son – was this: that the late Mr Carstairs had been the cousin of Isabel Brotherton's father: not a very close cousin, it is true, but of sufficient proximity for there to have been dealings between the two families. These, for reasons that nobody could now remember, had ceased some fifteen years before. Yet Mrs Carstairs, as she now poured out a third cup of tea for the young lord sitting before her, knew that she was driven by something more than considerations of mere loyalty. It occurred to her, for she was a shrewd and purposeful woman, that something was amiss about the entire undertaking – she could not at this point say what it was, but something nonetheless – and that justice, let alone the memory of the infant Miss Brotherton in her pinafore, required it to be investigated.

Shrewd and purposeful as she was, Mrs Carstairs was not so sanguine as to suppose that she would secure the ready assistance of her son. For Mr John Carstairs – this his mother had known for some years – was a weak man: a gentleman, a kindly man according to his lights, but a weak one. Three years previously the electors of a parliamentary borough in the Midlands had petitioned him to stand against the sitting member – for Mr Carstairs was a political young man – but he had havered, vacillated, begged time to consult with his friends, &c., and when the election came the sitting member had been returned unopposed. Then again, a year since there had been talk of a young woman, the daughter of an East India merchant living in Russell Square with ever so many thousands a year, whose hand in marriage Mr Carstairs might have commanded, it was said, by a single snap of his fingers. But somehow that snap had never been administered, the merchant's daughter had gone off to be consoled by an earl's grandson and Mr Carstairs remained in a state of bachelorhood. All this Mrs Carstairs had observed, and from it drawn certain conclusions. Knowing the nature of the man with whom she dealt, she now replaced upon its spigot the teapot that she held, gathered her hands before her, smiled fondly upon her son, who continued to drink his tea, and resumed her discourse in a rather more comfortable tone.

'I declare, John, it's uncommonly pleasant to have you for company at breakfast.'

'Well, I suppose it is – uncommonly pleasant.'

'And let me see, at what hour are you expected at the office?' Mr John Carstairs was employed in an under-secretary's chamber at the Board of Trade, where it was not thought that he fatigued himself very greatly.

'Eleven o'clock. That is, perhaps half past.'

'Well, I wish you would oblige me – you know, you are the head of the family now and such words must come from you – by calling at Mr Crabbe's chambers and enquiring . . .' – here Mrs Carstairs faltered just a little – '. . . enquiring of the matter of which we spoke. It will take no more than a moment and I should count it a great kindness, indeed I should.'

'D——t, Mother! I beg your pardon' – John Carstairs corrected himself hastily, seeing the expression on his parent's face – 'but I cannot see that it would do any good. I know old Crabbe. I meet him at the club and . . . and at other places. He is the civillest old file in Christendom, but I don't doubt that he'd think it a piece of interference. In fact I should swear he would. There – I do not mean to be severe! I shall call at his chambers as you wish, but I'll lay even money it's a fool's errand.'

And with that he picked up his hat, saluted his mother affection-ately on the cheek as was his custom and quitted the house before further words could be exchanged, leaving Mrs Carstairs to superin-tend the disposal of the breakfast things and reflect on the excellence of her understanding of human nature.

For myself I am inclined to believe that Mrs Carstairs had not arrived at a true estimate of her son's character. He was a weak man, but not perhaps as weak as his mother supposed him. In his heart he believed that there was something amiss in the matter of Miss Brotherton – Mrs Ireland – and that it behoved persons such as himself to take an interest in her well-being. And yet his experience of the world told him that information about Mrs Ireland would be difficult to come by. 'After all,' he said to himself as he raised his hand for a cab on the pavement of Marylebone High Street, 'old Crabbe has been the family lawyer for nigh-on half a century and will know what he is about.' Nonetheless he had given his word to his mother and so, not without all private misgivings, he directed the cab to Lincoln's Inn Fields, sent in his card, was smiled upon by Mr Crabbe's clerk and conducted to Mr Crabbe's chamber to await that gentleman's arrival.

It was here, however, that his courage began to fail him. I do not know that Mr Crabbe's office was any more forbidding than other legal chambers in which John Carstairs had at one time or another sat, but there was something about its arrangement, its faded damask hangings and its shelves of dusty law reports, that seemed to impress upon him the futility of his task. Five minutes passed, then ten, not one of which did anything to raise John Carstairs' spirits. After a while he sprang up from his chair and walked restlessly around the room with his hat in his hand, stood irresolutely before the great long window looking out over the square, peered into one of Mr Crabbe's black-backed law books with a kind of horror and examined the row of invitations on the mantelpiece, which told him nothing more than that Mr Crabbe dined out perhaps three nights in the week. It was in this attitude that Mr Crabbe discovered him as he came into the room, gliding in so silently and with so slight a disturbance to the door-handle that John Carstairs gave a start, rather as if he were a burglar who proposed to make off with one of Mr Crabbe's deed boxes.

'I must – must beg your pardon – that is, I am very pleased to see you, Mr Crabbe.'

Mr Crabbe was a hale old gentleman of seventy-five, white-haired and demure, of whom it was said that he knew many secrets worth the knowing. Forty years ago he had written books and exerted himself in the legal reviews, but those days were long behind him. There were young men, doubtless, who appeared in court and presented petitions in Mr Crabbe's name, but Mr Crabbe, here in the twilight of his years, contented himself with offering opinions. Again, I do not know whether Mr Crabbe's judgements were particularly scintillating, or whether it was merely the gravity of the demeanour with which he offered them, but it was felt that these opinions were worth the having. At any rate Mr Crabbe was a circumspect old man, and it was apparent to him – apparent from the moment that he entered the room – that John Carstairs' visit was something out of the ordinary, and that what-ever the nature of his business he was doubtful of his ability to pros-ecute it.

'Delighted to see you, Mr Carstairs. I hope I find you well?'

John Carstairs' health, which was excellent, having been disposed of, Mr Crabbe pressed on.

'And is there some way in which I may be of service?'

'As to that, Mr Crabbe, I – well, in fact, I have come about my cousin, Miss Brotherton.'

'Miss Brotherton?'

'That is – Mrs Ireland.'

'Indeed? Mrs Ireland.' Mr Crabbe's face as he said this was quite without expression, so that Mr Carstairs, who had assured himself when the conversation began that at any rate the old gentleman could not eat him, now feared that he might be devoured on the spot. 'What is it that you wish to know about Mrs Ireland?'

And here John Carstairs felt that he was placed in a quandary. He too believed that there was some mystery surrounding his cousin's whereabouts, and yet this belief was not something that he could exactly put into words. Indeed he scarcely knew what he did believe, or suspect, about Mrs Ireland's apparent disappearance, other than it was a subject of popular remark and had excited the general curiosity. So he contented himself by saying rather lamely:

'My mother and I – my father is dead, you know – would be very glad to hear the terms of Mr Ireland's will.'

'Mr Ireland's will?' Mr Crabbe, who had hitherto been standing, now seated himself in a chair on the further side of a large deal table littered with documents and pieces of paper bound up with coloured tapes, hooked one black-clothed leg over the other and stared at his visitor as if the question of Mr Henry Ireland's will was quite the gravest matter to have come before him in fifty years of legal practice.

'Well, as probate has been granted, I think I may say something of Mr Ireland's will. But in which particular?'

'Well – in the provisions made for his wife, let us say.'

Mr Crabbe – wholly disingenuously, it may be said, for he remembered the terms of Henry Ireland's will almost as well as he remembered the names of his children – took a file from the shelf that ran behind him and made a pretence of examining it.

'Mr Carstairs. Do not think me impertinent' – John Carstairs shook his head, as if he could not for the life of him imagine Mr Crabbe guilty of impertinence – 'but are you at all acquainted with Mrs Ireland's state of health?'

'We had heard that she was not well.'

'Not well! That is one way of putting it. I regret to say that the last doctor who examined her pronounced her – mad.'

'Mad, you say?'

'At the time of her husband's death and for some months previously, I am reliably informed, she had lost her reason to the extent of being unable to recognise him when he entered a room. Naturally this state of affairs was foremost in her husband's mind when he made his will.'

'Naturally.'

'At present she is residing with her husband's kinsman, Mr Dixey, who is responsible for her care. You will appreciate that she is not at all able to appear in society.'

'I feared it was so.'

There was a silence in the room so profound that each of the other sounds that had formerly run in counterpoint to Mr Crabbe's voice – a church clock striking the hour in the distance, the old clerk scuttling up the stair – seemed magnified and made unreal by it.

'And really, Mr Carstairs, that is all I am prepared to say about Henry Ireland's will. But perhaps you have some other question?'

John Carstairs shook his head: he had no other question. He was aware that what the old lawyer had said had been perfectly reasonable, and yet he was conscious, too, that in some way he could not perfectly fathom Mr Crabbe had had the better of him, that he had failed to extract certain pieces of information that, through skill and persistence, another man might have been able to acquire. All this irked him, for he felt himself placed at a disadvantage – feared, too, that all the business with Mr Crabbe's files was a sham. But he was a man who was disposed to accept what was told to him, especially when the teller was so lofty an authority as Mr Crabbe.

At the same time he was now definitely oppressed by the atmosphere of the room – Mr Crabbe's dusty papers, his damask hangings, his dinner invitations, the framed testimonies to Mr Crabbe's juvenile accomplishments dating from ever so many years ago – and determined that he would take his leave. Consequently he picked up his hat, shook hands with his host, escaped down Mr Crabbe's staircase through the gate of Lincoln's Inn and had himself driven away to the Board of Trade.

And Mr Crabbe, having watched him go across the square, stalked around his chamber pulling first one book from his shelves and then another but always failing to discover whatever it was that he wanted from them, then summoned his old clerk and informed him that he would see no callers, sat in apparent abstraction for half an hour, and finally slipped away down the staircase to his club, as demure and confidential a shadow as ever passed beneath the portals of Lincoln's Inn Fields and out into the City beyond.

III

Some Correspondence

Mr Dixey,
Easton Hall

Dear Sir,

This is a line as requested to notify you that the young woman as was spoken of has been put into my care.

She may be collected from this house at any time convenient.

The sum of four guineas in respect of her board and lodging would be gratefully received.

Your respectful servant
Sarah Farthing

*

Jas Dixey, Esq.,
Easton Hall,
Nr Watton,
Norfolk

Dear Sir,

I am commanded to inform you that a bill bearing your signature in favour of Mr Jabez Zangwill of Leadenhall Street, to the value of 500*l*, due on the 17th ult., is in our possession, and that we should be glad of either a prompt settlement or any terms that you may care to propose.

Most faithfully yours,
J. Grace
Clerk to Mr Pardew

Jas Dixey, Esq.,
Easton Hall,
Nr Watton,
Norfolk

Dear Sir,

I am commanded by Mr Pardew to inform you that he is in
receipt of your letter of the 14th inst., and will communicate with
you at his earliest convenience.

Most faithfully yours,

J. Grace

Clerk to Mr Pardew

*

Jas Dixey, Esq.,
Easton Hall,
Nr Watton,
Norfolk

Dear Dixey,

I have your cheque for 200*l*. Come now, it won't do! The bill
was picked up from Zangwill in our usual way, as you well know.
And here is some more paper with your name on it for 300*l* drawn
on our mutual friend Mr Ruen! Look here – I must have specie:
another 200*l* and your promise to pay at 6 weeks. That's about the
strength of it.

Yours, &c.

R. Pardew

*

Jas Dixey, Esq.,
Easton Hall,
Nr Watton,
Norfolk

Dear Sir,

We regret to have to inform you that as you decline to communicate with us in regard to settlement of the two bills bearing your
signature in our possession, the total value of which plus interest

now stands at 660*l*, we are reluctantly compelled to place the matter in the hands of our legal representatives.

Most faithfully yours,

Pardew & Co.

Bill brokers, Carter Lane, EC

*

Jas Dixey, Esq.

My dear Sir,

In accordance with your instructions, received by letter and stated verbally on the occasion that we met, I have taken the opportunity of observing the patient in the manner that you suggested. This period of observation, I may say, occupied the greater part of a forenoon, during which time I was able to satisfy myself, I believe, of the lady's innate condition, as opposed to any vagary of expression caused by the novelty of my presence before her.

A prolonged maniacal attack is not infrequently characterised by continual activity and a most ingenious disposition to mischief. In the case of Mrs Ireland I think it may safely be said that the majority of these symptoms have passed, notwithstanding a constant restlessness, eagerness to move about the room & so forth. From the strict medical point of view, the lady is somewhat emaciated and suffering from disorder of the stomach and bowels. I believe these afflictions to be consequent upon her mental state and not the result of any organic disease.

Her articulation is, I suspect, much impaired by her malady. She will begin a sentence and then break off at some quite arbitrary point. Her conversation, additionally, is disconnected – almost rambling: the Queen, her late father, the names of persons unknown to me, memories of her girlhood, &c. She seems conscious of this failing yet unable to correct it. She is reliably informed – could name several of Mr Dickens' novels, the Archbishop and his predecessor – but could do nothing with the information. Her recreations, while confined, have been of the most primitive cast. Thus I heard (from her attendant) that she will from time to time sing, not unmelodiously, to herself, or attempt to fashion small drawings on the sheets of paper that are provided for her. Examples of the latter, which I have seen, are incomprehensible. On one occasion, I believe, she asked to sit at a pianoforte, and, there being one available, looked longingly at the keys as if they stirred some recollection within her on which she could not quite bring herself to act.

I append a list of her responses to such questions as I put:

Q: What is your name?
A: Mrs Ireland.
Q: Your age?
A: I have passed my twenty-seventh year. (In fact, as I am led to believe, she is twenty-eight.)
Q: Who came before the present monarch?
A: The Hanoverian Elector.
Q: What is the bird that sits in the tree beyond the window?
A: A sparrow. (In fact it was a magpie.)
Q: Have you living relatives?
A: I have a husband.
Q: Where is he?
A: He is dead.

In the course of my examination I placed a number of objects before the patient with the aim of gauging her reaction. In a book – a volume of children's tales – she took no interest, yet the fastening of a horse's bridle, which I happened to have in my pocket, she shrank from, saying that it awakened in her the darkest fears and apprehensions. A handkerchief she received with the gravest solemnity, balancing it on the palm of her hand and inspecting it as if it were some rare token whose significance she appreciated without comprehending its function. A very sorrowful look came upon her as she did this.

As to whether this derangement betokens an outright imbecility, I am not yet in possession of sufficient facts to judge. I can see no reason for the use of the strait-waistcoat, the muff, the leg-locks and hand-cuffs, the restraining chair – or indeed any other form of material restraint. The arrangements which you propose for her seem to be admirable in every respect. The routines which I should additionally suggest are those of seclusion, quiet, repetitive yet undemanding work which may give the brain an opportunity to function without undue distress. A suitable sedative may perhaps be administered in the patient's food.

If I can be of any further professional assistance, or if a future consultation is thought to be advisable, then by all means apply to my secretary.

I am, my dear sir, yours most cordially,
John Conolly, MD
Late resident physician to the Hanwell Asylum

*

Jas Dixey, Esq.,
Easton Hall,
Nr Watton,
Norfolk

Dear Dixey,

Come now, there is a way out of this unpleasantness! Let me have that letter you spoke of (none shall know how I came by it, that I promise) and all shall be well. Why, you may have another 100*l* for all I care, and buy as many gulls' eggs as you choose!

Yrs, &c.
R. Pardew

IV

The Goods are Delivered

Early afternoon in Tite Street, and already the twilight is seeping up through the area steps and out into the grey pavements beyond. A bitter February day here in Tite Street ('that most respectable locality' as the house agents' particulars so truly represent it) with a raw fog hanging in the air since dawn, and little flicks of wind agitating the washing hung out in the smoky courts and byways – there is always washing in Tite Street, it will be there when all else has perished – like an unseen hand. Tite Street. King's Cross Station half a mile away and Somers Town hard by. 'Tite Street!' the cabman echoes his passenger, as if to say, 'You wouldn't go *there* if you knew about it.'

Tite Street. Forty stucco houses in varying states of dilapidation, a profusion of polished brass plates (apothecaries, insurance agents, water-bailiffs – Tite Street has them all), so many cards offering furnished apartments, pianoforte lessons and the like that to gather them up and deal them out would be to commence an all but interminable game of whist. Tite Street. At the nearer end an undertaker's parlour, with a couple of great horses, their plumes dyed nearly purple, stamping on the kerb. At the further, the Tite Arms and Refreshment Emporium, Jno Phelps, prop., the dreariest public house you ever saw, with a couple of smeary windows through which the melancholy figure of a man in a nankeen jacket and side-whiskers, possibly even Mr Phelps himself, can be seen polishing a row of pewter pots. A shooting gallery, a tobacconist-cum-newspaper-seller and a faded French milliner's whose door no customer has been seen to enter in the three years of the shop's existence complete the scope of Tite Street's amenities. Tite Street. Forty brass door-knobs, forty dark casement windows, for all the world like forty dim aquariums were it not that no fish swim inside them, on a grim, grey day in November and no one at home.

Or not quite no one. For old Mrs Farthing, seated at present in her back-kitchen with the lamps turned low and the shadows crawling consequently up the pale wall like so many phantoms, is always at home. One might as well expect the Sphinx to pick up its skirts and go hobbling across the desert as to conceive of Mrs Farthing quitting her roost in Tite Street where she has squatted these past twenty years and become so much a fixture that were she to depart on a little excursion to Camden Town or Marylebone market, Tite Street would feel itself robbed of an essential part of its character and get up a petition for her swift return.

Who is Mrs Farthing? To be sure, a queer old woman of seventy-five, with a queer old face whose nose and chin threaten to meet in mid-air like a pair of nut-crackers, peeping up out of shiny widow's weeds of black bombazine. There is no Mr Farthing, has not been for thirty years and nobody – least of all his relict – has anything to say of him. Perhaps he was a half-pay officer, or a commission agent, or took in lodgers – all occupations with which Tite Street is pass-ingly familiar. Perhaps his is the face, having a pair of mutton-chop whiskers and a sprightly blue eye, that gazes from the further wall of the back-kitchen, but Tite Street neither knows nor cares.

Had this putative Mr Farthing the ability to look down on his relict's back-kitchen, what would he see? Well, a monstrous old black-leaded range looking as if half a ton of coals at least were needed to keep it hot, a dreary old mahogany sideboard covered over with cups and plates and what-not, a quantity of copper saucepans, warming pans and chafing dishes piled in a heap, an old white-whiskered cat looking as if she were placed on this earth at approx-imately the same time as her owner. Everything old, ugly and inconvenient, and sitting amidst them perhaps the oldest, ugliest and most inconvenient article of all, namely Mrs Farthing, hunched up in a tall rocking chair above a smoky fire, with her face all shiny from the heat and the remains of some genteel refection (Tite Street inclines to pork chops and sweetbreads) lying on the rickety table beside her.

The capital's actor managers, did they know of this Tite Street faery's existence, would probably subscribe a respectable sum to induce her onto the London stage, so professed is her ability to reproduce the symptoms of inward agitation. There is no one in the room save the cat, but curiously Mrs Farthing's attitude suggests that she believes there to be a burglar, say, concealed under the fender, or a bailiff with an eye on the mahogany sideboard sat at the breakfast table before her. Twice in the course of ten minutes Mrs Farthing starts up in her chair and reaches forward, with who knows what constriction of her old bones, to stir the fire-irons and administer a wholly unnecessary prod to the slumbering fire with the poker. Twice, again, she rises to her feet, makes a half-hearted sally in the direction of the parlour door, thinks better of it and retires. A man delivering circulars comes and pushes one through the letter-box and Mrs Farthing pops her old head into the passage, catches sight of the white paper fitfully descending and mutters something scornful and unintelligible under her breath. Another glance at the parlour door, another rattle of the fire-irons, and Mrs Farthing resumes her seat.

Fast approaching four o'clock in Tite Street and the twilight is no longer a hint or a plausible speculation but an irrevocable fact. A few children, home early from the variety of select establishments in which the neighbourhood abounds, venture out to play at nine-pins on the area steps or make cock-shies in the corners of gloomy court-yards and are swiftly routed out and brought back by their nurse-maids. A muffin man marches up Tite Street clanging his bell, to depart a few moments later with ever so few pence for his trouble. A mad old lady with a rolling eye and a ragged umbrella lingers before the door of the French milliner's, thereby awakening all kinds of unrea-sonable hopes in the breast of its proprietress, before skipping girl-ishly away in the direction of Somers Town.

Within the walls of the back-kitchen, now practically drowning in a sea of inky shadows, Mrs Farthing, who has spent the past ten minutes staring very vigilantly into the fire, as if it formed an addi-tional door to the premises, rises once more to her feet and begins to shake out her skirts in a way that suggests thorough-going ill-humour, one ear cocked like a bad-tempered old fox hearing the huntsman's horn borne up on the wind. What is it that Mrs Farthing hears? A footstep creaking this way and that on an uncarpeted floor? A voice – a female voice, by the sound of it – murmuring ever so softly somewhere? Whatever it is, Mrs Farthing doesn't mean to put up with it. Taking a last angry glance at the clock-face, in whose powers she has long since ceased to believe, Mrs Farthing steams off in the direction of the parlour door like a fearful old battleship, pushes it half open and stands balefully under the lintel.

'No good will come of it, ma'am.'

The noise, which might be that of a person – a female person – walking up and down, ceases abruptly. Surer now of her ground, Mrs Farthing, in what she imagines – heaven knows why – to be a kindlier tone, extemporises further:

'No good at all, ma'am, in taking on so. There is nothing to be done.' The silence is by now so absolute that the ticking of the grandfather clock a dozen feet distant, very tall and ominous in the dark, seems to run away like some mechanical demon capering off in pursuit of an inventors' prize plate.

'Nothing to be done, ma'am,' Mrs Farthing remarks, darting sharp little glances at the room's interior, at the shadows wreathed around the principal armchair, and the solitary hand – very pale and delicate and tremulous – tapping restlessly away on its edge. 'Will you take anything? A glass of sherry, or a biscuit?'

The hand taps a little less feverishly, but there is no reply. Thoroughly disgusted, Mrs Farthing bustles back into her kitchen, chivvies away the cat, which impetuous and foolhardy creature has taken possession of her rocking chair, seizes a taper and lights a pair of tall wax candles that very soon begin to gutter and fizz, and settles down to brood. There is a letter lying on the kitchen table with a scarlet seal on its reverse side, and Mrs Farthing takes it up and reads for the thirtieth time the assurances of a certain legal gentleman that this day evening Mrs F's services – for which his friend Mr D is very grateful – will be at an end. But what if Mr D don't come, Mrs Farthing wonders? What if nobody comes? These are disagreeable thoughts, and Mrs Farthing doesn't care to entertain them.

Outside in Tite Street the evening draws on. Lights go on in upstairs windows, smoke rises from the ancient chimneys to mingle with the darkening air. The faint melodious clatter of a pianoforte can be heard somewhere, as if to say 'Why, d——, despite it all we *can* still be comfortable.' Cats begin to appear around the area steps and athwart the chimney pots, their eyes full of nocturnal purpose. Meek papas, thither conveyed from clerking offices in High Holborn and Fleet Street, are met at their front doors, relieved of their gloves and clerkly appurtenances, regaled with mutton chops brought in hot and hot and given babies to dandle while their supper beer is fetching.

Such is the press of servant girls and stout matrons around the door of the Tite Arms and Refreshment Emporium that Little Sills, the celebrated comic tenor, engaged that evening to delight the company with the ballad of Villikins and his Dinah, and arriving early in a tall hat and a sateen waistcoat, grows suddenly sanguine of his prospects and imagines a roseate future in which he is summoned to Windsor, appears before the Lord Mayor's banquet and can introduce Mrs Sills (at present with the children in Hoxton) to, as he puts it, 'the kind of society that a woman of her refinement, sir, demands'.

It turns colder, and a flake or two of snow – grey snow, soiled by the reek of a thousand chimneys, but snow nonetheless – drifts down over the street, where it is seen from out of the window of the Tite Arms and Refreshment Emporium by Mr Phelps as he descends to the kitchen to relay orders for beefsteaks and whisky-punch, and by the ancient proprietress of the milliner's shop, now retired to a comfortable back bedroom with her hair done up in curl papers and a copy of the *St James's Chronicle* in her ancient hand, and Mrs Farthing, who, knowing that it means wet underfoot, and pattens and footbaths, and all manner of inconveniences which Mrs Farthing isn't prepared to countenance, drats it with all her heart.

The person concealed in Mrs Farthing's parlour sees it, and twists her shawl more tightly around her shoulders and thinks – but who knows what she thinks? – of certain former passages in her life, in which predominate the figure of a pleasant-faced old gentleman wielding a quill pen above a sheet of paper quite as if he means to stab it through and through, until her thoughts altogether sail away with her, go running up the wallpaper of Mrs Farthing's parlour – which is all coy shepherdesses and their bucolic swains – to take sanctuary on the curtain pole.

It is at a late hour, unconscionably late for Tite Street – the meek papas, arrayed now in night shirts and slippers are yawning crossly for the candles while their wives wonder how it is that the winter nights *do* go on so, little Sills, his engagement concluded and the landlord's half sovereign clinking against the farthings in his breast pocket, is riding home to Hoxton on the top of a twopenny omnibus (it is a triumphal carriage in Little Sills' imagination, with a phantom crowd huzzaing at the street corner) – when a cab comes briskly into view at that thoroughfare's nearer end. So muted is its passage through the receding slush – the snow has vanished now, gone to fall on

Clerkenwell and Whitechapel and Wapping Old Stairs – that no one in Tite Street hears it except Mrs Farthing who, like an old bloodhound taking the scent, sees it from her front door and steps out into the road almost before the vehicle pulls up and an oldish gentleman in a wide hat and an Ulster begins to descend laboriously onto the pavement.

'D——d cold for the time of the year, I should say,' the gentleman remarks, and Mrs Farthing bridles, as if to say 'This is not language I would use, but the sentiment is, at any rate, sound.' A casual observer, overhearing them, would perhaps deduce that the gentleman and Mrs Farthing were formerly acquainted. Certainly Mrs Farthing gives a little bob, hinting at great things in the curtseying line were further encouragement to be offered, while the gentleman gives her a glance that might be interpreted to mean 'I would not dream of being so impolite as to suggest that I never met you before.' This impression is reinforced in Mrs Farthing's hallway, an immensely gloomy passage lit by a single lantern. Here the gentleman, having declined Mrs Farthing's offer of refreshment, fixes her with a look and presumes that the patient – the young lady – has passed a pretty comfortable day.

'Pretty comfortable, sir,' Mrs Farthing assures him. 'Leastways, nothing *I* would complain of.'

'She has been quiet, has she?' the gentleman continues.

'Quite quiet, sir. Except that she took on once or twice, sir, which I never could abide, sir, and told her plainly that I would not.'

'Took on, has she?' The gentleman's voice is very low now, very low and confidential.

'Crying, sir! Walking about the room! Not answering when spoken to!' Mrs Farthing particularises these failings as if each of them should be dealt with at Snow Hill by Mr Ketch in front of a baying crowd.

'Indeed? Well, I am obliged to you, Mrs . . .'

'Farthing, sir,' says Mrs Farthing eagerly, as if to say that she knows this game exactly. 'And now, sir, perhaps you would care to come inside?'

The gentleman duly comes. The parlour door shuts behind him. Mrs Farthing lingers hesitantly before it for a moment, like a duenna uncertain what the young people are up to, before stumping off to the kitchen with the thought that it is no business of hers, which indeed it is not. Presently the parlour door creaks open, the gentleman and his companion – her shawl drawn up very tight over her face – are borne away (it is very late now and the lights in the surrounding houses are all but extinguished) and Mrs Farthing slips out of our story and back into the cramped and melancholy annals of Tite Street.

*

'You'll find Mr Dixey an uncommonly peculiar gentleman,' Dunbar said, drawing the collar of his ulster close against the drizzle.

'Pecooliar?' Dewar rolled the word around his mouth and made a tentative step on the path before him. 'In what way pecooliar?'

'Well, I don't exactly know how to put it. Nothing out of the ordinary to look at, perhaps, but uncommon strange all the same.'

'Ten guineas is ten guineas,' Dewar suggested hopefully. 'Pecooliar or not.'

They were standing on the verge of a small country back-road, poorly surfaced, against which wound an ancient brick wall, very worn about its extremities, which rose up to a point almost level with their heads. Above them, and to the right, tall trees – firs and spruces – hunched into near-impenetrable thickets, with only a glimpse or two of pathways running on into the wood. To the left the land sloped down through fields and pasture to a low-lying plain, apparently devoid of human habitation, on which the weak late-afternoon sun shone faintly. Save for the drip of rainwater from the trees and the receding jingle of the cart that had brought them from Watton – now on the point of vanishing beyond the bend in the road – all was silent.

'Will he be expecting us?' Dewar went on. His eyes were red and inflamed from want of sleep. 'This Mr Dixey.'

'There was a wire sent saying the goods shall be delivered,' Dunbar told him. 'Just that. Rather neat, don't you think? But, see, we must be getting on. There is a gate here, to my recollection. And have a care for that d——d casket.'

They passed on along the road under the high trees, to a point where a five-barred gate, secured to its stanchion with a piece of rope, broke the wall's uneven course. Behind it a track, no more than a few feet wide, led away through the wood. Dewar would have climbed the gate but Dunbar, gesturing at the burden he held under his arm, jerked at the rope and opened it to let him pass.

'I saw a man drop a sea eagle's egg,' he explained, 'on the doorstep of the clergyman that was booked to buy it.'

'This Mr Dixey,' Dewar went on, whose curiosity had been pricked. 'What does he do?'

'What does he do?' Dunbar stood for a moment with his hand on the topmost bar of the gate while he looped the rope-end around its post. 'Why, he is a squire. Owns the land around here. That village where we put up our traps too, I shouldn't wonder. What does any gentleman do? Why, he has his occupations like any other man. Mr Dixey here is great in the dog-breeding line. Keeps a whole pack of them chained up in a barn – you shall hear the noise of them presently. Why, when I was here last a great mastiff jumped a four-foot hurdle and made fair to tear out my throat.'

'What did you do?' Dewar wondered nervously.

'Do? Why, I dealt it a blow on the nose that had it howling for a week, I shouldn't wonder. I never could abide a venturesome dog. But see, we are getting well on into Dixey's estate.'

Following the cast of his arm, his companion saw that the tall avenue of trees was thinning out into a more random assemblage of grass and outbuildings. In the distance, perhaps a half-mile distant, the outlines of a substantial residence could be dimly glimpsed. To Dewar everything that he saw was possessed of great novelty, and yet he was conscious that there was something lacking in the vista that lay spread out before him. Great piles of green-coated timber lay piled up on either side of the path, looking very much as if they wanted a woodman to come and take them away, and there was rank, knee-high grass in the paddock. Presently they passed a long, low barn, sheltered on three sides by banks of fir trees, from which, as Dunbar had promised, a cacophony of barking ascended to the pale sky.

'Grim kind of a place, ain't it, though?' Dunbar remarked, as if following his thoughts. 'But there is no one lives here you know. Just a servant or so and a man to open the hedge gates to carriages. Not that there's many of them. The gardeners have been sent away, I believe, for Dixey don't care about the height of his grass. As for what he owes in London, why your guess is as good as mine.'

'And yet he'll pay five guineas for an egg?'

'More than that sometimes. And not just eggs. Why, I brought him a pine marten last year, which I took in a wood in Carmarthenshire, that he paid twenty pounds for. There's no accounting for the rarey things he delights in.'

'But he don't keep up his estate and the gardeners is all gone?' Dewar's sense of propriety was offended.

'A solitary old gentleman he is. Why' – Dunbar's eye searched for some point of comparison – 'like one of those rooks up there on the fence. You shall see. Here, we are almost in sight. That is the servants' hall, behind the long window. Dixey's butler is a decent old fellow, but the housekeeper is a regular tartar, so no chaff, you know.'

They came now to a rectangle of bare, flattened earth, hedged around by currant bushes, that abutted the back parts of the house. Here some faint signs of human activity declared themselves. A man in a shabby suit of green, who might have been a gamekeeper, one foot braced against a tree stump, was sharpening up the points of a trap with a little whetstone, while a maid with short yellow hair was taking in washing that had been spread to dry over the bushes. Dewar, staring about him, thought the scene a very dreary one – there were old harnesses piled up by the porch that seemed as if they had been there ever so many years, and what looked like a fox's pelt nailed up on the barn door – but he approved of the servant girl, who nodded unblushingly to Dunbar as he went by.

'That's a nice-looking girl,' Dunbar observed as they passed out of earshot. 'And here is old Randall. How are you, Mr Randall? Tolerably well, I take it?'

Dewar, still registering the first impressions of a dozen other things that he saw, could not separate the butler's face from his surroundings. A row of pewter pots on the long sideboard behind him; a line of prints on the further wall, over which the soft rays of firelight played, a sheet of newspaper pale in the murk of an armchair – all these seemed to him elements of Mr Randall's being and his worn old face. An elderly woman with shiny black hair looked up from a chair by the fire where she sat stitching a cushion cover and Dewar, thinking that some gesture was expected from him, touched his hat. The woman turned her head away, whether pleased or offended he could not tell.

'Quite an adventure,' Dunbar was saying to Mr Randall, as they proceeded into a wide, panelled hallway where portraits hung in dirty gilt frames. 'But there is not much sport left in these isles. Why, Mr Cumming says he thinks of taking his guns to Africa.' A tall footman

47

carrying a tray before him came hurrying down the staircase, bobbed his head to Mr Randall as he passed and disappeared into the silence they had left behind them, and Dewar thought of the grocer's shop in Hoxton, with the great blinds drawn low over the window and the drift of white dust upon the lids of the flour barrels, and the two assistants all attentive behind the counter, and the pleasure it had been to command them.

A staircase of twenty-seven steps, a serpentine corridor whose lamps had not been lit, a man's face, hard and accusing, staring out at him from a picture frame, a closed door from whose lintel soft light gleamed – all this Dewar saw, and did not see, for his mind was lost in the airiest speculations over what lay around him: the footman with his tray, the casket in his hand, the murmur of a voice, whether above or beneath him he could not tell, elsewhere in the house. The door from behind which the soft light glowed having been wrested open for him by Mr Randall, he tumbled into the room over a ridge in the carpet, regained his footing, assured himself that the casket was secure in his grasp and then looked around him.

Dunbar, in whom the strangeness of their surroundings produced no obvious disquiet, was already on his way towards the wide desk that lay at an angle to the fireplace. Dewar followed dutifully behind him. In the course of his commercial career he had attended upon many gentlemen in their studies – he had brought in his little bill, defended it, conceded alterations to it and negotiated its settlement – but he was conscious that he had attended upon no such person as Mr Dixey and in no such surroundings. The gentlemen of Hoxton had sat, for the most part, in small, ill-favoured rooms with cash boxes on their desks, whose windows afforded a view of mean little gardens and stunted trees. Mr Dixey, alternatively, sat in a great wide room before a high window affording glimpses of a receding gravel drive and an ornamental pool, around which the wind whistled and careened, and on his desk there lay not a cash box but what appeared to be a human skull. He was – and this could be inferred even from his seated position – a tall man, elderly but apparently vigorous, in a suit of black with a white stock tied around his throat and bony hands that, resting curiously on the desk before him, looked as if they might have concerns of their own and be about to go scuttling off across the veneer in defiance of their owner's wishes. There was a little tuft of grey hair on the point of his chin which, whether left there by chance or design, enhanced this singularity, and Dewar became instantly fascinated by it, watched it as its owner rose to his feet (he did this cautiously but in a manner that suggested much steadfastness of purpose) and marked it as it moved up and down in response to the opening and closing of his lips.

'You are very punctual, Dunbar,' Mr Dixey said. 'It is not a week since I received your letter.'

'When goods are procurable, why, they should be delivered,' Dunbar remarked. 'That is a principle for the retail trade, I take it.'

Pressing closer to the desk, Dewar gazed wonderingly at the paraphernalia that surrounded it. The bear he had anticipated and regarded only cursorily, but the great cabinets – some displaying pieces of stone, others with stuffed birds and animals set up in what seemed to him the most lifelike attitudes – captured his attention and he began to inspect them out of the corner of his eye. The movement drew Mr Dixey's gaze upon him for the first time.

'This gentleman is not your brother, Dunbar? I don't believe I ever saw him before.'

'No indeed, sir. Why, William is laid up at Twickenham with a hacking cough. This is Mr Dewar, as came recommended to me by an attorney with whom I have dealings, and has given great satisfaction.'

There was a small grey object on the desk, nestled in the delta formed by a pair of randomly cast books, which, as Dewar watched, came to life and, now revealed as a mouse, ran off towards Mr Dixey's bony hand, was scooped up by it and deposited in his pocket. Dewar was conscious that something in the room – he could not tell what – oppressed him, and to counter this feeling, perhaps even to distance himself from the transaction on which they were engaged, he found himself placing the casket squarely down on the lip of the desk. Picking up a pair of spectacles which lay atop a third book and settling them on his nose, Mr Dixey bent forward to examine it. There was an eagerness about him, Dewar saw, that contrasted very markedly with the diffidence of his greeting.

Rolling the eggs from side to side in their bed of moss, he balanced one finally on the palm of his hand and balanced his forefinger upon it:

'There are only two?'

'Two is difficult enough, sir,' Dunbar observed. 'It is indeed. Why,

49

there were two fellows, to my knowledge, that spent a week in Easter Ross not long back and came away with nothing. Besides, the folk there have turned cunning. They know the value of the things. The help's not gratis, if you take my meaning.'

Looking at the old man as he peered over the desk, the spectacles balanced on the bridge of his nose, the egg in his hand, the light in his eyes, Dewar was aware that what oppressed him was Mr Dixey. He looked out of the window, where a faint greyness had begun to fall over the late-afternoon sky and a wind had got up above the tops of the trees, and then back at the tuft on Mr Dixey's chin. There was a pat-pattering of footsteps above them and a noise that might or might not have been laughter.

'These will do very well,' Mr Dixey said. 'I am obliged to you, Dunbar.'

'When goods are delivered, they should be settled for,' Dunbar rejoined, in a tone that suggested there might previously have been some slight oversight in this department.

'And so they shall. See, the note is here in my hand. But there is another commission I should have you execute, if you are agreeable.'

'Oh, I am always agreeable. What is it?'

'Did you ever see a wildcat in these islands?'

'I saw one took in Lincolnshire twenty years ago. A great thing that fell out of a tree and set the keeper's dog yammering into the bushes. The keeper himself, who was a man six feet tall, said he would not have cared to get in the way of it. And when we laid it out it measured thirty inches from nose to tail. There are none of your farmyard tabbies that size, I'll guess. But there are no wildcats left in Lincolnshire, nor anywhere else that I heard of.'

'But they could be looked for? In the Scots forests, say?'

'Oh, they could be looked for. Like the wolves. Looked for and not found. There was a gentleman shot a bustard the other day in Suffolk and everyone said it was the last to be seen.'

Mr Dixey nodded. If he was displeased by this impediment he did not say so, but contented himself with removing his spectacles and polishing their lenses with a handkerchief. The tall footman that Dewar had seen on the stairs came beckoning at the door.

'You must excuse me. There is an urgent matter to which I must attend.'

Dewar found that the feeling of oppression had left him, that he stood not in the premises of some sinister theatrical showman but in a spare, angular chamber tenanted by an old man in black with a grey head who wheezed as he passed on his way to the door. Mr Dixey and the tall footman disappeared immediately into the upper parts of the house. Dewar had a last glimpse of a pair of oddly truncated legs vanishing into shadow. Dunbar whistled crossly to himself as they negotiated the lower staircase and came again into the great hall.

'He'll find no great cats in Lincolnshire. Not if he drew every wood from the Wash to the Humber, for they are all gone.' Thinking that some explanation was required for this access of temperament, he remarked: 'A man gets tired of this work. I have been too long about it, I daresay.'

There was no one in the servants' hall. The maid who had been bringing in the washing was still outside, with her laundry basket. In the distance the noise of the dogs came borne on the wind towards them. Dewar saw that twilight was stealing up through the tall trees.

'Cheerful kind of place, ain't it?' Dunbar remarked again. He hunched his shoulders more tightly into his great-coat. 'Ugh, but this Norfolk air chills the bones. I could not stay a week here. Let us be away.'

Dewar stared back over his shoulder. Something in the appearance of the dismal house, its outlines now settling into the darker space beyond, caught his eye and he rested his gaze on the row of windows, some lighted now against the encroaching dusk, others gathered up in shadow. The place, he now saw, was not quite devoid of activity, for a woman's face – at this distance he imagined it to be the housekeeper's – could be seen at one of the upper windows. It looked out for a moment or two and was then withdrawn. The noise of the dogs came up again on the wind. Dunbar pressed his arm and they set off hastily through the trees.

*

She stood in the gathering twilight, on the wet grass. Behind her the men's voices receded into the shadow of the wood, dark now and silent but for the cries of the dogs. Through the lighted window before her she could see William, his jacket half-pulled onto his shoulders, moving through the house to answer a summons from some distant room. The sight cheered her and she bent to retrieve the wicker clothes-basket: heavy and unwieldy, but no trouble to her for she was a strongly built girl and relished the work that was put before her.

The voices had altogether disappeared, and she lingered for a moment with the basket balanced on her hip, watching the last streaks of daylight diminishing over the far-off plain. Some arrangement of the drifting clouds, some gleam of the fading sun briefly issuing out of the dusk, awakened in her the memory of a time when Easton Hall had not been her home, its secrets not hers to speculate on, when all that she now saw with the eye of half a year's experience was novel to her, quite fresh and full of wonder. She brooded on these phantoms for some time, as the streaks of light faded almost to nothing, leaving only a vast diffusion of variegated shade.

Then the sounds from the house – sounds of tea-things jangling, low voices and slammed doors – woke her from her reverie and, clutching the basket in her outstretched arms, she went inside.

V

Esther's Story

(i)

She stood on the station platform, watching the receding train. The white steam curled above the few bushes that hid the curve of the line, evaporating in the pale evening air. A moment more and the last carriage would pass out of sight, the white gates at the crossing swinging slowly forward to let through the impatient passengers.

There were but few of these. A labourer with a pair of kids, one lodged under each of his elbows, their startled faces peering uncertainly out into the light, attested to the agricultural character of the place. A young clergyman, bespectacled and high-foreheaded, with a superfluous umbrella dragging at his feet, directed the passer-by's attention to a church – round-towered and built of miscellaneous stone – poking up above a file of distant elm trees. Behind them came a girl of perhaps twenty, stumbling over an oblong box, rust-coloured and bound with twine. This she was attempting to propel before her, rather in the way that a brewer's man drives a barrel. She wore a faded brown dress and a calico jacket too warm for the day, and her burden, together with a faint nervousness about her face and in the movements of her hands, suggested a servant bidden to her new situation. It was a plump face, rather pinched at the nose and with wary eyes, a trifle sullen when in repose yet capable of a warm expressiveness when brought to laughter. She was laughing now, the porter having asked if she wished to leave the bundle she carried strapped around her shoulders with her box. Both, he ventured, could travel

53

in the donkey-cart which came down from the hall each evening to fetch parcels.

'Is it far?' she asked. 'Only I should rather walk than wait for the cart.'

The young man regarded her favourably out of pale, watery eyes. 'Not what you would call far. That is, if you are used to walking and don't mind keeping off the roads.'

'I am used to walking,' the girl replied, with an odd solemnity not perhaps demanded by the question.

'Two or three miles, then, if you keep your wits about you.'

He would have spoken further, but that the stationmaster, who stood taking tickets along the platform, had his eye upon him, so he contented himself with a vague little gesture of his hands in the direction of the church. 'There's a gate beyond the trees.'

She thanked the man and strolled along the platform, gazing across the low-lying fields and the strew of houses from the nearby town, still deliberating whether she should leave her bundle with the box. The last of the passengers had by now departed – she could see the figure of the clergyman hastening along the upland path towards the trees – and the stationmaster, his duty all done, stood almost forlornly by the platform's edge, his eye fixed on the horizon of pale sky and far-off hedgerows. Unfamiliar with her surroundings, her sensibilities yet more aroused by the novelty of her position, she was struck by the silence of the place, the low, brooding hills before her and the faint oppressiveness of the early evening heat. There was dust in the air, borne from the chalk road that flanked the station approach, and she stopped for a moment feeling the motes rise against her skirts. Only the church clock, striking the hour across the empty fields, stirred her from her reverie. Seven o'clock! And the letter bidding her to arrive by eight! She must make haste. Abruptly she swung the bundle down from her shoulders and, settling it in her arms – these were muscular and spoke of much early labour – set off in the direction recommended by her guide.

She was twenty years old and coming to Easton Hall. Of these facts she was sure, the one through frequent study of the dates inscribed on the flyleaf of her mother's Bible, the other through Lady Bamber. Of Easton Hall she knew nothing, as this was not a subject Lady Bamber had wished to pursue. For a moment Lady Bamber's face – aquiline, and with infinitely wrinkled skin – drifted into her imagination, only to be gathered up and lost in the dust motes that beat against her skirt and the flat horizon. She was beyond the level-crossing now and approaching the incline over which the clergyman had hastened five minutes before. To her right lay a row of houses, newly built, with uniform gardens and gates looking out onto the unmade road. These finally conquered her confusion of spirit, banished all thoughts of Lady Bamber and the three hours' journey she had just accomplished, and brought her mind back to earth. She knew these villa houses, for she had worked in others like them. They were the kind of houses in which only one servant is kept, to whom, consequently, all the duties of the establishment are devolved. Unsummoned, the voices of half a dozen of her former mistresses rose to clamour in her head. 'Esther! Have you nothing better to do that you should sit there in idleness?' 'Esther! There is Mr John calling for his shaving water, surely?' 'Esther! Be quick and take this letter to the post.' Esther had not resented these intrusions on her time, for she knew that they were occasioned by necessity and that the women drove her hard because they were driven hard in their turn. Nonetheless she was glad to be rid of them.

But Easton Hall! Easton Hall would be different. And its vast remove from any situation she had yet occupied awakened in her both an unwonted confidence and an instinctive dread. There would be a butler, she supposed, and a cook, and a parlourmaid who dressed in the zenith of fashion, walked with the footman to church and looked with scorn on a kitchenmaid with twelve pounds a year. And yet twelve pounds a year was a fabulous sum of money to one who has worked for seven and been grateful for eight, and again, unbidden, the image of a dress rose before her, to be bought with the surplus of her first quarter's wages, once the greater part had been remitted home.

Comforted by these thoughts, Esther wandered on through a sombre, tree-lined avenue that skirted the back of the church. The bundle, which contained two or three books given to her by her mother, a pair of pattens and her second-best dress, had already become irksome to her, and she put it down at her feet and rested for a while, casting her gaze through the trees to the fields and hummocks of land beyond. A black, ugly bird whose true name she did not know but called a cadder flew out of a hedge and she followed the line of its flight with her eye. She had come, she saw, to a point in the path at right angles to the churchyard, and some instinct prompted her to step inside the wicker gate and examine the stones.

There was not, indeed, a great deal to see – a fresh grave newly dug by the sexton, in the shadow of the tower, with the digging tools still laid out on the grass, and a few bunches of parched flowers – but the place had an attraction to the girl and she roamed here and there for a moment or two, remarking such peculiarities in the names of the deceased as took her fancy. Seeing that the hands of the church clock had now reached a quarter past the hour, she seized up her bundle once more and marched back fiercely to the avenue, where the path veered round to the right and a tall young man lounged by the fence palings smoking a pipe.

'Please, sir, is this the way to Easton Hall?'

'Certainly it is. Through the stables over there, and beyond the trees.' Glancing down, his eye took in her perspiring face, the shabby dress and the squat bundle clasped in her arms. 'But see here! I'm going that way myself. You must let me carry your things.'

Esther gratefully surrendered her load, which the young man swung over his shoulder with no apparent effort. In doing so he rose up to his full height, which, she saw, was even greater than she had first thought.

'Gracious, but you're a tall one.'

The young man smiled at the compliment. 'Six feet two in my stockings. But then footmen's always tall, ain't they?'

'Are you one of the footmen at the hall?'

He smiled again, but less humorously. '*The* footman. There's only one. Though old Randall, the butler, will wait at table sometimes when there's company. But it's a poor thing to be in a house where only one footman is kept. I shall be off presently, I daresay, to London or somewhere. Mr Dixey knows my feelings and says he won't stand in my way, which is decent of him, I must say, for there's some masters you know as will move heaven and earth to keep a footman in his place.'

Awed by this display of vigour and, it seemed to her, sophistication, Esther said nothing. The footman – his name was William, he allowed – she judged to be a year or so older than herself. Looking at him now, she saw a sallow, bony face, a shade too small for the broad shoulders on which it sat, with a pair of dark eyes whose glint suggested that you would do very well if their owner were friendly but less so if he had cause to distrust you. They were walking now across a long, low hillside path, where amid gaps in the trees the flat Norfolk plain ran on in the distance, the air growing cooler and with a faint intimation of approaching dusk. As they went, William pointed out various sites of interest to those who worked at the hall: a certain meadow in which a servants' pic-nic had taken place the previous summer, a stream from which capital perch could be taken, a particular field in which Sarah the parlourmaid had fallen into peril with a bull. 'It was a sight to see,' William explained, laughing. 'Her running off over the grass with her skirts pulled near unto her ears!' Not quite liking this exultation in another's misfortune, but perceiving that he meant only to be friendly, Esther smiled gravely back.

'They said at the station that the cart would bring up my box later on.'

'The cart isn't going to the station tonight – that is, I don't believe so. But Sarah will help you make do. She's a good sort, is Sarah. But what brings you to Easton, eh?'

His interest was of such a frank and ingenuous kind that her natural reserve was swiftly conquered.

'It was Lady Bamber that got me my place.'

'Lady Bamber! I knows that name. An eye that you could take out and hammer on an anvil if so that you had a mind. Comes to stay in the winter and makes no end of trouble. Tips bad, too.' He bent down to prise out a stick from the hedgerow and balanced it thoughtfully on his palm. 'Can you read, Esther?'

'Certainly I can.' The thought that he might be making fun of her caused her to knit her brows in anger. 'Why should I not?'

'I meant no offence. Truly now.' He flung the stick high in an arc above his head and watched it fall. 'Sarah can't read. She can't, though. She sits and looks at the stories in *Bow Bells*, but it's all shamming, really it is. She can't read no better than one of Mr Dixey's dogs. Sarah and me are great friends,' he went on, in answer to Esther's speculative glance. 'Friends, that is – and no more. But if you can read you will be starting on the right foot, for Mrs Wates, the cook, is always wanting the maids to read to her.'

This glut of information – Sarah the parlourmaid, Mrs Wates the cook, Lady Bamber's visits – served to depress Esther's spirits, for the protocols of which they spoke seemed altogether beyond her

57

understanding. Yet they awakened in her a curiosity about her new situation which she was anxious to satisfy.

'Who is Mr Dixey?'

'Mr Dixey? Why – Mr Dixey is the squire. Owns all the land hereabouts.' He swept his arm over the plain visible beyond the hedge. 'But you mustn't fear about him. Regular recluse he is. Shuts himself up in his room for weeks on end. Or wanders about the grounds as if there were no one there but himself.'

Young as she was, Esther had distinct ideas as to how gentlemen should manage their estates. 'Don't he take no interest in the place then?'

'Not he! There's an agent to manage it, you know. They say he has lost ever so much money, but that's not footman's business. Old Randall would know, I daresay. He and the master is very thick, sometimes.'

But Esther was still puzzling over the notion of a squire who took no interest in his land. 'But what does he care about then?'

'Oh, he's a great naturalist you know. There's a stuffed bear in his study and cases full of eggs and such things, and none of the maids likes it a bit. I shouldn't care to go in there myself after dark, when the lamps are out. Here! We're coming to the house right enough.'

She saw that the hedge path whose line they had been following for the past half-hour had now begun to descend through high banks of summer foliage, knots and clumps of tall trees beyond which outbuildings and stableyards could now be glimpsed. After the heat of the level path, this downward progress was very pleasant to her: there were great outcrops of swollen ferns that seemed to conceal sunless woodland glades, dense interiors far below the tree canopy. The effect of this new landscape, and of William, who continued to talk of Mr Dixey's dogs, of a great hound he had bred for the chase in Europe, four feet high, of all kinds of things both strange and familiar, was to produce in her a sense of dissociation, so that she might have been walking into some magical faery land altogether detached from the world she knew. The sensation was such that she clutched anxiously at the rough cloth of her dress and the pointing of her calico jacket as if to reassure herself that some vestige of the old world had come with her.

But it was so: the man at her side was simply another servant from the hall; her mother's books were in the bundle that he carried; the

58

railway station lay three miles down the path behind her. There was no mystery, except that she comprehended that a certain part of her life – the life of nagging women in suburban villas, her mother's cottage and her brothers and sisters – was at an end, and that a new one whose lineaments she could barely discern was about to begin. Humbled by this realisation, she found herself taking a sharp, obtrusive interest in the unfamiliar territory into which they now passed, in the curve of the tall poplar trees that hung over the path and the plumes of smoke rising from unseen chimneys in the middle distance.

'What are those sheds beyond the stable yard? There seem a great many of them.'

'Them? That's where Mr Dixey keeps his dogs. You'll hear them in a moment, I daresay, as we go past. But it's not a place to linger. Jack Barclay, as was footman before me, lost his place on account of interfering with the master's dogs. But look here, it's past eight and Mrs Wates is just the sort to make trouble over a lost half-hour. You had better say the train was late.'

Esther knew that this was a falsehood, and was troubled on that score, but she consented to nod her head. They came eventually, by way of certain vegetable gardens and glasshouses, into a little cramped square, its surface made of bare earth stamped flat, abutting the back parts of the house. Here a stout, red-faced woman with bare, mottled arms stood shaking out a tablecloth while contriving to suggest by the attitude in which she stood that this arrangement was not to her satisfaction.

'So you are Spalding, are you?'

'Yes, ma'am, I am.'

'But it is half-past eight. You were to have been here on the hour.'

'The train was late, Mrs Wates,' William cheerfully interjected. 'Indeed it was.'

'And you taking the girl idling out of her way, no doubt, William Latch. Well, it can't be helped. You had better come inside.'

Meekly Esther passed behind her into a long, low kitchen, its air made stifling by the heat of the range and the log fire that burned at its further end. She had an impression of squat, heavy furniture, a cat darting suddenly away from the hearth, muted light spilling from the half-shuttered windows. Standing on the flagged floor, the bundle silently returned to her grasp, she became aware of several persons seated around a vast mahogany table, all eyeing her with a profound curiosity. A grey-headed old man who had been reading aloud from the Bible stopped halfway through the verse, slotted his finger in the page and looked at her open-mouthed. A woman with a lined face, glistening black hair and an air of authority brought her hands, both of which had been extended onto her chair-arms, sharply together. A thin girl in a maid's dress and a lace cap bobbed up from her seat and then sat down again. Somewhere in the near distance a bell rang. And so Esther came to her new home.

(ii)

Esther awoke in a room suffused with light: light that poured through the open window a yard or so from her head, bounced and reflected off the coverings of her bed and made bright patterns on the bare, distempered walls beyond. For a moment, half unconscious, she was unable to recollect where she was: a stump of candle, half-melted upon a metal saucer at her bedside, seemed a thing of horror; the noise of birdsong from beyond the window jangled alarmingly in her ears. Gradually these apparitions passed and she became aware of her surroundings. She lay in a narrow bed, with a second bed jammed hard against its side – the arrangement leaving a gap of no more than a foot between the adjoining walls – in an attic room with a sloping ceiling and a low beam from which someone had hung a nosegay of withered flowers. A sound – not the birdsong from beyond the window, nor yet the noise of her own breathing, to which she had become keenly alert – disturbed her, and with a start she sat upright against the bolster. Sarah the parlourmaid, whose quarters she had been bidden to share, loomed half-dressed in the space between the end of the beds and the door posts, washing her face and torso in a basinful of water.

'Gracious,' she remarked, acknowledging Esther's presence with a shrug of her bare shoulder. 'In my last place the housekeeper would have been ashamed to have two girls squeezed together in a room where there's no space to swing a cat. I declare we shall smother each other in the night without knowing.'

'I'm very sorry to be a trouble to you.'

'Oh it's no trouble. Indeed it's a pleasure to have company. I have been alone up here for a month, and the last kitchenmaid was a

60

mouse.' Finishing her ablutions, she turned towards Esther and began to dry herself with a morsel of towel. 'But, Esther, why did you quarrel with the cook last evening? Everyone remarked it, and she is sure to mention it to Mr Randall.'

In her curiosity at Sarah's conversation, and the novelty of her situation, Esther had forgotten the events of the previous night. Now a fount of remembered bitterness welled up inside her and she gripped the edge of the bedspread with her hands.

'It was she that quarrelled with me! To expect a girl to set to work on the instant peeling potatoes, with no dress to change into on account of a donkey-cart that never came.'

'I don't doubt that you're right, but you must see it from her point of view. Cooks are cooks, you know. And now she'll have her revenge, you mark my words. Why, you'll spend a morning sanding saucepans if she has her way.'

Judging her to be a friendly girl, Esther climbed out of the narrow bed and began to put on her own clothes. Her good opinion of Sarah was confirmed a moment later when the latter said: 'Look, it is only six o'clock. I have not to boil the kettle until half-past. Let us go downstairs and I can show you about the place before Mrs Wates is afoot. She is very bad in the mornings, you know, and rarely shows herself before eight.'

They went silently along the passages of the upper part of the house to the back staircase. Here all was quiet. A mouse ran over the uppermost step and disappeared into the wainscot. Down below them, in the hallway, they heard a door close.

'That will be Mr Randall. They say there are nights when he never goes to bed at all.'

'Why should he do that?' Esther wondered.

'Oh he is a sly one, always poking about the place and turning up when you least expect him. How many of you are there at home, Esther?'

'Why, my mother and my four brothers and sisters. My father's dead.'

'Now, you see, there's another reason why you must be civil to Mrs Wates. Even if she does wear a moustache and drink gin out of her teacup.'

Presently, talking all the while in subdued voices, they came through the back part of the house to the servants' quarters. Whether or not the retreating figure seen from the stairwell had been Mr Randall, the kitchen was empty. A fragment of the fire still glowed in the grate and Sarah busied herself with its reconstruction. She had quick, agile movements but moved uncertainly on her feet, Esther noticed, on one occasion coming within an instant of toppling into the hearth.

'I have got a stiffness in my leg,' she admitted, when Esther commented on this. 'Indeed, at my last place the footmen used to call me dot-and-carry.'

'If they did, then that was very cruel of them,' Esther burst out.

'Cruel? Then I have known crueller things than that. But look, here are the knife drawers and the pots for the vegetables. The meat safes are in the back cupboard. If you wish to redeem yourself with Mrs Wates, then you must give her your beer. We are allowed a pint each at lunchtime and dinner. And if she sends you to the far orchard for apples, say that the distance is too great and she should send the keeper's boy instead. She'll respect you for that.'

'You are very kind,' Esther said, blushing.

'No, not kind. But you should know these things, and there are others that will grudge you the telling.'

In this way Esther and Sarah became very intimate. Indeed, by the time that the servants' breakfast things were laid out on the table and Esther, under Sarah's direction, had a crock of porridge boiling on the range, she had acquired a substantial stock of information bearing on her new position. Thus:

Mrs Wates, the cook, drank.

Mrs Finnie, the housekeeper, was a tartar. Mrs Finnie had got Sarah her place, but perhaps she might find that she preferred a place that Mrs F. had *not* got her.

Mr Randall, the butler, was a Godfearing man, and the elder of a dissenting chapel nearby. 'Indeed, we are given sermons morning, noon and night. And he has such a down upon the maids.' A girl couldn't look at a young man without Mr Randall finding out and making himself objectionable.

Margaret Lane, the housemaid, was a goose. 'It is unkind to say so, I know, but indeed she is. Why only last week Jem Raikes, Mr Dixey's gamekeeper, was with us at tea and to quiz her he said that he had shot a seraph that happened to be flying across Easton Wood, and she believed every word.'

As for William, Sarah informed her, 'He is a nice fellow, but he don't mean anything. Why, he and I kept company for three months last winter and were ready to have the banns put up in church, but it came to naught.'

Esther, wondering about William and what tasks he might be engaged upon that morning, found herself interrogated by Mrs Wates who, coming down to breakfast in a bad temper and seeing her stirring the porridge, wished instantly to know if it had been made according to her exact specifications. Having managed to satisfy her in this, Esther had hoped to escape to the scullery (this she had been given to understand was her private domain) and the peeling of the luncheon vegetables, but Mrs Wates called her back.

'Now, Esther,' she began. 'I trust that you are truly sorry for your wilfulness yesterday evening?'

It was on the edge of Esther's tongue to tell the red-faced cook that she was not sorry, but she resolved to curb her temper. 'Indeed I am, ma'am, very sorry.'

'Very well. Then we shall say no more about it. I like all my girls to be hard-working girls. Are you a hard-working girl, Esther?'

'I hope I am, ma'am.'

'Well we have been without a kitchenmaid for a month, and there is much to be done. You had better leave those vegetables for Margaret and come with me.'

The consequence was that, as Sarah had foreseen, Esther spent the morning at the scullery table cleaning a quantity of saucepans greater than it seemed probable that any single kitchen could accommodate. They were copper saucepans of the previous century, whose interiors required scouring with chains and whose surfaces must be burnished up until they shone. And yet Esther did not repine, for it seemed to her that there was much in her mind that she wished to consider. The scullery window looked out onto the earthen square and she stood, as if rooted to the spot, gazing out at the patch of grass beyond, where two small boys – the sons of the keeper, whose cottage lay hard by – played with a dog and threw quoits at a peg in the ground. The sunlight fell over the long table, burning off the copper and the bundles of knives, and she was not displeased to be drawn back to her work, which now seemed to her a consuming thing of great seriousness and importance.

At eleven, very red-faced and perspiring, Sarah fetched her a cup of tea.

'You have quite melted Mrs Wates' heart. What do you think? I just overheard her telling Mr Randall that she thought you were a hard worker after all.'

'Gracious, Sarah, you look tired. What have you been doing?'

'Oh it is Mrs Finnie. She always gives me disagreeable jobs. Just now I have been beating out carpets on the lawn.'

A little later Margaret Lane, the housemaid, stole into the scullery to prepare the vegetables. She was a small, dark-haired girl with a face like a doll's, disposed, in the light of Esther's treatment of Mrs Wates, to regard her with some awe.

'I declare,' she said, giving a nervous little glance at Esther's strong arms as they moved over the copper, 'that you are so fierce I quite expect to be eaten.'

'But I am not fierce at all,' Esther said, putting down the saucepan she was scouring. 'Indeed I am not. And I am sorry you are to do my work.'

'Oh it is nothing,' Margaret replied meekly. 'This is not a big establishment, you know, and we're all girls together. There are some houses where the parlourmaid won't speak to the housemaid. But we are not like that here.'

Watching the girl as she sat peeling vegetables, with her brow furrowed in concentration, Esther thought that she would like to talk to her, but Margaret seemed reluctant to speak further.

The servants dined at one. Mr Dixey, being an old-fashioned man, had his dinner sent up at four. There were guests at the hall but twice in the week, the other servants said. Seated at the lower end of the table, between Sarah and Margaret, her plate filled with beefsteak pie and greenstuff, Esther let her mind wander over the events of the previous day: her arrival at Easton, Sarah, William, the light burning through the bedroom window. William was absent from the table, having accompanied Mr Dixey into Watton in the gig. Before the meal began, she listened wonderingly as Mr Randall, hands clasped in front of his face, offered up an extemporaneous prayer.

'Oh Lord, we're all sinners here. I'm a sinner. Sarah and Margaret, Esther, who has just joined us, they're sinners too. Protect us, dear Lord, from the wrong that we do, and the wrong that is done to us, and bring us all to your table that we may eat with you in safety, and lead us to your eternal rock that is cleft for us that we may shelter there in comfort. Amen.'

After luncheon, Mr Randall took himself to his parlour to smoke his pipe and, it was thought, to sleep. Mrs Wates was driven into Easton in a dog-cart by one of the gamekeeper's sons. Margaret was summoned to an upper chamber by Mrs Finnie to sort linen ('It's a precious hard time she'll have of it,' Sarah explained to Esther, 'with the old cat always finding fault.'). Left to themselves, the two girls cleared away the lunch things and brought in fresh logs for the fire from the timber store in the yard.

'You must not think that anything happens here,' Sarah told her, 'for it does not. I never knew a duller house.'

'Oh but it is very beautiful,' the other replied. 'I think I should like to walk in the woods for hours at a time if I had the chance.'

'Well, perhaps you shall. Look, there is a whole hour until Mrs Wates comes back. Let us go to the orchard. It is my favourite place.'

And so they walked past the kitchen garden and the glasshouses along a dusty path where the grass grew six feet high against the hedges to a sad little half-acre apple orchard, very ragged and overgrown, where last year's fruit lay rotting beneath the trees.

'Why is there no one to pick it?' Esther asked.

'Because there's no men left to work on the estate, you know. Mr Dixey discharged them all last Michaelmas quarter-day. They say he is pressed for money.'

Esther made no comment. Of the resources required to finance a gentleman's estate she knew nothing. Lady Bamber lived in a villa of the kind that Esther had seen on the station road, and bullied her servant. But Lady Bamber, she knew, was the widow of a naval commander, lived on three hundred pounds a year, and had no property. The Dixeys, she had been led to believe, were an old county family. This paradox had the effect of quickening her interest in the solitary files of apple trees, some of them so choked with foliage that it was impossible to pass between them. Turning to Sarah, in search of further information, she found the other girl seated on a tree stump with her apron drawn up to her face.

'Gracious, Sarah, what is the matter? Ain't you well?'

'Oh it is nothing. Indeed it is very nice here, and I am glad to have you with me.' She dabbed at her eyes once or twice with the sleeve of her dress. 'If Joseph were here he would tell me not to take on, I know he would.'

'Who is Joseph?'

'He is my brother. But he is in China with the army and I have not seen him these two years.'

'And have you no other family?'

'None to speak of. But he writes to me, and that is something. Look, there is that gaby Margaret Lane. Mrs Finnie must have grown tired of sorting the linen and sent her out to find us. Hollo, Margaret! You would never guess what has happened to us since we sat here.'

Margaret's face stared anxiously at them from the path. 'What has happened?'

'Why a great swarm of bees from Farmer Mangold's hive across the field fell upon us. Indeed I think they would have stung us to death had not Esther here yelled at them and driven them away.'

Seeing the girl's open mouth, Esther could not resist a smile. Margaret frowned. 'It is very bad of you to hoax me in that way. Mrs Finnie says you are both to come instantly to the house.'

'Cheek of Mrs Finnie to send you her orders,' Sarah muttered under her breath, 'when everyone knows that the kitchenmaid answers to the cook. You should say you will wait to hear from Mrs Wates.'

Nevertheless, she made no move to prevent Esther from accompanying her back along the path. As they came through the kitchen garden, a slither of displaced gravel and the noise of hoofs announced the return of the gig. A moment later William's tall figure, his arms laden with parcels, could be seen in the kitchen doorway.

'Let us not go into the kitchen,' announced Sarah, who had stopped to adjust the pinafore of her dress. 'Look, there are the shutters of the dairy half-open. Ten to one the cat has got in. Will you come with me, Esther?'

Wondering, Esther followed her. There was no sign of the cat.

That evening after supper Mr Randall read from the Psalmist:

> *Behold, he travaileth with iniquity,*
> *And hath conceived mischief, and brought forth falsehood.*
> *He made a pit and digged it,*
> *And is fallen into the pit which he made.*
> *His mischief shall return upon his own head,*
> *And his violent dealings shall come down upon his own pate.*

VI

Singular History of Mr Pardew

There are some men whose lives are altogether mysterious. How do they come by their daily bread? No one knows, and yet they are always respectably dressed, seen stepping briskly out of hansoms or into their box at Astley's. Their very wives, perhaps, are ignorant of the paths they tread in the course of a morning's business, the company they keep and the hour at which they are likely to return to their familial hearth. They are glimpsed at the opera, at race courses, at boxing matches, at all the genteel diversions which England affords its citizenry, and yet the friends gathered round them are as mysterious as they. Their absence – should they cease to appear in these public amphitheatres – is seldom remarked, for there is no one sufficiently near to them to remark it. They bring legal suits, occasionally, and win them, they sit in Parliament or are active at the patent office, without one iota of this mystery ever separating itself from their elusive forms, and their fellow citizens can spend twenty years in their occasional company without ever forming a clear idea of their character, opinions and temperament.

Such a one was Mr Pardew. At the time of which I write he was a man of perhaps fifty years of age – but there had been no one with him at a school or a college or a regimental mess to confirm this speculation – tall, long-jawed, his hair still jet-blacked and with a hard grey eye that suggested its owner would brook no interference in any scheme on which he was legitimately engaged. As his voice assumed at moments of emphasis a somewhat curious intonation, it was thought that he had spent some time on the Continent, and might even have been born there, but this, as in the matter of his age, was the merest conjecture. As for the other appurtenances by which a man's stature is generally judged, scarcely anything could be said. He had a house in Kensington, but it was not thought that he was often at home there, and when he entertained his friends it was at a public room or at a theatre. There was a Mrs Pardew – at least he spoke of such a lady – but no one had ever seen her. Of his antecedents, his business and the nature of the ravens that fed him, all was as dark as pitch. And yet it was said at clubs, and in drawing rooms, by those who if they did not know him well at least knew of him, that Mr Pardew was a warm man and that he knew what he was about.

At the same time, a man cannot spend half his adult life on the margin of polite society without one or two incontrovertible facts arising from his dealings, and so it was with Mr Pardew. The sum of what was known about him may have been unconscionably small, but there was at least – something, and what there was encouraged Mr Pardew's fellow men to regard him with a certain circumspection. Ten years ago he had featured in the commercial directories as a stockbroker with an office in Pump Court EC and a certain Mr Fardel as his associate. Of this Mr Fardel even less was known than his partner, and yet his notoriety was, for a brief moment, altogether remarkable. In short, Mr Fardel was found one morning lying dead in an obscure alleyway not far from Pump Court with the back of his head stove in by some blunt instrument – a life-preserver or bludgeon, it was suggested by Captain McTurk of the City Police Force, who attended this melancholy scene. It was first presumed that Mr Fardel had been robbed, until a search of his person disclosed that neither his notecase, his diamond tie-pin nor his gold watch-seals – not even the silver-knobbed cane that lay by his side – had been disturbed.

Some enemy, then, who had waylaid him in this dark corner at dead of night – the hour of Mr Fardel's demise was put at between one and two in the morning – to prosecute a personal vendetta? And yet Mr Fardel's existence, diligently investigated by Captain McTurk and his men, proved to be the most blameless that ever a man had lived. A bishop, as the inspector observed, would have been flattered by the encomia pronounced over his catafalque. And here the matter would have rested, had it not been for a statement offered to the police some months later by a gentleman who had been abroad and only lately returned to hear news of the murder.

This person alleged that, walking in the vicinity of Pump Court on the night of the murder – very late it was, he believed – and passing the office of Pardew & Fardel, he heard loud voices coming from within. It was then suggested by persons who had had professional dealings with Pardew & Fardel that the two principals had for some little time been in dispute about certain matters relating to the firm's business. A clerk summoned to give evidence to Captain McTurk deposed that on the day preceding Mr Fardel's murder, during the course of an argument in the doorway of the office, he had seen Mr Pardew raise his fist and shake it at his partner's retiring back. All this was very bad, but it was not perhaps conclusive.

Mr Pardew, in the course of his several questionings, replied in his blandest manner. Certainly he and his late partner, the absence of whose capital he very much regretted, had had their differences. Certainly they had quarrelled that day in the office. Certainly they had remained there until a late hour on the evening that Mr Fardell had met his end. Equally certain, however, was that between one and two in the morning, and indeed for two hours before that, he had been playing cards at his very respectable club on Hay Hill in the company of half a dozen very respectable gentlemen, all of whom were ready to swear to his never having left the room.

And there, inevitably, the matter had to rest. Captain McTurk declared himself satisfied – more or less – of Mr Pardew's innocence. The office in Pump Court continued to trade for some months and then shut its doors, and no more was heard of Mr Pardew for the next half-dozen years. It was thought that he had engaged himself in commercial speculations on the Continent – some said at Leipzig, others at Prague – but whatever commercial speculations they were no hint of their nature was ever breathed in London. There were one or two people – possibly the gentlemen with whom Mr Pardew had been playing whist on the night of his partner's misfortune – who said that he had been harshly done by, and that base calumny and foul slander had conspired against his reputation, but these defenders were not notably numerous. When Mr Pardew returned into the public gaze, whether from Vienna, Prague or some other foreign capital, it was as the proprietor of a manufacturing process which, various quidnuncs had asserted, might altogether revolutionise certain aspects of commercial engineering. No one quite knew how Mr Pardew had come by his expertise, or his capital, but for a short time at any rate his stock was in the ascendant. And then there came another gentleman, a professional engineer, which Mr Pardew was

not, who alleged that in the course of their association, at some manufacturing works in the north of England, Mr Pardew had – defrauded
him of a patent? Appropriated some idea to which he was not entitled? The legal point was obscure, but it was generally held by those
who knew about such things that Mr Pardew had behaved badly. A
Chancery suit was brought at great expense, whose result was not
quite satisfactory, either to Mr Pardew or his former associate, and
the manufacturing process altogether lapsed. All that had taken place
four years ago, after which no more had been known of Mr Pardew's
whereabouts, or his undertakings, than Captain Franklin's.

On this particular morning – it was a raw, brisk morning in the
early part of the year – this Mr Pardew could be found seated in an
office in the modest thoroughfare of Carter Lane, London, EC. It
was a somewhat humble premises – no more than a single room with
a couple of tables crammed together and a fat, shabby clerk grooming
his nails with a paper-knife in the corner – but Mr Pardew's demeanour
suggested that it was his to order and command. Beyond the window,
which looked out onto the lane itself, the great dome of St Paul's
spread across the skyline, and Mr Pardew, lounging on his tilted chair
at such an angle that it seemed he must topple over and go sprawling
in the dust, regarded it sardonically, as if he altogether saw through
it and declined to be hoodwinked by its bulk and solemnity. The clerk,
whose attitude to Mr Pardew suggested a familiarity not often found
in City functionaries, completed the paring of his nails and flung the
knife down onto his desk, where it rattled ominously and lay quivering for a full half-minute.

'Are you a-going out this morning then?'

Mr Pardew continued to stare sardonically at the cathedral dome.
'I may very well do so. What is it to you?'

'Nothink. Nothink at all. I mind my business like anyone else. But
what am I to say if Donaldson comes?'

'You may give him a civil answer, show him the paper and remind
him that it's due three weeks hence.'

'Shall I now?' exclaimed the clerk with a horrible, bogus enthusiasm. 'And I don't doubt he'll pay us the fifty sovs on the instant.
Cash down, I shouldn't wonder. Oh yes indeed.'

From which conversation it may be gathered that whatever business Mr Pardew had previously undertaken he now dealt in discounted
bills – the discounted bills, moreover, of people who were very anxious

that they should not be redeemed. The look which Mr Pardew gave his clerk at the conclusion of this exchange was a curious one, for it spoke, on the one hand, of a very definite obligation to him which Mr Pardew could not ignore, and, on the other, of an absolute determination to have done with this indebtedness, and it was perhaps as well that the clerk did not see it.

It was now about midday, the time at which if men of business are to perform any useful activity they are generally about it, but still Mr Pardew sat, swaggering, it might be thought a little uneasily, on his chair. Once or twice he took a letter from his waistcoat pocket and read its contents through very thoroughly, made various abstruse calculations on a second piece of foolscap and then pushed the first document into the pocket of his coat. Once, again, he picked up a walking-stick that lay against the table, weighed it in his hand like a man who tests a weapon and then replaced it.

The clerk, meanwhile, ate his luncheon out of a paper bag while regarding his master with a vigilant eye. Finally, in a movement that for all its purpose seemed to suggest some inner uncertainty, Mr Pardew rose to his feet, jammed his hat on his head and thrust the stick under his arm.

'I'll not be back. If Carey calls, you had better have a message sent to me at the club.'

The clerk having signified that he would do this, Mr Pardew opened the office door and stepped out into the street. Very spruce he looked in his grey morning coat and tall hat, with the cane wedged under his shoulder like a swagger-stick, and several passers-by remarked him as they went along Carter Lane in the direction of the City. Had any one of them continued to stare, they would have observed him walk in a leisurely fashion along the lane and its adjacent thoroughfares until he came to New Bridge Street. Here, in sight of Ludgate Circus, he boarded an omnibus, tendered his twopence to the conductor and was conveyed along High Holborn to the vicinity of Lincoln's Inn. A further walk of two minutes brought him to the chambers of Mr Crabbe, where he sent up his card via the clerk and asked if he might have the pleasure of speaking to that gentleman. Had there been a third person present in Mr Crabbe's sombre vestibule that person might perhaps have deduced from their familiarity that Mr Pardew had had previous dealings with the clerk, and that they were sufficient to admit the transfer of two sovereigns wrapped up in a twist of paper.

Mr Crabbe, sitting in his room, with its fine view out over the gardens – very frosty now, with the trees altogether black and leafless – and the wall of books surrounding him on three sides, knew all the little there was to know about his visitor, did not like it at all and had half a mind to send back the card with a short answer. By chance, however, a great nobleman who had intended to spend that morning at Lincoln's Inn had found himself unexpectedly detained at the House, and Mr Crabbe, tired of poking his fire and bullying his clerk, was eager for diversion. Accordingly he sent down word that he would be happy to see Mr Pardew, and, having done so, placed himself before his bow window, the better to receive his visitor.

If Mr Crabbe had expected that Mr Pardew would be awed or made otherwise respectful by this piece of condescension he was mistaken, for Mr Pardew stalked into the room as if Mr Crabbe's deigning to see him was a simple acknowledgment of his genius. Upon my word, Mr Crabbe thought to himself, he is going to hit me with that stick! However, having exuberantly flourished his cane practically under the old lawyer's nose, Mr Pardew secured it beneath his arm and bobbed his head.

'It is very good of you to see me, Mr Crabbe. Truly I am obliged.'

Mr Crabbe, bobbing his own head, and silently acknowledging that it was good of him and that Mr Pardew in considering himself obliged spoke only the truth, looked carefully in front of him. He noticed the shine of Mr Pardew's hat and coat, the jut of his jaw and the grip of his fingers on the walking-stick, but he did not as yet form any judgement save to wonder idly what possible errand, or request, or supplication could have brought Mr Pardew to see him.

'I believe, Mr Crabbe, that we have a mutual friend. His Grace the Duke of —— has mentioned your name to me.'

At this Mr Crabbe pricked up his ears. He was indeed a friend of the Duke of ——, knew every secret of the great man's that there was to be known, had presided, in fact, over the ducal family's affairs for thirty years. In addition he was jealous of his friendship, and it irked him that such a man as Mr Pardew (a man who, as he reflected, was supposed to have murdered his own partner!) should presume to allude to it. At the same time, such was the discretion with which Mr Crabbe conducted his affairs that he had an idea that the only way in which Mr Pardew could have come by this information was if he had been told it by the duke himself. Consequently he did not bristle up in anger but contented himself with smiling rather stiffly.

'His Grace is very kind.'

'His Grace,' said Mr Pardew, 'is a d——d old fool. He has a great heap of money which he will not invest, an estate which is falling around his ears and some highly expensive habits which he will not curb. But doubtless you know him better than I.'

And here Mr Crabbe's eyes opened very wide indeed – not merely because he was shocked at hearing his noble friend, the proud bearer of sempiternal strawberry leaves, jocularly abused in this way, but because Mr Pardew's estimate of his foolishness was so manifestly correct.

'You must forgive my asperity,' Mr Pardew went meekly on. 'But I find that in dealing with persons such as His Grace, one is always being pressed to offer advice, whereas advice is generally the last thing that is wanted.'

'That may well be the case, Mr Pardew. It may well be the case indeed. What is it that I can do for you this morning?'

'I shall be perfectly frank, Mr Crabbe. I have money, rightfully mine, in the hands of others, that I need to reclaim.'

A prudent man – and Mr Crabbe was such a man – knowing something of his visitor's history, and hearing this pronouncement, would have taken the opportunity to bid Mr Pardew good morning. And yet for some reason – it may have been the ghostly presence of His Grace, or some greater fascination of which he was not perfectly aware – Mr Crabbe did not ring the bell for his clerk or go and stand by his fire in such a way that even so thick-skinned an animal as a rhinoceros would have understood the interview to be at an end.

'Am I to understand, Mr Pardew, that you are asking me to collect a debt?'

'In a manner of speaking. I am asking you, in the first instance, to write a letter.'

'But the retrieval of a debt is your ultimate aim?'

'Certainly.'

'But surely, Mr Pardew – you will forgive my bluntness – any attorney of your acquaintance could write such a letter? And might indeed be better suited to its execution than such a person as I.'

Mr Pardew bared his teeth ingratiatingly in a manner that suggested he forgave Mr Crabbe the bluntness entirely. 'If you will permit me to say so, Mr Crabbe, there is no one better qualified to execute such a commission as yourself.'

'That is all very well.'

Mr Crabbe was aware that all this was very mysterious, and that he did not quite like it. Most men, in visiting a lawyer's office, are specific in their desires. They wish a document to be drawn up, or a transgression punished, or a claim pursued. Mr Crabbe fancied – nay, Mr Crabbe knew – that something was amiss. Still, though, he did not voice his suspicions but stood on his Turkey carpet with his thin back to the fire considering what had been placed before him. Mr Pardew sensed something of his disquiet and turned in his chair to face him.

'Perhaps I had better explain myself, Mr Crabbe. I am at present engaged in the trade of bill-discounting' – Mr Crabbe nodded his head at this – 'but until fairly recently I was active in a branch of commercial manufacture. At the commencement of this business, which I may say was not unsuccessful, I had several associates – men of a humbler station than my own – whose practical help I needed but whose financial means were necessarily limited. Accordingly, it was decided that though they might withdraw funds out of the busi- ness my own capital should remain within it, with the prospect of future redress.'

'No doubt there is documentary proof of these agreements?'

'No, there is not. Such was the closeness of our association that each of us thought our word sufficient. Doubtless it was very foolish.'

Mr Crabbe nodded his head to signify that it was very foolish.

'But I am convinced,' Mr Pardew went on, smiling in a very sugges- tive manner, 'of their essential good nature and their willingness to return what is rightfully mine. The business closed a year or two since, but the profits were considerable. It is my aim to retrieve a propor- tion of those profits.'

'Trusting to your former associates' essential good nature?'

'And to lawyers' letters, Mr Crabbe. Which are sometimes more efficacious even than that.'

This was of course the moment at which Mr Crabbe should have taken full possession of his Turkey carpet, turned his back on Mr Pardew and wished his visitor good morning. The story about Mr Pardew's cred- itors he did not believe for a moment, for he could think of no man so situated as Mr Pardew – and certainly not such a man as Mr Pardew

– who would not have taken better steps to protect himself. It appeared to him, in so far as he could judge from the fragmentary materials before him, that Mr Pardew was playing some game in which the name of a lawyer, and especially such a lawyer as himself, would be useful to him, but he could not be sure. Above all, he was suspicious of Mr Pardew's manner, which, however deferential and respectful, seemed to him – false. Still, though, he did not ring the bell, summon his clerk or inti- mate to Mr Pardew that he would get better advice elsewhere. There was something about the situation, still more perhaps about the man himself, that intrigued him and that he wished in some manner to keep within his grasp. Consequently he continued to stare at Mr Pardew as he sat easily in his chair, wondering what could be done about him and what could profitably be said.

'Of course there is no guarantee that you would achieve your object.'

'I suppose not.'

'No guarantee at all.'

'I have no doubt it is as you say.'

'And you would wish to proceed immediately?'

'No. That is, not quite immediately.'

'Indeed! Then you have a very emollient nature, Mr Pardew. I confess that if I were owed money over such a long period I should be pressing my creditors. I should be very pressing, indeed I should.'

Again Mr Pardew smiled his ingratiating smile. 'It is a question merely of information . . . I will admit, Mr Crabbe, that there is one gentleman of whose whereabouts I am altogether ignorant.'

Once more Mr Crabbe hardly believed a word of what was said to him. Men, he knew, can usually be found, especially if the pursuer was such a one as Mr Pardew. Yet he was aware that, having tempo- rised in this way, it would be difficult for him to draw back. Without precisely acknowledging the fact, he feared that Mr Pardew had been too much for him, and while this understanding irritated him it also served to quicken his interest. At the same time he was determined, for these and other reasons, that the interview should cease forthwith.

Mr Pardew, observing this, was aware of the workings of the old lawyer's mind. He realised that if he were to play his trump card he had better play it now. Accordingly he reached into his breast pocket and brought forth a sheet of paper folded into two, very grimy about its extremities and bound up with a red ribbon.

'Here is a letter,' he said in the easy tones of a man who entreats his friend to examine the evening paper. 'Perhaps you had better read it.'

Mr Crabbe accepted the proffered piece of foolscap and sniffed at it. If the set of his eyes betrayed the fact that its contents were a source of profound disquiet to him, the tone of his voice did not confirm this impression.

'Where did you get this?'

'Dear me, I hardly recollect. Let us say that it came to me in the course of my professional dealings.'

'You are no doubt aware that it is a forgery – a most impudent forgery.'

'No doubt. And yet I believe you are acquainted with the Mr Dixey to whom it was written?'

'That, sir, is none of your business.' And yet still, for some reason, Mr Crabbe hesitated to ring for his clerk.

'Perhaps it is not.' Mr Pardew's smile was, Mr Crabbe thought, the most infuriating thing he had ever seen. 'But there is a deed-box with his name on it in your strongroom, or I am the old duke's ghost.'

Something in Mr Crabbe's eye divulged that there was such a box. But Mr Pardew was a clever man and did not on this occasion press home his advantage. 'It is a small world is it not, where a client of yours may also be a connection of mine? These things must be expected, I suppose.'

There was a silence, while Mr Crabbe, absolutely outraged by this treatment, yet still calculating what had better be done about it, stared at his desk and at the letter, which Mr Pardew now prudently retrieved and dangled between his fingers.

'You had better come to me again when there is anything to be done,' he said eventually.

Mr Pardew rose to his feet and bowed. If he felt that he had achieved a great object he did not by the manner of his voice and eye betray it. Having flourished his stick once again, he placed it under his arm.

'I am very much obliged to you, Mr Crabbe. Very much. One does not always enjoying dealing with lawyers, but when one does it is as well to find one whom one respects.'

'No doubt.'

'And perhaps you would do me the honour of conveying my compliments to His Grace?'

Now Mr Crabbe did not like this at all. Mr Pardew's observations about lawyers were, to one who had been in the profession for a half-century, disagreeable to him. He was aware, too, that by dwelling once more on those ducal strawberry leaves, Mr Pardew intended to signify that they had some bearing on what had passed between them. And invisible above their heads, yet burning all the while in the pale air, lay the outrage of the letter. Accordingly, he neither agreed nor disagreed with this request, merely nodding his head as he waved Mr Pardew towards his staircase and the escort of his old clerk. Still, though, hearing the noise of Mr Pardew's departing footsteps on the stair – jaunty feet, as they seemed to him, belonging to one who has attained some private goal – the matter was unsatisfactory to him, and rather than seat himself once more at his desk he remained on the Turkey carpet thinking hard and wretchedly on what he had done. There were various books lying to hand, thick tomes of the kind that decorate lawyers' offices, and he delved within them for a while, hoping that they might provide the reassurance he sought. Finding that they did not, he did take finally to his desk, but the letter he began to write seemed equally unsatisfactory and at length he flung its torn fragments into his waste-paper basket.

It was by now about half past one in the afternoon, the time at which most legal gentlemen are at their clubs or at legal eating houses near the Inns of Court or – anywhere save inside their chambers. But Mr Crabbe was not deterred by the obscurity of the hour. He had an inkling that the person he thought he wished to consult would be at home, indeed never was anywhere but at home, and that he could safely go and seek him out. Thus, having spoken a word or two to the clerk, he put his hat on his head, left his premises and walked along the gravel paths at right angles to each other until he came to a somewhat shabby building in the very far corner of Lincoln's Inn inhabited for the most part by youthful barristers fresh from their pupillage and that sad species of middle-aged attorney on whom the light of professional fortune has ceased to shine.

Here, at the very top of the utmost flight of stairs, in rooms that it was jocularly supposed had not seen a charwoman's broom since the days of the Chartist demonstrations, lived a gentleman named Mr Guyle. Of Mr Guyle, with whom it was thought that Mr Crabbe had been at school long centuries before, it may be said that he was in his way quite as legendary a figure as his boyhood companion.

And yet his celebrity was of an entirely different character to the man in whose company he was alleged to have been flogged when the two of them absented themselves from their desks to pick raspberries from a nearby market garden at about the time of the Battle of Austerlitz. Mr Crabbe went everywhere in the world and was esteemed for his worldliness. Mr Guyle, on the other hand, went nowhere and was equally esteemed for his detachment. Mr Crabbe knew dukes and duchesses, dined at grand soirées and administered the affairs of landed estates. Mr Guyle knew only his immediate neighbours, dined in a public house and had his most intimate conversations with the old woman who darned his shirts, and yet it was to Mr Guyle – humbly and with a due sense of the latter's expertise – that Mr Crabbe went when he needed an opinion.

Indeed Mr Guyle's opinions were famous. The claim to an earldom, it was said, had perished on account of what Mr Guyle had to say about it, and a bevy of old men quartered in a municipal alms-house had been awarded ten guineas a year for life as a consequence of an ancient will that Mr Guyle had grubbed up in some overlooked depository. All this Mr Crabbe gratefully acknowledged as he nodded at the lounging porter, who, knowing Mr Crabbe of old, greeted him with the most reverential bow, and made his way up Mr Guyle's four rackety staircases to Mr Guyle's room.

Entering this sanctum, at whose door stood a jug that had pretty clearly contained Mr Guyle's pint of midday porter brought across by a potboy an hour since, Mr Crabbe was immediately conscious of an almost Arctic chill settling around his limbs. Mr Guyle had never been known to have a fire, even in January, and disdained warmth as he disdained all social invitations. No coy blandishment, not one dispatched by royalty itself, had ever seduced Mr Guyle. He sat now as he always sat, at a little desk beneath a great shelf of books – books differing from those in Mr Crabbe's chamber by virtue of their shabbiness and torn bindings – with further books piled around him almost to the level of his knees, and a great tray of legal papers laid out on a second desk at his side, a little old man with a shock of white hair and a palsied hand that yet moved over the page beneath him as if pursued by Mr Guyle and anxious to evade his grasp. There was dust everywhere: dust on the cracked and rheumy window; dust over the drugget that made shift as Mr Guyle's carpet; dust on the framed portraits of my lords Eldon, Coke and other luminaries that hung on the wall; and dust, it may be presumed, in the ventricles of Mr Guyle's ancient legal heart.

'How do you do, Crabbe?' Mr Guyle enquired when he saw him, in a way that suggested that the exploits of their youth still lay before them, would not perhaps be referred to but could not altogether be discounted in any colloquy that they might undertake. 'Keeping well, I take it? My clerk's ill, or I'd have him bring you tea.' And he laughed mercilessly, as if to imply that this was the merest jest.

'It's a very cold day,' Mr Crabbe observed, gingerly availing himself of a chair that harboured some very ancient copies of the *Law Review*.

'Cold, you say?' Mr Guyle's breath as he said this rose in a little cloud above his head. 'I suppose you've a fire in your chambers, eh? And a young man to bring in the coal?'

Mr Crabbe acknowledged meekly that he did.

'I never saw the need of such things myself. Never indeed. A lot of d——d nonsense. Well then, Crabbe,' (it was alleged by certain young barristers that in a moment of conviviality Mr Guyle had once addressed his friend as 'Adolphus') 'what is it that I can do for you?'

And here Mr Crabbe hesitated. He had come to Mr Guyle not for a legal opinion but for advice – information even. And yet he knew from long experience that even should Mr Guyle possess this information, and even should he care to divulge it, such intelligence would not be given up without a struggle, in which the yielding up would become a kind of triumph on Mr Guyle's part. Accordingly he decided to advance by stealth.

'I hear,' he said, 'that Lord —— was most heartily obliged by your opinion of the Darrowby affair. Indeed, I have heard it said that the case could not have been prosecuted without your aid.'

As Lord —— was the gentleman who currently sat upon the wool-sack, and whom Mr Crabbe and Mr Guyle each regarded as the leading luminary of their profession, this might have been taken for the prettiest of compliments. Mr Guyle, however, was not to be won over by compliments.

'Hm – well! Darrowby was a fool to think that he could bring the affair off uncontested. And Lord —— was a fool to think the busi-ness could be concluded in a lower court. But come, Crabbe, you are not here to talk pleasantries I'll be bound.'

Mr Crabbe, looking at his fingers as they lay in the lap of his black lawyer's suit, thought that they were nearly blue with cold, and that even minor humiliation at Mr Guyle's hands was perhaps preferable to the discomfort of sitting in his room even a few moments longer.

'Very well. I merely wish to put a question to you. Have you ever heard of a man named Pardew?'

Mr Guyle examined the quill pen he held in his right hand with apparent incredulity, as if he had never seen such an implement in his life before and rather doubted its function. 'There was a judge of that name on the northern circuit in, when would it have been? Thirty years since, I don't doubt.'

Mr Crabbe sighed gently. Mr Guyle was in one of his captious moods. 'Your memory, Guyle, is really remarkable. No, I have just had this gentleman at my chambers. A bill-discounter, stockbroker, that kind of thing.'

Mr Guyle placed the quill pen wonderingly down on the foolscap page beneath him and bent his hands over it as if he intended to worship it as a fetish.

'The man who murdered his partner? Farrell? Fardolf? McTurk came within an inch of taking him. He told me so himself.'

'Nothing was ever proved.'

'And nobody ever saw the poor wretch who shot at Her Majesty in the park, but when found he had a pistol in his shirt and a spent cartridge at his feet. Well, what did the man want?'

Again Mr Crabbe hesitated. He was aware that he was not quite getting the better of this exchange, not quite indeed being treated with the respect that the Mr Crabbes of this world demand from their Mr Guyles. A part of him, consequently, did not altogether wish to reveal to Mr Guyle why it was that Mr Pardew had come to him. Accordingly, he once more moved the equipage of his conversation onto a subsidiary track.

'Well then, let us say that Pardew did murder his partner, although nothing was ever proved. Presumably that would not debar him from taking legal advice?'

'The man who is due to be hanged tomorrow morning is not debarred from taking legal advice, as you well know.'

'At any rate he seems thoroughly respectable,' Mr Crabbe went on, thinking as he did so that he knew Mr Pardew to be thoroughly unrespectable. 'I believe him to be a friend of His Grace the Duke of —— '

'You may take it from me that His Grace keeps some pretty queer company.'

All this, Mr Crabbe acknowledged to himself, was hard. He had never boasted of his dealings with the Duke of —— to Mr Guyle. Nevertheless, Mr Guyle was as familiar with them as he was with the names of Mr Crabbe's wife and daughters. He was aware, too, that in mentioning that nobleman, in advancing his name as the touchstone of Mr Pardew's respectability, he had betrayed himself. The realisation made him bitter, more bitter than he perhaps cared to admit, and he shifted his neat little lawyer's boots uncomfortably on Mr Guyle's dusty floor and resolved that at any rate he would stay no longer in this ice-house. Something of this resolve communicated itself to Mr Guyle, for he shuffled the papers that lay before him, exhaled another mighty spout of condensed air, and stared levelly at his friend.

'Now see here, Crabbe. I don't know what this man may have told you. He may very well not have murdered his partner. He may be head nursemaid to Lord John's grandchildren for all I know, though I must say I doubt it. All I can say is that a lawyer has a duty to be – circumspect. As for Pardew, I believe I heard that he had been at Prague or Vienna, though what he did there who knows? From what I hear of him he would not be the kind of person to tell you. And now perhaps you'll excuse me as I have a deal of work in front of me. You had better give my regards to Mrs Crabbe and the girls.'

Mr Crabbe, thinking that he had got off rather lightly in this exchange, nodded his head and made his way down Mr Guyle's Arctic staircase and across the frozen garden to his own chambers, where he immediately ordered his clerk to stoke up the fire to its fullest extent and instructed that a glass of brandy should be fetched from the public house beyond the Inn's gate, so great was the extremity of cold into which he had been plunged. And Mr Crabbe, as he drank the brandy and sat with his feet practically in the flames, such was the chill that he had brought back with him from Mr Guyle, and thought of Mr Pardew, who had been at Prague or Vienna, but about whom nothing was known, was struck by a feeling of disquiet that he could not quite fathom, the thought that he had plucked from its shelf some container that had better stayed unopened.

Presently he fell asleep over the fire – the old clerk, stealing into his room, watched him for a moment and then crept silently away – but the dreams he dreamed were not pleasant ones. A cat that in fine weather sunned itself on the steps came loitering through the half-open door to curl up next his feet, a cracked old gentleman with a suppositious interest in a Chancery case who had been bringing Mr Crabbe his petitions these twenty years or more got a quarter-way up the staircase before being smartly repulsed by the old clerk, but Mr Crabbe heard neither of them. When he awoke it was gone four o'clock, the fire had burned down, the cat was investigating the crevices of the wainscoting and there was snow falling beyond the window onto the dark trees. And Mr Crabbe watched it in silent wonder, as he and Mr Guyle had watched it fall on the turrets and pinnaces of old Windsor in the days of King George III.

*

Mr Pardew, when he emerged beyond the high stone gate of Lincoln's Inn, did not, as he had suggested to his clerk, make his way to his club. Instead he boarded a second omnibus at the corner where Chancery Lane meets High Holborn and had himself conveyed along the Marylebone Road and then northwards in the direction of St John's Wood. Once arrived at this desirable locality, and having brushed from his boots several pieces of straw which he had brought with him from the omnibus, he set off in a purposeful manner along two or three side-streets until he reached an avenue of secluded villas, each set back from the road and established behind hedges of laurel and cedar. It was growing steadily colder, and Mr Pardew as he walked pulled the collar of his coat up to his chin. An onlooker who had studied his passing, here on this grey January afternoon beneath a darkling sky, would perhaps have noted that he appeared to be in a remarkably good humour, smiling to himself and on one occasion, such was his apparent delight, stopping at the pavement's edge to laugh out loud. Turning in at the gate of one of the laurel-shrouded villas, and having been admitted by a servant girl in a white cap and a pinafore, he made his way into a drawing room, very daintily furnished, with pink and white paper on the walls and copies of pictures by Frith and Etty hanging in gilt frames, where sat a woman of perhaps twenty-nine or thirty years with a complexion as pink and white as the paper, reading, or perhaps only affecting to read, the *Pall Mall Gazette*.

'Why, Richard,' this person remarked when she saw him – her friendly tone perhaps masking a faint anxiety – 'you are quite a stranger here.'

'I don't believe that I am quite – that,' replied Mr Pardew, standing on the hearthrug and jingling his money in his pocket. 'It is but a week, surely?'

'Nine days. Ten days. But I declare, had you come only a little later you would have found me out.'

'Indeed? And where would you have gone?'

'I had thought of going to see the people in Islington.'

'Had you now?' Mr Pardew's face as he said this was set in the same cast as when he had discussed the little matter of Donaldson's bill with his clerk. 'You know I don't care for you paying such calls.'

'It is only my sister, Richard. And besides, what else is there for me to do? I declare, since I last saw you I have left the house only once, and that was to visit the milliner in Marylebone High Street.'

By way of an answer Mr Pardew looked down his nose, took off his coat and scarf, both of which he placed on the sofa, and seated himself in an armchair. An onlooker who observed this scene – one of the cupids, perhaps, gazing down from the frame of Mr Etty's picture of the Crystal Palace Exhibition – would possibly have drawn two conclusions from it: first, that the young woman with the pink-and-white complexion, though dressed in accordance with the latest dictates of fashion, was not what is generally known as a lady; second, that though his relation to her might not be outwardly clear, Mr Pardew brought to his surroundings the same proprietorial air that had been in evidence at his office.

'But let us not say another word about that, Richard,' continued the young woman, whose name was Jemima, 'for I am very glad to see you.'

Mr Pardew did not reply, but the look on his face seemed to suggest that he, too, was glad. Jemima hastened to press home her advantage.

'You will take tea?'

'Tea? Certainly I will. Let the girl bring it in. Upon my word, Jemima, you're looking uncommon handsome.'

Jemina laughed, but there was something in the laugh that suggested she did not find Mr Pardew's compliment wholly to her liking. The tea having been brought by the very respectable maid, she busied herself with its infusion, rattling the tongs against the sugar basin and standing meekly at Mr Pardew's side as he accepted his cup. Drinking a certain portion of his tea off at a gulp, Mr Pardew looked at her sardonically.

'Upon my word! Anyone would think that you had been a parlour-maid once. There's a way they deal out the sugar, I have remarked it.'

'That is very ill-natured of you, John. A girl can't help where she comes from.'

'I don't suppose she can. I meant nothing by it, so don't take on. Shall I tell you what I have been about?'

'If you will.' She hovered attentively by his side, not knowing whether he desired her to remain or to return to her seat.

'Well, today I hoodwinked an old lawyer. Well – not hoodwinked him. Played upon his vanity rather.'

'Gracious, Richard! Do you mean you took his money?'

'Nothing so grievous. Let us say that I placed him in a position where he may be able to do a service for me.'

'What kind of a gentleman was he?'

'Don't be a goose! The most respectable old lawyer in Lincoln's Inn. Lives in a big house at Belgravia and dines with half the Cabinet, I shouldn't wonder. Should you like to see him? Why, we could call upon him if you like.'

'No indeed! I should like nothing less.'

But there was a colour in Jemima's cheeks as she said this, over and above the pinkness of her complexion, that suggested she liked to hear such stories, and that Mr Pardew's tales of the world he inhabited were among her greatest solaces. 'But, Richard, how can he be of service to you if you have – hoodwinked him, as you say?'

'Why, he has a name you see. That's the beauty of dealing with men who have names. Have a Treasury lord vouch for you and you've twice the credit you began with. It's a trick I wish I'd learned long before.'

'But why is it that you need – credit, as you say?'

'Well . . .' Mr Pardew was always circumspect in his dealings with the persons around him, but Jemima's pink-and-white complexion was so agreeable to him that he was perhaps less cautious than he should have been. 'Let us say that I have a little scheme in mind, with which this gentleman may be able to assist me.'

All this conversation was very pleasant to Jemima and she hung upon it, wishing in fact that it could be indefinitely sustained. In truth she knew very little of Mr Pardew's affairs – he was perhaps careful that she did not – but what she did interested her beyond measure, interested her, it might be said, rather more than did Mr Pardew himself. But it could not, of its nature, be indefinitely prolonged, or perhaps it was merely that on this particular afternoon Mr Pardew did not wish to prolong it. At any rate when the servant girl had returned to the drawing room to clear away the tea-things he ceased to talk affably of his affairs and stood by the window looking out into the gathering darkness.

'I declare it is starting to snow. You had better tell the girl to go.'

Jemima did as she was bidden. Presently there came the sound of a door closing and footsteps receding into the distance. Returning to the drawing room, Jemima placed herself in its very centre, in the manner of one who awaits some signal. Finding that Mr Pardew continued to stand by the window, she angled her head in a gesture that he appeared to understand as he twitched two or three fingers of his left hand and she retired once more. Presently her movements could be heard in the room above.

Mr Pardew continued to watch the snow keenly: soft, regular flakes of snow, beneath which the summit of the laurel hedge had already begun to disappear. In his mind he could see it falling elsewhere: down the river at Greenwich, up on the heath a mile or so distant from where he now stood, upon the strawberry fields at Hammersmith, piling up in drifts upon the islands of the Thames at Twickenham and Teddington. It reminded him of certain other snowfalls he had witnessed, several thousands of miles distant, and of times when fate had not smiled on him in the way it seemed now to be smiling and there were no grand schemes in his head on which to brood.

The noises from above him had ceased. The house was altogether quiet. Seizing a lighted lamp from where it lay on the sideboard next to the door, he began to move soundlessly up the staircase.

VII

Curious Behaviour of Mr Crabbe

I will own that I am a curious man. And yet my curiosity is, as it were, of an altogether curious kind. A sealed casket holds no charms for me. A locked door seldom makes me yearn for a key and the right to admittance. Rather, my fascination lies with great people and the moment when their greatness has, albeit temporarily, been put aside. How does a bishop conduct himself when, retiring to the bosom of his family, he divests himself of his mitred hat? What does Lord John, coming back from the Treasury chambers, say to his wife, his butler or the domestic who hands him his tea? Half the charm of fiction resides in these imaginings. Write a novel about a ploughman in his field or a City Croesus striding about the floor of 'Change with his hands plunged into his trouser pockets and no one will read it, but let a distinguished nobleman, the heir to broad acres and the confidant of half the Cabinet, tell his wife that he has the gout or that he will lend no more money to her scapegrace brother and the public is instantly agog!

Say by some chance that a spyglass could be brought to bear on Mr Crabbe's innocent recreations: what would it show? It is late, very late indeed, on a black January night in Lincoln's Inn, yet still a light burns in the upper storey of Mr Crabbe's chambers. Three hours have passed since the sucking barristers and the high-collared young men went home to their families and their landladies, and all that time Mr Crabbe has sat absorbed among his books and his solitary lamp so that even the old clerk, now waiting at the foot of the staircase and noting the crack of light under Mr Crabbe's door, now descending to some bolt-hole of his own in the building's lower depths, marvels at it and thinks it odd. Lincoln's Inn is shut up and deserted, with the shadows marshalled under the great door and the wind bristling over the inky grass, and the old clerk wonders if his master has fallen asleep over the fire, or some other eventuality. But no, here is Mr Crabbe's footstep on the stair and the sight of Mr Crabbe's fingers buttoning his waistcoat and the lamplight spilling from his room to illumine his downward passage to the door.

'Decidedly cold,' Mr Crabbe murmurs in his soft voice to the old clerk as he steps out into the night air, and the old clerk nods, for it is cold, decidedly cold indeed, and watches his master pad cautiously away in the darkness like an old ghost rising out of his catafalque until a black wall of shadow looms up to swallow him and he disappears (Where does the old clerk sleep? I declare I think he doubles as nightwatchman and lives on the premises.). The great gate of Lincoln's Inn is shut, but Mr Crabbe avails himself of a side door and emerges with his hat in his hand and his coat pulled up to his chin into a public thoroughfare dominated by a cab rank, a workmen's brazier and a baked potato stall. Given his age and eminence, Mr Crabbe might be forgiven for resorting to a hansom, but no, he scuttles off, rather in the manner of his namesake, in the direction of High Holborn. On the corner of this thoroughfare there is an ancient law dining house named the Eldon – very sombre in its furnishings, with grim grey waiters in black stocks – and here Mr Crabbe stops almost without knowing that he does it, scuttles inside, hangs up his coat and under the approving eye of the head waiter – Mr Crabbe has been coming here since before that head waiter was born – orders a chop and a pint of watered sherry.

But there is something agitating Mr Crabbe. Why else does he pull a slip of paper from his waistcoat pocket, stare at it and replace it, only to repeat the operation two minutes later? An elderly legal acquaintance, so old and shaky in his movements that one almost expects to see a periwig on him and a pair of knee-breeches, totters over to shake his hand, but Mr Crabbe, though he is civil, has no eyes for him: his mind is bent entirely on the slip of paper, now lodged again in his breast pocket but soon brought out once more to be dandled in his white old palm. The head waiter notices that Mr Crabbe don't eat much of his chop, the wine waiter remarks that he don't drink much of his sherry (excellent Marsala it is, that you or I would willingly entertain) and presently Mr Crabbe rises from his table, leaving chop and sherry to be carried back into the kitchens, and sets out once more into the night.

It is very cold now, past nine o'clock – the legions of the street have all but gone away – and Mr Crabbe's breath rises into the dark air in a veritable fume of condensation. There is a cab bowling along High Holborn towards him and Mr Crabbe considers it for a moment before raising his hand and with the slightest imaginable movement compels it to stop. Where to? the cabman wonders, and Mr Crabbe tells him Grosvenor Square in a tone so mild and coming from so deep inside his coat that the man has to ask him to repeat the name of that very distinguished neighbourhood. But even now, in his cab, whipping off in the direction of Oxford Street, Mr Crabbe does not seem at ease. There are workmen out on the road, grubbing up a portion of the pavement, with a stretch of lanterns suspended over their heads like the illuminations of the Chinese pantomime, and Mr Crabbe stares at them altogether indifferently, as if to say 'So this is how the world conducts itself? Well, I neither approve nor disapprove' before returning to his meditations.

At Oxford Circus he takes an old lawyer's brief out of some inner pocket, very grey and curled up at the edges, and dabs gingerly at it with a pencil-stub, and halfway down Bond Street he puts brief and pencil-stub back into the same recess inside his coat, and that is the solitary diversion of Mr Crabbe's journey. At Grosvenor Square the cabman puts him down in front of a grand house positively a-swarm with carriages, policemen, bowing butlers, and Mr Crabbe steps down from his chariot, sniffs the air like an old charger about to re-enter the fray after long years in the paddock and feels himself rejuvenated, tips the cabman threepence, to that gentleman's great disgust, and marches up the great steps to the vestibule, where amidst a chaos of human traffic – ladies in evening dresses, gentlemen furling and unfurling umbrellas, perilously borne trays and suchlike – a servant divests him of his coat and scarf and murmurs that His Grace is in the drawing room. Mr Crabbe nods his head at this intelligence, accepts a glass of champagne from a flunkey in a gorgeously damasked tailcoat, strides out across the wide hall, where so many ladies are standing fanning themselves that the candles burning on the marble tables about them are in danger of being extinguished, and proceeds up the great staircase.

Many of the great people clustered on the landing at its summit know Mr Crabbe, and he them. Here he shakes a hand, there he listens attentively as a lady whispers something in his ancient ear. And

I should have as many headaches as I liked and no one to scold me.' And here, somewhat to her surprise, Sarah put her head in her hands and began to cry. Esther stood over her for a while, uncertain as to which of these demands had the greater claim on her time. Then, with the fingers of her right hand still clutched around William's letter where it lay in her apron pocket, she sped back down the stairs.

(xiii)

In William's absence an air of dereliction had fallen over the place. It was as if his departure had brought some greater upheaval among the lives of those who remained there that none of them could fathom. Mr Dixey went on his errands alone; the hot water for his shaving was taken up by Margaret Lane in a tea-kettle, for, as she said, she could not manage the great china ewer with which William had ascended the stairs each morning a half-hour after dawn. An occasional gentleman or lady came to call or to eat luncheon, even more rarely two of them together, but the dishes that Mr Dixey ordered up were of the plainest kind, and Mrs Wates despaired, for, as she truly remarked, what was the point of having a receipt for a Hollandaise sauce if one was never allowed to make it? Hastening down the back-stairs and into the servants' hall – very desolate in the daytime with the fire unlit and the last night's crockery still lying on the table – Esther found Mr Randall in his pantry. He was seated in the big armchair, comfortably enshawled in a wolfskin rug, so comfortably in fact that he might almost have been asleep, but when he saw her he stood up, pulled the rug from his shoulders and rose to his feet.

'I am glad to see you, Esther. Will you sit down?'

Esther did as she was bidden, wondering what Mr Randall wished to say. He had a doubtful look on his face – very creased, it seemed, from his half-slumber – and his fingers turned over an iron key that he held in the palm of his hand.

'Now, Esther,' he said, moving the key between his fingers so that, try as she might, Esther could not but look at it. 'Here is a question for you. How many people reside in this house?'

'There are six. Now that William has gone.'

'There are seven,' Mr Randall corrected her. 'How are there seven?

135

I shall tell you, Esther. You shall not think you have been deceived, I hope, for there has been no deception. You know the west wing of the house?'

'I have never been there.'

'No. The rooms are empty and shut up. They have not been used since before I came here, and that is many years ago. But see, one of them is not empty and not shut up. Or rather . . .' The key was very ancient and antique, Esther saw, with a large, much-ornamented hinge. 'There is a lady lives there. Mr Dixey's ward. An invalid.'

Feeling that something was expected of her, Esther said: 'What is the matter with her?'

'What is the matter with her? It is hard to say. The master has had doctors to see her. Their opinion is that her mind is troubled, that she does not know herself. That is why she lives as she does. Do you understand me, Esther?'

Esther nodded.

'Naturally it is Mrs Finnie that looks after her. Who attends to her wants. But we are short-handed, Esther, and there is need for another . . . I wish you only to take up Mrs Ireland's meals and attend on her. Just as if she were a guest in the house.'

'Her name is Mrs Ireland?'

'Did I not say so before? Yes, that is her name.'

As Esther listened, Mr Randall explained the nature of her duties. These were that:

Twice a day, at one and seven, she should take a covered tray supplied by Mrs Wates to Mrs Ireland's chamber.

On reaching the chamber she was to knock at the door. If Mrs Ireland did not answer, she should wait a short time and then unlock the door.

Once inside the room she should lock the door behind her.

The key should at all times be left in her pocket and returned to Mr Randall when not in use.

If, at any time, Mrs Ireland seemed disturbed, alarmed or in any other way altered from her usual manner, she should leave the room immediately, locking the door behind her, and inform Mr Randall.

Any questions put to her by Mrs Ireland that were not immediately answerable should be referred to Mr Randall.

The door should be locked at all times.

Any suggestion by Mrs Ireland as to leaving the chamber should be referred to Mr Randall.

Twice a day, at two and eight, she should return to the chamber and collect the tray. Again, she should knock at the door. If Mrs Ireland did not answer, she should wait a short time and then unlock the door.

The key should be kept in her pocket.

The door should be locked at all times.

(xiv)

One spring morning, when the wind blew crazily against the upper storeys of the house, Esther went into Sarah's room and found her gone. For a moment, standing in the doorway with her hands plunged into the pocket of her sacking apron and the light spilling over her face, she saw nothing strange in the vacant bed, the half-open skylight window and the patch of angry blue sky beyond, supposing that Sarah had already gone downstairs to light the fire or, as was sometimes her habit, risen early to perform some mysterious errand of her own. And yet there was something about the room that seemed to her odd, beyond the roar of the wind and the neatly drawn coverlet. Not altogether knowing why she did it, Esther tugged open the topmost drawer of the chest in which Sarah kept her clothes. It was quite empty. So, she discovered, was the drawer beneath it. Instantly half a dozen other tiny vanishments and discrepancies became apparent to her – the square of mirror that had hung on the wall, the portrait of the Crystal Palace Exhibition cut out of an illustrated paper, Sarah's pattens gone from beneath the bed – and the room's secret declared itself. Carefully shutting the drawers of the chest and hauling the skylight window to, Esther considered the implications of this discovery. It occurred to her that Sarah might still be in the house – it was, she calculated, barely half past six – and with this expectation growing in her mind she rushed downstairs into the hall, practically colliding with Mr Randall who, very white and shabby at this early hour, was winding up the grandfather clock with his butterfly key.

'Why, Esther! Whatever is the matter?'

'It is Sarah, Mr Randall. It's my belief that she's gone.'

Together they moved around the ground floor of the house opening doors and throwing open closets but there was no sign of anything save the kitchen cat, who looked up resentfully from its slumber on the parlour sofa as if to say that it very much deplored the intrusion. Then Mr Randall discovered that the bolts of the kitchen door had been drawn and that the door itself lay half-open on its hinge.

There was no doubt about it, Mr Randall said, standing uncertainly in his shirt-sleeves, with the wind rushing into the kitchen through the open door, but that Sarah had gone.

Subsequently Mrs Wates bustled downstairs with her hair done up in curl-papers, conducted a rapid inventory of the kitchen and confirmed that a two-guinea piece left in a box by the outer door and intended for payment of the butcher's bill had also vanished in the course of the night.

The master had best be told, Mrs Wates suggested.

At lunchtime the remaining servants sat in conclave over the absentee.

Mrs Wates deposed that Sarah was a bad girl, who in the manner of bad girls would undoubtedly come to a bad end. It was not for her to judge, for judgement lay in the hands of the Lord, but a girl of that sort, who crept out of the house in the middle of the night without a word to anyone, would certainly have a baby, and the baby would die, or be taken from her, and this was on balance a good thing.

Mrs Finnie said that she was a sly one and no mistake, that she had had a look on her face this past week that was a sure clue to her intentions to anyone experienced in these matters, that it was a wonder, what with people sneaking downstairs in the middle of the night and opening doors, that they had not all been murdered in their beds, and that Mr Randall ought to unlock his strongbox and ensure that the plate had not been stolen.

Margaret Lane said that she did not wish to speak ill of anyone, least of all those that were not there to defend themselves, but she had always thought the way that Sarah had made eyes at William downright shameful.

Mr Randall said that it was all a great pity, and that he hoped Sarah would be happy.

Esther said nothing.

That afternoon Mr Randall went into Watton to make enquiries, asked at the railway station, put his head into the bar of the Bull and returned empty-handed. It was not, he explained to the audience of the servant's hall, and notwithstanding the missing two-guinea piece, as if Sarah had committed a criminal act. She had merely quitted her situation, albeit in mysterious circumstances, and there was nothing that could be done.

'Oh Lord,' Mr Randall prayed aloud that evening as they sat before the fire, 'we commend to thy care thy servant Sarah, and we hope that we may remember her as we should and have no cause to repent of the treatment we allowed her, and that no harm shall come to her on the path she treads. Amen.'

And that was all that was said of Sarah, the parlourmaid at Easton Hall, who could not read and whose brother had died in China.

X

The Confidential Clerk

It will perhaps be allowed by those who have gone into the matter that in late years our idea of London has altered somewhat, and that a metropolis previously known for its stink and its monotony has blossomed forth in all kinds of unexpected colours. In short, the place has been taken up and turned romantic. Somers Town, as sketched by Mr Dickens, stands revealed as the most charming of localities; Islington is a sooty paradise; even Limehouse Hole has declared itself full of the most interesting byways and peculiarities that polite society had formerly not imagined to exist. A penny gaffe, beneath the gaze of these new explorers, is the most delightful refuge for the curious seeker after pleasure, and a threepenny theatre with a conjuror and a line of young ladies in Turkish trousers practically the acme of popular entertainment. Neither must it be supposed that this transmogrifying hand, once directed at a Clerkenwell, a Whitechapel or the vicinity of the Borough, can be stayed from touching the inhabitants of these respectable purlieus. The very beggars and the street acrobats have grown suddenly picturesque, and behave as if they wished to appear in those representations of 'London Characters' that decorate the print-sellers' windows, and the costerwomen have the vanity of artists' models. For myself, I altogether abhor and repudiate this false alchemy, whereby base metal, wrested out of the foulest pits and mines, is brought forth as human gold. Limehouse Hole, where Rogue Riderhood dwelt deep and dark, is no doubt a fascinating and fashionable place, but I for one would not go there, and one were as likely to meet a footpad in High Holborn as a soft-voiced old apple-woman with a sentimental eye. Dirt is dirt and squalor is squalor, that was what I was taught, and a waistcoat held together by one precarious button less efficacious than that secured by three.

The number of persons rendered more humorous and idiosyncratic by their privations is a dismally small fraction of gross humanity.

Certainly the eye that lingers in St John's Square, Clerkenwell, on a fierce morning – fierce, that is, in point of view of rain, fog and other elements – in early February will be hard put to distinguish any redeeming features. For a start, there is the general aspect of the place – a great ragged confluence of shabby thoroughfares quite cut in half by the Clerkenwell Road, the whole bleakly laid out and disposed beneath a flint-coloured sky suggestive of impending cloudburst, such light as there is dissolving into misty radiance. Then there is the teeming throng of people: each omnibus that clatters by is laden with passengers; tarpaulins gleam over the knees of those who sit outside. Labouring men in mufflers and shabby jackets, with billycock hats pulled low over their brows, go shambling past to their places of work hard by in Goswell Road or Aldgate; small boys with pieces of wet sacking drawn over their already wet shoulders slip past bent on God knows what errands, darting out of the little shops and places of manufacture. The commercial genius of Clerkenwell, it may be said, does not hanker after the grand scale. Warehouses, factories and the like are there none. Rather, each dwelling house and shop is divided into a myriad of individual concerns, three or four at a time. The house that stands yonder, within a yard or two of the public wheel-track, squeezed in between a corn chandler's and an ironmonger's and looking like a very small man quite domineered over by two burly companions, a house that in Kensington might harbour a family of five plus a cook and a maid of all work, contains, in Clerkenwell, beginning at its uppermost storey, a dye-stamping business, a sign-painter's, a glass and enamelling establishment, a mysterious enter-prise engaged in the distillation of black lead and, in its basement, a room in which six children are employed twelve hours a day manu-facturing colour-paper fans at three-halfpence the dozen. Thirty-seven persons pass in and out of these premises on a specimen day (there is an old woman, dying of the dropsy, locked up in a gaunt back bedroom who goes nowhere at all), all of them liable to tumble head over heels amongst the corn chandler's stock or scarify them-selves upon those of the ironmonger's wares proudly displayed on the narrow pavement. There is no space, you see, in Clerkenwell, and a shop is not a shop until half its contents are on view beyond the doorway, and a house not a house until two dozen people are crammed into its five rooms. No space, only dirt and decay, and ash-ridden streets, and a blackness of night which no lamp can penetrate, and nocturnal policemen going two by two, and poverty and pestilence taking turns as to which shall more advantageously dispose itself.

Loitering keenly along the corner of the square, a dilapidated umbrella allowing a miniature cataract to descend on his uncovered head, Mr Grace, Mr Pardew's confidential clerk, was in no way discountenanced by what he saw. He had been dealing with Clerkenwell and its regions for the greater part of his professional life. Clerkenwell, it might be said, was in his blood. Set down in it, he knew exactly where he was bound, what he might find there, and what in strict monetary terms might be the issue. In this spirit, forgetting the particular errand that brought him here, he browsed impressionably for a moment on the crowded pavement, put his head in at a pastrycook's and reluctantly withdrew it, stood for a while before a down-at-heel stationer's displaying copies of the *Raff's Journal*, the *Larky Swell* and other publications, and took a determined interest in the back part of a sofa, from which the horsehair had begun to sprout in little melancholic tufts and follicles, that some enterprising dealer in furniture had crammed into his window. The sound of a bell, clanging from the tower of St James's Church, cut short this reverie, and negotiating his way past the lower outcrops of a kind of Parnassus of willow-pattern crockery, over which the rain dripped and tumbled, he passed around the western edge of the square into a street of tall, nondescript houses dignified by the name of Clerkenwell Court. A casual observer who monitored his progress might have remarked that he examined not the house numbers but the brass plates set at head height next to their doors. An apothecary's, a day school and a dealer in hides and tallows – from whose frontage came a reek that made even Mr Grace, Clerkenwellian that he was, shy his head – were rejected, until finally he stopped before a plate whose inscription read: 'J. Snowden, Dial Painter'. Having ascertained that this was the place he sought – for he was a near-sighted man – he rolled up the tattered umbrella, gave a couple of smart raps on the dusty front door with the ferrule and stood back from the step the better to appraise whoever might appear upon it. The door having been opened by a young woman in a shawl carrying a baby on her hip, Mr Grace bared his teeth and enquired:

'Name of Dewar?'

'Second floor back.'

Experienced enough in these visitations to know that the woman's sullen tone denoted not impertinence but the dignity of proprietorship, Mr Grace raised his umbrella by way of a salute and proceeded across a negligently swept hallway to the staircase. He was a calculating man – long years in the service of Mr Pardew had taught him the value of calculation – and as he ascended he looked diligently about him and calculated both the degree of the squalor that he saw and the likelihood of his errand's proving successful. That there was a connection between the two, Mr Grace well knew. 'No staircarpet anyhow,' he said to himself as he gained the first landing. 'Not that one expected it anyway. But holes in the timber big enough to put your foot into, and not even the sight of a coal scuttle' (this observation was provoked by a heap of coal piled up on a sheet of newspaper) '– dear me, that's bad.' Proceeding up the second flight, he grew suddenly conscious of the noise his boots made on the bare slats and wondered proudly at the effect such irruptions might have on the equanimity of persons inhabiting second-floor back-bedrooms in Clerkenwell Court. Standing finally on the second landing, he beat a miniature tattoo on the door that caused it to rattle dangerously in its frame and then, barely pausing for the weak cry of acknowledgement that came from within, pushed his way inside.

He stepped into a room which was not disorderly or unclean but presented merely the chill discomfort of poverty. The bare boards of the floor space were decently swept. Upon them could be found a high brass bedstead of the old-fashioned type pushed back almost to the window, a wash-hand stand, a couple of cane-backed chairs and a small occasional table. A tiny fire burned in the grate, composed of three glowing coals and so insubstantial that the air by the door where Mr Grace now lingered seemed quite unwarmed. On a shelf affixed to the nearside wall sat a beer jug, a white china cat from whose mouth issued a spray of coloured paper, and a copy of *All The Year Round*, so dusty and time-worn that it seemed that, in deference to its title, it had always lain there from January through to December. A few miscellaneous items – a plate, the half of a quartern loaf and a teapot – lying in the grate completed the picture. All this Mr Grace's beady eye took in as he stood in the doorway. So fascinated was he by the meagre inventory that it was a moment before he could begin to appraise the room's human populace. This consisted of a thin, pale-complexioned woman who, although dressed, lay on the bedstead in an attitude of extreme fatigue, and a pasty-faced, unhealthy-looking man wearing a dressing gown over his frayed shirt who sat awkwardly on one of the cane-backed chairs. Seeing from their faces, in which curiosity combined with great alarm, that he was master of the situation and that no voice would be raised against him, Mr Grace brought his hands smartly together and made a little bow.

'Name of Grace. That put you in the way of Lewis Dunbar. Recollect me?'

Receiving no answer, other than a vacant nod of the head from the man, he delved into the inner pocket of his coat and brought out a wad of grimy paper, much folded and secured with a piece of ribbon.

'See this? Bill for thirty pounds in favour of Hodge, dry-goods merchant, Pentonville. Know anything about it?'

Dewar turned a doleful pair of eyes towards him. 'On my honour, sir, the money was paid . . .'

'Very likely! Very likely indeed, with me standing here a-holding of it in my hand. Did I say thirty pounds? More likely thirty-five, what with the interest owing. More like thirty-seven pound ten shillings, I shouldn't wonder. Question is, Mr Dewar, what do you mean to do about it?' He stopped for a moment, his attention fixed on some incongruity in the room, in the set of Dewar's face even, that he could not quite fathom. 'Great heavens, man! What have you done to your hair?'

'He's dyed it.' The woman spoke for the first time, indistinctly, with her hand drawn up to her breast.

'Dyed it, has he?' Grace rocked back on his heels, as if this were the most singular thing he had ever heard. 'Now why should he want to do that?'

The woman coughed, in a way that brought a crimson flush to her otherwise pallid cheeks. 'He thought one of the reasons he couldn't get work was his looking so old.'

'And so it was!' Dewar interjected. 'Once your hair's turned there's no chance for you. The governors don't want old men, or them that they think is old. I was working in a chop-house in Hanover Street, first job I'd had in a month. Come the second day I saw the man who owned it talking to the head waiter. "We don't want no old men," he says. "Better turn him off." So they turned me off and I went away and had my hair dyed, though precious little good it's done me.'

The woman began to cough again and he broke off and regarded her helplessly.

'Had to dye your hair?' Grace wondered. 'Dear me, that's bad. That's bad indeed.' Although he continued to stare around the room with benign amusement, as if the sight were a kind of tableau expressly designed for his entertainment, he had already begun to recalculate his strategy. His original scheme had been to browbeat Dewar, threaten him even, and thus to secure some small portion of the debt contracted to Mr Hodge of Pentonville some eighteen months before and now transferred to his own master. Experience told him, however, that such a game was not worth the candle. Accordingly he began upon a second scheme which Mr Pardew had suggested to him earlier that morning in Carter Lane.

'Now see here, Mr Dewar. I don't doubt there's paper of yours all over the City. There may be a dozen Mr Pardews after you. I don't know. P'raps there's more. However many there are, it's no good to me. Still, there's a way we might help one another, indeed there is. If the lady don't mind perhaps you could come along of me to somewhere we could talk more private-like?'

Dewar looked at him curiously for a moment, but in the end assented, muttered something in an undertone to his wife, drew off the tattered dressing gown and replaced it with an equally thread-bare topcoat which he took from a pile of clothing heaped at the end of the bedstead. Thus arrayed, he stood uncertainly in the doorway for a moment while Grace, tipping his finger to his forehead in salute to the occupant of the bed, led him out onto the landing.

'Your wife's bad, ain't she?' he remarked conversationally as they descended to the level of the street.

'Don't take no nourishment from her food,' Dewar gloomily assented. 'Thin as thin.'

'Consumption I should say. I seen that kind of cough before. When the spots come to their cheeks. She'll die on you, I shouldn't wonder. I means no harm,' he admonished, catching the look in his companion's eye. 'Neither does Mr Pardew, for all he's a hard man. But there's truth and there's lies, you know. Now, from the look of you I should say that you could do with something 'ot. Am I right?'

Dewar nodded his head. Glancing sideways at him as they passed through the door of the house into Clerkenwell Court, Grace satisfied himself that he seemed to shuffle rather than walk.

'Here,' he said. 'How long since you had a square meal? Come on, you can tell me, you know.'

'Yesterday. That is, the day before.'

'And that bread and tea, I shouldn't wonder. Never mind. Just step along this way.'

On the corner of Clerkenwell Court, where it verges on the green, there was a public house, empty now against the anticipated dinner hour, but emitting gusts of beer and spirituous liquor from its half-open doors. A pot-boy, one of those insouciant, devil-may-care pot-boys with a black eye and a cap pulled down low over his forehead, looking as if he had lately escaped from Mr Egan's *Life in London* and needing only the attentions of a beadle or two to drag him back, stood at the entrance polishing the dark windows and whistling horribly through his teeth. They passed into a dark, cavernous chamber, lit by a blazing fire which winked and glinted off the pewter mugs as if it were having a kind of round game with itself and these utensils were in the habit of passing the message on, where Grace, leaving his companion at one of the tables, returned from the bar carrying two steaming tumblers of brandy and water.

'You'll find this warm enough,' he observed, jangling the change from the transaction in his palm and turning over the coins as he did so. 'D—— it, will you look at that?'

'I don't see anything amiss,' Dewar commented, examining the florin that Grace threw down on the table-top between them. 'What's the matter with it?'

'Coiner's silver,' he elucidated. 'See the colour of the metal next to a real two-bob. Probably made of one of them pewter pots. Now, as to our business. I daresay you're finding the wind blows just a trifle cold around your legs at the moment. Would that be the case?'

'It does blow cold – very cold.'

'Well now.' Grace brought his face to within a foot of Dewar's. 'What would you say if I were to offer you a week's work as could strike out Hodge's bill *and* leave you with five pounds in your pocket? You'd be agreeable, I take it?'

'Naturally I should.'

'Very well. But there's one or two particulars that I need to assure myself of, see. Mr Pardew' – and here Grace paused, as if he somehow expected that his employer would take visible shape in the spirit fumes that rose above their heads – 'Mr Pardew don't like sending good money after bad. It's a thing he can't abide. First point: have you a decent, respectable set of clothes as you can set your hands on?'

'I think I have.'

'In quod I suppose?' Grace deduced, more or less sympathetically. 'How much needed to take them out?'

'Twelve shillings . . . Twelve shillings and sixpence. I haven't the tickets with me.'

'Very well again. Second point, and no offence meant or taken in return: can you play the gentleman? Meaning, if you was sent into a bank and asked to collect money that was due, could you act the high feller, come across haughty-like, and that kind of thing?'

'I suppose I . . .'

'Come along! You've kept a shop in your day. You'll have made a particular study of the breed, I'll be bound. Yes or no?'

'Yes.'

'Excellent! Couldn't be beat. Now, there's one or two peculiarities of the case as you should know of. First item, for the purposes of this job your name ain't Dewar, it's Roper. R-o-p-e-r. Got that? James Roper. Second thing: you're a gentleman of means. Three days from now you'll get a letter with a banknote in it. You're to take that note to Bulstrode's Bank in Lothbury – as Mr Roper, mind – and open an account. Know the place?'

'I think I do.'

'Excellent again! I knew as we should be able to do business. Now, there's one other thing. When you're opening the account in Lothbury – and it'll all be quite in order, no fears on that score – you're to say that you're paying a visit to Yarmouth (no, not the one on Wight, Yarmouth in Norfolk!) and that the money should be transferred to Gurney's, as are their agents in the town. Once that's done, you're to go to Yarmouth – as Mr Roper, mind – and make believe as you're taking the sea air.'

The look on Dewar's face as he stared up into his companion's eyes suggested that this was a piece of jocularity too far. 'You are making fun of me, Mr Grace. Indeed you are.'

'I was never more serious in my life. Listen to me. You're a gentleman that's on holiday – well, on business then. Anything as looks respectable. You takes lodgings somewhere, and pays for them cash down. You go for walks along the promenade. Take a look at the sands – I b'lieve they're very fine. And await our communication.'

'A letter?'

'That's the ticket. A letter giving full particulars of what you're to do. Couldn't be easier – hey?'

It now wanted but a few minutes to midday, and the tavern in which they sat had lost its recherché air. Half a dozen workmen, come from manufacturing shops in the vicinity, now clustered by the bar ordering pots of porter. The musicians of a German band, their instruments propped against their feet, were regaling themselves with faggots purchased from a metal plate kept hot by jets of steam that surged beneath it, and a villainous old woman in a shawl and a poke bonnet was going among them selling exceedingly waxen apples. Seeing the crowd of people – none of whom, as is the habit of the Clerkenwell work-horde, took the slightest notice of him – Grace grew taciturn, replying to Dewar's questions in monosyllables and affecting a great interest in some sporting prints that hung from the further wall.

'See that Silver Braid? Now that was an 'oss, that was. Ten guineas I've won on that animal in my time. But perhaps you aren't a betting man?'

'I confess I'm not.'

'And with the Derby coming up again too! Well, never mind. Now see here, Mr Dewar' – and here Grace lowered his voice significantly – 'all this is going to cost money. Naturally it is. Couldn't not. Now, what I suggest is that we go somewhere a bit out of the way of the generality.'

At the rear of the tavern there was a small ante-room set aside for the benefit of gentlemen who might wish to wash their hands or engage in other ablutions. As, however, very few gentlemen seemed eager to avail themselves of this amenity, the room was generally vacant. Here, beckoning Dewar to follow him, Grace unostentatiously repaired.

'Stinks to high heaven don't it? Never mind. Now, a sovereign to take your things out of quod and spruce yourself up – for you must look the part, you know, be able to tip your tile to the quality. Then there's travelling expenses, lodgings and so forth. Five pounds should cover it.' And to Dewar's astonishment – for there was a part of him that still believed their colloquy to have been an elaborate game, got up to mock him – he produced a battered purse from his pocket and counted out this much in gold coins. Then, abruptly, his manner changed.

'There you are. I don't need no receipt – ha! You'd best go away and do what needs to be done. Ain't no need to seek me out, for I shan't be found. One more thing: anyone asks if you know anything about me or Mr Pardew as employs me, you're as silent as the grave. Anything goes amiss, and we never met, never spoke, never so much as nodded in the street.'

Seeing the look on Dewar's face, he brightened and clapped him on the back. 'Never say die, though, eh? Why, we shall see the Derby together maybe, you and me. Now, don't cling so tight as all that while we make our way out of here, do you see?'

Grace's anxiety appeared to be misplaced. Certainly no one – not the workmen, now conversing animatedly among themselves, or the members of the German band, or the old woman selling apples – so much as raised an eye as they made their way to the door. Outside the sky retained its singular, slate-grey shade. The dolorous bells of St James's, pealing across the square, disclosed that the midday hour had come. At the tavern door Grace halted, plunged his fist into his trouser pocket to jingle his change, and caught the eye of the pot-boy, who, having completed his polishing was pushing a wretched broom listlessly across the flagstones.

'Here,' he said, producing a florin from his pocket and flinging it across in what Dewar, who followed the coin's arc, registered as a single movement of his arm. 'Something to remember me by.'

At the street corner he turned and brought his face, now grinning from ear to ear, to within an inch or two of Dewar's. 'Ha! Fancy the look on his face when he goes a changing of that, eh?'

Dewar shook his head. 'Why should that be?'

'Why? For it was the snide that I gave him, don't you see?'

He laughed again, turned his head and was gone, and Clerkenwell knew him no more.

*

Dewar's behaviour, once he became aware of his companion's disappearance, was of a very singular kind. Having witnessed the trick played upon the pot-boy, which seemed to him in his mild way a very cruel piece of spite, he was struck by a sudden anxiety that the coins given to him might be similarly false. For a moment this possibility affected him so forcibly that, standing alone on the street corner, with the midday crowd flowing around him, he began to shake with fear.

Yet a glance at the five sovereigns, which he now took out and arranged in his palm, reassured him. Indisputably the coins were real. Still nervous of his good fortune he put one into his mouth and bit down on it, but no, all was as it should be. For a brief second the action reminded him of other experiments, carried out behind the counter of his grocer's shop, and his frame shook once more. Then, in an instant, his head cleared and he realised – something that had scarcely occurred to him in the time since he and Grace had passed out of the tavern – that he was standing on a street corner in Clerkenwell, very wet now, to be sure, yet with money in his hand.

Several thoughts now crowded in upon him: that the nature of the business that Grace wished him to transact both now and in Yarmouth had altogether escaped him; that he was exceedingly hungry; and that he was now in a position to assuage at least some of the sufferings of his wife. However, for some reason that he could not properly fathom it seemed to him that it was inadvisable for him to return home at the present moment, that there were things that he needed to establish to his inward satisfaction and that, above all, more pressing than any of these concerns, he needed food.

There was a luncheon bar ten yards down the street – a poor place, his eye told him, catering to the lowest navvies and street women, but no matter. At this moment it seemed to him the most delightful refuge on earth. In a few seconds he was inside it, pressing his fingers into the breast of his coat to feel the outline of the coins within its threadbare lining. A cup of tea or coffee, the proprietor, a gaunt man in an extremely dirty apron, proposed? No, he was half-starved. He must have something to eat. What was there? Seeing the fearful, flustered look in his eye, the man regarded him suspiciously for a moment until he saw the glint of gold in his hand. Why, what – sweeping his hand above the giant urns and the metal trays kept hot by various patent apparatus – would he have? Within a further few seconds, it seemed, Dewar found himself at a table at the rear of the shop dining off a plate of fried ham and eggs, the luxury of the poor. No sooner had the last morsel passed his lips than he called for a second plateful. He ate with relish – no food he had ever tasted seemed so good – and yet he was aware, as he did so, that his thoughts were not pleasant ones, and that the figure of Mr Grace, with his smile and his fascinating jargon, wandered through them like a ghoul. By now he had finished his second meal and the proprietor was bearing down on him again. Would he take anything else? Let him say the word and a dessert should be brought. But Dewar's euphoria had altogether evaporated, to be replaced by a feeling of the deepest trepidation. He rose up from his table, paid the man and strode out into the street, there to brood on the tasks to which he had committed himself.

It was by now about half past twelve – early still for Clerkenwell, much of whose business, it may be remarked, takes place in the hours of darkness. The rain had ceased; a ray or two of watery sunshine penetrated the flint-hued cloud wall to the north. All of this Dewar ignored. His duty, he knew, directed him to Clerkenwell Court and the woman to whom he had bade farewell an hour or so before. Such, though, was the pitch of Dewar's disquiet, a paroxysm of nervousness that could only be quelled by the rapid movement of his limbs, that he began to walk not westward towards his home but northwards across the square and to the dim and even less respectable regions beyond. With the food that he had eaten he felt better, physically, than he had done for many a day, and yet inwardly his mind was altogether restless. He saw Grace everywhere – on every street corner, grinning from every omnibus, his coat-tails descending every area step. He moved on rapidly, taking due care of such hazards that lay in his way but, it later seemed to him, blindly, with no thought of the direction he took. In this way he traversed great areas of the northern city. He walked to King's Cross and stared at the railway work. He wandered through Somers Town, along shy, empty streets where it appeared that no man before had ever trod. All sorts of queer things caught his attention and held him mesmerised: a street clown turning lugubrious cartwheels; a bolting cab horse that had overturned hansom and driver into the road and now lay quivering beneath the press of onlookers; a white-faced prisoner, with a grim woman pulling at his arm, led out of a house by three policemen.

All this Dewar saw, or rather did not see, for his mind was lost in ceaseless calculation. He knew little of the money world, the world of Grace and his master, but he knew sufficient to be aware that the tasks he had been commissioned to perform could not, of their nature, be legitimate. He knew, too, that should he prove unsuccessful – should some authority take an interest in his masquerading as 'Mr Roper' – his protestations of ignorance would be altogether disbelieved. At the same time he was conscious that having taken Grace's money, spent two shillings of it and having nothing with which to replace it, he had, perforce, incriminated himself already. Seeing that he could not go back, he could only go forward. And meanwhile what was he to tell his wife? How to explain the five sovereigns, the requisitioned suit of clothes, the 'playing the gentleman' and the going to Yarmouth? On this he brooded fruitlessly, yet not altogether unhappily, as the afternoon wore on, the sky darkening by degrees as he did so, until at length, scarcely knowing how he had come there, he found himself on the summit of Primrose Hill looking down on the distant city.

A Londoner for half his forty years, he swiftly identified the various landmarks that lay before him. Far away, rising from the lower masses of buildings, there stood in black majesty the dome of St Paul's. Scraps of murky vapour, softening its outlines as they flew around it, gave it the appearance of something less than solid, floating almost on a sea of penumbral brick. Nearer, amongst a myriad of spires and steeples, lay the bulk of Newgate, its countless little windows glittering out of the shadow. Nearer still Smithfield, St Bartholomew's Hospital, the glimmer of the railway line, like an enormous artery, which spreads between Clerkenwell Road and Charterhouse Street.

The enormity of the scene, and his own insignificance in the face of it, impressed him and he began rapidly to descend the slope, reaching decisions of which he had not formerly thought himself capable as he went. He would find some form of words that would satisfy his wife without telling her the exact truth. As for himself, he would shut his mind to all extraneous thoughts and fix his concentration on the task in hand.

Reaching the foot of the hill once more he plunged south-eastwards into more familiar territory. Dusk had fallen now, and the pavements – garishly illumined by the flaring gas-lamps – were crowded with costers' barrows and roadside shops. Here he wandered for a while, his hand tightly clutched once more in the pocket of his top-coat, in search of some inexpensive delicacy that might be a comfort to his wife. A handful of shrimps and a tin of salmon having completed his purchases, he moved off in the direction of the Farringdon Road. The house in Clerkenwell Court was quite dark. Entering his room he found it unlit, the fire extinguished in the grate; only the sound of his wife's breathing denoted that any living thing inhabited it. Presently, although he had been silent in his movements, merely squatting by the hearth and with infinite patience attempting to rebuild the fire, his wife stirred.

'Is that you, John?'

'Yes, but don't trouble yourself. Look, here is the fire nearly alight. And there shall be supper presently.'

'I declare I do feel that bad. As if my head would tumble off my shoulders. Supper, you say?'

The lamp lit and the flames taking hold in the grate, he displayed his purchases to her.

'But I thought the gentleman had come after a debt?'

'Well – yes. In a manner of speaking. But there is money, too. And work, of a kind. Let me explain it to you.'

'Well, John!'

The fire rose in the hearth. With an effort, his wife hoisted herself from the bed and began to decant the shrimps into a saucer. Let it be hoped that, between them, the Dewars did not spend an altogether comfortless evening.

*

Somewhat to his surprise – for there was a part of him that still believed his dealings with Mr Pardew's clerk to have been entirely chimerical – Dewar discovered that the events of the succeeding days fell out largely as Grace had predicted. On the next morning he proceeded to an establishment in the Clerkenwell Road, with whose proprietor he had in recent weeks become exceedingly intimate, and for the sum of thirteen shillings and sixpence took his suit of clothes out of pawn. It was a good suit, purchased shortly before the end of his grocering days, and examining it as it lay on the brass bedstead in Clerkenwell Court – where it seemed to flaunt its superiority to every other garment in the room in a very vulgar and indiscreet way – Dewar thought that it would do. He was not sanguine enough, however, to imagine that this would be the limit of his expenditure. His boots, as he knew from his excursion to Primrose Hill on the previous afternoon, were falling into pieces and his tall hat, run to earth in a cupboard that contained the fragments of a defunct mangle, proved to be rent nearly in two. Accordingly, taking one of the four sovereigns that remained, he went out again to an emporium in Rosamon Street and laid out a further ten shillings on a pair of shoes. A hat, seen in the window of a second-hand shop, subjected to the most devious negotiation and eventually knocked down to him for five shillings and ninepence, completed his wardrobe.

'How do I seem?' he demanded of his wife, having struggled into these garments and, finding no mirror, being forced to make do with his reflection in the tea-kettle.

'Indeed, John, you look very well.'

'A band for the hat? But no, that's scarcely necessary. What about gloves?'

In the end it was decided that a pair of gloves could be procured from Mrs Hook, a seamstress who inhabited the room above. Throughout this investiture Dewar's expression, which he was careful to disguise from his wife, was of the most melancholic cast. He knew that, however ignorant he might be of the ultimate purpose of Grace's scheme, he was engaged on what he had assured himself inwardly was some kind of 'dodge'. This feeling was made doubly worse by the clothes in which he was now caparisoned and the silk hat that hung from his hand. It seemed to him that he could scarcely venture into the street beyond his house without risking exposure, that the very policemen who directed the traffic would look upon him with eager eyes. Gradually, by slow degrees, this feeling left him. He had, as far as he knew, not yet committed any crime. It might be – and to this hope he clung like a condemned man who has been offered one last hope of pardon – that the task before him was less suspicious – more honest – than it seemed. It was inevitable that something of this disquiet should communicate itself to his wife, and on the evening of the day in which his sartorial transformation was complete, Mrs Dewar observed somewhat gravely:

'It does not seem to me, John, that you are happy about this work that you've to do.'

'Well – no. Perhaps I am not. Not very. You see,' he improvised, conscious of his inability to communicate any of the fears that burned within him, 'it is such a deuce of a way. And of course I don't like to leave you.'

'I shall do very well.' (Mrs Dewar's face, which was chalk-white, belied this assertion.) 'Mrs Hook has promised to see after my meals. And, you know, John, it is important that you should make a success of this chance.'

'Well yes, there's that of course.' But Dewar's countenance, as he said this, did not make it appear as if he regarded success as a very probable outcome.

Two days passed, at the conclusion of which Dewar's nervousness had reached such a pitch that he had almost determined upon selling the suit and other appurtenances with a view to returning the five sovereigns. Then, on the morning of the third day after his encounter with Mr Grace, the postman – not an official seen very often in the vicinity of Clerkenwell Court – could be heard ascending the rickety stairs to deliver a letter. Sent from an address in Carter Lane, it contained, as Grace had promised, a bank note for fifty pounds, a summary of the instructions previously tendered and an injunction to convey himself to Great Yarmouth as speedily as he could. The letter was received at nine in the morning. At ten, dressed with a punctiliousness that won the instant approval of Messrs Bulstrode's commissionaire, which gentleman swept open the vestibule door with a respectful flourish, Dewar presented himself at Lothbury. Nothing, it appeared to him from the warmth of his reception, could be easier than the opening of a bank account in the name of Mr James Roper or the concluding of an agreement with Messrs Bulstrode's East Anglian agents, and by eleven he was on his way to the Shoreditch Railway Station. Here he paid eleven shillings and threepence for a return ticket to Great Yarmouth, surrendered his valise to a porter and was installed in a second-class carriage curiously impregnated with the scent of aniseed and containing an old woman with a Pekinese dog in a wire travelling basket.

'He's a very good dog, sir,' this lady said. 'Never bitten a person yet. Not even when he was a puppy.'

Dewar remarked that he was very glad to hear it.

'And yet it's a fact, sir, that he can't abide travelling. Never could, and never will yet.'

Dewar observed that this was very surprising.

Eventually, in a great hiss of vapour and disturbed air, the train bore them away out of Shoreditch into a queer hinterland of smoke-blackened chimney stacks and meandering tributaries of the river, their surface rainbow-hued with oil, past warehouses whose sombre frontages hung low in the water, and ancient manufactories whose windows had known no glass and whose roofs had known no slates, beneath great, black-bricked viaducts tilted monstrously against the sky, alongside immense, sprawling cemeteries where the gravestones lay all tumbled together under fantastic outgrowths of sooty foliage. Everything – the chimney stacks, the greeny-black skirts of the warehouses, the ledges of the viaducts and the gaunt palings of the cemeteries – dripped rainwater, off which the rays of a weak sun intermittently flashed, so that the effect was of a dozen little candles suddenly gleaming into life out of a fog of greyness and being just as suddenly extinguished. The old lady sucked caraway comfits for a while and then went to sleep with her mouth open, exposing a row of yellow teeth the colour of pianoforte keys, and the dog, howling a little at this abandonment, burrowed deep into his basket as if he genuinely believed that he might contrive an escape through the square of tin sheeting that constituted its base.

All this Dewar watched, without finding any salve for his dissatisfaction. There was a conspicuousness about his position that he wholly distrusted. It seemed to him that, clad in his black suit, silk hat balanced on his knees, he was a kind of exhibit at a public gallery that men might be invited to step forward and appraise. This self-consciousness preyed upon his mind and made him nervous. Were the guard to come tramping along the corridor, he shrank into the corner of the carriage like a man pursued. Were, at the several stations along the line, an old woman to put her head in at the window offering newspapers and trays of hardbake, he started up in his seat in terror. At Ipswich the old lady woke up, pronounced a final encomium over her wire basket and was escorted away across the platform by a female relative, but her successor, a dark and silent man who trimmed his nails into a pocket handkerchief, Dewar did not like at all, believing him to be a police inspector travelling incognito who desired only the obscurity of a tunnel to leap up and apply a set of handcuffs.

It was no better at Norwich, where he was compelled to wait two hours for a connecting train and skulked miserably around the city in the grasp of a zealous porter, examining an ancient cathedral and a castle-cum-prison whose gardens were tended by men in zebra clothes with equal indifference. It is a scant twenty miles from Norwich to Great Yarmouth, across a great bare flat covered by a myriad of windmills, and yet Dewar wished the distance were two hundred. However, on reaching his destination he was pleased to discover – something that would have seemed impossible to him four hours before – that he was at any rate alive, that no lions had eaten him, or attempted to eat him, and that the porters, railway men and tourist touts whom he encountered treated him with an agreeable civility. In this way his spirits improved and, carrying his valise out of the station – it was by now about four o'clock in the afternoon – he absolutely stopped to ask an old man in a smock holding the bridle of a dray horse where in Yarmouth he might stay and if, in addition, there were anything in the town worth seeing? Finding that persons of quality generally put up at Bates's Hotel and that the beach contained a wonderful houseboat that Mr Dickens had put into one of his novels, he determined to be taken instantly to the former and to spend a part of the next morning examining the latter.

Alas, Great Yarmouth out of season is a dreary place – at least I have always found it so. There is a promenade, running in parallel to the sea for nearly a mile, over which the spray gusts with unappeasable ardour; there is a north wind which blows directly down from Jutland; there are a couple of theatres which, though displaying the most inviting notices of past and forthcoming attractions, are always shut up; and a Thursday bazaar, always threatening to break out into a rash of 'sixpenny sales', 'shilling auctions' and the like, but, in point of fact, closed on all seven days of the week. Quite how the inhabitants of the town may be thought to occupy themselves between the months of October and March I do not know, for the shops are always shut and the streets always empty.

Having risen early the next morning, proceeded to the telegraph office, where he communicated his address to Carter Lane, investigated the sailors' reading room, which contained a rheumy-eyed copy of the *Yarmouth Mercury* and a cannon ball supposedly discharged at Trafalgar, and examined the exterior of the houseboat on the beach that Mr Dickens had put into one of his novels (the interior proving unnavigable as it contained a family of nine persons) Dewar felt that he had exhausted the town's possibilities. On the next day, however, there came a further letter from Carter Lane. This he examined with great alarm, for it disclosed to him the precise nature of his business in Great Yarmouth. Specifically, he was to visit that morning in the character of Mr Roper the offices of two of the town's solicitors. At each he was to represent himself as the creditor of a gentleman named Nokes, living at an address in Peckham, and request that a letter be written soliciting the payment of debts to the value of £150. He was then to retire to his hotel and wait until such time as the solicitors communicated with him. All this – and in truth there was not much more than a page of it – Dewar read half a dozen or even a dozen times, so anxious was he to commit these instructions to memory.

Then, with his hat in his hand and the gravest foreboding in his heart, he stepped out into the high street with the aim of executing his commissions. Again, though, as with the bank at Lothbury, nothing could have exceeded the civility that greeted his appearance at these legal portals. In each case he was swiftly admitted, inducted with the merest delay into the presence of a partner in the firm, heard respectfully and assured that the letter would be written forthwith. He was staying at Bates's Hotel? Well, it would be their pleasure to communicate with him there. At the second of these offices discreet mention was made of the need for a reference. Dewar, though he felt sure that the beating of his heart could be heard by passers-by outside in the street, gritted his teeth, referred the questioner in his blandest manner to Messrs Gurney, with whom he believed his own bankers corresponded, and was bowed out onto the staircase in the manner of a modern Croesus. All in all, Dewar reflected, as he made his way back to his hotel, through air that now seemed to carry a rank odour of fish, it could all have been a great deal worse. Again, no lion had eaten him, or even attempted to eat him. In all his undertakings he had met only lambs.

It was in this spirit that, stepping out of the hotel after luncheon with the aim of taking another turn along the beach, he met with a calamity of such a nature as to send all his former fears flying once more about his head. Idling in the lobby, having transacted some minor piece of business with the desk-clerk – a certain shovel of coals that might or might not have been added to his fire, a certain dish that might or might not have been added to his supper menu – he became aware that a man who had just entered the vestibule was regarding him with the keenest of looks. Dewar turned aside, intending to return immediately to his room, but in an instant the man, whose features Dewar now believed that he half-remembered, was at his elbow.

'Now here's chance. I said to myself when I came into the place that it was you, and d——d if I wasn't right.'

'Well, yes indeed. How are you?'

Searching the man's face, Dewar recognised a commercial traveller with whom he had had dealings in his Islington days, one, moreover, to whom every detail of his commercial misfortunes would be known. Striving vainly to compose himself – for he was conscious that he had gone very red in the face – he became aware that the commercial traveller was observing him with more than usual interest.

'Here on business, I suppose? Well, you look as if the world was treating you pretty comfortably. By the way,' the other continued, 'didn't I hear the fellow at the desk call you Roper, or some such name?'

It was an innocent enquiry, but to one of Dewar's febrile state of mind sufficient to goad him almost to frenzy. Stammering some excuse – he could not subsequently remember what he had said – he rushed from the vestibule into the street and, having ascertained that he was not being followed, took himself off to the promenade. Here, aided by cool air and the absence of onlookers, his head became clearer. He had met with a misfortune, he assured himself, but there was no reason why it should prove fatal. Doubtless he could no longer remain in a hotel where his assumed name might come to be generally known, but there were other establishments where the name of 'Mr Roper' would attract no such suspicion. Accordingly, having allowed the greater part of an hour to elapse, he returned to Bates's Hotel and, having made sure that the commercial traveller was nowhere to be seen, presented himself at the desk with the intelligence that a letter recently received required him to leave town instantly. Five minutes saw the matter concluded, and Dewar found himself out in the street once more with his valise in his hand. Fear, he now perceived, had made him cunning. Rather than transferring himself to a rival hotel – the thoroughfare in which Bate's lay contained two or three – he walked to a rather out-of-the-way part of the town, somewhat beyond St Nicholas's Church, and engaged a room in the house of a fisherman and his wife. Here he straightaway wrote to the two solicitors' firms and to Carter Lane informing them of his removal though not, in the final letter, offering any explanation for it. He spent the remainder of the day walking the shore line (a presentiment having told him to avoid any region where he might chance upon the commercial traveller) and eating the frugal supper of sprats with which his landlady had seen fit to provide him.

Alas, Dewar's troubles were far from vanished. Time hung heavy on his hands. Dull, rainswept mornings, which might have been tolerable in a commercial hotel, with a fire and the society of other men, were infinitely tedious to him in a fisherman's cottage in Southtown. He took to wandering the beach, far down by the water's edge beneath the flight tracks of the gulls and the murky sky, and in this way walked solitary miles along the coast path. There was a town to the south named Gorleston, full of picturesque cottages built of stone from the beach, and a lonely lake – the Breydon Water – populated only by herons and silent trees, but in neither of them did he find any solace. He had got into the habit – he remarked it during the course of these excursions – of muttering to himself as he walked, and the realisation was not pleasant to him. At the same time, labouring through the wind with his collar turned against his face, hands plunged deep into the pocket of his coat, he assured himself that his ordeal was nearly at an end, that another day – two days – would see him home. The tenement in Clerkenwell Court now seemed a kind of Elysian field and the clanging of the bells of St James's was celestial music when set against the endless sand and the harsh cries of the gulls. He was a Londoner, he told himself, and the placid Norfolk faces that dogged his every step mystified him.

On the third day of his sojourn in the Southtown cottage, two letters arrived for him by the first of the morning's posts. Each was from one of the firms of Yarmouth solicitors he had engaged. Each begged to inform him that £150 had been received from his debtor, Mr Nokes of Peckham, and that the money, less the firm's commission, was there for him to collect. This intelligence, which Dewar had calculated would only raise his spirits, had, curiously enough, the effect of deflating them still further for they offered proof – if further proof were needed – that the scheme on which he was engaged was altogether fraudulent. No creditor, he reasoned, having experience of creditors in his own line of business, would remit a sum of such magnitude in such a brief space of time. Surely such rapidity would arouse the deepest suspicion in those he had employed to collect it? There was nothing to be done, however, save to obey the summons, and into the town, carrying himself very circumspectly and with his hat pulled down over his eyes, Dewar went. Again, at both establishments, he – or rather Mr Roper – was greeted with the greatest deference. In each case he was invited to read a letter in a fine italic hand, signed by Mr Nokes of Peckham, berating him for his exigence but nevertheless acknowledging the extent of his obligations. In each case he quitted the premises with a cheque, drawn on the firm's account, for slightly less than £150.

There remained only a single task to perform. Dewar's money was by now nearly expended. Only a shilling and a few pence remained of the five sovereigns which Grace had given him a week and more ago. Yet each of the Yarmouth solicitors had, in addition to the cheque, presented him with a bill for six shillings and eightpence. Further funds would be required to pay his rent in Southtown. Following the advice of the most recent letter from Carter Lane, Dewar resolved to apply to Messrs Gurney for some portion of the funds lately transmitted to his account from Lothbury. Calculating that half an hour would see him gone from the town, arming himself with the two solicitors' bills by way of a reference, he stopped a passer-by to enquire directions. Gurney's Bank? Yes indeed, Gurney's Bank lay in the very next street.

It was by now nearly midday. Knowing that the businesses of Great Yarmouth, such being the case in provincial towns, clung to the habit of a dinner hour and that the doors would soon be barred against him, Dewar made haste. Whether it was the flustered state into which he was thrown by his rapid transit or the general air of light-headedness which had afflicted him for some days past that was responsible for what now befell him is perhaps arguable. Nevertheless, it is certain that on reaching the teller's desk, the following exchange took place:

'I should like to draw on some funds which I believe have been transferred here by your London agent.'

'What is the name?'

'Dewar.'

He corrected himself in an instant, but the instant was too late. The clerk's eye was already raised in enquiry. Worse, a senior clerk with a beard and an eye-glass who happened to have overheard the exchange from his own desk to the rear now rose up and made his way across the room. Another man might perhaps have brazened it out, made a joke of his absent-mindedness, produced incontrovertible proof that he was Mr Roper, but Dewar was not that man. He merely took to his heels and fled. Making his way wretchedly back to his lodging, he cursed himself for his incompetence while demanding of himself the question: what am I to do? A search of his pockets realised the sum of fifteen pence. There was only one thing that he could do. Reaching the house at Southtown, he made the welcome discovery that his landlady was absent: a moment later and he and his valise were once more out into the street. Sweat pouring from his forehead, looking wildly around him as he went, he walked hurriedly to the station. Four hours later, followed only by a fog that had risen up in the Norfolk fields and pursued his train westward across the flat, he was back in London.

*

MR THACKERAY'S TOUR
Norwich – Hingham – Watton

. . . Within, except where the rococo architects have introduced their ornaments, the cathedral is noble. A rich, tender sunshine is stealing in through the windows and gilding the stately edifice with the purest light. The admirable stained glass is not too brilliant in its colours. The organ plays a rich, solemn music. Six lady visitors, each with her guidebook and her attendant gentleman, were parading up and down the nave in the company of a fierce-looking verger whose eloquence was such that I declare I felt ashamed of my ignorance of my ecclesiastical history and slunk away to the gate of the cathedral school hard by. Here half a hundred young gentlemen in tight black jackets and trowsers were playing tag or cockshies or purchasing hardbake off a tart woman's tray, watched over by a kindly young master in a stuff gown who clearly envied them their relaxations – I know I did.

At noon we left the city by its western approach, passing the great house of Earlham, seat of Mr Gurney, and the pretty village of Colney before emerging once more onto the hard Norfolk road. This is, I believe, a charming country, where the river winds through water-meadows and osier-beds, with little neat churches rising here and there among tufts of trees and pastures that are wonderfully green, and yet the whole curiously empty and forlorn. Where the people had gone, unless it were to help with the harvest, I do not know. At any rate I saw none, except a solitary boy playing by the roadside at Wymondham who enquired: 'Would your honour like to see a big pig?' 'Titmarsh,' I said to myself, following him into a sad little maze of allotments and yards of scuffed-up earth, 'you *shall* observe the agricultural delights of the county and be a farmer yet', but I must confess that the animal, found staring complacently from its sty, seemed a very unremarkable specimen. Still it was a pleasure to hear the rascal prattle of the thirty shillings his mother *would* get for the carcass and the plate of pig's fry he *would* have on slaughtering day and I confess quite reconciled me to the twopence which constituted our fee for the viewing . . .

Beyond Hingham – a neat town with a fine mere rippling at the wood's edge – the land turned morose and dreary. A cart rattled by bearing half a dozen old men and women with shabby luggage piled up at their feet and not a tooth between them – paupers, said my friend, who knows the county well, bound for the workhouse at Watton. A brewer's dray passed us, drawn by two great stamping horses, and I thought of its journey's end: mine host in a white apron standing at his door, the barrels rolled down into the dim, cool cellar, the pretty barmaid drawing the drayman's tankard. No such welcome, alas, awaited the old paupers. Towards Watton we came to a big house half-hidden by trees with its boundaries fenced off by a high flint wall. This I was interested to see, being the abode of Mr Dixey the celebrated naturalist. A smart lodge lay at the gate, with white ducks and stockings hung up to dry on the currant bushes, but there was no sign of life. The gates themselves were locked and barred, and it seemed to me that Mr Dixey, however strong his ardour for butter-flies, does not care much for visitors.

Indeed this part of the country has a desolate aspect: tall trees shading the roadside, a horrid old ruined house that could have been the setting for one of Mrs Radcliffe's romances, and always the great brooding flat stretching on into the distance. A wind had got up and came soughing through the reed beds in the most melancholy way. Passing a gap in Mr Dixey's wall, where the stone had crumbled, I could not resist taking a peep into his parkland, but there was nothing except a pack of hounds chained up in an enclosure and a woman's figure fluttering silently in the meadow before the house . . .

And so at length to Watton, a wide old market-place with ostlers attending to their beasts at the rails and the George Inn, with its fragrant beds and the liveliest parlourmaid I ever saw, and an impe-rious old housekeeper to whom I would only say 'Madam, my chop would have been sweeter still had the serving girl's thumb-print not stared up at me from the plate . . .'

W.M. Thackeray, 'A Little Tour Through the Counties of East Anglia', *Cornhill Magazine*, 1862

XI

Isabel

Whenever I think of the life I led before I came here, it is always Papa to whom my thoughts return. Indeed, I sometimes imagine that of all the things I have seen & all the people I have known it is only Papa that is real, that all the others are mere ghosts tapping at a door through which they shall never be admitted.

Papa has beautiful white hands with pink knuckles & long nails. His eyes are soft & large. His voice is slow & gentle. He holds down his cheek to kiss & he presses my forehead.

I can see him passing his hand through his hair laughing at the children pouring out his tea.

I can see him swinging his arms as he walks. I can see him looking out over the ship's side & replacing his spectacles that are always slipping.

When Papa wrote his stories he would draw the pictures for them as he worked: gentlemen on horseback, fine ladies conversing, all upon the margins of his manuscript book. Once when we were at tea there came a tap at the window & looking out we saw Mr Hannay, that Papa knew, waiting on the step. 'That is the man I need,' Papa cried & set to work at once with his pen. And that is how the face in Papa's *Cromwell* is not Cromwell's at all but Mr Hannay's as he stood on our doorstep.

When I was one-and-twenty Papa gave me a birthday dinner at Richmond. Such a bad dinner, Papa said, but we liked it so much, the two of us. When the things were cleared away Papa called a little carriage & we drove home past the river through clouds & clouds of mist, & came through Barnes & over the bridge, & all the people were out in the street at Kensington, & I was so very happy.

All this is very vivid to me, very particular in its dimensions, as if the years that followed had never been. And yet I know that had I foreseen them then I would have wished them gone.

*

'When I am an old man,' Papa used to say, 'you shall be married to a grand gentleman, & living in a fine house with company calling in carriages & footmen in powdered wigs, but perhaps I shall be allowed to sit & drink my glass of claret & watch my grandchildren grow.'

But now Papa is gone, there is no grand gentleman & no fine house, no company calling in carriages or footmen in powdered wigs, & the claret is all drunk up.

*

This morning Mr Conolly comes. He is brought to my room by the butler, who waits outside until he is done.

I am sure that I saw Mr Conolly before. But there is so much that is gone from my mind that however long I dwell on those old pictures I cannot find his face within their frames. Papa & Mr Hannay, & Mr Smith that was Papa's publisher coming up to see him in a cab, but not Mr Conolly. Who is a white-haired, civil, old, thin-legged gentleman of a kind I do not like. Who presses my hand and looks very searchingly into my eyes as he speaks.

I would that Mr Conolly's eyes looked elsewhere. At the butler waiting in the doorway, or the water-jug & the teacups (they do not allow me a drinking glass, tho' I have often asked for one). Anywhere but at me.

How do I find myself, Mr Conolly begins by asking.

'I am perfectly well, sir, I believe,' I tell him.

You will excuse me, madam, he next says, if I ask you a question or two.

'If I can answer you, sir, I shall.'

I do not mean to answer Mr Conolly. Who still presses my hand as he looks into my eye. Who is very impertinent.

'How long has the Queen reigned?'

'A dozen years. A hundred. I am sure the Queen would know, if there is a doubt.'

'If I wished to journey from London to Bristol, through which counties would I pass?'

'Indeed, sir, I should travel by air balloon. It is said to be most agreeable.'

I am surer now than ever that I saw Mr Conolly before. Who proceeds in this manner for some time. Who finally takes his eyes, and his soft hand, and his thin little legs away from me and shuts the door behind him. Whose carriage, shortly afterwards, can be heard grinding up the gravel in the drive.

I am Isabel Ireland.

I am twenty-seven years old.

The Queen has reigned twenty-eight years.

If I wished to journey from London to Bristol I should pass through Berkshire, Oxfordshire and Gloucestershire.

The number of states of the American Confederacy is thirteen.

The Prince Consort is four years dead.

How do I find myself? Alas, I am altogether lost.

*

A conversation with my guardian, Mr Dixey.

'Have you diversion enough, madam? Is there anything that can be got for you?'

'I should much like to read Miss Brontë's novel *Agnes Grey*,' I say to test him.

'I believe we have it in the library. Randall shall bring it up to you. But something other than a book?'

'Indeed, sir,' I tell him, 'I should like to see company.'

To this he says nothing. The book comes with my supper. I fall on it as hungrily as the food.

*

Papa hated to see me idle. If he found me in the drawing room with my feet among the sofa cushions he would say, 'Come, miss, let us take a walk around the gardens' or bid me to fetch a block from the study floor (it was on these that Papa did his drawings before they were taken away to the engraver). So I am always careful to occupy myself. I read my book. I mend my clothes – that is, when they are in need of mending. I study my situation. A man should make an inventory of any new place in which he finds himself, Papa used to say, and this I have accomplished. Thus:

I have two rooms for my private use: the one a sitting room, the other a bedroom.

The dimensions of the sitting room are twenty-four feet by eighteen feet; the dimensions of the bedroom fourteen feet by nine feet.

The dimensions of my sofa are six feet by two feet; of my desk four feet by three feet; of my table the same.

I am brought my breakfast at eight, my luncheon at one, my supper at seven.

I read my book. I mend my clothes. I study my situation.

*

Papa and I often talked of the man I should marry.

He will be an archdeacon living in the country, Papa would say, & you will have ten children, & write his charges, & make puddings, & be very severe on the dissenters.

Nonsense, I would say in return, he will be a navy captain with only one leg, & a great telescope fixed to his eye, whom I shall see but once a year when his ship is in harbour & who will shock me with his oaths.

Nonsense again, Papa would say. He will be Professor of Greek at Oxford & you will turn bluestocking & have solemn parties for the undergraduates & be very down on ladies who have not read Homer.

I think that Papa joked in this way because he feared that I should leave him, & that I joked with him because I feared it too. 'Alas,' he would say, whenever a young lady's banns were read in church, 'another old gentleman turning his face to the wall and wondering who shall bring in his slippers.'

'The old gentleman,' I would say, to twit him, 'should bring in his slippers himself.'

All that was five years since. And now all those that I loved are gone from me, & there is no power on earth that shall bring them back.

*

I have been very ill. That is what they tell me, & I daresay it must be true, for there is so much that has vanished from my mind that only sickness could have dragged it from me. It is not for want of thinking – oh no, not that! Once, indeed, I tried to set down on a sheet of paper all that has passed since Papa's death, yet found myself altogether defeated. The essentials were there in my head, I knew, but it seemed to me that I could not grasp at them & that they drifted through banks of vapour whose depths I could never penetrate.

167

I remember Papa dying, and the silence in the bedroom above our heads, and the servant rushing in crying, 'Oh he is dead, miss!' and myself running to fetch Dr Collins from his breakfast.

I remember the motion of a boat upon the water & Henry's face – very white and grave – next to mine, & a ribbon fastened about my waist that, try as I might, I could not undo.

And – much later it seems to me – a woman's voice saying, not unkindly, 'Now put on your bonnet', and I, very meekly, putting on my bonnet & stepping out into darkness & a jolting cab, tho' where it took me I could not say.

For I can be good – oh so very good – when I wish it.

*

When I was a child I had scarlatina. It was in Italy, with Papa, who was unwell too, & the two of us lay on our backs in adjoining rooms overlooking the sea with our arrowroots & our lemonades & were, I think, very comfortable together. Now I lie on a sofa with a view of Mr Dixey's wild garden, & my treatment is this:

I have a draught of medicine, brought to me morning & night, which I am bidden to swallow.

I have Mr Conolly to press my hand & ask me how I find myself.

I have the door locked behind me, for fear that I should injure myself.

I am glad that the door is locked behind me, for I should not wish to cause inconvenience.

Not to myself or to anyone else.

*

As for Mr Dixey's establishment, seeing that I have never been permitted to explore it, I have scarce an idea of its design. There may be a dozen rooms or a hundred: I have no means of knowing. And yet I have a vision of myself stealing about the place at night, a candle in my hand, opening doors that should not be opened, prying into chambers where Mr Dixey would not have me go. No doubt it is very wicked of me to think these thoughts. But they have crept into my head unbidden, while there are other thoughts I would have kept there that have stolen away.

Yet though I may not turn keys & steal down staircases, I have eyes & ears, & there are things that I may deduce within the confines of a locked room. Thus, I calculate with certainty, there are nine of us in this house.

Mr Randall, the butler, brings me my meals. He does not speak, except to ask if the food is to my liking (it is not!). Once, indeed, he pressed upon me a small book, saying that I should do well to take its contents to heart. When he had gone I looked & saw that it was a tract, *Some Paths for the Craven Spirit*, of the kind that Aunt Charlotte Parker favoured. And which, knowing it to be dull, I did not read.

William, the footman, Mr Randall's viceroy, says not a word. Indeed, he lays down my tray and refills my water-jug, scurries to the door and scrabbles with the key in such hot haste that I believe he fancies me to be a young sorceress ripe to turn him into a toad.

Mrs Finnie, the housekeeper, attends on me each morning at eleven, there being certain feminine wants that a butler and a footman cannot between them be expected to supply.

Who is a sour old woman with hair of such a blackness of jet that it cannot be her own.

Who declines to be drawn by the most amiable pleasantry.

'It is a fine morning, Mrs Finnie.'

'Indeed, ma'am.'

'But not so fine, I think, as it was yesterday.'

'Perhaps not, ma'am.'

There is no conversation to be got from Mrs Finnie.

Then there is a cook, Mrs Wates, on whom I never set eyes, & three maids, whose voices I hear about the house & whose figures I have glimpsed at a distance in the grounds. I confess that I should like to speak to them, to sit in a parlour with them, even, & listen to them as they talk. Yet such are the ways of this house that I know they would not wish to speak to me.

Sometimes I hear the scrunch of gravel on the drive & the sound of voices far below & know that visitors are come. Once there came a clergyman, for I stood on tiptoe to look out of my window & saw his shovel hat. Another time an old lady came walking at a great distance through the gardens & passed round the side of the house. What business she had I cannot imagine.

I am forbidden company, Mr Conolly says, for there are foolish fancies in my head that conversation may excite. I confess that this makes me very unhappy.

But perhaps it is for the best.

This evening Mr Dixey again comes to visit me. He says nothing at first, but merely regards me as if there were some question he wished to put but could not bring himself to ask it.

'I have finished *Agnes Grey*,' I tell him. 'Are there other books I might see?'

'I shall have some brought to you,' he says. 'Is there anything else you would wish?'

'Indeed, sir,' I say, greatly daring. 'I should like to write a letter.'

'A letter! To whom would you wish to write?'

Alas, so hastily was the thought plucked out of my mind that I cannot immediately answer him. 'I should like to write to my husband's lawyer.'

'There is nothing that he can tell you that cannot be told by me.'

'Nevertheless, I should like to do so.'

He bows, but says nothing. Later, with my supper, Mr Randall brings me two books. They are Mr Trollope's *Framley Parsonage* and Mr Jerrold's *The Story of a Feather*. Knowing how much Papa disliked Mr Jerrold, I leave the latter unread.

*

A dull morning, overcast & with rain. Mrs Finnie arrives punctually at eleven.

'It is a fine morning, Mrs Finnie.'

'Indeed, ma'am.'

'Even finer, I think, than yesterday.'

'As you say, ma'am.'

There are other fools in this house than I!

*

I confess that I have begun to make a study of Mr Dixey. A study of the set of his features. Of the way he stands before me. Of the way he sits in his chair.

What is there to say?

My guardian is a tall man, somewhat elderly yet vigorous in his demeanour. He has grey hair & grey eyes that sit in his head like pieces of flint but conceal, I judge, a kindly & industrous nature.

He is very active in his pursuits, wears a pair of gaiters, seems ever to be returning from some walk, has on riding boots or carries a dog-whip, &c.

There is no Mrs Dixey, nor I think ever was.

He has read Papa's books & indeed those of other literary gentlemen that Papa knew.

Yet there is something mysterious about him. Viz: his habit, when asked some question, of not replying; his habit of regarding me as if I possessed some piece of information of which he was dearly in want; his habit of casting his grey eye around my chamber as if something was hid there that he could not discern.

Henry, as I now recollect, used to talk of him occasionally, saying he was a man to whom he owed much, that the Dixeys were thought to be 'queer people', whatever that might mean, that this Mr Dixey had some reputation as a naturalist & scholar, &c., that his name could be found in the catalogues at the British Museum and so forth.

This is all that Henry said, & having little interest I asked no more.

My guardian's face is clean-shaven with deep lines etched into the loose skin. He has long, delicate fingers and a way of saying 'That will do very well' or 'I had not remarked it' when something is drawn to his attention – trivial expressions, no doubt, but as they are part & parcel of the man I set them down.

As to his interests, the other day he fetched a slow-worm that he had found on the path & concealed in his pocket for his amusement; the week before, a bat nestled in moss upon a saucer that he believed he could nurse back to health. When I shrank from these objects – the bat with its pinched little face & evil claws I could scarce stand to look at – he expressed surprise, saying that he supposed certain things were not to others' tastes. This I thought very singular, but somehow characteristic of him.

And then last evening a most curious encounter, whose elements will long remain with me.

It was very late – gone eleven indeed – pitch-dark outside with a high wind blowing, but I had been amusing myself by singing snatches of old songs – it was something Papa and I used to do in days gone by – & had not thought of going to bed. Just as I assured myself that I absolutely must retire, there came a knock at the door, very loud and distinct, & in answer to my enquiring a turning of the key & my guardian's tall figure standing in the doorway. Again, he stared at me for a full half-minute without speaking, went to the window & stared into the night, & finally remarked:

'The hour is very late.'

'I had not noticed it,' I lied.

'You are quite comfortable here?'

'Indeed, sir. Very comfortable.'

'I cannot offer you company. But there is conversation, if you wish it.'

'I do wish it.'

I had thought he would seat himself on one of the armchairs in my chamber. Instead he bade me follow him through the open door – he had a lighted candle set near the wainscot which he now retrieved. In this way – he leading, myself following, with my skirts seized up in my hand to guard against the dust of the bare boards, our two shadows in monstrous relief against the wall – we proceeded along a corridor to a great silent landing, with moonshine streaming through the window onto the balustrade, climbed a flight of stairs & came eventually to a far-off room where lamplight glowed under the door.

His study, my guardian explained. He seemed very anxious that I should explore it and stood by my shoulder, indeed, as I examined it, like a small boy with his boat that his female relatives are bidden to admire.

Indeed my guardian's study is a very singular place, unlike any other gentleman's room that ever I saw. Picture, if you will, two or three great high bookcases extending almost to the ceiling, so that it must take a step-ladder at least to ascend to their top-most shelves. And then a number of squat glass cabinets, all a-gleam with the light from the fire, and filled with the queerest objects: a stuffed pine-marten poised on the bough of a tree; several animal skulls and pieces of bone; lichens and ferns set under squares of glass. Several of these exhibits I confess I did not over-like – viz., a wolf's head on a plinth, a stoat preserved so ingeniously that he seemed ready to strike the grey mouse that lay at his feet. Turning from them I all but fell into the arms of a great brown bear who stood in the corner of the room in such a lifelike attitude that I could scarce prevent myself from crying out.

I must not mind old Bruin, my guardian said. Who in life craved but tender shoots and honeycombs.

There were, in addition, several little tables set against the wall on which lay trays of what I could not fail to remark as birds' eggs, all neatly labelled, thus: *Philomachus pugnax; Rallus aquaticus; Circus aeruginosus*. These, I will admit, took my fancy & I browsed among them for some time.

'What, pray, are these sir?' I enquired of a pair of reddy-brown specimens, reposing on a saucer of moss.

My guardian seemed gratified by my interest.

'They are osprey's eggs. A bird the Scots call the eagle fisher, and very hard to come by in these times.'

Much as I admired the eggs, there seemed something sad in this admission. That it were a great tragedy for the hen bird who returned to her nest to find them gone.

'It is a pity,' I said, 'that they could not have hatched, and allowed the world two more ospreys.'

'As to that, madam,' he remarked, 'I fear that I cannot agree with you.'

After that no more was said about eggs.

I suppose that I must have remained in that room an hour. I remember that there was a moon shining on the garden & an owl that flapped at the window, & the warmth of the fire being very pleasant.

My guardian is a restless man. He does not sit easy in his chair but stands up repeatedly to poke the fire, take down a book, inspect one of his cabinets, &c.

He is the possessor of a great fund of curious information, so that I should now think myself tolerably able to answer the most searching questions on the breeding habits of the lynx, the manufacture of otter snares, &c.

One very droll incident occurred, which I must not omit. By my guardian's chair, as he sat, I noticed there lay a saucer of milk. This I supposed the perquisite of some cat that I had not yet seen. Presently, though, a tiny mouse popped its head through a hole in the wain-scot, darted forth to the saucer & began to lap up the milk, appar-ently oblivious to the fact that great people were talking above its head. When I drew my guardian's attention to this – for I confess to a slight horror of mice – he smiled & said Sir Charles (he is named after Sir Charles Lyell, the great geologist) was a pet & had the run of the place, & stooping down put out his forefinger, which the mouse saw & scrambled up almost the length of his shoulder, so that I could not help but laugh, it being so very humorous to hear a gentleman talking while a mouse ran in and out of the folds of his coat.

*

A very curious aspect of our conversation, which I here set down as fully as I can recollect it.

'Who made the world?' my guardian asks.

'Why, God made it.'

'And yet there are those who say he did not.'

'Indeed then, who else would be able to form us in the manner that we are and give us life?'

This was the answer that Papa always gave his friend Mr Lewes in debates of this kind. My guardian acknowledges it with a nod of his grey head.

'Some men would say that the world made itself.'

This seemed to me such a blasphemy that I cried out:

'But out of what materials? And who placed them there?'

At this my guardian seizes up Sir Charles, who has been polishing his whiskers in the region of his master's collar, and continues:

'And mice? Did God make them? Or were they once some other thing?'

'A mouse is a mouse.'

'But he might not always have been so. The rocks are older than the Bible.'

'And yet, sir, they are all a part of God's purpose.'

As am I, & my position here, & what will become of me, of which I would know more, when it pleases God to tell me.

*

And then a greater mystery even than my guardian's questionings.

Waking early this morning, at six of the clock, with the wind still beating against the eaves and a grey dew beyond the window, I entered my chamber to find a white rose upon the desk. A single white rose lying upon a silver dish, the thorns neatly trimmed from its stem.

I enquired of the servants – Mr Randall, who fetched me my breakfast, Mrs Finnie, who came to me at eleven, the tall footman who brought my lunch – yet none of them could account for it.

*

I have been thinking of Mama.

Although, to be sure, it is twenty years since I saw her & fifteen since she died. Which I remember above all, the funeral at Kensal

Green, and Papa in his black coat, and Sir Henry Cole, Papa's friend, standing at the grave, & all of us quite broken down with our grief. At the thought of poor Mama, who would never again laugh or comb out her red-gold hair as she sat on the terrace, or kiss me & tell me to be a good child, & all the other things that we recollected her for.

Papa and Mama met at Worthing, where he had gone to write his book & she to take the air with Aunt Charlotte Parker. Their carriage broke its axle on the Brighton Road & Papa was very gallant, summoned a cab & escorted them to their hotel, which I thought a very romantic story. When they were married they lived in an old brown house in Kensington. One day when I was a girl Papa told me to put on my hat & I walked with him across the gardens to a house where a gentleman in a travelling cloak with a great beard coming down over his shirt-front sat at breakfast over a silver teapot. This Papa said was Mr Tennyson.

I remember Mama reading to me from the beautiful silk books that lay on the round drawing-room table.

And Mama sitting on the terrace with all her hair tumbling about her shoulders & our servant Brodie combing it out.

And Mama putting me to sleep in a dear little room with two little beds & some pictures. One was of a good boy doing a sum & another of a sleepy boy yawning on his way to school, & then over the door hung Daniel O'Connell, who I fancied would make the most horrible faces to frighten me.

And Papa's figure in the doorway as he regarded us & his shadow in the firelight as he stooped down to bid us goodnight.

And then we were at Paris & Mama was ill & she went to live with a doctor in a big house with a great garden full of little paths, & sometimes I would spend the day with her & run after her down the long slopes. And Mama would become quite like a girl again & play with me for hours at a time until Papa & the nurse came out to find us. And Papa would say that we were his two darlings & that the happiest moment of his life was when he came along the Brighton Road (Mama said that he had his head in a book & scarce noticed her) & saw the carriage with its broken axle.

Sometimes Mama would fly into a temper & throw the cup that she had in her fingers to the ground or beat her hands upon her chair in a passion, tho' it was a puzzle to me that anything could distress her. Yet I was never frightened of Mama at these times, for I knew that she loved me & would not bring me to harm.

Mama herself said as much.

Then the doctor said it was better we should not go to see her any more & we came away to England. I remember Papa's face in the diligence that fetched us from Paris, & the lamp swinging from the jolting road, & Papa scolding me for some trick I had played, & thinking that I should see Mama again & be consoled.

And yet I never did.

And when she died – I was twelve then & had a great friend called Tishy Cole, & Papa was writing his life of Sir Thomas More – it was as if someone I had known long ago & then forgotten had come back to haunt me. And I resolved never again to forget Mama, & her red-golden hair, & running down the slopes of the doctor's gardens. Which I have not done to this day.

It seems to me that I am very like Mama.

I too have a room where I sit & am brought things & people are very kind to me.

I too have my tempers & my frets.

I too have my red-golden hair, which is like Mama's, altho' I think not so long.

And yet Papa, & all the others on whom I might rely, are gone from me for ever.

*

Once, before Henry & I were married, I tried to explain to him about Mama, & the doings at the French doctor's house, & other things – of Mr Farrier, even, & what had passed between us – but he shook his head, smiled & said that it did not signify.

*

Of all flowers, there is nothing I detest so much as a rose.

*

And now, all unexpected, there is *an addition to my circle* (as Mrs Brookfield, who we knew in the old Kensington days, & was very kind to us, would say when she had some lion to tea).

This lunch-hour, instead of the tall footman who never speaks, there comes bearing my tray one of the maids, the yellow-haired girl whom I recollected seeing from my window. Very sturdy & carrying her burden before her as if it weighed no more than a teacup.

'Where is William?' I asked, the tray having been set down & the girl bobbing her head.

'Please, ma'am, he has gone away.'

I fancied that William's going away was not to her liking.

'And you are to take his place?'

'If you please, ma'am.'

Upon which she gave me a look such as I have often seen in the faces of those that serve me: as if she were wary of what I might say or do & wished that the door were open behind her.

'You must not be afraid of me,' I said. 'Indeed you must not, for I mean no harm. What is your name?'

'Esther, ma'am.'

She would not say more, but busied herself about my desk & shook out a sofa-cushion that had disarranged itself, in such a way that I was very grateful to have her company. Plainly my situation – the room, my papers, &c. – interested her for I saw her dart several eager looks as she went about her work.

When she had gone I listened to her footsteps tripping along the passageway until there came a moment when I could not distinguish them amid the other noises of the house, & then another moment when they were altogether gone.

XII

Dealings with the Firm
of Pardew & Co.

15 May 186–

Wm Barclay, Esq.,
Director,
South-Eastern Railway Company

Dear Sir,

I refer to the meeting of the 11th inst, at which it was desired by
the directors that our position regarding the conveyance of bullion
to the French banks should be formally set down. The arrangements, which I have examined with the aid of representatives of
the firms of Abell, Spielmann and Bult, and of Mr Sellings,
stationmaster of the London Bridge terminus, are duly summarised
herewith.

As you are no doubt aware, the company's overnight mail-train
departs for Folkestone each evening at 8.30. The ferry service is
naturally dependent on the hour of high tide, when the steamer
may be brought further in to embark heavy cargo. It may be
observed that the safe may even be lifted aboard the steamer,
should this prove necessary, such is the vessel's proximity to crane
and gantries at high water.

Naturally, our dealings with Messrs Abell, Spielmann and Bult
are of the most confidential nature. Mr Spielmann informs me that
Mr Sellings, a most trusted and respectable employee of the
company, is kept ignorant of their intentions until such time as a
representative declares himself at the station office. Under Mr

Sellings's express supervision the bullion chests are escorted by the railway police to the stationmaster's office. Here each is weighed. Subsequently the chests are taken under escort to the baggage van of the ferry train.

I must here emphasise the strenuous efforts of both ourselves and Messrs Abell, Spielmann and Bult to guarantee security. Mr Chubb has provided the company with three copies of his patented 'railway safe', constructed of steel plate to a depth of one inch and with dual locks. (It may be noted that at a recent exposition Mr Chubb fixed one of his patent locks to a hotel door and invited the assembled company of locksmiths to pick it. None could do so.) As a precaution, copies of the keys are held by separate individuals of the company at London Bridge and Folkestone. Further, although all three safes are opened and closed by the same keys, only one is in use at any given time. The bullion boxes – each of these contains perhaps a hundredweight of gold – are of course locked, each additionally bearing the merchant's individual wax seal.

The company's engine having arrived at Folkestone, the railway safe remains under constant guard until such time as the bullion boxes can be removed for checking and shipment. One key is held by the station superintendent; the other is kept under lock and key at the company's office on the harbour pier. The weight of each chest is checked against its measure in London. Additionally, the station supcrintendent has been instructed to conduct a close inspection of the seal. Once placed in the care of the captain and crew of the steamer, the bullion is thenceforth conveyed to Boulogne. Here it passes into the custody of the Messageries Impériales and is once again checked with regard to its weight before proceeding to the Gare du Nord and the Bank of France, where the boxes can be collected by the Paris merchants.

I should add that Messrs Abell, Spielmann and Bult, with each of whom I had some private conversation, professed themselves thoroughly satisfied with these arrangements, Mr Bult in particular being convinced of the impossibility of any larceny being perpe- trated while the shipment was in the company's hands. The merit of Mr Chubb's safe, I am assured, is that a cracksman has nothing to work upon save the keyhole. Further, a fully loaded bullion box requires two men to carry it. In the unlikely event of any theft being committed, the outrage would become apparent as soon as the safe was opened at Folkestone. To lay hands on the stamps of merchants such as Messrs Abell, Spielmann and Bult would, as Mr Bult asserts, demand nothing less than the burglary of their vaults.

I trust that this information is of use, and would be glad to supplement it with any further details that may be required.

Having the honour to remain your most obedient servant,

I am, sir, yours most faithfully,

James Harker

Secretary to the Board

*

Spring had come, finally and after much hesitation, to Lincoln's Inn Fields and there were daffodils out upon the green grass and gilly-flowers blooming in the window-boxes of the ground-floor sets. This being Lincoln's Inn, where an air of general severity prevails, they did so with an unconscionable meekness, as if they feared that some legal eminence – Mr Crabbe perhaps – would descend in wrath from his chambers and present them with a writ for unlicensed blossoming or occupying too great a proportion of space. Mr Pardew, hurrying through the great black gate on his way to see Mr Crabbe, saw neither the daffodils nor the gilly-flowers, saw nothing, in fact, other than the several phantoms that rose up and stalked through his imagination. Though he strode with his customary vigour, had walked all the way to High Holborn from his office in Carter Lane brandishing his stick as if all manner of unseen enemies were about to leap up at him, Mr Pardew was not happy in his mind. There are some men who pride themselves on their autonomy, of having their progress through the world laid out in a manner that they themselves have arranged, and Mr Pardew was such a one. He was the kind of man who, if he wished to have the pleasure of dining with a certain gentleman, would make sure that the invitation came from himself, or if he wished to pursue a certain course of commercial action would insist that the business was of his own devising. Such a resolve to follow his own inclinations had perhaps contributed, some years before, to his falling out with the late lamented Mr Fardel.

Just at this moment, on the other hand, Mr Pardew was on his way to an engagement to which he had been summarily bidden not once but twice, and he did not like it. To be sure, he had begun by treating the affair with his customary insouciance. A letter had come

180

from Mr Crabbe suggesting that he might present himself at the former's chambers at such and such a time and Mr Pardew had – ignored it. Then a second letter had come repeating the suggestion advanced in the first in such a way that it became a request. This too, after a certain amount of reflection and calculation, Mr Pardew had ignored. Finally a third letter had come, whose tone was so unambiguous that not even Mr Pardew, however insouciant the remark he pronounced over it to his clerk, could deign to throw it in the wastepaper basket. This, consequently, was the chain of events that brought him to Lincoln's Inn Fields on a bright March morning with the breeze springing this way and that through the newly risen grass, gnawing savagely at his finger-ends and waving his stick at the shifting air in a manner quite worthy of Don Quixote with the windmills.

In truth Mr Pardew was not greatly alarmed at the prospect of facing Mr Crabbe in his den. He had taken up arms against Mr Crabbe before and knew that he had had the better of him. The letter whose production had so enraged and cowed Mr Crabbe lay still in the pocket of his coat. This repeated summons to the old lawyer's presence was but a consequence of that victory. Moreover, he had an idea of what Mr Crabbe might say to him and what he himself might say in reply. Yet there were other anxieties revolving in his mind, other schemes on which he hesitated to embark but which could not long be postponed, which agitated him to a much greater degree. The conflict that these precipitated in his mind became so great that at the door to Mr Crabbe's chambers he halted, made a great slash with his cane at some chimerical adversary and muttered to himself something to the effect that he could not be eaten by Mr Crabbe, and that this gentleman might, if he did not take care, be eaten himself. Having taken himself in hand in this way, he rapped noisily on Mr Crabbe's brass knocker, was admitted with such alacrity that it appeared the old clerk had known of his coming and been expressly stationed behind the door, divested himself of his coat – the stick he retained in his hand – and whipped smartly up the stairs to Mr Crabbe's room.

Mr Crabbe was awaiting Mr Pardew. In fact, having seen him coming across the grass from his window, he had been able to make certain preparations in advance of his visit. In particular, he had envisioned a ruse not uncommonly thought up by gentlemen who wish to interview other gentlemen and appear to some advantage: he had with his own hands taken the chair that stood in the centre of his room for the use of visitors and propelled it behind a screen that faced onto one of the bookcases. This meant, according to Mr Crabbe's reasoning, that Mr Pardew would be compelled to stand in front of him and should, additionally, find it very difficult to avoid Mr Crabbe's gaze. In this assumption Mr Crabbe was, as it turned out, altogether wrong. Mr Pardew, coming into the room with the old clerk panting at his heels, saw immediately the nature of the ruse and decided that he would have nothing to do with it. Shaking hands with Mr Crabbe and muttering some civility, informing the clerk that, yes, he would have a cup of tea if such were procurable, he took himself first to the fireplace, where he stood for a moment warming his hands, and then to the window, where he appeared to take a very keen interest in a cherry tree whose burgeoning upper branches could be seen perhaps twenty yards away. Mr Crabbe, seating himself behind the desk from which he had risen to shake Mr Pardew's hand, was not quite put out by this cavalier treatment but he was aware that his preliminary stratagem had wholly failed and that an advantage could only be secured by the ingenuity of his tongue. Accordingly he shuffled the papers on his desk – papers which related to his recent dealings with the firm of Pardew & Co. – and did his best to attract Mr Pardew's attention.

'A very fine day,' Mr Pardew observed from the window, where he was still engrossed in the cherry tree. 'Upon my word, I think I never knew it so fine for March.'

'I don't doubt it is a fine day,' Mr Crabbe deposed, with a blandness that he did not at all feel.

'By the by, I saw His Grace the Duke of —— the other night. He seemed to be in extraordinarily good spirits.'

Mr Crabbe, staring at his visitor's back, the front half of him still being turned towards the window, felt that this allusion was too much to be borne. He laid the papers down on the desk in front of him with a little crash of his fingers and coughed.

'Mr Pardew. I have asked to see you because a very serious matter has arisen with regard to your affairs.'

Mr Pardew turned abruptly from his station by the window. 'Indeed? Anything that concerns my business is serious to me. By all means say what you have to say and you shall find me a willing listener.'

Mr Crabbe nodded at this courtesy, which was far more like the kind of thing to which he was accustomed, but at the same time he hesitated, for there was a difference between what he knew or suspected of Mr Pardew's affairs and what he could decently insinuate. A gentleman, after all, does not invite onto his premises another gentleman with whom he had business dealings and accuse him of being a thief. On the other hand he may very easily introduce into his conversation a presumption of thievery which the presumed thief can either acknowledge or deny as he chooses, while being aware that this presumption exists. Mr Crabbe, to be blunt, remembering the course of their last meeting, was wondering how far he could go and what might be the consequence if, in a manner of speaking, he went too far.

The facts of the case were these. In the course of the past two months, relying solely on information provided by Mr Pardew, Mr Crabbe, or rather Mr Crabbe's clerks, had written letters to perhaps half a dozen persons at addresses in the north of England requesting payments of debts owed to the firm of Pardew & Co. Somewhat to Mr Crabbe's surprise these debts had all been paid, either by cash, cheque or a combination of the two, the payment being made either by post (the letter generally lamenting Mr Pardew's exigent attitude towards his creditors) or by emissary to Mr Crabbe's office. In each case the money or moneys having been received by Mr Crabbe and transferred into Crabbe & Enderby's bank account, where all the firm's receipts were customarily deposited, Mr Crabbe, having first deducted his commission, had written a further cheque in favour of Pardew & Co. How Mr Crabbe now regretted having written those cheques! For in the fullness of time word had come back from Mr Crabbe's bank that one of the cheques had been inscribed on a form that, it was alleged, had been stolen from the person on whose account it was drawn, and that two of the banknotes were forgeries. All this was necessarily a source of horror to Mr Crabbe. The loss to the bank had been instantly made good out of his own pocket. The circumstances – the promptness of the payments, a certain consistency in the tone of the letters lamenting Mr Pardew's harshness – made him deeply suspicious. But still he had accepted Mr Pardew's instructions in respect of his creditors – something that he now greatly deplored – and there was, he thought, a limit to the crimes of which Mr Pardew might legitimately be accused.

Divining something of the thoughts that were oppressing the old lawyer's mind, Mr Pardew, prowling now in the region of the fire, determined to make them work to his advantage. Smiling in the friendliest manner imaginable, he remarked:

'I suppose it is something to do with those creditors of mine. I presume one of the cheques has not been honoured, or something of the sort?'

'It is worse than that,' Mr Crabbe told him grimly, wishing for all the world that the interview was over and he could go back to his copy of *The Times* and the devising of errands on which to send his clerk. 'One of the cheques was written on a stolen form, and two of the notes were false.'

At this Mr Pardew opened his eyes very wide. 'Indeed? How very provoking. But then I suppose a man to whom a debt is owed can scarcely be held responsible for the honesty of his creditors.'

'Perhaps not.' To allow even this concession was a source of pain to such a one as Mr Crabbe. 'Naturally the police have become involved.'

'Oh indeed?' said Mr Pardew again, with perhaps rather too studied a nonchalance. 'And what have they managed to discover?'

'Only that the address from which the forged notes were despatched was a poste restante.'

Despite his nonchalance Mr Pardew, standing on Mr Crabbe's Turkey carpet with his legs opened against the warmth of the fire, was engaged in a rapid calculation. He knew, of course, that the banknotes were forgeries and the cheque written on a stolen form because, in an assumed hand and using anonymous messengers, he had sent them to Mr Crabbe himself. But that such transactions could be traced back to the office in Carter Lane he thought unlikely. Should anybody – the famous Captain McTurk, say, or any representative of Mr Crabbe – take it upon himself to investigate any of the addresses to which Mr Crabbe had been directed to write, Mr Pardew was confident that they would find nothing in the least incriminating. Having assured himself of this, but reminding himself that there was still one favour he required of Mr Crabbe, he drew himself up to his full height, made a little feint with his stick at the fire and said in a meditative tone:

'Indeed? This is very shocking. I can only apologise, Mr Crabbe, for the inconvenience to which you have been subject.'

This was too much for Mr Crabbe. 'Inconvenience, sir? It is more than inconvenience! Why I have had a man from the bank absolutely asking me – asking *me*, sir! – if I knew of the money's provenance.'

'And how did you reply, I wonder?'

'I said what I believe to be the truth. That I had been requested to write a letter in connection with a debt, quite in the usual way, and this had been the result. I tell you what, sir' – and Mr Pardew observed that Mr Crabbe was genuinely angry, much angrier than he had been at the start of their interview – 'this had better be the end of any dealings between us, indeed it had. If you have any further debts to be collected you had better take them to some other firm and see what they say.'

Hearing this opinion, which would have had many a legal colleague with whom Mr Crabbe dealt positively abasing himself on the carpet, Mr Pardew hesitated. He did not believe, in the last resort, that Mr Crabbe would altogether throw him over, for he knew – and he knew that Mr Crabbe knew – that if questions could be asked of himself regarding the stolen cheque and the forged notes, then they could also be asked of Mr Crabbe. Behind their conversation, as ever, lurked both the stupendous figure of His Grace the Duke of ——, and the letter which Mr Pardew had waved in front of Mr Crabbe's face on their previous encounter, but Mr Pardew acknowledged that there was a limit both to the power of His Grace's ducal strawberry leaves and the power of the letter. He might threaten to drag Mr Crabbe down, but he fancied that Mr Crabbe might wish to drag him down also. He needed to appease Mr Crabbe, but he could not afford to leave him conscious of any triumph.

'Well, if it is any consolation to you, Mr Crabbe, that money from my former business associates is pretty much in. There is no need for me to trouble you with any further labour in that line. But there is a chance that in a month or so I shall require you to write me another letter.'

'There is, is there?'

'It may not be necessary. Indeed I trust it will not. It is a client of mine who has been sadly neglectful in the restitution of his obligations. Perhaps you have heard of him. It is the Earl of ——.'

Mr Crabbe, brooding savagely in his chair, looked up at this. He had indeed heard of the Earl of ——, and from what he had heard imagined him exactly the kind of gentleman likely to fall into the hands of Mr Pardew. Instinct told him to request Mr Pardew to leave his chambers immediately, and yet something stayed him from issuing this demand. Mr Crabbe could not exactly locate the source of this unease, but he told himself that he did not quite like the look in Mr Pardew's eye, which seemed to him both mocking and complicit, as if Mr Pardew knew other things about him, things quite beyond those contained in that awful letter, while being altogether indifferent to any revelations that Mr Crabbe might make with regard to his own dealings. Therefore Mr Crabbe did not summon his clerk and have Mr Pardew ushered away. He merely sat and stared at the fire and at the papers on his desk and at Mr Pardew, who was now swaying luxuriously from one foot to the other like a cat that is getting ready to pounce, finding solace in none of them and feeling older than he had felt for many a year.

'As I say,' Mr Pardew continued, with an unmistakable note of deference in his voice, 'such a course may not be necessary. It may not indeed. And even if it were not, I should of course be delighted to return that piece of property of yours of which we spoke . . .'

Mr Crabbe made some feeble motion of assent with his hands and muttered something. It was not intelligible to Mr Pardew, but its meaning was clear. Mr Crabbe, if absolutely entreated and compelled to, would write the letter. For the moment, however, he would do nothing other than to have Mr Pardew take his leave at the earliest possible juncture, would be glad, in fact, if he never had to set eyes on Mr Pardew again. Mr Pardew understood this as well as he understood the rates of interest in that morning's *Financial Gazette*, and was quick to depart, shaking the single finger that the lawyer extended to him from behind his desk and stalking down the staircase into the vestibule at such a rate of knots that he altogether forgot his overcoat and had to be followed out of the door by one of the clerks with that garment gathered up in his arms. Mr Crabbe, watching him go, felt so wretched that he flung a pen-wiper into the fire and sent his clerk out to a law stationer's in Carey Street to fetch a copy of the *Legal Review* that he did not in the least want to read. Such was the wretchedness of Mr Crabbe.

Mr Pardew, now striding away across the green grass towards the gate, congratulated himself on the result of his dealings with Mr Crabbe, but he did not linger on this congratulation. Having gained his immediate object, his mind was bent on the greater purpose which he had been considering half an hour before and on which, it is fair to say, his mind had been bent for many months. Mr Pardew was not a timid man and yet the boldness of the scheme greatly alarmed him. It was an enterprise, he was aware, that might crash without warning over his head, one that would involve extraordinary risks and dangers, the principal danger being to Mr Pardew and his liberty. Half a dozen times, as he sped over the grass, past the daffodils, through the great gate and into the street beyond, Mr Pardew declared to his inner self that he would not do it, that the risk was too great. Half a dozen times, too, he corrected himself, slashed at the thin air with his stick, settled his hat more advantageously upon his head and plunged on again. In this way, arguing furiously with himself, at one point calm, confident and assured of his abilities, at another cast down, unhappy and sure that all would fall instantly into ruins, he walked back down the long expanse of the Farringdon Road and bent his steps in the direction of Carter Lane. It was mid-morning now and the streets, especially those side-streets through which Mr Pardew walked, were not unduly crowded. Turning into the lane, he saw on the other side of the pavement from his office door, smoking a pipe and staring up and down the street, an exceedingly ill-favoured man in threadbare clothes with a cotton handkerchief tied round his neck. When this gentleman saw Mr Pardew he gave the faintest perceptible sign – no more than a movement of his eye – that he recognised him. Mr Pardew, even less perceptibly, acknowledged this and then turned into his office.

Here he found Bob Grace, feet up on a chair, hat pulled low over his eyes, eating his lunch out of a pastrycook's carton. Seeing his employer he removed his boots from the chair and cocked up his hat, but did not otherwise salute him. Mr Pardew smote his desk hard with the ferrule of the stick.

'Upon my word, Grace, I never knew such a one as you for eating. Well, has anything happened?'

'Davidson undertook to pay ten now and renew for another month. Here's the stamped paper. And that Pearce is outside. Brought a letter here, which he says you'll want to see. I told him as you'd want to see the letter first and him second, most probably.'

'Most probably is right. Where is it?'

Grace flicked a piece of rough white paper across the desk that Mr Pardew immediately picked up and smoothed beneath his fingers. He knew, as soon as the paper passed into his hands, that it was not in fact a letter but a copy of one, or rather the first attempt of a clerk working to dictation, for there were several crossings-out and emendations by a second hand. Nonetheless the paper was entirely sufficient for Mr Pardew's purpose and he examined it with great interest. The letter was signed by the secretary to the South-Eastern Railway Company and addressed to its directors. Such was the care taken with the alterations that Mr Pardew declared himself certain that the information contained in it was accurate and that a final document would soon after have been prepared.

Much of what it had to say was known to Mr Pardew, but a certain proportion was not. These parts of the letter he read over two or three times, committing them to memory as he did so, before placing the piece of paper on the table before him. As he did so he became aware, once again, of his surroundings, the shabby room in which he sat and the saturnine figure of his clerk, and resolved to himself that whatever steps might be necessary to remove himself from Carter Lane, its bleary window, the piles of stamped paper and Bob Grace would be worth the taking. Again he picked up the paper and read through it once more, lest there were some detail that had escaped his eye. But there was nothing, and having assured himself that he had the words by heart, and thinking such a course of action prudent in the circumstances, he crumpled the paper quickly between his fingers and flung it into the waste-paper basket. As he did so his gaze fell upon his clerk, who had ceased all pretence of eating his lunch and was sitting with his hands drawn up over his chest regarding him keenly.

'Now,' said Mr Pardew, looking up again at the bare, distempered ceiling of his office and thinking that he hated it. 'Now, Grace, what hour would you say it was?'

Grace licked some gravy from the ends of his fingers, staring all the while at these appendages as if he fancied that they might serve as his dessert. 'It's a few minutes after midday, I daresay.'

'Where is Latch?'

'Out collecting. Gone after the swell in Monmouth Street as was supposed to have renewed this day fortnight.'

'You had better go and find him. You needn't trouble to come back this afternoon.'

'Not come back! Why, who's to lock up the shop I should like to know?'

'I think you'll find,' Mr Pardew observed tartly, staring at the bleary window and hating it, 'that I can turn a key in a lock if I have to. Now, be off with you. And ask Pearce to step in on your way out, if you please.'

With the expression of one greatly wronged, Grace rose to his feet, scattering a fine spray of crumbs negligently on the desk as he did so, jammed his hat as low over his brow as it would go and took his leave, taking care to slam the door smartly behind him as he went. In truth he was not unduly displeased by the turn that events had taken, having grasped the opportunity to read the letter before it passed into his master's hands, and also to have spoken several words to Pearce when that gentleman first presented himself in Carter Lane. Armed with this information, and with certain other hints that Mr Pardew had let fall, deliberately or otherwise, over the past month he had a fair idea of what his master was about, and the advantages that might accrue to himself from this knowledge. 'He is a sly one and no mistake,' he said admiringly to himself as he lumbered out into the street, 'and yet I'll be even with him too.'

Left on his own in the office, Mr Pardew got up immediately from his desk and performed several rapid actions. First he took a small notebook from out of a drawer and laid it open before him. Then he inspected the contents of a metal cash box that sat upon his clerk's desk, replaced the lid but did not lock it. Finally he took Grace's chair and, lifting it easily in one hand, placed it in the centre of the room. This done, he returned to his own chair just as Pearce, following the instructions given to him by Grace, came through the street door.

Mr Pardew laid his hands out squarely on the desk before him, stuck his chin up at an angle and gave his visitor a glance. On close inspection he seemed even more haphazardly attired than he had appeared in the street. The cotton handkerchief looped round his neck was stiff with grease and his hands, half protruding from his trowser pockets, were extremely dirty. Seeing Mr Pardew, he raised his eyebrows slightly in a gesture that spoke of an intelligence greater than that suggested by his outward demeanour and accepted the prof-fered chair. He smelled very strongly, Mr Pardew now noticed, of beer and tobacco smoke.

'It's a Friday afternoon,' Mr Pardew said, without preamble. 'Why ain't you at work?'

'Sick,' Pearce rejoined, hoisting one leg over the other so that Mr descended in his absence that the corner on which Cursitor Street meets Chancery Lane had all but vanished into the gloom. There were pale lights beginning to shine in the windows of the law stationers and the copying shops, a young woman's startled face appeared suddenly behind a curtain ten feet above his head and drew it shut, a great clatter of milk churns being rattled downstairs rose from a dairy hard by, and John Carstairs wrapped his muffler about his face, secured the fastenings of his great-coat and set off in the direction of Whitehall and the society of the Honourable Mr Cadnam. He was thinking about a young woman to whom he had once behaved very much in the way that Mr Farrier had done to the mother of his natural child and the thoughts, though they at first awakened in him an agreeable nostalgia, were not in the end pleasant to him. In Cursitor Street, meanwhile, the afternoon wore on without further interruption in Mr Devereux's chambers and their tenant, having spent half an hour recruiting himself over a copy of *Punch*, went out searching for tapers, there being nothing with which to light the candle and no clerk to send out in his stead.

XVIII

Sub Rosa

There is much that I would remember that I have forgotten. And there is much I remember that I would forget.

*

Last evening I had a curious presentiment that my guardian would come to my room & indeed it was so. He came bearing an ulster thrown over one arm & said if I wished it he would take me into the grounds & show me his dogs. Tho' I have no great liking for dogs – certainly not of the kind my guardian breeds – & no great liking for my guardian's company, I said I wished it very much. This seemed to please him, for he remarked that they were unusual dogs & I should not regret my choice.

'But you must be very quiet,' he instructed. 'Indeed we must be altogether silent while we are in the house.'

I said that I would be very quiet.

Such a queer excursion! First we stole down the back-staircase, where the moon shone through a great window & enveloped us in white, ghastly light. Passing through the servants' hall we came upon a room behind whose door a lamp still burned. 'That is old Randall's pantry. He has fallen asleep in his chair I'll be bound,' my guardian explained. Making not the least sound he drew open the pantry door – I could see the old man fast asleep with his head on the table – & returned with a key that would admit us to the gardens.

I confess that I am of a singularly nervous disposition – altogether frail & fearful, Papa used to say – & that had I not had my guardian beside me & his arm to lean on I should have been very much afraid. Viz., the trees rattling above us in the wind, a dark, cloud-strewn sky & not a spark of light to be seen. As to where the dogs might be kept, I had no need to enquire, for we could hear them howling from afar. They are housed in a great barn, a full half-mile from the house. This we approached – my guardian taking up a lantern which lay in one of the ante-rooms – whereupon the barking & snarling rose in a crescendo, & I wondered that the people in the house did not think there were burglars on the property.

For myself, I did not care for the dogs, which seemed to me great wolfish beasts, of a kind I never saw unless they are some breed of mastiff. My guardian, however, exulted in their company, reaching his hand through the bars of their kennels – they are all chained up against the hours of darkness – flinging them biscuits, &c., which he had brought in his trowser pocket.

I enquired – for it seemed to me that such animals must take a deal of labour – did Mr Randall or any of the servants engage in their care?

My guardian said no, that he would not have the servants 'interfering' – that was his word – in such business.

Seeing that I shivered at the cold, he immediately became solicitous. Would I take his coat to add to my own? Would I return to the house? Hearing that I should, he locked the door of the kennel-room behind him, extinguished the lamp – the dogs seemed subdued & silent at his going – & set off across the darkling lawn. Next to the barn, I noticed, a high thorn hedge grew up in a square, with a wooden gate set into it, curious to see, yet even in daylight, I should guess, impenetrable to the eye.

'What is that?' I asked, as we passed there.

'It is nothing,' he said. 'A part of the wood that I keep shut up.'

And yet it seemed to me that others of my guardian's hounds must be kept there, for I am certain I heard a noise of movement & a snuffling that did not come from the barn.

And so we returned to the house, taking ourselves once more to my guardian's study, where a fire still burned (for which I confess I was very grateful) & I was bidden to recruit myself with a glass of wine. It was by now very late – half past midnight – yet my guardian seemed disposed to talk, showed me a pair of avocets under glass. They are curious birds with turned-up bills, which he said had been taken at the Breydon Water and set up for him by Mr Lowne, the Yarmouth taxidermist.

I thought the avocets pretty birds, but did not see why they should not remain at liberty on the Breydon Water. However, I said nothing of this.

Neither – though it was on the edge of my tongue – did I speak to him of the rose.

Sir Charles came out of his hole in the wainscot & ran silently about the floor, coming rather close to my skirts, which I did not like.

My guardian continues to observe me in the most marked manner. Looking once more at his display cases, at his insistence, I caught for a moment in the reflection of the glass his face regarding me. The look Papa's face had when he drew his portraits, only, it seemed to me, less agreeable.

'Sir,' I said, when half an hour had passed, 'I wish very much to write the letter of which I spoke.'

'Which letter was that?' he enquired, affecting forgetfulness.

'The letter to my husband's lawyer,' I replied.

'Why do you wish to write to him?' he asked, by no means unkindly.

'There is much that I wish to ask him,' I faltered.

'You may ask me.'

'I would ask him.'

'Then you may do so.'

Nothing more was said. Presently he escorted me back to my chamber, pausing only to bow as he quitted me at the door.

It occurs to me that I am another of his avocets, set up by Mr Lowne, for him to inspect at his leisure.

*

And then this morning another flower. The same white rose on the same silver salver. With no hint as to how it came here.

Yet I am not without resource in these matters.

Thus, when Esther arrives with the lunch tray, having first secured the rose in my desk, I enquire:

'Were any flowers brought to the house yesterday, Esther?'

'Indeed, ma'am, the master brought some from Lynn.'

'And what kind were they?'

Esther looks up from setting down the tray. 'Why, roses, ma'am. & grown under glass, too, for there be none outside in this weather.'

I see. Or rather, I do not see.

*

Esther & I are very confidential. Indeed we talk for as much as ten minutes whenever she fetches my tray, or retrieves it: I sitting in my chair; she performing certain little duties around the room for which I am exceedingly grateful. Thus I believe I can state with confidence of Esther that:

She is twenty-one years old.

She earns twelve pounds a year.

She has never left the county of Norfolk.

She has a mother & four brothers & sisters living at Fakenham.

She has read the Bible, & *Foxe's Book of Martyrs* & *Maria Monk*, but little else.

To be sure, her manner of speaking often bewilders me. She says 'mawther' when she means 'mother' & 'du' when she means 'do' & 'dicker' when she means 'donkey'.

But I must not mock her, for she is very kind to me, sympathises with my wants & wishes to ameliorate them.

The footman, who is her admirer, has gone away to London. Where, she says, he will write one day & 'send for her'.

What should she do, I asked, when this summons came.

'Why,' she said, 'go and do as he bade me.'

'What?' I said. 'And give up your situation here?'

This, however, she would not answer. Feeling, perhaps, that I am confederate with Mr Randall.

Once I asked her: 'What should you do, Esther, if you could leave here & do exactly as you chose?'

'Why, ma'am,' she said, 'I should take a husband, & have six children, & live in a cottage, & be happy I hope. Only I should take care that I wasn't poor.'

And where should I go if I left here & could do as I chose?

I have not the least idea in the world.

I am lying in bed in the old house at Kensington, though it is not yet dark.

It seems to me that I have lain there for hours, waiting for the light to fade & the noises around me to cease.

Then I see that, though I have not been aware of her coming, Mama is standing at the door watching me. Mama, in a brown dress with her red-gold hair standing out from her face, & something in her hand which the light catches & plays with. How long she stands there I do not know, until Papa, coming briskly into the doorway, catches her in his arms & whatever she has in her hand tumbles down to the floor.

And Papa smiles at me.

I set this down exactly as it came into my head this morning, at about half past ten, as I sat at my desk with bright sunshine – for the spring is come – pouring in through the window.

*

Esther is my spy.

No, that is not quite true. Rather, there is much that Esther tells me, all incautious, that I would not otherwise know. It is like Papa, who would come back from the meetings of the committee at his club (which proceedings were of course secret) & talk endlessly of them from sheer amusement.

Of the other servants. Of the house. Of my guardian & his habits.

Thus I learn – something I might perhaps have guessed – that Mr Randall, the butler, is a religious man, constant at his meeting, &c., pressing tracts both on those who would have them & those who would not.

That Mrs Wates, the cook, was found dead drunk in her room last Sunday: a great scandal that was somehow kept from the master, despite there being no dinner that night.

That Mrs Finnie, the housekeeper, 'gives herself airs', is very hard upon the maids & in consequence much disliked.

I enquired of Esther: had she ever seen my guardian's dogs? She said no, 'but we hears them, ma'am, whenever we are about in the gardens or on the paths, & 'tis not a sound you would want to hear close by you'.

Esther says that she is happy in her work. That she has known worse. That she has been able to buy a dress out of her wages – she has promised to show me this dress! – & that a complement of six servants is better than a solitary employment. 'For then, ma'am, the mistress is always around you, finding things for you to do, & making tasks where none existed just for the pleasure of it.'

There is a Lady Bamber, who got Esther her place, 'but I do not see her now, for she does not come here. Indeed, Mr Dixey sees no company.'

My guardian, I hear, is pressed for money. Indeed the men who worked in the garden have all been paid off & William the footman has no substitute (much to the other servants' annoyance, Mrs F., in particular, thinking it a disgrace to occupy a situation 'where no footman was kept'). Last week, it seems, there was very near an execution in the house, for a bailiff came from Lynn in pursuit of some debt & could only with difficulty be begged to leave.

Esther says that it is 'well known' that my guardian owes 800*l* in London, & that the servants worry that their quarter's wages will not be paid.

'In which case, ma'am,' Esther says, 'what will become of us all?'

And to the untended gardens, & the dogs in their kennels & Sir Charles Lyell in his hole in the wainscot.

And what will become of me?

*

Not all is lost from the world I once knew.

Thus in the recess of my desk there is a little japanned box that Papa once gave me. How it came there I know not, for I do not recall its being with me in the days before I came to Easton. And yet it must have been, for the contents are such that only I could have put them there. Viz.:

the old, blunt-nibbed pen with which Papa wrote his *Marlborough*

a silhouette of me as a little girl, done by Papa's friend Sir Henry Cole & framed on a square of white card

a lock of Mama's hair, placed in an envelope, still rust-red & dated 17 May 1848

a jet brooch that I had from Henry when we were married

Henry's ring, the seal from his watch-chain, the locket with his mother's portrait, &c.

a receipt that Aunt Charlotte Parker wrote me once for hardbake & which I always kept

a set of verses that Richard – Mr Farrier, that is – gave me ten years since, & which ditto.

To place these objects on the desk before me is to fall prey to the queerest sensations, as if I stood at a little window looking in upon a crowd of people who smiled at me, waved & spoke all manner of things that I, alas, could not hear.

I see Papa writing at his book, with the ink staining his white fingers, & calling out for tea & bread and butter, & a printer's boy waiting in the hall for some paper that Papa had promised.

I see Sir Henry cutting the silhouette & exclaiming, to quiz me,

'Why, her nose is so snub that I shall never match the set of it, try as I may!'

I see Mama once more, seated on the terrace, with her hair tumbling around her shoulders & Brodie combing it out.

I see the jet brooch in Henry's hand & the ring on his finger, the watch-chain peeping from his waistcoat pocket.

I see Aunt Charlotte Parker's white curls & her cap above them, which she says was very fashionable, only she meant the fashion of Queen Adelaide.

I see Mr Farrier standing at the garden gate in his cutaway coat – being what the young men then used to call a 'swell' – with the paper in his hand.

And then I see the room in which I sit, with its desk & its window & its locked door, & a little japanned box with a trinket or two & an old pen & some scraps of paper – nothing of the least consequence in the world.

*

The estate is in sad decline, Esther says.

The timber, cut two years ago & seasoned now, lies rotting in the woods for there is no one to take it away.

The grass grows up six feet high in the garden & the panes in the glasshouse window crack in the winds & are never replaced.

The rats run wild in the barns & the keeper no longer preserves.

Mr Dixey cares only for his dogs, Esther says.

*

When I was a girl I flew into the queerest passions. A drawing that I could not frame to my satisfaction, the thought that Tishy or some other girl did not love me – such things would anger me beyond measure & Papa would say that there was a devil in me & that at these times I knew not what I did or said. Dear Papa, who meant only kindness & would not blame me if he could.

Last night I flew into a passion.

All evening as the twilight faded into darkness & the wind buffeted the eaves, I had been thinking of the roses & how they must be placed in my chamber while I slept in the other room, struck all the while by a presentiment that this morning I should find another, mocking me on its silver dish, burning into my skin. Finally as the clock came near to midnight I could bear this apprehension no longer & resolved to combat it as best I could. In the corner of my bedchamber there was a ball of twine, which I fancy had once secured the cover of my trunk. Taking this, & greatly surprised by my own ingenuity, I seized a chair & placed it to one side of my door, took up the fire-irons & placed them to the other side, connecting the two by means of a piece of twine stretched across the doorway at a height of six inches. Anyone crossing the threshold, I assured myself, would perforce tumble over it, or at the very least greatly inconvenience himself. This done, & making sure that a candle & a box of lucifers (these are kept in the recess of my desk next to the japanned box) were to hand near my pillow, I retired to bed.

Naturally, being plunged into a state of nervous exhaustion, I was scarce able to sleep. Half a dozen times in that first hour of slumber I was awakened by what I conceived to be some stirring in the other room, only to find that it was the merest phantom of my imagination. Once indeed, so definite did the noise appear, that I rose up in my nightgown & went in my bare feet into the other chamber, but there was nothing there, only the tap of some branch against the window & the rush of cold air beneath the door, together with those creakings & groanings of timber in which the house customarily abounds. I confess that I felt more than a little foolish that these imaginings had crumbled into dust, but not I think frightened, for the passion was still upon me & an ogre from a fairy-book lumbering into the room would merely have excited my scorn. Still there was no ogre, only the wind & the tap-tapping of the twigs, & so I retired to my bed, pulled the covers around me & once more lay down to rest.

How long I lay there I do not know, but the hour cannot have been much before three or four. Half-wakeful & half-asleep, I was yet conscious of being able to *see* very wonderfully (this I supposed a further consequence of my nervous state) & that I fancied Papa was there in the room making little remarks & observations that I strained to hear, that several other persons known to me were present but just a little way out of reach. It was then, again with a presentiment that it was *about to happen,* my senses all stimulated by the novelty of the situation, that I heard with utter distinctness the creak of a footstep & the turning of a key in the lock. Scarce daring to breathe I lay still as a third & more prolonged sound – the noise of the door being drawn open – broke the silence. It occurred to me that still I must make no sound myself. Accordingly I lay silent in the darkness, only reaching out my hand so that I should be able to grasp candle & matches at the first opportunity. On the instant there came a mighty crash, as of a person tumbling over, accompanied by the noise of other objects falling to the floor, sharp intakes of breath, &c. Jumping to my feet & crying 'Who is there?', my heart all the while beating like a drum, I hastily struck a match – my shadow, rearing up against the arc of the flame I confess did alarm me – lit the candle & moved to confront the intruder.

I was too late, for whoever it was had vanished in an instant. Footsteps echoed in the corridor, causing me to marvel at the resourcefulness of such a one who could gather his wits & make good his escape in the few seconds granted to him. The door was wide open. The key hung from the lock. Before it lay proof of the excellence of my stratagems: a silver dish rolled against the chair & a single white rose fallen nearly as far as the fireplace. The fire-irons, much to my satisfaction, were strewn everywhere about. For a moment I considered the advantages of stepping out into the corridor. Yet it seemed to me that my point had been proved, & no good would come of any nocturnal ramblings. Instead I busied myself in rectifying the damage that I had caused: restoring fire-irons & chair to their rightful places, gathering up the twine into a ball, casting the abandoned rose into the grate. It occurred to me that anyone who glanced into the room – some witch passing on her broomstick, perhaps – would have seen the most curious sight: a woman in her nightgown, candlestick on the desk before her, tidying the disorder around her yet laughing as she did so.

It was then that I remarked that there was something else in the chamber with me. Not something that I could see, but something that I could hear: squeaking & scuffling & making fierce, evil little movements in the shadow beneath my desk. At this my anger grew to a pitch, for I knew that this was Sir Charles Lyell, which my guardian had carried upon his shoulder or in the pocket of his coat & left behind in his haste to depart, & I resolved to have my revenge, if not on my guardian then on the creature that he had brought with him, for a mouse that runs across the floor when I stand there in the dark is a thing that I dislike very much. He was, as I say, running this way & that beneath the desk, but I am the equal of a MOUSE & seizing the poker from the stand to which I had returned it I stood all silently until such time as he should show himself. Presently, lulled by the silence & (as I now think) having no terror of human beings, even those that stand barefoot in their nightgowns, he poked his head out into the circle of soft light & in a trice I had brought the poker down upon him.

Nasty scuffling thing! A dozen times I belaboured him. When I had convinced myself he was quite dead I picked him up with the fire-tongs & cast him out into the corridor, where whoever searches may find him.

There shall be no more mice scampering in *my* chamber.

Afterwards, when the passion left me, I was properly remorseful, shed tears even at the thought of poor Sir Charles lying dead in the corridor where I had thrown him, for it was not his fault, poor thing, only that of the PERSON who brought him.

Papa always said that it was a sin to take a life, however humble. And yet I know that Papa liked to shoot a pheasant, which he said was there to be eaten & served no other purpose.

When all this had passed & I had arranged the room to my satisfaction, the door still hanging open on its hinge, I returned to my bedchamber, much alarmed now at what I had done, yet so exhausted that I fell almost instantly asleep. He will come in the morning, I told myself, though what I am to say to him & he to me I cannot tell.

*

He did not come. When I awoke it was exceedingly late. Bright sunshine streamed through the window of my chamber, the door had been locked & a breakfast tray left on my table (the tea altogether cold & insipid). Presently I fancied that I could hear voices far below, that the maids – Esther, & Margaret whom she thinks a goose – were out in the garden & I was filled with an inexpressible longing to be with them, to run over cut grass & walk wherever I choose.

All the rest of the morning I sat at my desk thinking that he would come, but he did not.

After some time there was a twisting of the key into the lock & I sprang to my feet, my heart pounding. And yet it was only Esther bringing in my luncheon & some foxgloves that she had picked in the wood next to the garden & placed in water, which I was very glad to have.

Esther.

Who gave me a very mischievous, sidelong look as if to say that she knew all about me, indeed more perhaps than I knew myself.

Who seemed disposed to talk.

'Has William written lately?' I enquired, knowing that this is a question she likes to be asked.

It appears that William is working in some capacity for an associate of my guardian's in the City. Of his duties & the manner of their execution Esther knows little, but it is clear that she is impressed. 'For he is making a mint of money, ma'am, truly. And, as his letter says, is stopping in rooms' – there is pride in Esther's voice as she pronounces the word – 'at Seven Dials. Do you know of it, ma'am?'

'A very respectable locality,' I tell her.

'And he says again that soon he shall write to me, and I am to go to him.'

'And shall you go?'

'Certainly, ma'am, I shall go.'

And who shall I talk with, I wonder, when Esther goes? Not Mr Randall, assuredly, with his tracts (he brought another one, a week ago, on the West African Mission) or Mrs Finnie, to whom I have not spoken ten words in the past fortnight. But it occurs to me that if I take every care it may yet redound to my advantage.

I must be cunning.

He does not come & he does not come.

*

I took out the verses that Richard – Mr Farrier – wrote me, which I had not done for half a dozen years & read them & was so very sad.

To Miss Isabel Brotherton

Last night I wasted hateful hours
Uncalmed by the peace of a college bed
I thirsted for brooks, and for tender showers
Instead of the policeman's patient tread
On the pavement yonder, beyond the gate
And the fruits of a life lived all sedate
Away from the river in foaming spate
There are distant sights that I would see
Untouched by the light of an English sun

I yearn for the roar of an ancient sea
And the ancient race that I would run
Yet the rose from the gardens in the south
I crush on my breast, and upon my mouth
Ripe to appease my burning drout.

RF fecit, July 1856

A week passes & he does not come. And then, all unexpected, one afternoon as I lie on my sofa – for I have been greatly fatigued in these last days – there comes the sound of footsteps in the corridor beyond the twist of a key in the lock.

I mark some great change in my guardian. His eyes seem more set in his head, his hair more grey, his face more lined, though only a week has passed since I last saw him & I did not then observe these things.

He says nothing of our last encounter, nor anything of Sir Charles Lyell. I, too, am silent. After regarding me in his customary way he proposes – greatly to my surprise – that we walk in the garden.

'The servants are all away,' he says, as if a gentleman can only walk out with his ward in the absence of domestics, 'or I should not have suggested it.'

And so we walk down the great staircase, through rooms that I glimpsed before only at night, & into the back of the house, emerging from it onto that lawn at which I have stared so long from my window.

My guardian's attentiveness is a wonder to behold. He takes my arm as we come to the gravel path, as if such an accumulation of tiny stones might cause me to fall, slashes with his stick at a nettle bush that threatens to impede my progress, draws my attention to the natural wonders in which the place apparently abounds. Thus I am bidden to admire a jay, a crossbill & a most curious, comical bird named a hoopoe, orange-plumaged & very bright-eyed, that trips across the grass to examine me as if he never saw my like before.

My guardian, it occurs to me, is a black crow, hopping over the grass in his rusty black vestments, cawing his pleasantries in my ear.

It is a day of bright sunshine, very pleasant in the shadow of the trees, & yet it seems to me very desolate & melancholy. Nothing blooms inside the great glasshouses; the cats run in & out of the dairy door. Yet my guardian is more eloquent than I have known him before. He says:

'I have lived here nearly half my life. My uncle, from whom I inherited the estate, died when I was thirty. Though I travelled when I was a younger man, since I have grown old I have rarely left it.

And yet soon you may have to leave it, I tell myself, with the timber rotting in the woods & the bailiffs coming from Lynn.

'Where did you travel, sir?' I ask.

'In Europe a little. Beyond the Danube & as far east as Kiev. And then in Araby.'

As we turn about the side of the house, in sight of the gravel drive – which is full of great ruts & puddles left by the spring rain – & the circles of uncut grass & an old fountain rising out of a mermaid's head, very cracked & worn, something of the melancholy of the place seems to strike him, for he says:

'My uncle used to give great parties here in his time. *Fêtes champêtres* with a quintain for the gentlemen to tilt at & archery for the ladies & a line of carriages stretching all the way to the gate & a marquee for dancing. But all that was forty years ago.'

'I have no taste for parties,' my guardian says.

What does my guardian have a taste for? Why, for little white eggs that lie in his cabinets & will never hatch, & for birds that will never move because they are stuffed & dead, & for staring at me as if I were one of his specimens preserved under glass.

We are standing before the front of the house now, where the sun slants low over the gardens & the frontage is gathered up in shadow.

'Sir,' I say, 'I very much wish to write that letter.'

'You shall write it,' he says. 'For there is much that can be said in it.'

And then, not greatly to my surprise, for some instinct had been at work within me before our excursion commenced, he takes my hand.

*

He wishes to marry me.

He says that during the course of our association he has formed a great affection for me, extending beyond that which a guardian naturally feels for his ward.

He would make me mistress of Easton Hall.

He is a stooped old man in a black suit, cawing at me like one of the rooks in his field.

266

There will soon be no Easton Hall to be mistress of.

I would rather be mistress of myself.

*

Mr Conolly has prescribed more medicine for me, which I am bidden to drink. Half a teacup full, which Mrs Finnie brings to me each morning. It is colourless, like water & at the same time unlike it. I drink it as I am bidden.

Today, as Mrs Finnie stands before me – it is a bright, clear morning but I know better than to quiz Mrs Finnie about the weather – I ask:

'Mr Dixey was not ever married, I think?'

'Not to my knowledge, ma'am.'

Mrs Finnie's hair is so very like black patent leather that I have a vision of her polishing it each morning before the mirror.

'But was he ever engaged?'

And here, quite unexpectedly, Mrs Finnie does not deny, ignore or deflect that which is asked of her. She says:

'There was a young woman that he offered for five years ago, ma'am. A Miss Chell, the daughter of the brewing people that live at Bury. There was talk of lawyers & settlements & old Mr Chell, as was the young lady's father, came over several times to see the master. Indeed we thought that it was a settled thing. There was even a rose garden that Tom the gardener had orders to plant out. But then something happened between them, & the banns that were to have been put up a month after were never said & the turf as had been grubbed up for the rose garden is where the maids do bang out their carpets.'

I declare that I never heard Mrs Finnie make such a speech. Mrs Finnie, too, seems conscious of the novelty of the situation for she clasps her hands nervously before her, hangs her head – so shiny indeed that the sunlight nearly bounces off it – & declines to offer another word.

I find myself greatly fatigued. Doubtless it is the strain of these days that has wearied me so. I sleep in the afternoons, yet am not refreshed.

He does not come & he does not come. And though I am glad of this I confess that I grow more nervous of the time when he shall arrive.

Thinking of this, I recollect a day once when I was a little girl –

it was just after Mama had gone away – & had been spiteful & bad-tempered. Whereupon the nurse had said to punish me, 'Your Papa shall be told of this, miss, when he comes home!' This was a source of great anxiety, for I loved Papa & would not make him unhappy if I could. By some miracle Papa did not come home, dining unexpectedly at his club or being summoned to the table of some friend. And yet I was not in the least consoled, knowing that the reckoning was merely delayed & that every hour which passed before it had the power to distress me more.

*

Today I did a wicked thing.

Its wickedness was not in the aim I proposed but in the means by which I effected it.

I had determined that another day in this room – Mrs Finnie's sour face, Mr Conolly's draught, the sun streaming in through the open window – would be intolerable to me. Thus when at midday I heard the noise of Esther turning her key in the lock I retired to the sofa & lay there in a piteous manner, clutching my hands to my sides. Then as Esther moved into the room, the lunch-things balanced on the tray before her, I turned upon my back & groaned aloud.

'Why, ma'am, whatever is the matter?'

In bringing me my luncheon, Esther has an infallible routine. First she unlocks & pushes open the door. Then she places the tray on the ground at her feet. Then she pushes shut & locks the door, placing the key in the pocket of her pinafore. Then she retrieves the tray & places it on my desk. But she has grown easy with me over the weeks & I, sly minx that I am, resolve to exploit this ease.

'Oh Esther,' I moan. 'I feel most dreadfully unwell. A pain in the stomach – truly.'

As I foresaw, Esther's first thought was for myself. Placing the tray on the floor, but omitting to lock the door, she came immediately towards me.

'What is it, ma'am?' she asked again.

Whereupon I beckoned her to me & as she bent over my recumbent form gave suddenly a violent push with my hand that sent her stumbling backwards into a heap. How much it pained me to do this I cannot say. Then before she could rise up I sprang away & out of the door.

As to what took place in the ensuing minutes, so airy-headed was

I at having attained my goal that I can scarce recollect their passage. I know that I tumbled down a flight of stairs, came into the hall, where Mr Randall looked up from winding the grandfather clock, saw me & cried out, that I ran across the gravel at the front of the house, across a road – conscious all the while of a person or persons following at my heels – & into a field, where I asked the way of a girl out scaring the birds, & would have run further but that a man whom I had not seen approached from nowhere & caught me up in his arms & not unkindly brought me home.

It is a mystery to me why I did it, knowing full well, of course, what should be its end.

*

I sleep an entire day & wake with a great vacant space in my head where my thoughts should be.

*

'Esther,' I say, when next she comes, 'I beg that you will forgive me for the trick I played, which was not meant to injure you.'

'Indeed, ma'am,' says Esther, who has locked the door as she steps into the room quite in the old way, 'I was not hurt. It was only the suddenness of the thing that startled me.'

The teacup with Mr Conolly's medicine sits on the tray. A question occurs to me which I have several times shied away from asking.

'What is said about me in – the house?' By this I mean the servants' hall. A distinction Esther appreciates.

'In the house, ma'am?' She sets down the tray & stands regarding me.

I do not mind when Esther stares at me. It is her master I abhor.

'In the house. Between Mr Randall & Mrs Finnie.'

'They say, ma'am, that you are . . .' Esther removes the cover that lies on my dinner-plate. 'That you are . . . not in your right mind.'

'Do you think I am not in my right mind?'

'No, ma'am.'

The teacup with Mr Conolly's medicine sits on the tray.

'Esther. Will you do me a great service?'

'If I can, ma'am.'

'Take up that teacup which is on the tray & drink what is in it. I promise it shall not harm you.'

'Very well, ma'am.'

Esther picks up the teacup & drinks the contents. Then she makes a most welcome & consoling gesture.

She smiles.

*

'I ask you only to think of it. That is all.'

I am seated in my guardian's study once more. It may be eleven of the clock or midnight – I do not know. I have been here an hour & would be anywhere else.

But there is nowhere else.

'I assure you,' my guardian continues, 'of the sincerity of my feelings. If they did not exist, I should not declare them.'

When I glimpsed him first, as he stood in my doorway an hour since, I saw that some change had come upon his person which I could not at once fathom. Then I remarked it. The old black vestments were gone, & in their place was a quite juvenile costume of a white jacket & a tie fastened with a sailor's knot.

I fear that I preferred the old rook.

I remark, too, his nervousness. His hand darts now & then to his mouth to finger his yellow teeth.

Yellow as the keys of a spinet that I saw once in my aunt's house at Dover.

He talks of Easton Hall. Of what lies in its chests & strongboxes & beneath the ceilings of its attics. All this shall be mine to command, he says.

Three times in my life I have been paid court to by gentlemen. First Mr Farrier – Richard – with his verses & his walks in the rose garden, & of whom indeed I was very fond. Then Henry, to whom I was married. And now this grey-haired old man with his rusty voice & his creaking politenesses.

Whose singularities Papa would have marked down in a trice, as was his habit, written up in one of his books &, as was also his habit, gently mocked.

'Say only that you will think of it,' he says again, patting my hand.

I will think of no such thing.

*

It is as I suspected.

270

Esther says that in the hours after she drank Mr Conolly's draught she grew unaccountably tired, could not keep from yawning, indeed fell near-asleep on her chair in the scullery, from which she was routed out by Mrs Wates, crying that she was a lazy good-for-nothing & a slut that no man would marry, &c.

The next draught that Mr Randall brings me I shall throw into the chamberpot!

*

Today a letter was brought up on the tray with my breakfast.

He asks only that I may think of it. But he desires an answer.

I would that I had cracked open his grey head with the poker rather than poor Sir Charles Lyell!

*

And now a great crisis is upon me! The letter from Esther's lover has come & she proposes to join him in London. This she confided to me very gravely – yet suppressing, it seemed to me, a great excitement – as she stood in my room this forenoon (the door locked very thoroughly behind her) with the luncheon tray.

'When shall you go?' I ask her.

'He says for me to go immediate, ma'am.'

'And shall you give notice?'

'There was a man come from Norwich this morning, ma'am, & stayed ever so long with the master, with another man who came & stood in the drive looking at the house quite as if he meant to take it down brick by brick.'

Which I construe thus: *What is the point of giving notice when the house is to be sold around us a month hence?*

'And what will you feel when you get there, Esther?'

'As to that, ma'am, I shall have to take it on trust.'

But there is my plan. For which I do not require Mr Dixey's aid, nor anyone else's save Esther's.

'Esther,' I say, 'you must help me. Sit in a chair and wait, just a moment, while I think.'

And so Esther perches on the chair, regarding me very curiously, as I sit at the desk & write a letter to Mr Crabbe, Henry's lawyer, explaining where I am, & what is happening to me, what my guardian proposes, &c., & much else, & how I would not stay here a moment longer. There is no envelope but I twist it across & write on the back: MR CRABBE, LINCOLN'S INN, & Esther says she will deliver it.

'And Esther,' I say, as she folds it up & places it in the pocket of her apron, 'I hope you will be very happy.'

'I hope it too, ma'am.'

'And Esther . . .' But before I can say more I have taken her in my arms & kissed her.

Esther smiles, saying that she will come on the next day & bid me goodbye.

I listen to her footsteps, moving off along the passage.

The next day dawns but she does not come.

She does not come & she does not come.

*

Twice he has asked me for an answer. Twice I have said nothing. The second time he grasped my hand & said loudly that I was a foolish girl & he would not be gainsaid in this.

Mr Randall brings my food now.

She does not come & she does not come.

I am so very tired.

Part Four

XIX

North of Sixty

He awoke each morning just before dawn, groping about on the floor of the cabin for his mittens and his muffler before tugging open the door and staring out at the eaves of the forest, pale and grey in the half-light. At first, because he was new to the land and inexperienced in these matters, he had assumed that its contours were unvarying. Gradually, however, his eyes had grown keen enough to register faint variations in the landscape: the frown of the spruce trees softened by a fall of snow; a line of tracks not yet obliterated; the bent white branch of a fir sapling which would, in time, release its load with a snap like a pistol-shot. All this reassured him, for he was a man who relished movement and the sense of things happening around him, and he knew, even in his inexperience, that the wild hated all movement, knowing it to be a symbol of the life-force which it seeks to extinguish and subdue. Yet at the same time he feared what he saw around him, for he knew that he did not understand it and that his ability to conquer it depended on the ingenuity of others. And so he stood each morning in the doorway of his cabin, twenty yards from the boundary of the forest, cold in spite of his mittens and his muffler, looking out at the frown of the first spruce trees and the pale sky with all manner of doubts and suspicions forming in his mind.

He was a resourceful man in his way and he had devised certain routines to allay these doubts and suspicions. By the time that the short, sunless day was an hour old he had attended to the embers of the previous night's fire, boiled a kettleful of melted snow, made coffee and chopped more wood to add to the pile beneath the cabin's lean-to. Then, with a second cup of coffee in his hand, he would sit on the solitary chair and run his eye over the provisions that remained there: the grey sacks that contained their flour; the box of sun-cured fish; the

strips of fat salt pork in their metal chest. As he did so he congratulated himself on his thoroughness. The boys would be pleased at how
well he had kept the place in order, he told himself. They had left traces
of themselves which he came upon with a pleasant sense of recogni-
tion: a deck of cards face down upon the snow; a clasp-knife that had
rolled out of sight behind the flour sacks; a silver Canadian dollar lost
underfoot. He collected these objects carefully and placed them in the
pocket of his fur-lined jacket, anticipating the moment when he could
return them. Later, as the day wore on and the sky to the south warmed
to rose colour, he moved restlessly around the interior of the cabin,
feeling at the little imperfections and blemishes of the wood with his
fingers, or sat reading and coughing over the fire, whose smoke rose
through a chimney made of a tin pail. At four the last of the grey light
drifted into dusk and the pall of the Arctic night descended.

The boys had been gone two days now. Another two – at the outside,
three – would bring them back. He could hear in his head the sound
that the sled would make as it came through the dried-up water-course
on which the canopy of spruce trees frowned and the barking of the
five dogs drawn out in a wide fan before it. They had come here to
the Powder River country in search of a supply of logs which, come
the spring, could be floated back south as far as Fort Mackenzie if need
be, or further. And those logs, he had been told, would make their
fortunes. And this assurance, though he had no real need of money,
having plenty of it in the land from which he had come, cheered him
and invigorated him as he went about his tasks. And yet he knew,
newcomer though he was to the land, that the winter was drawing on
and there remained only a little time in which those logs could be
found. Never mind! The boys would be back soon from their reconnoitre in the white country that stretches all the way north as far as
the Arctic Sea and they would return along the trail they had come,
eighty miles to Fort McGurry, where the traders and the Hudson Bay
Company men put up for the worst of the snows.

Thinking that the boys would be pleased to find fresh meat waiting
for them, he took the rifle and several cartridges from his store and,
winding the scarf carefully around his face so that only his forehead
and the tip of his nose were exposed to the raw air, plunged off
beneath the canopy of the forest. Such was the silence around him
that the noise of his breath and the sound that his moccasins made
as he padded over the soft snow oppressed him. It was like no silence

that he had ever known, immense, chilling and elemental, and for the first time in the course of his journeyings in the wild he began to wish that he had stayed in Fort McGurry. He corrected himself on the instant, telling himself not to be so foolish, that the boys would be back shortly, that the next morning, even, would see them home, and they would want a couple of snowshoe rabbits or a hare rather than a companion who took fright at so little a thing as silence. And in this way he recovered his spirits, settled his rifle more comfortably in the crook of his arm and moved deeper beneath the tall trees, taking care, however, to remember which way he had come and always keeping a sight of one very tall spruce tree, taller than any of the others, which he knew lay in reach of the cabin.

A half-hour's search, though, turned up nothing and he was forced to retrace his steps through the snow, wondering that the game should have vanished from a country that when he had first come to it two months before had been teeming with life. There was a famine in the land that had followed the cold but he did not know this. He knew only of the cold, which it seemed to him had become a great deal more irksome since he had first come to the cabin. At last, in the deep undergrowth aside from the forest path, he turned up a ptarmigan that went squawking and fluttering from her nest. The noise startled him and he stood for a second or two gazing stupidly at the bird as it took flight into the trees before he raised his gun. But his fingers, even in their fur-lined mittens, were chilled to numbness and the shot whistled away into the depths of the forest. After this he grew sober and reflective. It certainly was very cold out here, and there was clearly no game to be had. The boys would have to make do with salt pork and biscuits. He went back to the cabin in the fading light along a path devoid of all living things and comforted himself by taking out from amongst his kit certain prized possessions which he had brought with him from home. There was a keepsake book that his sister had given him and a volume of Tennyson's poetry, with an inscription in it that was not his sister's, and he brooded over them by the fireside as he ate his pork and biscuits. Later the wind got up and he lay in his shakedown by the dwindling fire listening to the creaking of the spruce trees.

Next day he woke at exactly the same time but with a feeling of expectation in his mind that he could not at first identify. The boys were coming! That was it! Another half-dozen hours would see them back and the sled rolling into view along the dried-up water-course that did service for a road here in the extremity of the wild. There fell on him a feeling of grave responsibility, and he attended to his chores with more than usual determination, building up the fire until it seemed to pulse with heat and chopping yet more wood with which to feed it. As he chopped he rested occasionally with his foot on the axe and looked into the forest, thinking that he saw something moving within it and then deciding that it was merely a trick of the light. It certainly was very cold, he thought. At first, when he had begun on his log-splitting, he had taken off his thick jacket and draped it over a juniper bush, but within two or three minutes, despite the warmth brought to his limbs by the action of chopping, he could feel the numbness creeping into his body and put the coat back on. All the time that he did this he strained his ears for a sound, but there was nothing. Oppressed once more by the silence he took to contriving small ways to break it, humming to himself as he worked and stamping his feet vigorously on the surface of the frozen snow. After a while the immensity of his solitude struck him once more and he fell quiet. He was not an imaginative man – his skill lay in practicalities, in the devising of tasks and their accomplish-ment – but it occurred to him that there was something romantic in his situation here on the margin of the world. The wind had got up again and he listened to it soughing against the trees and sending little flurries of snow to patter against the cabin door, and was thankful to hear it. Later, when the hour or so of rose-tinted sky had been and gone, he strode down the frozen hill to the point where it met the water-course, along which the boys and their sled would come, and looked down the trail for a long time.

There was snow during the night: only an inch or two but enough to cover the tracks that he had made the previous day in walking down to the trail. As he ate his breakfast, sitting over the embers of the fire with his coffee cup balanced on his knee, he reflected that the boys certainly had been gone a long time. He was aware as he did this that two thoughts existed simultaneously in his head: the one that the boys must have found something unexpected with which to occupy them-selves along the further reaches of the trail; the other that there was something sinister in this absence. It was a windy day, with more snow drifting in almost horizontally across the grey landscape, but several times he tied his muffler about his ears, put on the raccoon-skin hat that he had purchased from the factor at Fort McGurry and walked down to inspect the trail. Each time that he returned he added another log to the fire and sat by it warming his hands and brooding.

In this way two or three more days passed. His sense of anticipation, he now discovered, had become all-consuming. Half a dozen times in an hour he found himself wandering down to the trail and staring out into the distance to the point where it lost itself in the horizon of trees and leaden sky. The strangest thoughts ran through his head. One was that the boys had simply deserted him. And yet he fancied that had the boys wished to do this they would not have left him to guard their provisions. Another was that they had lost themselves on the trail. But he knew, too, that the one to whose leadership they all deferred had come this way half a dozen times before. It was all very mysterious, he assured himself. Thrown back upon his resources he became suddenly absorbed by the environment in which he found himself. He began to notice things. He noticed that when he cleared his throat and spat, for in common with most men in that region he had taken to chewing plugs of tobacco, the spittle cracked when it hit the ground. This suggested to him that it was very cold indeed. Separating the bark from one of the logs that lay piled up in the cabin's lean-to, he saw that scurrying beneath it there were insects of a kind he had never seen, and observed their bewilderment as they were exposed to the chill air. He saw, too, the way in which the time of the rose-coloured sky grew shorter and the hours of daylight continued to diminish. All this told him that winter was coming perilously close and that it would be as well for the boys to return.

And then he would tell himself that he was an old woman, that he had food, firewood and a rifle, and that soon there would be an explanation of the mystery. It occurred to him that he had better take an inventory against the boys' arrival and so, laying out the items on a square of tarpaulin as the fire burned and crackled beside him, he made a list of everything he could find in the cabin. There were, he discovered, at least a dozen strips of fat salt pork, a couple of canisters of biscuits, a sack of flour, beans, a large box of sulphur matches and a dozen cartridges, together with the sun-cured fish, intended for the dogs but which a man could eat if he had a mind. This reassured him, and yet he knew that the pile of foodstuffs had substantially diminished since he had last examined it. The theory of existence in the wild had been explained to him by an old-timer he had met at Fort McGurry. This was that one subsisted on iron rations, supplemented by such fresh meat as was available. But what if there was no fresh meat? This was not something that the old-timer had cared to speak about. When he had finished counting the provisions he laid them out upon the upturned tarpaulin and counted them a second time.

One morning he awoke with a sensation of deep unease. Previously he had known exactly how long it was that the boys had been gone. Now he realised that he had forgotten the precise number of days. Was it seven, or eight? He could not be sure. It occurred to him that he should make a mark with his knife on the door-frame to remind him, and so, drawing the blade from its covering, he cut a series of notches into the timber, seven at first, then adding an eighth as he became certain that eight days had passed. When he had finished he sat down and admired the notches, which were deep and evenly spread, only to be assailed by another spasm of unease. It was seven days, surely, that the boys had been gone? Very well, he would remind himself not to cut another notch on the following morning. Placing the knife back in its leather scabbard, he went and stood by the door and looked out across the snow towards the eaves of the forest. There were tracks in the snow, he noticed, that had not been there the previous night, but, newcomer to the land that he was, he could not tell which animal had made them. He supposed that he should take the gun and go looking for meat, but the sky threatened more snow and he acknowledged that he felt sluggish and out of sorts. He would sit by the fire, he told himself, and read and brood, and perhaps as he read and brooded he would hear the noise of the sled bowling down the trail of the dried-up water-course, and the boys would come.

Accordingly he spent half an hour chopping more wood until a pile of split logs three feet high lay beneath the canopy of the lean-to, and then sat by the fire reading the keepsake that his sister had presented to him and the volume of Tennyson's poems. The poems, of which he had formerly taken no great notice, seemed to him extraordinarily fine. He read several of them two or three times, and thought in a very melancholic way of the person who had given them to him. It occurred to him that it would be amusing to read them aloud, as he had used to do at school, standing up at his desk as the master watched him from his dais, and so he opened his mouth and spoke a few words of one, looking as he did so into the depths of the fire and seeing the schoolroom and the faces of the boys and the great window and the meadow behind it. As he did so he saw, quite distinctly, the face of the person – the female person – who had given him the book. But his voice seemed small and pitiful in the silence that surrounded him and after a line or two he stopped, rather shame-facedly, and put some more wood on the fire. The day wore on and he continued to sit by the fire, alternately brooding and dozing until darkness fell. He was aware, as he rolled out his blanket and settled himself to sleep, that something he had expected to happen had not happened. The boys had not come! Never mind, they would come tomorrow. Outside he could hear the wind howling in the trees.

In this way more time passed. Quite how much time he could not say, for he found that he became lax at cutting the notches into the timber of the door-frame. Or rather not lax but cautious. He would stare at the neat line of indentations unsure as to whether he had added to their number that day or not. Sometimes at the conclusion of this staring he would add a notch, sometimes not. It was the same with his routines. Sometimes he would awake from his half-doze before the fire to find that he had let the pile of wood run down almost to nothing, and then a panic would seize him and he would spend an hour or more chopping a great pile of logs and arranging them in the lean-to. He supposed that he was becoming a little out of sorts, a little jittery at the silence and the grey landscape beyond him. And yet he continued to look ahead, to plan intricately in his mind what should be done in the days after the boys arrived and they set off back along the trail to Fort McGurry. He found a fragment of mirror, no more than an inch square, in the pack in which he stored his bedding and, examining himself in it, discovered that the beard he had begun to grow when he had first come to the wild reached down almost to his breast-bone. Well, he would shave that off when he got back to Fort McGurry. The thought tickled him and he imagined himself calling for soap and hot water and the boys laughing at him as he set about his task. He continued to smile about it as he chopped the logs, built up the embers of the fire, read at his little volume of Tennyson and made an inventory of the pile of provisions.

One day – he did not quite know how long had passed since he had last done this – he found himself standing before the timber door-frame and counting the notches. There were twenty-one. The number star-tled him and he counted and recounted, thinking that there must be some error in his computation. The realisation of his predicament stole upon him by degrees. He was in a jam, he supposed, a high old jam, and he must settle down and decide what was best to do. In the meantime, though, he would chop more logs and make a further inventory of the supplies. The calmness of his demeanour as he did this surprised him as much as the long row of notches on the timber door-frame. It was as if the person chopping the wood and calculating the extent of his provisions was someone else at whom he stared from above. The situation did not seem to have anything to do with him. But he was startled, again, by the sparseness of his inventory. Only a single canister of the biscuits remained, together with half a dozen pieces of pork, twice that amount of fish and some flour. Had he really eaten that much while the boys had been gone? Looking at the food as it lay on the tarpaulin he conceived a notion of himself living frugally in the cabin through the winter, of being found by the first horseman who came riding along the trail in the spring and explaining modestly how he had survived. But the dwindling supplies scared him. That night he ate only a couple of biscuits and the half of a sun-cured fish before unrolling his blankets and settling himself to sleep.

In the morning he felt more confident than he had done for many a day. It seemed to him that he knew more about the functioning of his body than he had ever known before. He watched his fingers as they moved over the buttons of his coat. Sitting by the fire drinking his cup of coffee he was conscious of his heart beating and a vein pulsing in his forehead. This comforted him, for it spoke of life and movement rather than the inertness that lay beyond the cabin door. Then, turning to refill the coffee pot, he made an alarming discovery. There was no more coffee. For a moment he brooded over this discrepancy, even searching a little among the canisters and the provision packets to see if he had overlooked anything, before, as it seemed to him, resigning himself to this new feature of his existence. He would have to do without coffee. Outside in the grey light there were a few snowflakes falling and he watched them for a while, thinking how sombre and melancholy the land seemed. The sight reminded him of the routine he had previously followed and he made his way down to the river-bed and stared northwards along the trail. With the snow the track had all but disappeared, he noted, only a faint depression in the lie of the land showed that it had ever been there.

A sudden sense of purpose overcame him. He would have to do something, he realised, take some decisive step before the snows came and covered him as they had done the trail. Surprised at himself, for he did not quite know from where the impetus had come, he found himself seizing an armful of discarded branches and an axe and fashioning a makeshift sled. There was a length of rope in the cabin and he used this to lash the pieces of the frame into place. With what remained of the rope he constructed a harness that he could fasten over his chest and shoulders, enabling him to drag the sled behind. The sight of the sled lying on the patch of ground before the cabin door cheered him. The light was beginning to fade and the outlines of the trees receded into darkness. Tomorrow, he thought, he would rise at dawn, pack what remained of his provisions onto the sled and set off down the trail towards firelight, warmth and human voices.

Somehow, though, he did not do this. It was difficult to explain how this came about, how he had conditioned his mind, as he thought, to do one thing and yet how another, unconscious conditioning had compelled him to do something else. Mid-morning on the next day found him once again sitting before the fire and brooding over the little volume of Tennyson. Wondering at his behaviour, he went and examined the sled again, silently appraising the curve of the birch-bark runners. The sky, he noticed, had already turned grey, which meant that there was snow coming. It would be foolish, he thought, to attempt anything today. Much better to stay by his fire. Wandering over to the lean-to he was puzzled to find that only a handful of logs remained. Reproaching himself for this negligence, he set to work to replenish the pile.

The fire had burned almost down to nothing when he woke the next morning and there was a great numbness in his limbs, despite the blankets and the coat that he had thrown over himself before he went to sleep. Thrashing his arms against his sides and stamping his feet on the ground he built up the fire once more and the numbness receded, but the memory of it remained. It really was extraordinarily cold. He had heard of there being terrible cold snaps in the wild when birds fell frozen from the sky and animals survived only by burrowing under the drifts of snow and he wondered if this was such a cold snap. There was no wind today and though he was not an imaginative man it seemed to him that the land had a terrible gauntness, a desolation that he could no longer bear to observe. Again, not quite knowing from where the impulse came, he found himself assembling his belongings – his tea-kettle, his canisters of food, his box of sulphur matches, his store of cartridges – on the sled. When he had arranged them to his satisfaction he took the tarpaulin and fashioned it into a cover. The sound of the snow crunching beneath his moccasins reminded him of something else that he needed and, plunging off into the eaves of the forest, he returned with another armful of brush-wood. From this, with the aid of various twists of rope and twine that remained to him, he constructed a pair of snowshoes.

Curiously, having finished these preparations, his sense of resolve began to recede once more. He looked at the fire again and at the timber of the cabin door, felt for the little volume of Tennyson that was stowed in his jacket pocket and reflected that perhaps he was being a trifle hasty. He wondered how far away Fort McGurry was, wishing that he had paid more attention to the maps that the boys had examined in the early days of their excursion. It could not be more than seventy miles, he thought, say eighty at the outside. And even walking over fresh snow and encumbered by snowshoes a man ought to be able to travel at fifteen miles a day. These calculations reassured him, but they did not reassure him as much as he wanted them to do and he wished that he had a proper sled and a team of dogs such as those which the boys had taken with them when they disappeared up the trail all that time ago. He wondered idly – it was something he had not considered for several days – what had become of the boys and why they had not come back to find him, glancing all the while at the timber of the cabin door and at the embers of the fire. He wondered if he ought to leave a message for the boys, and so, tearing out a flimsy blank sheet from the back of the little volume of Tennyson, he settled down by the fire, so that his fingers would not become numb, and scribbled on it with a stump of pencil: *RETURNING TO FORT McGURRY – R.F.* This he secured to a rusty nail on the back of the door-frame. Seeing the note emboldened him in a way that his previous preparations had not. Casting a final glance around the cabin, strapping the rifle over his shoulder and settling the harness of the sled on his chest, he set out down the short incline of the frozen hill and pulled out onto the trail.

The pale Arctic sun was at its zenith and a great silence seemed to have fallen over the land, even greater than the one he had remarked on his first day in the cabin. He was aware, as he moved, that he was frightened of the silence and yet, at the same time, feared to combat it, and that in setting his feet onto the surface of the snow he aspired to soundlessness. The noise of his breath irked him. He was forever dragging the runners of his sled into fresh grooves so that they would move more smoothly. The trail, he was relieved to find, was still discernible: a faint, sunken line in the snow that ran on past belts of dark fir trees and occasional banks of undergrowth. Once a white hare broke from cover and bounded nervously across the path. Aside from this, nothing moved. Two hours of daylight remained to him and in this time he calculated that he had covered five miles. Then at dusk he dragged the sled into a cluster of spruce trees to the right of the trail and set up camp for the night. He was methodical in this, for he was wise enough to know that his survival depended on it, that it was imperative for him to stay warm and by staying warm to recruit himself for the rigours of the next day. He was aware that even five miles dragging a sled over his shoulders had exhausted him and he knew that to over-exert himself would be a foolish thing. Accordingly he chopped a good pile of wood, lit a fire and cooked his frugal supper. When he had done this, his spirits lifted. He was out on the trail right enough. Four days or perhaps five would see him home. His only regret was the absence of coffee. He had never thought there would be a time when he would miss coffee so much. But apart from this, and the piercing cold, which caused him to huddle himself ever closer to the fire, he thought that he was comfortable enough. If the boys could see him, he told himself, they would be pleasantly surprised at how a *checaquo* could adapt himself to the land. Half-dozing over the fire he imagined himself striding into Fort McGurry and the look of surprise on the factor's face.

There was a patch of darkness just beyond the firelight and beneath the margin of the spruce trees and he watched it for a while, thinking that it looked remarkably like an animal stretched out and luxuriating in the warmth of the fire, like his own dogs lounging by the hearth in his guardian's house back in his own country. Interested in this singular phenomenon he found himself listening carefully into the night air, but there was nothing except the crackle of the fire and a faint hiss of steam from the kettle he had placed at the fire's edge. Having drunk some of the hot water that it contained he allowed his gaze to rest once more on the patch of darkness, but it seemed vaguer now, less distinct in his imagination. He wondered if here in the extremity of the wild, with each of his senses heightened to their utmost pitch, his eyes might be playing tricks on him. Sometime later he picked up a stick from the margin of the fire and threw it speculatively in the direction of the patch of darkness, but there was nothing there and he heard the stick fall hissing into the snow.

Next morning he awoke long before the rays of light had crept over the lines of spruce trees, ate his breakfast in darkness hunched over the embers of the fire, packed his things onto the makeshift sled and resumed the trail half an hour before dawn. No more snow had fallen and the surface beneath him was more tightly packed. In this way he made better progress than on the previous afternoon. Mid-morning brought him to a region of open country between two banks of firs where the trail turned south along the banks of a frozen water-course. The lack of cover oppressed him. It seemed to him as he moved forward that he was a tiny limpet-like creature clinging to the surface of an unending vastness, and he was glad when he returned a mile or so later to the bleak avenues of trees. He ate his lunch – half a slice of pork left over from the previous day and a biscuit – seated on the trunk of a fir tree that had fallen halfway across the path. He certainly was hungry, he told himself as he disposed of the food, but the dull ache in his stomach remained. Almost as the thought came into his mind a jack rabbit bobbed into view from the undergrowth twenty yards away and instinctively, such was his desire for fresh meat, he raised his rifle and loosed off a shot. But his fingers were awkward inside his thick mittens and the jack rabbit slipped away out of range. Seeing it disappear he wished now that he had not shot at it, for he had a curious feeling that by breaking the silence with that deafening report he had drawn attention to himself in a way that a more prudent man might have avoided. Some other impulse prompted him to examine the number of cartridges in his store. Finding that he had only seven, he resolved to shoot at no more rabbits.

Towards afternoon he reached another long low bank of spruce trees, sparsely arranged on either side of the trail. The forest was beginning to break up, he told himself, for the land that stretched away on either side was more variegated. There were hills in the middle distance, themselves mere spurs and outriders of yet more distant mountains. The discovery cheered him, for he understood that he must be closer to Fort McGurry, which, as he knew, lay in the dip of a stretch of higher ground. Gaining the avenue of spruce trees, where the trail ran for more than a mile, unerringly straight, like a road, some instinct – like the instinct that had urged him to shoot the rabbit and to examine his store of cartridges – caused him to glance over his shoulder.

There, thirty yards behind him, muzzle down in the snow, grey ears pointed and alert, walked a wolf. He was not such a newcomer to the land that he could not recognise a wolf. Standing uncertainly with his feet planted on either side of the sled, he watched as the animal slid towards him, saw him motionless and came to a halt some twenty yards away, resting its paws on the ground before it and curling over its tail as a cover for them. He knew enough about wolves to realise that this was an impressive specimen – gaunt and showing signs of malnourishment, but fully five feet from nose to tail and perhaps thirty inches at the shoulder. It occurred to him that it had been following him since he had set out on the trail and the thought was not pleasant to him. Still, he had a rifle at his shoulder and seven cartridges and he determined to be sanguine. Pulling the string of the sled against his shoulder and casting a last look behind him, he set off once more along the trail.

After an hour the shadows began to steal up among the spruce trees and dusk fell upon the land. He selected his camping place for the night with care: a patch of ground beneath the boughs of a particularly large tree. Having chopped a stack of kindling from the brushwood that lay to hand, he lit a fire and established himself in a declivity at the base of the tree with the fire before him. With warmth and food his spirits rose again. Two days or maybe three would see him in McGurry, talking to the factor and having his beard shaved by the fort barber. He could not see the wolf, had not done so since he commenced to build his fire, but he believed that it was there. As the darkness grew more complete his eyes grew sharper and he began searching through the murk beyond the arc of the firelight. He had almost convinced himself that the beast had gone, sprung fresh meat somewhere along the trail and pursued it elsewhere, when he realised that what he had thought to be a thicket of shadow thirty feet beyond the fire's edge was the shape that he had distinguished the previous night. As he watched, the wolf rolled over, like a dog that lies in front of a drawing-room hearth, and he saw its eyes flash like live coals. Without pausing to reflect he took the rifle from where it lay on the tarpaulin next to him and raised it to his shoulder, but the click of the safety catch alerted the beast and it slipped lazily to one side even before he could bring the weapon to bear. Looking up a moment or two later he saw that it had re-established itself quite comfortably a yard or two away from its original place.

He did not sleep much that night but dozed unhappily, troubled by a dream in which he ran steadily down a stony beach pursued by some white, flapping thing like a sheet whipped up by the air, always moving at the same speed, waiting only for him to flag. Waking once from one of these dozes he saw that the fire had burned low and the wolf lay only a dozen feet away, close enough for him to make out the bristling fur of its jaw and the twitching of its grey flanks. He watched it for a long while as he renewed the fire with brushwood and then settled himself once more in his position against the tree-trunk. In the morning – a very grey morning it was, with the promise of snow in the lowering sky – his first act on waking was to look for the spot where the wolf had lain but there was no sign of any living thing. This cheered him and he ate his breakfast with greater relish than he remembered eating a meal for days. Then, as he picked up his belongings and stood warming his feet at the embers of the fire, he saw from the tail of his eye the wolf come slinking out of a clump of whin bushes away to his right. In its absence the man had not ceased to reflect upon the wolf, and he now brought into his mind certain of the reflections with which he had comforted himself. If the wolf wished to follow him down the trail to Fort McGurry then he had a rifle and seven cartridges and he could build a fire beyond which the most obstreperous wolf in the northern territories would not care to venture. Let the beast wander after him if it wished! It was of no account to him. In this way he regained his composure, slung the string of the sled over his shoulders and pulled out once more onto the trail.

He was in luck that morning. The snow had kept off and the ground remained crisp underfoot. Moreover he recognised, or he thought he recognised, certain signs suggesting that Fort McGurry was not far away: a broken stirrup cast onto the side of the trail; a blackened camp-fire only half-covered by the snow. These convinced him that his journey might soon be at an end. In this access of high spirits he found that he could refrain from looking over his shoulder for as much as five minutes at a time. When he did so he saw that the wolf continued to plod thirty or forty yards behind him. Well, if it wanted to do this, let it! What did he care? It was while turning back from one of these scrutinies of the trail and the grey shape loping in his wake that he fell into danger. Scarcely seeing that he had done so, he had come almost to the outer margin of the trail, to the point where it was bordered by brushwood and bushes concealed by the snow. Here he put his foot upon a prairie hen's nest and the bird came whirling up in a frenzy into his face. Startled, he beat the creature away with his hands and in doing so tripped on a root and fell heavily onto his ankle. He was up in an instant – the outraged hen continued to flutter around his head – conscious, as he did so, that his foot would not support him. Standing on one leg and using the upturned rifle as a crutch, he examined the foot with the fingers of his right hand, gritting his teeth against the shards of pain that now coursed up his leg to the level of his knee. He had either broken the ankle or badly sprained it, he did not know which. What he did know was that he could place no weight on it and thus was all but unable to move.

It was by now about midday, and the weak winter sun had irradiated the trail with pale, phantasmal light. The wolf had stopped twenty yards away and, head down over its paws, was regarding him with interest. He stood there foolishly for a moment or so, sensible of the pain in his ankle, wondering what he should do. There was nothing for it but to build a fire and conduct a proper examination of the ankle. Accordingly, as the sun began once more to slip beneath the rim of the sky, moving awkwardly on his one sound foot, he constructed a small fire at the side of the trail, waited until the flames had risen up and then, with the tarpaulin spread out beneath him, removed his moccasin and his thick sock and exposed his foot to the raw air. It was bruised and swollen to almost twice its normal size and, believing that he had sprained it rather than broken it, he bound it up with strips of cloth, replaced sock and moccasin and settled down to consider what he ought to do. There was nothing for it, he decided, but to stay the night where he was and trust that by the time he awoke in the morning he would be sufficiently recovered to proceed. And so, working slowly and occasionally crouching in the snow the better to accomplish his task, he built up a great pile of brushwood next to the fire and, cursing over the exposed nature of the spot in which he found himself, sat down once again to await the coming of nightfall. The wolf, twenty yards away, regarded him keenly. As the shadows began to lengthen he noticed it sidle slowly nearer to him until it lay barely ten feet distant from the arc of the fire. Its languid movements here in the warmth of the fire were, he decided, deceptive, for he was aware that the beast watched and registered each move that he made, following the descent of his hand as he reached for the biscuit canister, flattening its ears and preparing to retreat if he showed signs of struggling to his feet. He spent a restless night, troubled by the pain of his ankle and the thought of the wolf stretched out beyond the circle of firelight, and his own defencelessness.

He started awake to find the fire almost extinguished and the wolf scarcely two yards from where he lay. He cursed, seized a glowing fragment of wood from the embers and threw it in front of him, causing the beast to back away. There was a great ache in his ankle, he realised, and it had begun to snow quite heavily: already a coating an inch or two thick lay over the surface of his tarpaulin. He told himself that he was not afraid, that he would lie up here on the edge of the wild until his foot was healed, that he had a rifle and seven cartridges, and yet he was conscious that if he stayed where he was the snow would surely cover him. His salvation, he knew, lay in movement, that movement that the wild despises, and yet to shamble even a few feet was agony. The wolf continued to watch him as he made his preparations, assembled his belongings beneath the tarpaulin on the sled and then, again using the upturned rifle as a crutch, attempted to pull out onto the trail. He managed perhaps a dozen yards and then fell over in the snow, cursing at his ankle and at the fate that had brought him here to the wild, taken the boys from him and sent a prairie hen to sprain his ankle. The wolf retreated a few paces at the noise of his cursing and then, seeing that he did not mean to move, settled down to watch him.

It was snowing hard now, and staring at his thick mittens he could see on each of them a layer half an inch deep. Hastily he brushed it off. Instantly further snowflakes descended onto the surface of the wool. He was startled by how calm he felt. Here he sat, amid falling snow, on the margin of the wild, with his ankle sprained and the boys mysteriously gone from him – he wondered idly about the boys and what had happened to them – and the wolf silently regarding him, and yet he had a curious sensation that he was somehow detached from his own body, looking down from some warm, airy vantage point in the skies at the figure sitting hunched up on the trail with the rifle cradled in his arms and the wolf a dozen yards behind him. The snow continued to fall.

XX

Roman à Clef

In the vicinity, though not quite the near vicinity, of London Bridge, halfway along Tooley Street and in sight of Hay's Wharf, at the junction of a crossroads of thoroughfares where pack-horses and covered wagons jingle at every hour of the day and night, much to the dissatisfaction of the Tooley Street inhabitants, lies an inn named the Black Dog. Quite where the Black Dog, a vivid representation of whom dangles from a square frame above the grey stone doorway, came from, the Tooley Streeters are uncertain, but he is generally thought to be of ancient lineage, for the establishment to which he gives his name contains, in addition to his stygian portrait, a box concealing half a dozen bullets fired by Cromwell's men into the statuary of the neighbouring church and a glass case harbouring an antique sword, its blade mottled with rust, which is generally assumed to have cut several heads from their shoulders in some remote era of Tooley Street history.

The attractions of its bullet box, its rusty cutlass and its dangling sign notwithstanding, the Black Dog wore at this particular moment in time – eleven o'clock on a May morning – a somewhat desolate and forlorn air. The shutters on the ground-floor window were only half-open, the door – upon which the Black Dog gazes down balefully, as if he had half a mind to gobble it up with his great jaws – only half-ajar and the potboy sluicing water upon the step, over which the fumes of spiritous liquor seemed to hang in a kind of fog, only half-awake. Within, all was similarly cast down and mournful: the public bar all grey and ghostly in the half-light, with the chairs still resting on the wooden table-ends, the dirt very prominent on the beams and the window panes and the floor very much decorated with last night's detritus of tobacco fragments, pieces of bread, shrimpheads and the like. That such an environment has a lowering effect on the temperament was clear from the behaviour of the landlord, who stood by the bar regarding an upturned beer barrel with an expression of such melancholy that Mrs Landlord, arriving downstairs in a muslin dress and a cap, somewhat greasy from a late breakfast, took fright and began to dart round the room, gathering up the spittoons under her arm and administering sundry little polishes to the tables with a duster.

Here, in a corner, flanked by a lugubrious print of the Tower and a faded bill dating from ever so long ago announcing that Mr Felix Benjamin's benefit is finally to come off under the patronage of the Honourable Mr Makepeace, JP, his face well-nigh hidden behind a newspaper, sat Mr Pardew, very demure in a frock-coat and peg-top trousers and his feet squeezed into the neatest little pair of lacquered boots you ever saw, which was a tribute to Mrs Pardew or whoever else dressed him that morning. A specimen Tooley-Streeter, a cabman from the rank up by the station forecourt, or one of the waggoners thundering past in the road outside, who poked his head through the Black Dog's half-open door (pushing his way past the pot-boy, who had now absolutely sat down and gone to sleep on the step) would perhaps have remarked that the relation between Mr Pardew and the landlord and his wife was rather peculiar, and that though each side was cognisant of the other both were trying deliberately to ignore the undoubted fact of the other's existence.

The specimen Tooley-Streeter might also have noted that Mr Pardew, though studiously absorbed in his newspaper – indeed with a pencil in his hand with which he made certain emendations in the margin – and with a glass of something (brought by whom? The landlord seemed to know nothing about it) before him on the table, was waiting for someone and that this someone had delayed his or her appearance to a point sufficient to cause him vexation. Certainly Mr Pardew had not come to the Black Dog to read his newspaper or to drink his glass of Foker's Entire, for he was forever squinting at his watch, comparing that instrument's progress with a clock that hangs on the far wall next to a facsimile of Sir Walter Raleigh and additionally patting the pockets of his frock-coat in such a manner as to reassure himself that something dear to him still lay within it. Eventually these signs of nervousness could be borne no longer and Mr Pardew jumped to his feet, jingled his money in his pocket and took a turn around the bar, looked at the print of the Tower and the encomium to Mr Felix Benjamin, ran his hand meditatively over the bullet box, shook it in fact as if it held dice, and came to rest alongside the glass case containing the rusty sword.

'Dear me,' said Mr Pardew, half to himself and half to the landlord, who stood, still regarding the beer barrel, a few feet away, 'but that's a fearsome weapon.'

'I daresay it is, sir,' remarked the landlord, to whom the sword, formerly one of the baubles of his tenancy, had now mysteriously become an item of no account. 'I daresay it is.'

'Feel that on your neck and you would know about it,' Mr Pardew observed pleasantly. Mr Pardew was about to say something more, but their colloquy was interrupted by the arrival of a timid young man with light-coloured hair who came marching hastily into the room, flung his gaze around with an expression of apparent horror and might almost, it appeared, have marched out again, had not Mr Pardew taken it upon himself to intervene. The landlord, had he taken any account of the proceedings, might have said that Mr Pardew's behaviour was masterful. Without appearing to make any decisive movement, indeed still seeming to take an interest in the glass case, he contrived to interpose himself between the young man and the door, not exactly standing in the visitor's way but positioning himself, so to speak, on the flank of his retreat. Again, the disinterested onlooker might have been forgiven for assuming that there was some peculiar relation between Mr Pardew and the landlord, for the latter instantly ceased his occupation of the bar and disappeared into his private quarters, leaving Mr Pardew and the young man alone in a silence broken only by the flap of the half-open shutter and the wagons in the street.

Mr Pardew hesitated, tapping one hand against the pocket of his frock-coat and getting a hint of something metallic concealed there in return and half extending the other before him. He was not sure of his man, was conscious, too, of the public nature of the place in which he stood and knew that he must proceed with very great caution. Nonetheless he fancied that if he could first succeed in putting the visitor at his ease the business might be done. Consequently he extended the hand yet further, to within a foot or so of the young man's stomach, so that he could not very well avoid shaking it.

'I believe I have the honour of addressing Mr Tester?'

'I – that is – I am Tester.'

Tester's eyes, as he spoke these words, darted around the room – at the sword in its case, at the windows, at the retreating figure of the landlord – as if it were alive with a movement that none but he could see. He was, Mr Pardew saw, a good-looking young man, light hair sleekly parted on his head, the set of his features only impaired by the suspicion of a twitch on his upper lip.

'Perhaps you would like to sit down,' Mr Pardew suggested, with the same pleasantness of tone as when he had drawn the landlord's attention to the sword, 'and take a glass? As you see, we are very quiet.'

Tester looked around him again, rather wildly, as if quietness were the last thing he desired and that only a German band with its instruments pitched to crescendo would have been sufficient to restore his spirits. However, he consented to sit down, passing a hand through his hair – his fingernails, Mr Pardew could see, were bitten down to the quick – and measuring the distance to the door with his eye.

'Will you take some brandy?' Mr Pardew wondered.

'No – nothing.'

They sat in this way for two or three minutes, Mr Pardew still smiling blandly and peering every so often at his newspaper. In the short time since the two men had greeted each other he had changed his opinion of the best means of handling the enterprise on which he was now embarked. Tester's nervousness and his apparent deference could, he believed, be usefully exploited by sheer firmness of manner. Thus he folded up his newspaper, glanced at the door (Tester's gaze following him as he did so) and said in a tone lower than that which he had previously used:

'You have the items with you?'

Tester nodded.

'I have a room hired upstairs. We had better go there.'

'Could we not . . . Could it not be done here?'

'What, and have a policeman come in and find us?' said Mr Pardew, meaning to frighten Tester. 'I hardly think so.'

After this Tester agreed to go upstairs. Ascending the wooden steps, which clattered beneath their feet in an alarming manner, they came eventually to a bedroom containing nothing but a bed, a wardrobe and an open window with an excellent view of the river and the towers and pinnaces of the distant city. This Mr Pardew went and inspected with evident delight. Tester, meanwhile, seated himself on the bed with an expression of blank terror.

'I should not be here,' he said at length. 'I had better go.'

'By all means,' Mr Pardew rejoined. 'Then you will have wasted my time as well as your own. You have read my letter?'

'Certainly I have read it.'

'Then it is necessary for you to know only that I stand by it. Where are the keys?'

Tester turned his head towards the doorway, as if there were some other person there whose help he might enlist in denying Mr Pardew his wish.

'I have them here in my pocket.'

'Give them to me.'

'On my honour, I never did a bad thing in my life before.'

'Who is to say that you are doing a bad thing now? They shall be out of your hands for half a minute. Half a minute, I promise. Then you shall have them back. Give them to me.'

With an audible sigh and an attitude of resignation – as if he could not help what he did and wished to emphasise this fact to any unseen eye that might be watching – Tester dipped his hand into the inner pocket of his coat and passed the keys across. Mr Pardew, placing them in the palm of his hand, gave them a quick, exultant stare and then dropped them singly onto the coverlet of the bed. The first key lay where it had fallen, but the second sprang up and clattered onto the floorboards. Mr Pardew gave a little exclamation and bent to retrieve it. Reaching into the pocket of his coat he brought out a small, square tin, not unlike a cigar-box, whose lid, prised off, revealed a layer of greenish wax. This Mr Pardew considered for a moment, pressing down the surface with his thumb once or twice to see whether he thought the depth sufficient for his purpose. Then, picking up first one key, then the other, he plunged each of them into the wax, drew them forth, established that the impressions were to his satisfaction and then placed them once again on the bed. All this Tester watched with the air of a man who observes a conjuror producing coloured scarves from a tall hat and cannot for the life of him see how the trick is done.

Seeing the keys once more within his grasp, Tester made as if to retrieve them. Mr Pardew frowned. Reaching into his breast pocket he brought out a white handkerchief, took up the keys for a second time in the palm of his hand and began carefully to polish them. In this way he was able to remove several traces of wax that still clung to the metal.

'Now,' he remarked finally. 'I think our business is concluded. You will not have been missed at your work?'

'Mr Smiles and the secretary are elsewhere.'

'And these are the keys that came from Chubb? You are sure of it?'

'I am sure of it.'

'Excellent. The terms stated in the letter will, of course, be fulfilled. One thing more,' said Mr Pardew amiably. 'I never knew you. You never knew me. This place' – he cast his hand around the room, Tester's gaze following wide-eyed in its wake – 'never was. That is all.'

When Tester had departed – flying down the stairs so rapidly that the boards resounded beneath his feet – Mr Pardew did not immediately follow. An onlooker, observing him, would have deduced that he had nothing in the world to summon him away. Picking up the tin from where he had left it on the bed, he replaced it in his pocket, moving as he did so to the window, where he stared for some while at the horizon of buildings and wharfs and tall ships' masts as if to reassure himself that no essential part of their arrangement had changed, the presumption being that if it had Mr Pardew would have had something to say about it. This done, he sauntered downstairs in the airiest manner, greeted the landlord, who had by this time repositioned himself at the bar, complimented Mrs Landlord (met in the passageway) on her fresh complexion, drank off a small glass of brandy with which this lady gladly furnished him, made a further inspection of the sword in its glass case, rather as if he would have liked to take it out and whirl it above his head, and finally wandered out onto the pavement.

It was now shortly before midday and the frenzy of Tooley Street – its wagonettes and its carts and its stern-faced gentlemen in rapid transit to the waterfront – had not abated, but Mr Pardew paid it no heed. With the little square tin in his pocket and a hand clasped protectively over that pocket, as if it guarded the greatest secret in the world, he crossed over Tooley Street, narrowly avoiding being run over by a great pantechnicon, and proceeded, by degrees, to the bridge, thereafter to the City, the vicinity of Clerkenwell and the workshop of a professional acquaintance in the business of metal-casting and die-sinking, where, it is to be hoped, he spent a profitable afternoon.

*

Five days had elapsed since the encounter in Tooley Street and Mr Pardew sat at his desk. The month of May was now well advanced and the weather warm, so that Bob Grace, who sat opposite him on his high stool, had taken off his jacket and in addition rolled his shirt cuffs up to the level of his elbows, but Mr Pardew cared nothing for such relaxations. He was examining a package which had lately arrived from Clerkenwell and which contained a pair of keys, very sleekly burnished up, and with the one attached to the other by way of a metal band. Thus far in his inspection Mr Pardew had not taken the keys out of their packaging but had merely looked at them as they lay nestled within it. In truth Mr Pardew, knowing that gentleman's perspicacity, hesitated to display them before his clerk. Grace, if he saw the keys and the manner in which Mr Pardew examined them, would certainly pass some comment. This Mr Pardew felt that he could not endure. At the same time Mr Pardew had a suspicion, born of long dealing with the man, that Grace knew a great deal more about his affairs than he had ever divulged and that any attempt to conceal even a small part of his business would be worse than useless. Consequently, having pondered the desirability of sending Grace out on an errand and then decided against it, and having reflected on his own anxieties with regard to the matter before him, he threw caution to the winds, delved inside the package and drew the keys out onto his desk-top.

If Grace noticed this manoeuvre of Mr Pardew's he did not acknowledge it, but continued to brood over a copy of *Bell's Life*. Mr Pardew looked at the keys. They had certainly been excellently turned, he thought to himself as he slid first one then the other into his hand, and would certainly serve for the purpose he had in mind. Something about their respective size and the set of their teeth struck him and, still with his eye on Grace, he placed the first key on the wooden surface of the desk with the second balanced on top of it. The suspicion that had lurked in his mind being confirmed by this experiment, he fetched a sheet of cartridge paper and a pencil out of his drawer and, laying the keys side by side, traced rapidly around their edges with the pencil point. Having accomplished this task, he stared for a long while at the resultant outlines, biting his lip and occasionally referring to the keys themselves. 'The fool,' Mr Pardew said finally to himself. 'He has brought me duplicates of the same key!' For a moment he tried to convince himself that this was not so, that there was some tiny variation in the metal which would differentiate them, but it was no good: the two keys, he now saw, were identical. For a moment Mr Pardew's spirits sank to the point where the enterprise he had determined upon scarcely seemed worth continuing. Then, after a short interval, during which time Mr Pardew looked out of the window and cast his eye over certain melancholy documents that lay on his desk, they revived. 'Well, I suppose I shall have to bring it off at Folkestone,' he said again to himself.

Looking up from his desk, and at the keys, from which even now he had some difficulty in removing his gaze, Mr Pardew saw that his clerk's eye was fixed firmly on him, and that the copy of *Bell's Life* had been scrunched up and hidden out of sight. There was something about Grace's expression that Mr Pardew did not at all like, for it spoke of shared confidences and painful secrets; nevertheless he determined to meet it head on. Still Grace continued to stare.

'What is it? Why do you gawp at me in that way?'

Grace drummed his finger-ends on the desk, took a fresh nib from a little box he had beneath the desk-top and inspected it as if it might be something good to eat.

'Keys is a blessed noosance,' he suggested.

'Eh? What is that? What business is it of yours if I have a pair of keys on my desk?'

Grace appeared not to hear. He was still evincing the greatest interest in the nib, which he now held between finger and thumb, preparatory to fixing it onto his pen.

'Mr File is a man who knows all about keys,' he continued meditatively. 'An excellent man to talk to, I believe, if there's anything wanting in the key line.'

'Eh?' Mr Pardew said again. 'Mr File? I will not have Mr File's name mentioned in this office, do you hear?'

'Certainly,' Grace replied. 'Mr File not to be mentioned. And his address in Amwell Street to be took out of the book, and no letter to be sent there, nor anything else I suppose.'

All this was horrible to Mr Pardew for he understood, or he thought he understood, exactly what Grace meant by it. For a moment he thought – and the imagining was very pleasant to him – that he might usefully dismiss the man on the spot. Prudence, however, as Mr Pardew soon acknowledged to himself, counselled caution. A Grace who sat in Mr Pardew's office, under Mr Pardew's eye, however great his impertinence or dirty his shirtfront, was preferable to one who roamed the world outside it and, embittered by harsh treatment, breathed all kinds of things to all manner of people. It occurred to Mr Pardew that the present moment would be a good one in which to take Grace into his confidence, and yet even here he hesitated. If he began to explain to Grace things of which the clerk was already aware he would appear exceedingly foolish. If, on the other hand, he imparted information to Grace which Grace did not know, he might compromise himself still further. Mr Pardew cursed under his breath and wished Grace at the bottom of the Thames.

'Perhaps,' he said, 'we had better have a little conversation. There are certain affairs on which I am currently engaged of which I don't doubt you are aware. I take it you have a fair idea of what I am about?'

'A pretty fair idea, sir, I believe,' Grace acknowledged meekly. 'Though of course Mr File's name is not to be mentioned.'

This, too, was horrible to Mr Pardew but still he persevered.

'I find that I am obliged to pay a visit to the coast. To Folkestone, in fact. Perhaps you had better accompany me.'

'It shall be as you say, sir.'

'We may very well set off this afternoon.'

'To Folkestone, sir?'

'Yes, to Folkestone.'

'Where the mail-steamers go across to Boulogne?'

'Yes. Where the mail-steamers go across to Boulogne.' The look on Mr Pardew's face as he said this was positively devilish, and once again he wished Grace at the bottom of the Thames. 'Now, is there anything outstanding?'

'Samuelson's bill is due for renewal. Forty pounds at six weeks I recollect.'

'Do you think he will pay it?'

'Last time he was a-talking of his cousin as is a clergyman that might put his signature to it.'

'I don't like clergymen's paper. No good ever came of it. You had better go round there. No, send Latch to call on him. By the by,' Mr Pardew enquired, 'how do you find Latch?'

'He is an obliging young man, sir, as does his duty.'

Mr Pardew said that he was very glad to hear it and again wished Grace at the bottom of the Thames.

*

Before departing for Folkestone on the early-afternoon train, Mr Pardew undertook certain preparations of a highly confidential nature. To accomplish these it was absolutely necessary that he should be undisturbed. Thus, having despatched Grace with a copy of Mr Samuelson's promissory note, and having instructed that gentleman that he would meet him at London Bridge at two o'clock, he shut the office door, turned the key in the lock, pulled down the blinds upon the bleary window and seated himself once more at his desk. Here he took a final look at the keys, holding first one and then the other up to his face, before replacing them in the packet and locking it in the office safe. This done, he wandered over into a little back room that adjoined the main part of the office where was a coat stand, a chair with a broken leg which nobody had ever troubled to have repaired and a box of miscellaneous items such as dusters, India rubbers and the like. Mr Pardew turned the contents of the box over in his fingers for some time before finding precisely what he wanted.

When he returned to his desk some moments later he carried in one hand a short length of candle stuck into a saucer and in the other two slender half-cylinders of metal resembling the halves of a very slim pencil split lengthwise. Placing the candle on the desk-top and lighting it with a sulphur match from a box that lay nearby, Mr Pardew took the first of the metal cylinders between finger and thumb and held it to the flame. When it was quite black from the heat he withdrew it, laid it carefully on a sheet of blotting paper and performed the same manoeuvre with the second. A lick of air coursing in from beneath the locked door caused the candle to flare up and scorch his thumb, but such was Mr Pardew's absorption in his task that he paid it no heed. A short while later both of the metal cylinders, each stained black with carbon, lay side by side on the blotting paper before him. Seeing them there Mr Pardew frowned. Then, reaching into the drawer of his desk, he drew forth an ancient tobacco pouch, poked his fingers into it to ensure that no strands of tobacco remained within, and very gingerly, taking care to handle the cylinders only by their extremities, pushed them inside. Stowing the pouch in his coat-pocket, extinguishing the candle, drawing up the blind and unlocking the office door, Mr Pardew, having fastened the door once more behind him, set off at a rapid pace in the direction of Blackfriars.

*

Wm Barclay, Esq.,
Director,
South-Eastern Railway Company

Dear Sir,

I refer to your communication of the 14th inst., in which the directors, while declaring themselves perfectly satisfied with the arrangements for the conveyance of bullion to the Continent, requested further particulars with regard to the procedures at Folkestone.

The railway office is situated on the pier, under the supervision of Mr Chapman. This gentleman has been in the company's service for five years and we repose the greatest confidence in his abilities and general trustworthiness. There is in addition an assistant, Allman, and a clerk. Our regulations state that the office is to be manned at all times. However, on such occasions when the officials are obliged to meet the steamer the room is left unattended but with the door securely locked. I am informed by Mr Chapman that this period is rarely longer than a few moments' duration.

The safe key is, of course, kept locked up in a repository on the premises. The key to this in the sole possession of Mr Chapman.

I should add that in addition to the precautions here outlined the pier is patrolled by the police on a regular basis during the hours of daylight.

I shall be delighted to supply you with any further information that you or other members of the board may require.

Having the honour to remain your obedient servant

I am, sir, yours most faithfully

J. Harker

Secretary to the Board

*

A disinterested observer, travelling down to Dover by way of Folkestone on the train from London Bridge that afternoon, would perhaps have observed the following. Mr Pardew and his clerk stepped into their carriage together – indeed the latter held the carriage door open for the former – but it could not be deduced from these civilities that they knew one another, nor that they were connected by any object other than their journey. During this transit Mr Pardew read a newspaper, made calculations with a bit of old pencil in a notebook and grasped his stick with a remorselessness that suggested the slightest loosening of his grip would see it dance off down the corridor. Grace, alternatively, looked out of the window, admired a young lady in a muslin frock being escorted to the seaside by an old gentleman in a billycock hat and finally went to sleep with his mouth open, much to his employer's secret disgust.

At Folkestone, where the sea breeze blew in across the platform and the young lady in the muslin frock, looking delightfully fresh-cheeked, clutched her straw hat anxiously to her head, it could have been assumed that there was some slight relationship between them, for they set off together in the direction of the town – or rather Mr Pardew stalked a yard or two in front while Grace strolled meekly in his wake, Mr Pardew throwing back certain remarks over his shoulder which his clerk either did or did not catch depending on the severity of the breeze. In truth, as the train had left London Bridge the confidence which Mr Pardew habitually felt in his abilities had altogether deserted him. He was aware that the mission on which he was now embarked involved a considerable risk, and the thought frightened him. He was also aware that he could not allow himself to impart any of these misgivings to Grace. In this way, Mr Pardew brooding with his eyes seeming to bore into the very surface of the road, Grace moving jauntily through the crowds of people pressing back and forth from the esplanade, they came eventually to the Pavilion Hotel, where Mr Pardew, having checked his watch and assured himself that the steamer would not be docking for a further two hours, proposed that they might eat an early dinner. For myself, I like nothing better than to dine early on a day in summer in sight of the sea, but I do not think that Mr Pardew enjoyed his meal. Certainly he was surly with the waiter and, having eaten his broiled fowl, lapsed altogether into silence. Grace, on the other hand, gave every impression of relishing the food that was set before him, ordered an extra chop and sent word to the orchestra – the Pavilion is a select establishment – asking: would they play 'Garryowen'?

Presently a ship's horn sounded in the distance. Mr Pardew broke out of his reverie, looked suspiciously across the table as if he could not imagine how the plates, serving dishes and glasses had got there, called for the bill and paid it. As he and his companion strolled through the hotel foyer into the busy high street and thence in the direction of the pier, it could be observed that Grace's demeanour had altogether changed, that he kept close to his employer and that certain words were spoken of which he took precise note. The pier, when they came to it, was thronged with people: passengers for the steamer, with porters bringing their baggage behind them, townsfolk come to patronise the refreshment rooms. At the further end they could see the grey bulk of the steamer moving slowly towards its mooring place. Mr Pardew's spirits rose, for he knew that a crowd was as advantageous to his schemes as solitude.

At the same time the scheme was dependent on a precise set of circumstances whose existence he could not at all guarantee. Thinking to reconnoitre, and indicating to Grace that he should remain a short distance behind him, he moved forward along the pier, walking quickly but affecting to take an interest in the lemonade stalls and the souvenir shops. Five minutes spent in this way brought him to the railway office. Here the press of people was less great, enabling him without difficulty to observe that the outer door was ajar and that a clerk in a railway company uniform was stationed at a counter within. Having noted this fact, and then turned his head to examine the hovering gulls and the grey sweep of the sea, Mr Pardew proceeded a little further along the pier, almost to the point where the docking apparatus began and men in oilskins and woollen jerseys stood ready to set about their business. Here the line of shops and stalls gave way to bare deck and he was able to stand with his arms on the pier-rail (Grace, meanwhile, occupying a similar position a dozen yards away) apparently entranced by the heaving deeps before and beyond him, but in fact keeping one eye on the pier walk that he had just traversed. He had been there but a moment or so when two railway officials came walking up very rapidly towards the steamer. Mr Pardew waited another moment until they had passed, still staring out over the grey horizon, and then, lifting his face skywards with the expression of one who delights in the briny air, walked purposefully back in the direction he had come. As he had anticipated, he found the railway office shut up and the outer door firmly closed and locked. Observing that there were several people in the near vicinity, Mr Pardew made a great show of trying the door and feigning exasperation when it did not yield.

'Why it's too bad,' he exclaimed to Grace, who had taken up a position at the pier-rail. 'The place is closed.'

'We shall have to wait, I suppose,' Grace answered him. 'That's all there is to it.'

Having, as he saw it, established his *bona fides* – those of a traveller frustrated by the absence of officialdom – Mr Pardew lingered a foot or so in front of the heavy oak door. To anyone passing it would have seemed that he was studying a notice advertising sailing times and tariffs. In fact, Mr Pardew was examining the lock. This, as he had suspected, was a substantial affair but primitive, consisting of a narrow opening and a spindle, over which the hollow of the railway officials' key would fit like a glove over a finger. Round this spindle were eight iron sliders pressed forward to the mouth of the lock by a spring. Each slider, Mr Pardew knew from certain other investigations he had undertaken in this line, had a tiny knob whose position corresponded with a notch in the central spindle. The key, consequently, would push each slider back to the point where the knobs and notches were in line. Mr Pardew had no key, but, he assured himself, he had a means of establishing how such a key would operate. Still training his eye on the notice, but reaching the while into his inner pocket, he drew out the tobacco pouch and delved inside. Moving the metal cylinders into his hand, he slid first one then the other into the lock, then turned them slowly against the enclosing metal barrel until he felt them rub against the eight notches of the sliders.

'There is no sign of anybody,' Grace now called out to him. 'We had best away, I dare say.'

Mr Pardew nodded. With the pouch now stowed back in his coat pocket he stood back and took a last look at the notice. Then he sauntered across to join Grace at the rail and the two men walked back along the pier. Here they conducted a conversation which, had it been overheard by any passer-by, would doubtless have puzzled this eavesdropper by its obliquity.

'Smoked?' Grace enquired.

'A tolerable job, I think,' Mr Pardew allowed. 'I did not care to see whether the marks corresponded. We had better go somewhere out of the way and assure ourselves.'

'Mr File knows what he's about,' Grace remarked. 'And then if it don't fit exact, we can always sand it down.'

Mr Pardew laughed grimly at his clerk's presumption of expertise. 'As you say,' he observed, 'we can always sand it down.'

*

A BRIEF MEDITATION ON KEYS BY MR ROBT GRACE . . .

. . . We had come a fair way, I will allow, but not far enough. We had a key that would open the door of the railway office but that was all we had, and a day spent in there might not have been enough to get what we wanted. But then Mr P, as is a clever man, whatever else may be said of him, hit upon a plan. It was this: that he should send himself a box of a hundred golden sovereigns by the South-Eastern Railway to Folkestone, to be collected from the railway office on the harbour pier. This to be sent down at the weekend, when there was no shipment to Paris and the safe, as we reckoned, would travel straight back to town. This was done – I took the receipt myself for an old cash-box with the money in it – and Mr P goes down to Folkestone, in a frock-coat and a silk hat, for it's as well to play the gentleman in a game like this, to collect it back. A quiet Sunday forenoon, you understand, with the folks at church and no one about and just the one clerk – as Mr P had wagered – in the office. What has the clerk to do? Why, he has to get the cash-box from the safe, while Mr P stands and waits in the office. Nothing there for him to steal, is there? In any case Mr P's a fine gentleman in a silk hat and he ain't a-going to be taking halfpence out of the charity box is he? So the clerk fishes a key out of his pocket, unlocks a cupboard on the wall, takes out another key – this one opens the second lock of the safe – and goes off to do his duty. When he comes back, there's Mr P still a-standing at the counter looking as cool as you please. Opens up the box, looks over the gold, sees it's all there, signs another receipt and goes back to his 'otel. What the clerk don't know is that Mr P has the tin of green wax in his coat pocket with the line of the wall cupboard key pressed into it neat as neat.

We don't need no Mr File for that key, bless you. Any die-sinker as knows his trade could make you a twin brother of that in half an hour. So now we has the key to the door and the key to the cupboard where they keeps the thing we truly wants. Two weeks later Mr P and me are on our way to Folkestone again. It's remarkable how regular a gentleman like Mr P needs a touch of sea air to keep his spirits up, ain't it? To be sure, Pearce has been with us – that's a conniving scoundrel as I'm sure you'll know – and I've a railwayman's uniform over my arm. It don't fit me, but who's to know it's not mine eh? When we get to Folkestone Mr P asks for the use of a bedroom at an inn and I go up and put it on. As we come down we hear the boom of the steamer horn. Sure enough, hurrying along the pier in the dark it's to find the clerks gone and the office locked up. Well, Mr P gives me the key to the outer door and before you can say jingo I'm opening up the wall cupboard with the key that lies in its lock. There inside is the key to the safe lying on a little saucer as a man might lay a teacup on. Half a moment later and I'm outside again, looking very serious and official-like. Heavens, I even stop to tell an old lady the time of the next steamer sailing though my heart's jumping into my mouth all the time. Mr P has his tin to hand, to be sure, and before you can say jingo again I'm locking up the cupboard with it safe back inside. Then I fastens up the outer door and we're away off down the pier again like a couple of sports with nothing on their mind but the path to the beer 'ouse. And yet it was a narrow-run thing, sir – those clerks coming back from the steamer can't have missed us by more than a few minutes – and I wouldn't do it again for all the guineas in Christendom . . .

XXI

A Morning in the Life
of Captain McTurk

About halfway along Northumberland Avenue, not very far from Charing Cross Station, reached by means of a tight little archway whose ancient flagstones have veered this way and that like pieces of crazy paving, hard by a stable yard whose ostlers must be the least occupied in all London, in that they are never seen to move from the hay-strewn approach to their place of work, waiting for horses that never come, lies a tiny square composed of small buildings in lugubrious grey brick. In one of these, reached by means of two flights of gloomy stairs, a long polished oak corridor and an ante-room tenanted by a neat, side-whiskered secretary, sits Captain McTurk. The public these days has romantic notions of the senior officers of Her Majesty's Metropolitan Police Force. If they are not lithe-limbed young men with cold grey eyes capable of wresting a vital clue from a dung-heap at a second's glance, then they are pictur-esque, snuff-taking ancients, hearty and comfortable yet thinking nothing of pursuing the doughtiest villain across, let us say, a couple of rooftops to grapple with him finally upon the pinnace of St Paul's. Captain McTurk belonged to neither of these categories. He was a tall, somewhat spare man in middle age, clean-shaven, with hair cropped very close to his scalp and with a prominent chin that no amount of razoring would ever quite keep clear of stubble.

How Captain McTurk had conducted himself in his previous life nobody quite knew, but he had occupied his present position for nearly ten years and it was said that his criminal adversaries, those gentlemen whose portraits appear with such startling regularity in the *Police Gazette*, were very anxious that he should cease to occupy it.

The public these days has romantic notions of how the senior offi-cers of Her Majesty's Metropolitan Police Force spend their time. If they are not routing out continental revolutionaries from their nests among the Soho attics, then they are attending upon the Home Secretary and establishing the security of the Royal person against the attentions of sundry garrotters and pistol-wielding assailants. Again, Captain McTurk was engaged on neither of these duties. Just at this moment he was sitting in his room with a cup of tea on the deal table before him examining the pile of post which, neatly opened, assembled and docketed, had lately been brought in to him on a tray by his secretary.

There was no letter from the Home Secretary. In fact the topmost communication on the first pile that Captain McTurk turned his attention to consisted of a complaint concerning an old woman who kept a toll bridge at Chiswick, which missive I am afraid to say that he crumpled up with his hand and flung into a waste-paper basket. The second packet, however, interested him greatly, so much so that he pushed the tray to one side as a way of making sufficient space to inspect its contents. The packet – in truth a substantial parcel – had been addressed to Captain McTurk by the police superintendent of Suffolk. It contained a life-preserver, something over twelve inches in length, fashioned out of a wood that Captain McTurk could not identify, so thick was the layer of varnish, weighted with lead at one end so cunningly that it was almost impossible to determine where the wood ended and the lead began. All in all it was a fearsome-looking weapon. Seeking to test its efficacy, Captain McTurk picked it up in his right hand and tapped smartly on the surface of his desk. To his surprise, for he had put no force into the blow, the glass veneer of the desk broke instantly into a dozen fragments. After this Captain McTurk put the life-preserver back into its covering and applied himself to the letter which had accompanied it.

The weapon, he now learned, had been picked up by a farm labourer from beneath a bush on the road between Woodbridge and Wenhaston. Having seen nothing like it before, knowing that such things were not likely to be the property of respectable citizens yet unable to connect it to any misdemeanour of which he was himself aware, the Suffolk superintendent now offered it to Captain McTurk with his compliments. Putting down the letter and at the same time sweeping aside certain fragments of glass, Captain McTurk retrieved the life-preserver from its wrappings and turned it over once more in his hands. He too, though familiar with every kind of nefarious weaponry, had seen nothing like it before, but he was aware that a blow delivered with it to a human limb would result in fracture and a blow to a human skull most likely result in death. Still holding the life-preserver in his right hand, Captain McTurk picked up the letter once more and read again the names of Woodbridge and Wenhaston. He was conscious as he did so, without being in any way able to verify the sensation, of some memory stirring within him, of something that he had read or mused over that had some bearing – he did not quite know what – on this discovery. Having pondered this for a few moments more, he pressed a bell on the side of his desk and summoned his assistant in to attend him.

The assistant, whose name was Masterson, surveying the broken glass, but knowing that Captain McTurk was not generally prone to offer explanations of his behaviour, remarked merely:

'There seems to have been some kind of accident, sir.'

'Accident? I suppose there has been. You had better send someone up here with a broom.'

Masterson having promised that someone should be sent, Captain McTurk plucked the life-preserver out of its wrappings.

'Did you ever see anything like this before?'

The assistant, on whose forensic skills Captain McTurk was accustomed to rely, weighed the instrument in his hand.

'Well, no. I never did. It is foreign, I should say.'

'Would you now?'

'Well, I should doubt it was made in Shoreditch. Or anywhere else around London. Look at those hieroglyphics or whatever they are around the base. Where did it come from?'

Captain McTurk explained about the Suffolk superintendent and his discovery on the high road between Woodbridge and Wenhaston.

'Do you know where the London Library is in St James's Square?'

Masterson acknowledged that he did.

'Well perhaps you'd oblige me by stepping round there and seeing if they keep a file of the *Gentleman's Magazine*. Say from the December of three years past to the December of two. But it may be that my memory is at fault.'

Masterson remarked politely that he doubted it and went off on his errand. When he had gone, Captain McTurk locked the life-preserver inside a little safe which reposed in a cupboard on the far side of the room and contained a great deal of material evidence gathered over the years, while placing it metaphorically in a compartment in his mind where it could lie undisturbed but be hastily retrieved when the occasion demanded it, and went back to his letters. Outside the clock chimed eleven, the ostlers in the stable yard continued to linger in the most hopeful manner, a janitor climbed up from the depths of the establishment to clear away the smashed glass and shake his head at the destruction, but Captain McTurk paid none of them any heed. One leg twisted awkwardly over the other, a cigar smoking between his fingers, the bristle on his chin waxing bluer by the moment in the soft spring light that now began to infiltrate the room, he continued to tear through his correspondence and the packets that various of his subordinates had thought worthy of his attention.

At least a dozen other letters – letters relating to specious applications for tide-waiterships, letters from gentlemen who considered themselves grievously wronged by the activities of Captain McTurk's lieutenants – went the same way as the custodian of Chiswick Bridge, but the thirteenth packet Captain McTurk found himself considering with almost as much interest as the life-preserver. At this juncture the capital had fallen victim to a succession of fraudulent impostures. All over the City, it seemed, gentlemen had been cashing cheques they were not entitled to possess, drawn on accounts to which they were not party, using signatures which were not theirs to sign. A great commercial concern in the City Road had had one of its cheque books stolen and £1,500 lost in this way. A firm of solicitors in Hampshire had been pillaged of £800 after retrieving debts for a mysterious client, the cheques used to remit these debts found to be stolen and the client mysteriously absconded. By all of this Captain McTurk was much exercised. He believed that there was a pattern to it, but he could not yet establish what the greater dimensions of the pattern were. The case before him seemed particularly suggestive. A solicitor in Bermondsey had been asked to write a letter in pursuit of a debt of £100 owed to his client by a defaulting creditor. An address had been supplied by the client, the letter had been written and the money very soon remitted – paid in to the solicitor's bank account and a fresh cheque drawn in the name of the client. Then it was discovered that the first cheque was a forgery. The client, to whom representations were made, had by this time vanished from the face of the earth. The creditor's address, when visited by the solicitor, had turned out to be a tobacconist's shop, kept by an old woman who knew nothing whatever about it.

A thought occurred to Captain McTurk and, taking up his hat from where it lay on a stand near the door, he determined to act upon it. It was now the middle of the morning, and there seemed little chance that Masterson would return before noon. Accordingly Captain McTurk descended the two flights of stairs, nodded his head to the seneschal at the door, avoided the ambitious stares of the ostlers and walked out through the tight little archway to the street beyond. Here he summoned a cab and had himself driven away across the river towards the Borough and the address to which the original demand for payment had been despatched and from which the fraudulent cheque had subsequently been returned. It became apparent to Captain McTurk as the cab bowled through the remoter quarters of Southwark that he could not expect very much from this visitation, and in this assumption he was correct. The tobacconist's shop lay at the end of a street of shy little houses, hunched beneath the outer wall of a tanning factory about whose premises hung an indescribable stench. Within could be glimpsed certain melancholy appurtenances of the retail trade: a very little counter – no more than a trestle stretched between two boxes – displaying three or four dingy little tobacco tins, a half-bin of Lataika so friable and ancient that it might have been dried pure awaiting distribution to the strawberry fields, and a fierce, dirty, little old woman with her jaw wrapped up in a handkerchief against the toothache seated in a rocking chair from which the rockers had unaccountably become detached.

All this Captain McTurk saw in a glance, divining as he did so the absolute futility of any interrogation. Nonetheless he placed his hat on the counter, rolled around in his fingers a fragment of the Lataika from the bin – very dismal stuff it was, that crumbled away to nothing – looked up at a dangling cage with a stuffed jackdaw suspended in it and announced, first, that he was a police officer, and, second, that he believed the old lady's premises had lately been used as an accommodation address. Having received the old lady's cautious assent to this, Captain McTurk further deposed that certain letters had doubtless been received at the address, and wondered who had come to collect them. The old lady remarking that it was a shame she should be so worried when plagued with the toothache and that it was no the night in question, remembered assisting two gentlemen lately debouched from a railway carriage with what had seemed to him an inordinately heavy piece of baggage, but the hour was late and the gentlemen so caparisoned in travelling cloaks that he could recollect nothing of them. A cab-driver, too, recalled picking up two men – again with pieces of heavy luggage – and depositing them on the edge of the City. Again, he could remember nothing other than both were tall, one stout and one with a prognathous jaw. Finally there came a money-changer near Blackfriars to reveal that very early on the following morning he had changed into sterling a quantity of Napoleons offered to him by a burly man in a travelling cape speaking in a low voice and showing every indication of wishing to conclude the transaction as swiftly as possible. Though he gave no outward indication of disquiet, these three pieces of information excited Captain McTurk very much. He ensured that representations were made to others of the capital's money-changers. Banks were asked to examine their records for that day and the day following it in search of unusually large cash deposits. Nothing further came to light, however, and again the trail ran cold.

All these enquiries proceeded during the course of the summer. Though the sensation did not die down in nine or even ninety-nine days it could not, by its very nature, be maintained at the same high pitch. Polite society was by this time in any case decamped to Baden-Baden or taking its ease on the grouse moors. The public likes variation in the criminal accomplishments offered up for its delectation, and it was thought that the murder of a nobleman by certain burglars engaged in the plundering of his ancestral seat rather had the edge on the robbing of the Folkestone mail. All this was observed by Captain McTurk, who did not apparently take holidays, sitting in his office in the square beyond Northumberland Avenue, sending Mr Masterson out on his little errands and continuing to ponder the suggestions offered up by the day's post.

It must not be supposed that the other enterprises on which Captain McTurk had been engaged before the scandal of the bullion robbery had now been placed in abeyance. On the contrary, he continued to revolve them in his mind even as he sat attending to the Home Secretary's wrath or questioning the Folkestone ticket-collector. It could be said, in fact, that Captain McTurk's mind, or that part of it which did not contain his wife, family and acquaintance, was a single stage

343

populated by an ever-shifting cast of criminal actors, this one now moving audaciously into the light to say his lines, that one now subsiding gently into a throng of scene-swellers. To this end he had continued to take an interest in the death of Mr Henry Ireland, had summoned a craftsman who might know something of the manufacture of life-preservers and sent Mr Masterson once more to Suffolk with instructions to submit all the evidence in the case to the closest re-inspection. At the same time he had recalled to mind the circumstances of certain other murders in which gentlemen had been bludgeoned to death. None of this, however, was of the slightest avail. The craftsman, bidden from his workshop in Mile End, shook his head over the bludgeon, agreed that it was a remarkable piece, speculated that it might have come from Prague or the region of the Danube, but could say no more. Mr Masterson, though he spent a further week in Woodbridge and retraced his steps along the Wenhaston Road, was unable to add to the stack of lore he had brought back from his previous visit.

And then there came to Captain McTurk a stroke of luck of the kind that were it to arise in a work of fiction would have mesdames and messieurs the critics wagging their fingers at its improbability but that is nevertheless a welcome concomitant to many an official inquiry. The public had lately become somewhat exercised by the imputation of dishonesty to certain representatives of the metropolitan force charged with the supervision of police cells. It had been alleged, to put the matter bluntly, that no watch, wallet or personal item placed in the pocket of a suspect left in such accommodation at dusk was likely to be there at dawn, and an evening newspaper had caused much amusement by suggesting that any citizen who wished to know the time should hasten right away to a police constable, as that gentleman was certain to be in possession of a watch-and-chain. Captain McTurk had, of course, read these claims, or rather they had been shown to him, and been made angry by them. He did not dispute that some of them were true, but by no means all of them he thought, and he determined when the chance fell to him to conduct certain investigations of his own.

Wandering one night through that part of the station headquarters in which prisoners are confined, he happened to encounter a constable who, it seemed to him, was very anxious to make his way past him along the corridor as quickly as he could. It seemed also to

344

Captain McTurk that, as he came upon him, the man was in the act of transferring some hard, glinting object from his hand to the pocket of his coat. Demanding that the object – as he had foreseen, a watch – should be given up to him, Captain McTurk rebuked the constable and took the contraband up to his room to examine it at leisure. It was a large gold repeater watch, very cunningly wrought and not at all the kind of thing generally to be on display in the labyrinths beneath Northumberland Avenue. But Captain McTurk was less interested in the watch's provenance than in the inscription engraved on its reverse side. This reproduced the name of the gentleman who had originally owned it and the name was *Henry Ireland, Esq.* Having read this, the police commissioner put the watch down on the desk-top before him and whistled sharply through his teeth. He was not so sanguine as to believe that the discovery of Henry Ireland's watch would offer him any immediate clue as to how it had been taken from its owner, but he knew that in however small a way the trail had been renewed.

The prisoner from whom the object had been abstracted was fetched from his cell, brought wonderingly into Captain McTurk's office and ordered to give an account of himself. He was a miserable and wretched-looking specimen who, Captain McTurk now saw from the charge sheet conveniently provided for him by the former's escort, had been arrested for loitering in a somewhat suggestive manner, together with a package containing two files and a chisel, about the area steps of a house in Notting Hill Gate. His account of how he had come by the watch was offered up with no apparent hesitation. He had been engaged at cards with certain acquaintances of his in a tavern at New Cross, and had won very heavily off one of these acquaintances who, declaring himself short of ready money, offered him the watch in payment. What was this man's name, Captain McTurk demanded, his gestures implying, if they did not exactly guarantee, that a softer view might be taken of the files and the chisel were a satisfactory answer to be received. The man thought that his name might have been Pearce, and that he was in addition perhaps five feet nine inches tall and wore a whitish-coloured great-coat. As to the address at which he might be found or what ravens fed him, the man at first professed himself ignorant, but then, thinking perhaps of the files and the chisel and the awful proximity of his person to the cell where the constable's hand had fallen upon his shoulder, suggested that he believed he might previously have been an employee

345

of the South-Eastern Railway Company. This fact, though Captain McTurk inscribed it dutifully on the sheet of paper before him, did not immediately strike him as significant, but a description of Pearce was circulated to each police station in the metropolitan district.

And then, within the fortnight, came a second stroke of luck. The public, whose sensibilities at this time appeared to be in a state of permanent crisis, had also been exercised by the dreadful preponderance of illegal boxing matches. Three thousand persons, it was maintained, had recently assembled in some quiet Surrey field to watch the Tutbury Pet belabour the Dorking Chicken for a prize of a hundred guineas, despoiling the crops and trampling down the very fence-posts in their eagerness to surround the ring. It was known in the county that a rematch of this Herculean encounter (the Chicken feeling rightfully aggrieved by his initial defeat and demanding satisfaction) would take place in a secluded corner of Epsom Downs. Infiltrating the course – from which the protagonists had already been spirited away in cabs – the police were concerned only to disperse the crowd that had gathered. In doing so they were obstructed by a drunken man who, protesting that he had had £20 on the match and was d——d if he would see it taken from him, eventually became so obstreperous that he was hustled off into custody. The man's name, it was now determined, was Pearce. Additionally, a search of his clothing produced not only a quantity of banknotes but a pair of Louis Napoleons. Both these discoveries were immediately communicated to Captain McTurk. There may of course be excellent reasons as to why a man found drunk on Epsom Downs should carry such coins in his pocket, but Captain McTurk, cynic that he was, thought otherwise. Pearce was ordered to be sent up to London in a police carriage under escort. Captain McTurk, to whom the coins had come in advance, placed them on the table before him together with Mr Ireland's watch and began to wonder, as he could hardly fail to do, whether the two might not have some very singular connection.

XXV

Esther in London

She sat on the edge of her seat in the corner of the third-class railway carriage and watched as the train rolled slowly into King's Cross Station. Dense vapour blew down over the grey platforms on either side of her, altogether obscuring the mighty overhang of stanchions and red brick, and for a moment she wished that she might not ever have to leave the carriage, which now seemed to her a very safe and comfortable refuge. Then, as the smoke began slowly to clear and the train juddered almost to a halt, this feeling left her and she glanced out of the window at the moving figures now revealed behind the glass. There were but few of these – a guard in a peaked cap with a red flag stuck into his jacket pocket, a pale-faced old lady clutching a small child by the hand, sundry boys and lookers-on – but she stared at them with a curious intentness, supposing that the secrets of London, where she had never come before, must surely lie within their grasp. The carriage was empty and Esther, realising that she had raised her knuckles to her mouth, such was the extent of her nervousness, was glad that there was no one to see her. From somewhere near at hand a whistle sounded and all around her could be heard a tramping of feet and a slamming of doors. A silent and solitary figure amidst this cacophony of noise and movement, Esther reached up to the rack above her head for her luggage, released the catch of the door with her free hand and stepped down onto the platform.

Caught up instantly in the throng of people leaving the train, she darted anxious glances at those who moved alongside her, wondering if any of them knew her for what she was: a servant who had thrown over her place and disappeared without leave. The anonymity of her situation reassured her – she had half expected to find a policeman on the platform waiting to summon her back – and she perceived that she was merely a girl in a brown dress with a canvas satchel strapped across her shoulders and a travelling bag dragging at her feet (she had left the unwieldy trunk at the Hall), one of countless similar girls in whom she imagined the metropolis abounded. The thought of this solidarity cheered her and she reviewed, for perhaps the twelfth time that day, the circumstances of her flight from Easton: waking before sunrise, her things concealed in the scullery the evening before; stealing down the back-staircase in grey, unearthly light; abstracting the key from the ring in Mr Randall's pantry to let herself out of the kitchen door into the silent dawn, her feet and the marks of the handcart leaving a trail on the dew-drenched grass. She supposed that Mr Randall, alone among the Hall's servants, would regret her passing and she brooded on this for a moment, conscious, however, that the Hall and its people had already begun to pass from her imagination and that her mind had begun to occupy itself with other things. On the wall above her was a poster advertisement showing a man in a tall hat and a morning coat drinking from a glass, and she marvelled at this thing, ten feet high, that stood in a public place inviting her, and those that passed with her, to admire it. Something in the man's gorgeous apparel – the set of his collar or his magnificent waistcoat – reminded her of William in his footman's uniform, and she added this to her store of imaginings and anticipations. And so, with the travelling bag bumping behind her and the dust from the platform hanging about her dress and forearms, yet intrigued and for the most part delighted by what she saw, Esther came at last to the station concourse.

Here, momentarily, her courage failed her again. Never in her life, she thought, had she seen so many people gathered together in one place or moving so rapidly about their business. Behind her three or four great engines smoked and steamed at the buffers. Porters ran on all sides propelling trucks of baggage. Before her lay almost a thoroughfare of coffee stalls, newspaper kiosks, barbers' premises, shoe-shiners' stocks and the like. Before her, arranged beneath blue-grey air, she could see the immensity of London – a vista of tall buildings and church towers moving away behind the teeming street. The effect on her consciousness was so bewildering that she hesitated to venture out into this turbulent world, electing for a moment to stand quietly by one of the coffee stalls, drink a cup of tea and ponder her next course. William had advised her to engage a cab, but this, even with the quarter's wages she had hoarded in her purse, was not something she could bring herself to do. She supposed that she should take an omnibus. The question was: which? Below the steps of the station was an expanse of stone pavement where half a dozen stood drawn up, their drivers and conductors recruiting themselves with tea, and this caravanserai she now timidly approached.

'Excuse me, sir. Can you tell me how I may get to the Strand?'

The demureness of her expression and the downward cast of her eyes as she asked the question commended themselves to the official.

'You want this one here, miss, as goes to the Eastcheap. Mind your skirts now, as you steps aboard.'

Again, as she sat on the lower deck of the omnibus with the straw rustling beneath her boots, looking back at the towers and pinnaces of the station, a memory stirred within her – of the evening when she had first come to Easton Hall, of walking with her bag across the hill as the twilight rose and settled around her, and the dust-motes rising up from the chalk path to strike her skirt, and of the faces turning to greet her as she came into the kitchen. Again, though, the outline quickly receded, like a dream that vanishes from the somnam-bulist's mind on the very moment of waking, to be replaced by the tall figure of William smoking his pipe as he lounged against the fence and saluting her as she passed by. And so she sat, as it seemed to her, very comfortably on her seat in the omnibus, joined presently by two workmen who chaffed her about her luggage and asked her was she running away to marry a marquis? She ate a bun that she had purchased from the coffee stall, was carried away into the heart of the city and ceased for a moment to think of Easton Hall. The books that her mother had given her banged together in the bag at her feet but she did not register that they were there. They were merely things that she carried with her, things that she would always carry. As to what her mother might think of what she was doing, the strictures that she could imagine her pronouncing left no impression. Her mind was too full, too crammed with the sensations stirred by her journey and the thought of what would await her at its end.

Quitting the omnibus at the bottom of the Strand – she knew that it was the Strand for she had taken the advice of the conductor – she stood by a cab-rank staring at the tall buildings set back from the road, wondering who inhabited them and what went on within their walls. All kinds of people and vehicles passed her as she lingered – gentlemen in tall hats, inky boys with bundles of newspapers under

349

their arms, clerks moving in and out of office doorways, costermen with their barrows – and she followed the ebb and flow of the crowd for a moment with her eye before once more taking out William's letter to study. This directed her, as she knew – for she had read it a dozen times – to a public house in Wellington Street named the Green Man, where she should ask for him at the bar and he could be sent for. Wellington Street, a passer-by advised her, was very near. Accordingly she fastened the satchel once more about her shoulders and, dragging the travelling case once again at her heels, set off along the dusty pavement. Her nervousness, she realised, had been replaced by a feeling of calm satisfaction: that her route had fallen out as William had predicted, that everything was where he had said it would be. It did not occur to her to wonder if he would be there to greet her or what she should do if he were not. She could see him in her mind's eye, just as she could see the dome of St Paul's a mile and a half distant rising into the azure sky.

Wellington Street was empty of people. The Green Man stood at its further end, and Esther, crossing the pavement to its open doorway, stared for a moment into its dark interiors, where a fat man stood at the bar caulking a barrel. As she entered, two or three other men sitting by the door turned to stare at her and she became aware of her face reddening. Never mind! William should come soon and they would stare at her no longer.

'Yes, miss?' the fat man wondered.

'I was told to ask here for Mr Latch.'

'He's not been in today, miss, but the boy can be sent. Hi, Joey!' There was a commotion from the passage behind the bar and a boy of perhaps twelve years of age with a strawberry birthmark half covering his face stuck his head through the doorway. 'Take yerself off to Shooter's Buildings – yer know the place – and tell Mr Latch there's a party asking for him at the bar. And now, miss, what will you take?'

Esther accepted a glass of lemonade and took it to a table that looked out through green glass windows to the street. She had finished half of it when there was a rush of boots upon stone and William came marching into the bar with the boy Joey loping at his heels.

'Why, Esther! So it is you! I am very glad to see you.'

He came over and stood by the table, as if uncertain how best to greet her, finally extending his hand for her to shake.

'I am very glad to see you, William.'

Looking at him as he stood before her, Esther noted the change in his appearance since they had last met. He was clad in a suit of black cloth, which she could see was a good suit made by a competent tailor, and the white stock around his throat was freshly ironed. In addition there was a white carnation in his buttonhole. He had put on more flesh, she believed, indeed was better complexioned since the days when she had watched him running into the drawing room at Easton Hall or bringing in Mr Dixey's parcels from the gig. William guessed the angle of her thoughts.

'They're a good set of duds ain't they, Esther? I fancied you should like them. But what's that you're drinking? Lemonade? Come, you should have something better on a day such as this. What shall it be?'

Esther consented to take a glass of porter.

'Something stronger, miss?' said the fat man, when the order was conveyed to him. 'Mr Latch drinks Irish.'

'Porter will do very well,' Esther replied.

'This is my friend Miss Spalding,' William said. He drank the whiskey in a series of gulps. 'Excellent stuff! But it don't do to have too much of it in the afternoon, eh? Now, Esther, you must tell me about yourself and the doings at the Hall. How are Mr Randall and Mrs Finnie, I wonder? And Sarah?'

As Esther explained about Sarah's disappearance, William composed his features into a look of suitable gravity.

'Run away hey? That's bad, that is. Run away and you get no reference. But then, you have done the selfsame thing. You're looking uncommon well, Esther.'

'I have nothing to complain of,' Esther said, to whom the enormity of her departure from Easton Hall had now become apparent.

'That's the ticket. We understand each other, Esther, you and I. As for myself, I'm doing pretty well. Mr Pardew – I have told you about Mr Pardew? – is pleased with me and says I shall do well if I stick to it. And Bob Grace – that's Mr Pardew's man-of-all-work – and me are regular pals. It's hard for a chap when he comes to a strange place full of things that he's not used to, but I fancy I shall make my mark in the end.'

Listening to these remarks, Esther was aware that the confidence William had shown in his abilities when they had talked together at Easton Hall had increased in the six months that they had been apart. Rather than alarming her, as being evidence of vainglory that could only lead to a fall, she was conscious that she approved of his delight in his success and wished, in so far as she could do so, to share it.

'You do seem very prosperous,' she told him, with her hand on the glass of porter.

'Ah, but you only ever saw me before in my footman's togs. Ugh, how I hate to think of them. But look, what say we go to my place? It's not much to be sure, but I shall be getting an apartment before too long.'

Esther nodded. There was a meaningfulness about his voice that she could not fail to apprehend, but she gladly allowed him to pick up her baggage and escort her out into Wellington Street. Turning into a lane of small shops and dreary office buildings, he led her eventually to a house whose lower window advertised rooms to let. William, who had said nothing during the course of their journey, now let fall the baggage and turned to her.

'I suppose you know,' he remarked, 'why we are come here?'

Again, Esther nodded her head.

*

Later they lay in a room beneath the eaves of the house, where pigeons clacked at the window and from beyond could be heard the implacable drone of the city.

'What a noise those birds make,' Esther said suddenly.

'Regular little nuisances they are. Like rats with wings. And never quiet. Not like the owls at Easton.' William was silent for a moment. 'What would old Randall say if he could see us now? Probably give us each a tract, eh?'

Despite her respect for Mr Randall, the image that this conjured up in her mind was too much to be borne and Esther laughed.

'Probably stand over us and fire off a regular prayer,' said William, rather less amiably.

'I'm sure,' Esther said, more demurely than she intended, 'that he would see nothing he had not seen before.'

'Nothing he hadn't seen! What do you know about it, Miss Pert?'

'I am not Miss Pert! And you should not mock Mr Randall.'

'And what about you?' William persisted, making a grab for the coverlet of the bed. 'What have you seen that you never saw before?'

352

'Nothing to startle me. Men always think that a girl has no notion of the world.'

'Well – perhaps they do. Hold on though, it is gone six and I have a fellow to see at eight. We had better go and eat, Esther.'

But Esther had her own ideas about this. William's fireplace, she noticed, contained several utensils, while the cupboards gave notice of one or two things that could be drunk or eaten.

'I could cook something for us,' she said, getting to her feet and standing uncertainly in the centre of the room, 'if you cared to eat it.'

'That's my good girl,' William said.

Presently there came the sound of a kettle boiling and the jingle of cutlery. William looked approvingly on.

*

The next day was one of the pleasantest that Esther ever remembered having spent. She woke late, with bright sunshine streaming in through the window and the sound of music in the street below. It was a bank holiday, said William, whom she now saw staring at himself in a fragment of mirror, a razor halfway to his chin, and they could do as they pleased. The sight of William shaving reminded her of the situation in which she found herself and she lay for a moment considering it, recalling certain scenes of the previous day to mind and taking pleasure in their remembrance. Was there anywhere that she would care to go, William persisted? Esther sat on the bed considering. The values of the city both fascinated and repelled her: she had not the faintest idea, as yet, of how time could be spent there or how people amused themselves.

'I think I should like to walk about,' she said, 'and see the people.'

William nodded, which as the lower half of his face was covered with soap produced a very comical effect.

'See them you shall,' he said. 'Why there will be thousands of them out on a day like this, I shouldn't wonder.'

Esther's clothes lay on a chair at the foot of the bed. Seeing her gaze move towards them, William became self-conscious. 'I have to see a chap at the Green Man for a moment,' he explained, scraping the final twist of lather from his chin and pulling on his jacket. 'There's water here in the jug you know.'

Glad of his consideration, Esther waited until he had gone and then

353

washed and dressed herself, examining the contents of William's chamber as she did so. In truth there was not a great deal to see – a few prints of racehorses that hung on the walls, a wardrobe containing his clothes and a pile of what she supposed to be business papers seemed to be the extent of his possessions. On a shelf above the fire-place she found a piece of cloth that she recognised as having fallen from her apron-string six months before. The realisation that William had hoarded this memento and taken it with him to London produced in her the queerest sensation and she sat down on the bed once more with her dress only half-buttoned to brood upon it. It was here that William found her ten minutes later as he sauntered into the room with his hat cocked back on his head and a sporting newspaper in his hand.

'Here's a stroke of luck,' he said. 'Who'd have thought the Tin Man would have won the Gold Cup after all that was said about him?' His gaze moved downward. 'Why, what's the matter, Esther? Sorry you're here?'

'Not in the least,' said Esther truthfully and hastily buttoning up her dress. 'Is that a horse that you had money bet on, William?' she enquired timidly.

'You sound like old Randall. It was just a trifle, and now I have a couple of sovereigns to spend today.'

Esther said that she was glad of it, and holding his arm descended into the street. Here it was as William had predicted. A great crowd of people swarmed here and there across the pavements bent on pleasure. The noise of the German band playing in the street grew louder and the public houses had already opened their doors. They breakfasted at a pastrycook's – a very gay pastrycook's, with little Saturnalian rosettes decorating the trays of tarts and muffins – and wandered in the vicinity of Covent Garden for a while. Then, almost without realising that they were a part of it, they were caught up in a throng of people moving through the dusty roads in the direction of Holborn Viaduct.

'What do you say, Esther?' William demanded. 'Shall we take a train and go to the Palace?' The look of bewilderment on Esther's face prompted him to explain. 'The Crystal Palace. There's grounds to walk round and the glasshouse to see if you've a mind.'

Esther thought that she would very much like to see the Crystal Palace, yet the size of the crowd on the station platforms frightened her. Men and women, all dressed in their holidaying clothes, with small children dragging at their heels, flocked around her with such eagerness to be off that she was thankful for William's protection. A man with a corked bottle protruding from his coat pocket stumbled into her and William tapped him on the shoulder and told him that if he played that trick again he should knock him into next week, see if he didn't. Then, all of a sudden, the train drew in and William was pushing her, much to her alarm, into a first-class carriage, where he remarked that it was a public holiday, was it not, and he should like to see the ticket collector as could turn them out. They sped away over the rooftops of South London, the universal glare of sunlight about them, the carriage dense with tobacco smoke, and Esther, nestling in the crook of William's arm, thought that she had never felt such delight.

Everything about Crystal Palace – or 'the paliss' as the other people in the carriage referred to it – impressed her. She marvelled at the grounds and the promenade, and the fair to which William escorted her, above which a white cloud of dust already hung kicked up by the multitude of feet, seemed to her even more splendid than the fairs of Norfolk. William, she noted happily, was all indulgence, standing at her side as she shyed for coconuts and handing her gallantly out of the whirligig into which they had ventured.

'I declare that's game of you,' William pronounced. 'Being flung about like a parcel in the back of a donkey cart. Tired are you? Well, I shall be glad to sit down, as there's a fellow or two as half-promised to look me up.'

The realisation that the trip had been in William's mind all along, rather than – as she had first presumed – something presented to her which she could accept or decline, did not distress her. It seemed proper to her that William should have things that he wished to do and schemes that he wished to prosecute even in the midst of this new life. So she went very happily with him to the shilling tea-room to be regaled with tea, bread, butter and cake in hunches, while William skirmished dextrously for milk-jugs and sugar basins and such items that needed almost to be fought for among the crowded tables. At the heart of the throng went serving girls, twisting this way and that through the tumult with trays piled high with crockery, and Esther sympathised with them in their plight.

'It's a shame those girls have to work on a day such as this,' Esther said.

'I daresay. Why look! That is Mr Grace coming now. And Dewar with him.'

'Who is Dewar?'

'Why he's a little fellow that works on the railway. Tremendously down in the mouth, you know.'

The two men, having ascertained through the crowd where they sat, were now bearing down upon them. Grace, Esther saw, was a big burly man, quite unlike his name, and wearing a dark suit that she thought must stifle him in the heat of the day. Dewar, who trailed behind him in the manner of a factotum, was shorter and stouter, with a crestfallen, woebegone face beneath hair that had at some point in its history been dyed.

'Why, Latch, taking the air I see,' said Grace affably to William, and then, nodding at Esther in a way that suggested he knew all about her, 'pleased to make your acquaintance, miss.'

William caught the eye of a waiter, more chairs were brought and the four of them sat down together, William and Grace immediately falling into a subdued conversation that Esther could not for the life of her comprehend. The afternoon sun, she now saw, had reached its zenith, there was a band playing in the middle distance beneath the walls of glass that sparkled in the glare, the crowd in the tea-room had somewhat diminished, and this, together with her own fatigue, gave her the feeling of one plunged into a state halfway between wakefulness and dreaming. A woman of about her own age wearing a yellow frock cut very low and with a little boy clinging to her skirts came hastily into the room, looked about her for a moment, swore in vexation at not finding the person she sought and then hastened out again, and Esther wondered at the sorrow in her face and her corn-coloured hair. Dewar, she noticed, said nothing. Now and again Grace would look up from his talk with William and address a remark to him, whereupon Dewar would nod or shake his head as the occasion demanded: no other response did he care to make. He seemed utterly cast down.

'How's your wife, Dewar?' Grace flung out at one of these junctures.

'Bad as bad,' Dewar rejoined shortly.

'Mind you take her something home then,' Grace said, not unkindly, and went back to his deliberations.

Something about Dewar's miserable face and the set of his lank hair awakened a memory in Esther and she said:

'Did I not see you before, Mr Dewar? You came once to Easton Hall I believe.'

Dewar turned to look at her as if he had only now seen her for the first time. 'I believe that I did, miss,' he said, and both of them were silent, she remembering the linen draped over the currant bushes as he went, he recalling Mr Dixey in his study and the mouse stirring in his palm.

'But your wife is ill, they say?'

'I'm afraid she is, miss. Very bad.'

'Has she not anyone to look after her?'

'There's Mrs Hook as lives above us promised to give her a bit of dinner. And then I shall be back by seven, I hope. But you're right, miss, it's a poor look-out for her.'

He seemed anxious to say something more, only for Grace suddenly to tug at his shoulder.

'And you'll mark the time you're to be on the look-out, Dewar. Late afternoon – or never.'

Dewar said he would mark it. Grace, his professional obligations apparently at an end, took another cup of tea prior to his and Dewar's departure and said that he hoped Esther was enjoying herself. 'Yes indeed, sir, very much,' she replied. The three men laughed good-naturedly at her simplicity and Grace bowed and said he hoped he would have the pleasure of meeting her again. The afternoon wore on. So much dust rose up above the fairground that it was as if a white cloud hung above the heads of the coconut-shyers and those who swung crazily on the pleasure-boats. There was dancing upon the grass in which William was eager to take part but Esther found herself too weary to do anything save cling to his arm. And so, by slow degrees, they came to the station and the train that would return them to Holborn.

There was but one embarrassment between them. It came as they sat in William's room in Shooter's Buildings and Esther, leaning over the fire to adjust the tea-kettle, remarked:

'If you'll direct me, William, there is a letter I must deliver in the morning.'

'A letter? What sort of a letter?'

'It was give to me by Mrs Ireland. Mr Dixey's ward that you must remember.'

'Certainly I remember Mrs Ireland,' William said, somewhat sharply. 'Who has she been writing to?'

Esther explained the circumstances of the letter's composition, William listening intently from his position on the sofa. He was especially interested in the mention of Mr Crabbe's name.

'That's a fellow Mr Pardew has dealings with. No end of a swell, that has a house in Belgravia. Grace knows all about it. But see here, Esther, it won't do. There's some mystery here as I won't be charged with the unravelling of.' There was a curious tone in his voice, Esther discerned, as if he knew more of Mrs Ireland than he cared to reveal. 'You had best give it up, indeed you had. Where is the letter?'

Wordlessly Esther went over to the travelling bag which contained her mother's books and the little packet of documents – a letter from Lady Bamber, a 'character' from a former employer – that she referred to as her 'papers'. It occurred to her that for reasons which she could not yet determine William wished to destroy the letter, and that if she wished to serve Mrs Ireland's interests she must deceive him. This thought did not distress her. She merely accepted it as one of the necessary subterfuges that her situation demanded of her.

'What shall I do with it?' Esther wondered, bending over her bag.

'You had better throw it in the fire. Or wait – let me see it. Never mind, that will do very well.'

For Esther, seizing an envelope from the bundle that she held in her hand, had cast it into the flames.

'I should not like to offend Mr Pardew, you understand,' William said, feeling that some explanation was required for this piece of high-handedness.

'Certainly not.'

'Grace says he is a real tartar at such times. You ain't cross with me, Esther, I hope?'

Esther, knowing that the letter lay concealed among her papers while the note from Lady Bamber burnt to blackness in the flames, shook her head.

*

Easton Hall ran through her dreams. Each night her imagination dwelt upon some aspect of her time there, twisting what she knew to have been real into ominous, phantom shapes. Sarah and she were running through the wood pursued by some silent, fleet-footed creature that burst out on them continually from the trees. The Master, turning to speak to her in the drawing room, had no face beneath his tall hat. Mrs Ireland, sitting in her chamber, changed suddenly into a great bird that flew blindly at the window and scored its beak across the pane.

William suffered no such hallucinations. He said:

'No, I don't think of the Hall. Why should I, unless it's to remember old Randall prosing and that cat Mrs Finnie making herself disagreeable? It was a place I had that I threw over – that's all! As for being a footman, why if you offered me a pair of yellow plush breeches and a cockade for my hat, I'd laugh in your face. There's other things in life than holding a door open for ladies as has come to call, or running up three flights of stairs with the master's shaving water.'

And Esther could not gainsay him.

XXVI

Thoroughness of Mr Masterson

It was at about this time that Captain McTurk came upon a piece of information – to be exact, several pieces of information – that interested him very greatly. Some months had now elapsed since the audacious robbery upon the South-Eastern Railway, and many another crime had risen to enflame the imagination of the public, but still Captain McTurk was sanguine of his ability to extract – something – from the mystery. He knew – long experience had taught him – that there are many ways in which a guilty man may be induced to declare his guilt. He was aware, too, that very pertinent and significant pieces of evidence may not be immediately available to authority's investigating eye. Consequently, Captain McTurk kept his counsel and busied himself, in the midst of half a hundred other matters, with what he believed might be a useful line of enquiry – that is, establishing what had become of the very considerable sums of bullion abstracted during the course of the theft.

These, he had been able to confirm from Messrs Abell, Spielmann and Bult, consisted of a quantity of gold bars, a nearly equal number of Louis Napoleons and a somewhat smaller amount of American eagles. Of the gold bars, Captain McTurk almost instantly washed his hands. Contraband of this nature, he knew, would be melted down, reconstituted and disposed of in half a dozen ingenious ways: whatever the nature of the transformation it was now beyond his grasp. But the Louis Napoleons and the eagles he thought he might do something with. Accordingly Mr Masterson was sent out into the City, instructed to renew the familiar acquaintance he enjoyed with certain major-domos of counting houses and banking establishments and urged to solicit their opinion with regard to certain transactions that these gentlemen might have witnessed in the course of the preceding two months.

Mr Masterson, though he went about this task with his customary efficiency, was, if truth be known, less sanguine than his superior. He himself did not believe that the money was in London. He thought it was in Paris, Dresden, New York – in any city where it could be passed through the banking system with the least remark. But he was a thorough man and he followed the instructions with which he had been entrusted to the letter. For a considerable part of that autumn, in fact, as the leaves fell on the grass of legal courts and inns and were gathered up in Charterhouse Square, as the lamps were lit earlier and earlier and the mud grew in the streets, Mr Masterson went diligently about his business, and in the course of these enquiries he found – something. A bank in Gutter Lane, a most respectable establishment, indeed a bank with which Captain McTurk dealt in his private capacity, but not one engaged in much foreign business, had at some point in the late summer received into its safe-keeping a considerable quantity of Napoleons. Mr Masterson's heart was not immediately uplifted by this intelligence, for he knew that there are many excellent reasons why an Englishman should think it prudent to pay foreign currency into an English bank, but he was sufficiently interested to enquire of his informant in Gutter Lane who had done the depositing. Learning that the customer was the legal firm of Crabbe & Enderby of Lincoln's Inn, Mr Masterson, though not a little awed by the lustre attaching to the name and reputation of Mr Crabbe, decided that an investigation had better be made.

As it happened Mr Crabbe was away, attending upon some grand nobleman at his estate, but an obliging young clerk, himself not a little awed by the lustre attaching to the name and reputation of Mr Masterson, looked into the matter and reported that the money had apparently (although it seemed that there was some faint mystery about this) been received from a firm of engineers in the north of England in settlement of a debt owed to one of Crabbe & Enderby's clients. And here Mr Masterson did prick up his ears, for he knew that the debts of engineering firms in the north of England are generally paid in coin or notes of the realm. However, he did not remark this fact, but, having obtained from Mr Crabbe's clerk the name of his client, he hurried back to Northumberland Avenue.

'The firm whose debt the money was intended to settle is called Pardew & Co.,' he explained to Captain McTurk, as they sat in the gloomy office looking out over the stableyard. 'A bill discounter, I believe, somewhere in the City.'

Although the name of Pardew was familiar to Captain McTurk, he did not immediately choose to advertise this fact. Instead he contented himself with enquiring:

'What was the name of the creditor?'

'A firm of engineers at Sheffield, I believe. Messrs Antrobus & Co.'

'Hm. Just oblige me, Masterson, would you, by stepping down to the reading room and bringing a commercial directory? Of the northern counties, if there is one.'

Mr Masterson did as he was bidden. The commercial directory was a large and compendious volume, but, as both men had suspected, it contained no mention of Messrs Antrobus & Co. Whereupon Captain McTurk became intrigued, slapped his hand upon his thigh, shut his door, placed his feet upon the table and cast his mind back to a case that had occupied him at an earlier stage of his tenure in Northumberland Avenue and which interested him very much.

*

'Well, I have heard from Farrier,' Mr Devereux remarked to John Carstairs at about this time.

'Have you indeed? It must be a great trouble to him to answer his letters.'

'It was more a case of the letter finding him. He has had the most tremendous adventures, I believe. Lost in a blizzard with his ankle broke, a wolf on his tail and the sled with his friends on plunged into the frozen river and all of them drowned.'

'You don't say?'

'He was found half-frozen in the snow and sent back east to recover himself – see here! I believe he writes from Montreal – and the letter reached him there. But the upshot is that he declares himself most interested to read it and, having settled one or two matters to his satisfaction, intends to return home within the month.'

Mr Devereux and John Carstairs sat in the former's shabby chamber in Cursitor Street. Some little time had elapsed since John Carstairs had visited the premises and the room seemed to him yet more sunk into decay. The bust of Lord Eldon boasted a layer of dust so thick that some enterprising person could, had he wished, have reached out and written his name on that jurist's august forehead, while the floor, quite half of which was carpeted with old legal reviews and law books, seemed to make a positive virtue of its untidiness. Mr Devereux, on the other hand, was more cheerful than ever, and poked up his fire and arranged his papers on his desk as if half a dozen clerks laboured in the broom cupboard and a ducal chariot lay drawn up at the kerb outside.

'Well,' said John Carstairs, taking a look in quick succession at Lord Eldon, Mr Devereux's variegated carpet and the somewhat cheerless prospect of Cursitor Street, 'that settles it I suppose.'

'Settles it? I would hardly go so far as to say that. What exactly does it settle?'

It may as well be admitted that the resources of John Carstairs' mind were not concentrated on Mr Devereux with the attention that was perhaps the lawyer's due. Only the previous afternoon John Carstairs had spent half an hour closeted with Mr Dennison, while the Honourable Mr Cadnam had kicked his heels in the newspaper reading room, and while that guardian of Southwark Conservatism had not exactly told his client that the nomination for the borough was his for the taking, yet he had contrived to leave him with the impression that all was not lost. In this way John Carstairs had been persuaded to bestow on Mr Dennison a cheque for £50 to defray certain additional expenses which that gentleman had accrued in pursuit of his candidature. And then that very morning had come news – well not news, but a rumour brought by a gentleman who had got it from another gentleman at his club – that Mr Bounderby was – to be promoted? Transferred to another position? Proceeding to dignified retirement at Richmond? At any rate to disappear from the Board of Trade in the very near future. All this had caused John Carstairs' mind to deviate wildly from the line on which it had been set following receipt of Mr Devereux's summons two days before.

'What exactly does it settle?' demanded Mr Devereux again, who perhaps had some inkling of this agitation.

'Eh? You must excuse me, Devereux. The fact is that there are certain things . . .' Intimate as he had become with the lawyer, John Carstairs did not quite wish to unburden himself to Mr Devereux on the subject of the Southwark nomination. 'What I mean to say is that if Farrier is returning to England, then something surely can be done.'

'But what precisely? No doubt he may call upon Mr Crabbe and take his opinion. No doubt he can write to Mr Dixey if he has a mind to. But that will not get him any closer to Mrs Ireland. Let a respectable medical man say that the patient is not to be seen, shock to her delicate sensibilities and so forth, and take it from me, seen she will not be.'

Perhaps a quarter part of John Carstairs' mind still dwelt upon Mr Dennison, the crack of that gentleman's knuckles, which seemed to him more obnoxious than ever, and Mr Bounderby's supposed departure, but it was an influential quarter.

'Then I don't see what we are to do.'

'Well – look here.' Mr Devereux gave the fire a tremendous poke and kicked over a couple of volumes of *Lorrequer's Commercial Law* in his eagerness to draw his chair closer to that of his guest. 'There are one or two things that I have picked up in the course of my own business. In my line of work one hears a lot about the stamped paper that is going around the City. Well, let me tell you that a great deal of it is Dixey's.'

'You don't say?' John Carstairs wondered again.

'I have seen no paper myself, you understand. But from what I hear he is properly in queer street. Trying to renew but at longer intervals, and then bringing in fresh bills to anyone that will accept them, which is not many in these circumstances. But that's not all.'

'No?'

'No. I chanced to be in Oxford the other day. A particular affair called me there, and I'm an Oxford man myself you know, whatever my present occupation may suggest to the contrary' – and here Mr Devereux laughed with what appeared to be genuine amusement. 'Well, I was walking past St John's College and something prompted me to step inside and call upon the cousin of Henry Ireland's that inherited the Suffolk property. Mr Caraway he is called, and you never saw such a man: I should think that to step outside his lecture room would be a great adventure for him and that a brisk walk would confine him to bed for a week. Anyway, he was pleased to send word that he would see me – I believe he thought I had come to trouble him about the property, and was relieved to discover that I had not. I was pretty frank with him – I always find that it pays in such matters – and he seemed quite agreeable to talk about Henry Ireland's will and its provisions.'

John Carstairs was now all ears, and Mr Dennison a mere speck in his mental cosmos. 'Did he indeed?'

'Well – yes. It appears there were two sums of money. I suppose the greater part of it must have come from old Mr Brotherton, for Henry Ireland was sadly embarrassed when he died. A certain sum to be laid out on Mrs Ireland's care and treatment, to be administered by her trustees, and a second sum – Caraway would not say how much, but substantial – set aside for her private use.'

'And so Isabel – Mrs Ireland – is an heiress? At any rate the money is her own?'

'It is her own if the doctors say she is fit to use it.'

'And now she lives in the house of one of her trustees, while her estate is administered by the other?'

'I suppose that is about the strength of it.'

'And not in sound mind?'

'That is what we have all been led to believe, at any rate.'

'It sounds d——d suspicious to me.'

'And to me. When we have Farrier here he may think there is a case to answer. Indeed I am certain of it.' Mr Devereux stood up from his chair and extended his arms in a gesture that, such were the dimensions of his chamber, nearly knocked Lord Eldon from the mantelpiece. 'By the by,' he remarked, 'I hear you are coming out for Southwark.'

'I – Let us say that it is not quite settled.'

'I should say that it was,' observed Mr Devereux, who appeared to know everything. 'Why, that Honeyman the brewer has given up politics, they say, to marry an earl's daughter. And as for Sir Charles Devonish, from what I hear the amount of his paper in circulation is well-nigh as great as your Mr Dixey's.'

XXVII

Flies and Spiders

'Is that you, Emma?'

'Yes, Mrs Latch.'

'I am still abed, I'm afraid. You had better bring me a cup of tea, if you would.'

'Certainly, ma'am.'

Esther lay in the big brass bedstead listening to the sound of the servant's footsteps descending the rackety stair. The fire, lighted three hours previously, had begun to go out and she could feel the cold creeping back into the room. She remembered William standing with his back to it as he had bade her goodbye. Turning towards the bedside clock, Esther found that it was nine o'clock. She lay motionless for a moment or two longer, her gaze fixed on a jacket that for some reason William had left draped over a chair-back, and then, rising out of the bed with an effort, got up and began to put on her clothes.

As she dressed she peered curiously out of the window. Six months in the metropolis had not dimmed Esther's interest in the complex organism of which she was a part. Even now, embarking on some solitary journey by train or omnibus, or out with William at some place of entertainment, she found herself mesmerised by the volume of people, the noise that they made and the costumes that they wore. 'How many people live in London?' she had asked, a fortnight into her stay at Shooter's Buildings, and William had told her a million or maybe two, but what did it matter eh? Curiously his matter-of-factness reassured her, gave her confidence in his ability to forge out patterns in the city's immensity. For her own part she remained awed, impressionable, and in the matter of window panes and the views from railway carriages ever inquisitive. Now, however, there was only

366

fog pressing against the glass and a handful of plane trees all but lost in vapour, and she turned regretfully back, curiosity quenched by a memory forming in her mind.

William had said something to her before he went out. What had he said? That he would be back late? That there was a message for Mr Grace that should be given to him if he called? She could not remember. Sitting on the bed once more to button her boots, she tried to imagine William's face as he had spoken the words, thinking that this would help her to recall them, but her head was still fuddled with sleep and she gave up the attempt, threw a last glance around the high, angular room and the window of fog and then went out onto the landing and carefully down the staircase.

A noise of fire-irons being clashed together told her that Emma, the maid-of-all-work, had transferred her operations to the drawing room. The promised tea lay sending up steam from the kitchen table and she drank it gratefully, the warm cup cradled in her hands, looking round the kitchen for signs of Emma's industry (experience had made her an exigent mistress, not a tolerant one) and finding them in the row of burnished saucepans and the tray of vegetables brought that morning from Shepherd's Bush market. Emma's wages were £12 a year and this both alarmed and comforted her, for she knew that six months before she had been earning the same sum herself, casting the same covetous eye over the remains of a joint that Emma cast as she carried it back from the dining-room table.

The noise of clashing fire-irons had now given way to a dull thudding sound suggestive of a mat being belaboured with a stick. A double rap at the door announced the arrival of the postman, but Esther, going to investigate, found only a single letter marked *Urgent: Mr Wm Latch*. In any case, as she reminded herself, no one ever wrote to her, for with the exception of her mother no one knew where she was. Returning to the kitchen, she poured a second cup of tea from the pot which Emma had left stewing, examined the bowl of lump sugar to assure herself that it had not been pilfered from and took the cup and saucer into the parlour where she sat down immediately in a chair and began to brood.

She became aware, without consciously registering the fact, that she was thinking of William. This did not surprise her, for she knew that this was, had been for as long as she could remember, the single topic on which her thoughts ran. In the half-year since she had left

Easton Hall she had come to acknowledge that William, if not the paragon of her imaginings, was a reasonably fair-minded and unexceptionable specimen of male humankind. This realisation, which had come gradually upon her, did not distress her, for she knew – years of observation had taught her – that there were worse than William, who did not at any rate mistreat her, take conspicuously more than was good for him to drink or swear more than ordinarily. Evidence of his regard, moreover, lay everywhere around her – in the house in which they lived, the third of a row of dwelling houses known as Cambridge Villas, in the person of Emma, whose deference Esther still found highly agreeable, and in the half-dozen dresses and other items of clothing, newly bought, that now constituted her wardrobe. In all, Esther declared herself more than satisfied with William. To be sure the 'Mrs Latch' with which Emma daily saluted her was a fiction – and she believed that Emma knew it to be a fiction – but, again, this did not distress her for she knew it to be a consequence of the step she had taken and the world in which she now moved and had her being.

And yet there were mysteries pertaining to her new life that she could not fathom, no matter how hard she tried. The first, and the most pressing to her mind, was the nature of William's business, how he came by his money, everything in fact that occupied him in the many hours that he spent beyond the walls of Cambridge Villas. Undoubtedly he worked for Mr Pardew – he was 'Mr Pardew's man' he told her proudly – and Mr Pardew, she understood, was a bill-discounter. Esther knew about bills – they had not been altogether absent from previous establishments in which she had worked – but what William had to do with their negotiation and collection she could not determine. Mr Pardew she had met but once, at a house to which William had escorted her in Kensington – a civil old gentleman, she had decided, with a jutting jaw, who had let fall the single remark that it was a fine day. Others of Mr Pardew's satellites – Dewar of the melancholy visage and a sharp-faced man named Pearce – she encountered but rarely. It was Grace that she saw most often and with whom, indeed, William seemed to spend the larger amount of his time. To meet with Grace, to talk with Grace, to plot with other persons in Grace's company: these, so far as she could establish, were the principal occupations of his day. To this end he went (she had picked this up from stray scraps of his conversation) on boat trips to Greenwich, to an office in the City – quite where in the City Esther knew not – and half a dozen other places. Yet the nature of the business on which he was detained she could not begin to elaborate.

'William,' she had asked at the end of the first month of their association, having already meditated the subject for some time, 'what is it that you do all day with Mr Grace?'

'What do we do?' William did not seem displeased by this enquiry, nor indeed by anything that she asked him. 'Why, we are Mr Pardew's men, you know, and we do his business.'

'Does that mean that you collect his bills? Or do you sit in his office? It is only interest that makes me ask.'

'Well now – not exactly. Today he and I were in Southwark, where we had an affair to settle, and then we had Mr Pardew's instructions to see a party at the Green Man.'

'And all this is to do with money?'

'Well, yes. That is – not exactly.'

More than this William would not say. Esther, seeing that some mystery hung over his silence, forbore to ask. And yet her curiosity was roused, still more at the time three months ago when they had exchanged the modest eyrie in Shooter's Buildings for the comparative splendour of Cambridge Villas. Of the financing and mainte-nance of Cambridge Villas – it was rented at £40 the half-year, for Esther had seen the receipt – William said not a word. He merely informed Esther of the change of lodgement, engaged a wagon for the transfer of their possessions and the deed was done. There were other changes that Esther noted at this time, quite apart from their removal to Shepherd's Bush. One was William's habit of darting up from his chair if a knock came at the door. Another was the look of vexation that passed across his face if he judged that a stranger was staring at him in the street.

'You won't guess who I saw today, Esther,' William exclaimed one evening at about this time, standing in the parlour with the dust from the street clinging to his clothes.

'No. Who?'

'Sarah! I was stepping out of the Green Man with Mr Grace and there she was, walking up Wellington Street towards me. It gave me quite a turn, I can tell you.'

'What is she doing in London?' Esther wondered.

'Ladies' companion. Upper servant. That kind of thing, she said. I took her address, so you must go and see her, Esther.'

'I should like to,' Esther said truthfully.

In the event the piece of paper with Sarah's address turned out to have vanished from William's pocket – it was quite mysterious, William declared, how it should have disappeared – and this desirable scheme had perforce to be abandoned.

Grace was frequently seen at Cambridge Villas. He had a habit of arriving in the early evening for supper, sleeping the night in the back bedroom and being found in the kitchen cooking himself an early breakfast in a frying pan.

It was with Grace, and at Cambridge Villas, that William had commenced on the most curious undertaking of all. Coming back to the house one afternoon after an excursion to Shepherd's Bush market, she had found a quantity of dark, rectangular bricks piled up on the kitchen table, together with a large pair of bellows. As she examined them, William came in from the parlour.

'Why, William, what are these?'

'These? Why, they are fire bricks. And that is a pair of bellows unless I am much mistaken.'

'Fire bricks?'

'Well – yes. The thing is that Grace and I have decided to go in for the business of making leather aprons.'

'Leather aprons?'

'I declare you sound like a parrot, Esther. Yes, leather aprons. The fact is that we have some capital secured between us and this seemed the best way of laying it out. Grace knows all about it.'

William explained that they intended to carry out the work in the back bedroom. As this involved the generation of a great deal of heat, it would be necessary to remove the stones from the hearth and replace them with fire bricks. He added that leather aprons were valuable items and much sought after, and that they fully intended to make their fortune. And yet Esther could not help noticing that the project was remarkably short-lived. A week, perhaps, was spent in this endeavour, during which the house grew so hot that Esther frequently retired into the kitchen. Afterwards nothing more was said of it and the back bedroom once more became Grace's occasional sleeping place and a store for the few things they had brought with them from Shooter's Buildings. Going in there on some errand in the days after the work had ceased, Esther found that the floorboards next to the hearth had been scorched quite black.

The tea had gone cold in her hand. Starting up in her chair, Esther became aware that the morning was now well advanced. Beyond the window the fog had risen, to be replaced by a weak and watery sun. The thoughts of William, Sarah, Bob Grace and the charred boards in the back bedroom still turning in her head, Esther went upstairs to her room and sat once more upon the bed. Driven by an instinct she did not quite comprehend, she got up and moved to the wardrobe where William kept his suits of clothes and plunged her hand into the pocket of the nearest. There was nothing in it, however, save a solitary guinea piece, which, having inspected it for a moment or two, she somewhat guiltily replaced. The instinct continued to oppress her, and presently she went over to a trunk that lay in the corner of the room and returned with a small packet of papers. Among these was the letter which Mrs Ireland had entrusted to her on the day before she had left Easton Hall, and she examined it carefully, allowing her mind to wander over the scenes it conjured up. Again, somewhat guiltily, she replaced the packet in her trunk, having first concealed the letter among several larger items, and retraced her steps to the vestibule. Here she selected an umbrella from the basket that contained William's walking-sticks and went in search of Emma, now at work in the kitchen.

'Emma! I am going out for an hour or two.'

'Yes, ma'am.'

'If Mr Latch returns, you had better say that I shall be back in the afternoon.'

'I can do that, ma'am.'

This instruction was superfluous. William, once he had quit the house after the breakfast-hour, was never known to return to it before the evening. Leaving Cambridge Villas, the umbrella swinging restlessly in her gloved hand, Esther wandered at first in the direction of Shepherd's Bush, where there were certain shops she might examine and certain necessary purchases she might make. The weather was less forbidding now, and she walked more rapidly, with a sharp eye for her surroundings and the people she passed, yet she knew that her journey had no obvious motive. Gradually, Shepherd's Bush market having no charms for her, she found herself moving eastward.

371

Eventually she stepped onto an omnibus which took her to the Charing Cross Road, and having alighted halfway along this thoroughfare – dense now with the noise of wagons and carriage horses stamping their feet as they waited at the crossings – continued into a vicinity that was familiar to her from her days in Shooter's Buildings. It occurred to her that such wanderings might bring her to William, much of whose business was still conducted in this former territory, but she forbore to approach the entrance to Wellington Street or put her head in at the door of the Green Man and instead walked along the Strand in the direction of Fleet Street. The memory of having come this way six months before now assailed her and she bit meditatively on her lip. The tap of her expensively shod boots on the pavement reminded her of the shabby footwear she had worn that day and she marvelled at the transformation that had come upon her. There was a flight of steps to her left leading down into a little shabby courtyard, and here a young woman of about her own age, rising to the topmost step, stopped and regarded her keenly.

'Esther! Is that really you?'

For a moment Esther could only stare at the girl's smiling face.

'Sarah! What a pleasure it is to see you.'

Sarah continued to examine her wonderingly. 'Isn't this a splendid piece of good fortune? But what brings you this way?'

Esther outlined, without any great conviction of motive, her journey from Shepherd's Bush. Sarah grasped her elbow.

'But I would scarcely have recognised you in your finery. You are looking very well, Esther.'

'Nor I you.'

Esther looked closely at her friend as she said this. In her six months in the metropolis she had acquired sufficient sophistication to comprehend that whereas she, Esther, was dressed expensively and respectably, Sarah's attire was perhaps a trifle too overstated for the season and the time of day.

'But come, dear, we must sit and talk now we have stumbled upon each other. You are in no hurry?'

'Not at all. I –'

Betraying by the manner of her walk her familiarity with the street and its environs – a glance into a shop-window here, a dart across the pavement there – Sarah led them to a decent-looking restaurant bar adjacent to St Bride's Church.

'The clergyman will want to come out and chase us away, I shouldn't wonder,' Sarah remarked mysteriously. 'Are you still a religious girl, Esther?'

'I suppose not,' Esther replied, acknowledging that she had not ventured into a church since her arrival in London.

'They are such flats, to be sure, those parsons.'

'What is a flat?' Esther wondered.

'Why, a gaby, a young innocent. Like Margaret Lane, to whom Raikes said that he had shot the seraph and she believed him.'

All traces of Sarah's previous melancholy had vanished, Esther noticed. Sitting in the window of the restaurant bar, with one dainty boot escaping from the folds of her skirts, she seemed in the highest of spirits.

'No,' she explained, in answer to Esther's question, 'I had a bad time of it when I first came here. Indeed I stayed once in a boarding house in the Borough where I scrubbed the stairs for my keep. But now I am with Mrs Rice and all is well with me.'

'Who is Mrs Rice?'

'She is a widowed lady who lives in Kennington, and was married once to a sea-captain, and I am her companion you know and have all the ordering of the meals and the carriage to take us driving, and it is all very pleasant. But Esther, what is all this about William?'

Dazed by the rapid flow of information that had been conveyed to her, Esther could only repeat mechanically:

'What is all what about William?'

'You knew that he had seen me? Indeed, I have seen him several times for I am often come this way on business.'

'On business for Mrs Rice?'

'Well yes – that is, in a manner of speaking. But is it true what they are saying?' She drew her head closer to Esther's. 'You mustn't mind telling me, dear, for I know when a secret is to be kept.'

'Is what true?' Esther said blankly. 'What secret is to be kept?'

'Oh I did not mean to upset you. Truly I did not. Only you know that William is often seen about with that Mr Grace?'

'Mr Grace? Yes, I know of him.'

'I never could abide that Grace. Well, they are saying . . .'

'Who is they?' Esther wondered in bewilderment.

'Why, Mr Farrow that keeps the Green Man for one. Dear me, I hardly like to tell you if you really do not know, but – you have heard talk of the bullion robbery in the summer? Everybody has been speaking of it.'

'The mail train going down to Folkestone? Yes, I have heard of it.'

'Dear me, it cannot be that you do not know – but they are saying that Grace – I cannot speak for William, of course – was in some way concerned.'

'You are saying this to hoax me, Sarah – you are indeed.'

'Certainly I am not. Why, let me tell you what I myself have seen. I was at the Green Man a fortnight ago – I have – business – that occasionally takes me there – when I saw Grace pass a French coin, one of those big Napoleons, to Mr Farrow, and heard Mr Farrow say that he would need to mend his bellows to deal with such an item.'

Esther became aware that her hands were gripping the table-top before her so tightly that it seemed almost that the wood must break apart in her hands. She said, shortly, for it was the only thing she could think of saying:

'I am sure William has nothing to do with this.'

'Very likely not. It is that Grace, I am sure.'

'He is Mr Pardew's man, in any case. The bill-broker that has an office in Carter Lane.'

'And Grace is Mr Pardew's man too, dear. Why, I declare that they are like perfect brothers together. But come, let us talk of something else. Indeed, that man over there has been staring at us these five minutes past. How vulgar people are!'

They talked idly for a moment or two more, but Esther had not the heart for conversation. Beneath her meek exterior she was consumed with nervous anxiety. That William, her William, should be spoken of in connection with this great crime seemed to her a terrible thing. The most terrible and unjust thing she had ever known. And yet as Sarah continued to put questions to her, to which she replied only in listless monosyllables, she was forced to consider certain incidents to which she had been party, certain fragments of talk passing between William and Grace that had come her way. All this frightened her further, and yet she was forced to acknowledge that the alarm was not disagreeable to her, that it gave a piquancy to the situation in which she found herself. As her mind worked in this way her interest in what Sarah was saying altogether lapsed, so that the other remarked:

'You are out of sorts I daresay, dear, and would sooner be alone.

374

But now we have found each other, we must not give each other up again.'

'What is your address?' Esther asked dully.

'Mrs Rice says she is tired of the house and means to sell it. You had better ask for me at the Green Man. That is the best way I think.'

Standing on the corner, the bells of St Bride's Church as they struck the hour quite obscuring their farewells, Esther watched her friend depart along Fleet Street, hobbling slightly with the odd irregularity of her gait. Thirty yards along the pavement a fat man with a red face and a waxed moustache stood staring into the window of a gentlemen's outfitter and Sarah stopped to speak to him. Something in her gestures now conveyed to Esther what trade it was that brought her to the region of Fleet Street in her best clothes on an afternoon in November. Not wishing to see the result of this chance encounter, she turned on her heel and moved disconsolately away.

Returning to the house in Shepherd's Bush an hour later she discovered that William had sent word to say that he should not be back until morning. It was by now nearly four o'clock and the vestiges of daylight had already begun to recede. Beyond the kitchen window dirty yellow fog was beginning to creep back into the dreary garden and she sat in a chair and watched it, thinking all the while of William, Sarah and the events of the morning. A thought struck her and she moved silently up the staircase to the landing, here proceeding past her own room and into the back bedroom, not inhabited since Mr Grace had last slept in it a fortnight since. Here the atmosphere was cold and damp. A jug of stale water stood on the dressing table and she trailed her fingers in it for a moment, brooding over the task that she had set herself. Then she bent down and, resting one hand on the iron fender, stooped to examine the hearth. This, it occurred to her, was unlike any other hearth she had ever seen. The fire bricks lay piled up around its interior where formerly the ordinary hearthstones had been. Beneath them a steel plate of some kind had been fixed to the floor. It was not, however, either of these novelties that drew her attention, but the boards on either side of the hearth. These were scorched almost black with heat, indeed at some points altogether burned up, the wood itself turned into a dark mass like charcoal. Squatting now on her haunches, she ran her hand curiously over the boards. They were not, as she had first assumed, quite uniform in their appearance for stuck in the surface here and there were several fragments of some yellowy substance. After a moment more Esther ran her finger over the wood and gently prised one of the fragments away with her thumbnail, placed it carefully on her palm – it was perhaps the size of the head of a pin – and inspected it closely. Whatever the metal was, it seemed clear to her that it had at any rate undergone some melting process in the hearth.

She squatted there for a long time with the yellow fragment in her hand. There was a brooch on the bosom of her dress that William had bought her a month since and she wondered if the money that had purchased it had been stolen. This thought gradually worked upon her to such an extent that she unpinned the brooch and placed it on the charred board before her. In this way another long period of time passed. She was woken from her brooding by the sound of the church clock striking five and a realisation that the pain in her legs was becoming unendurable. The room was now quite dark, she saw, and the landing beyond wreathed in shadow. It occurred to her that she could not stay here for ever, that she should find some occupation by which she could pass the next few hours. A part of her wished that William was in the room with her, and another part – perhaps the larger part – was grateful for his absence.

After a few more moments of reflection she got up and, walking carefully down the dark staircase, went into the kitchen and lit a lamp. Then, with the lamp in her hand, she climbed the stairs once more and turned into her own room. Here, again, she delved into the trunk containing her papers and emerged with Mrs Ireland's letter. The two things that preyed upon her mind were, she now acknowledged, connected. The connection, she once more acknowledged, was William. Again she wished that William were in the room next to her, and yet she shrank from the questions that she knew she would wish to ask him. The room, the bed on which she sat, the mirror by the wall in which she glimpsed her reflection – all these things were suddenly distasteful to her, and, pressing the letter into the pocket of her dress, she carried the lamp hastily downstairs. Still for a moment she stood uncertainly in the hallway. A sound came to her ears and she realised that it was a footstep beyond the door. A sudden apprehension overtook her and she shrank back into the corner of the vestibule, her face averted from the turning handle, and it was thus that William found her as he stepped hastily into the house, his silk hat pushed back from his forehead and a little cloud of condensation hanging about his features.

'Good gracious, Esther! You seem quite taken aback to see me. Whatever is the matter?'

'I did not think – Emma said – that you would be back until the morning.'

'A man may change his mind you know,' William said easily. 'The fact is that there is something of mine which I cannot do without, and I have to fetch it. There, will that satisfy you?'

He was an astute man in his way, and he knew, as he said this, that his return was not the cause of Esther's alarm, that there was something that agitated her beyond his unlooked-for knock at the door.

'Whatever is the matter?' he said again, pressing his hand against her arm. 'Why, you are trembling like a leaf.'

She felt the pressure of his hand without seeing it. Her eyes were searching his face, which seemed to be unnaturally pale in the half-light of the hall.

'I have seen Sarah,' she said.

'Sarah? Sarah Parker? What did she have to say?' Esther watched him as he said this, and it seemed to her that his face was paler still.

'She said' – Esther halted, for the words would not properly form in her mouth – 'she said that you and Mr Grace had stolen a great sum of money.'

'Did she?' William laughed. 'Then she is a greater fool than I took her for, and when I next see her she shall be told so.'

He made to move past her into the body of the house, but she clung onto his arm and restrained him.

'Oh William! I have been up to the back bedroom – where you and Grace were at work – where the hearth is all scorched – and there are pieces of gold on the boards.'

'It's a lie! Sarah has been filling your head with nonsense and you are fool enough to believe her.'

'But William – oh!'

She felt rather than saw his hand strike her cheek. The smart of it did not so much hurt her as startle her and she stood for a moment rubbing her palm against the side of her face, altogether bewildered by the sensations that stirred within her.

'I should not have done that,' William said with a curious remoteness, as if he were speaking to himself. 'But it is hard to bear such things – there!'

Again she was startled by the violence of his embrace, and she let out a little cry not of fear, exactly, but of some emotion that she could scarcely identify. Just as the thought that her brooch was contraband had failed to shock her, so she submitted – not unwillingly but with a curious feeling of excitement.

'That's my good girl,' William said, after a moment had passed. 'Now, do you believe what Sarah told you?'

'I do not know what I should believe.' Her head was still against his shoulder. 'But, William, are you in danger?'

'Nothing to speak of. But, see, I must be gone from here. Only for an hour or so, but there are things I must do.'

'Oh William, if you would only stay. Promise me you shall.'

'I can't, Esther. A couple of hours. I promise you. Look' – he caressed her with his hand and she followed the movement of his fingers wonderingly along her dress. 'Say you shall be here with supper on the table and a jug of beer on the hearth and I shall tell you everything.'

'That is an easy thing to promise,' Esther said, her eyes alight.

'Well – perhaps it is. Wait –'

Esther stood meekly in the hallway as he strode up to their bedroom. Here the sound of cupboards being opened and shut could be plainly heard. Then he hurried back down the staircase, pausing only to rest his hand upon her hair.

'I'm sorry that I struck you, Esther.'

'It is nothing,' she said.

When he had gone she moved into the parlour and sat by the fire in a reverie. Curiously the thoughts that rose in her head were not of the previous five minutes but from far back in time. In her imagination she was back at Easton Hall, hanging out linen on the currant bushes before the kitchen garden, with the sun slowly declining over the edge of the wood and the cries of the rooks echoing in her ears. She brooded over this picture for some time, the faces – William, Sarah, Mr Randall, the master in his black garments – rising and falling before her, until she became aware that an hour had passed, the fire had burned low and that the evening was well advanced. Hastily she donned her coat and bonnet and, purse in hand, went out in the empty street. A walk of three minutes brought her to a row of shops, where she made various necessary purchases – a particular sweetmeat that she knew William favoured, a particular relish that might garnish his beef. Then, stopping at the public house at the end of the row, whose entrance emitted an enveloping glare of yellow light, for the filling of her jug, she sped away home. The house was dark and the silence within broken only by the tick of the clock. Swiftly she placed her purchases upon the kitchen table and went to light the lantern in the hall. There was a noise beyond of footsteps approaching the door and she went eagerly to open it.

*

In the region of Newington Butts, hard by the Walworth Road, squeezed in behind a pair of factory chimneys and altogether dwarfed by a gasometer lately installed by an optimistic gas company, lies a row of mean little houses, very tottery and shaky in their appearance – as if they were about to tumble over and might need propping up with some giant crutch – named Bright Terrace. From an upper room in one of these properties, at a window quite half of whose panes had fallen away and been stuffed up with rags and pieces of old brown paper and beneath which the wind passed unhindered, Sarah sat looking out across the dismal street. An hour had passed since she had concluded her transactions in the Strand – it was now about four o'clock in the afternoon – but she had not yet divested herself of the costume in which she had sallied forth that morning or indeed even taken off her bonnet. Instead she crouched almost motionless in an armchair looking first at the street, which was altogether devoid of human life, then at the two white hands that lay in her lap and finally at the mantelpiece a yard or so from her head. There was nothing remarkable about the mantelpiece other than the fact that it supported a tea caddy with the representation of a royal personage on its side, yet an onlooker who sat beside her might have observed that the gloomy street and the pair of pale hands held no joys for her and that it was to this unremarkable object that her gaze returned.

The room in which she sat was perhaps more commodious than the servants' quarters at Easton Hall, but not much better furnished. There was a stout iron bedstead jammed up against the wall, a little wardrobe and an occasional table on which reposed a water jug and a basin. A handful of coals – very small coals they were – lay on a sheet of paper in the grate, but the fire had not yet been lit. Upon this somewhat melancholy scene there looked down a couple of prints of gauzy dancers in the correct Parisian manner and a picture of a bowl of peonies bought at the threepenny stationer's. All this Sarah saw, or rather did not see for by now her gaze was concentrated almost exclusively upon the tea caddy. Ten minutes or a quarter of an hour went by in this way, until there came a sound – very faint and tremulous at first, then mounting in volume – of footsteps ascending a staircase, a knock at the door and an old woman with a hard eye and the lower part of her face wrapped up in a comforter put her head into the room.

'Oh it is you, is it, Mrs Mayhew?'

'Your light wasn't a-shining,' this lady observed. 'I was wondering whether you was still hout.'

'Well I am not. It is too fatiguing for a girl to be out the entire day.'

'Hoity toity. When there's work to be done.'

'There shall be a half-sovereign for you in the morning, indeed there shall be.'

'Those that wants supper should know where supper comes from,' Mrs Mayhew remarked, as if pronouncing a general truth which every inhabitant of Bright Terrace would do well to take to heart. And then she went away again in a flurry of crashings and cross little door-rattlings, the wind rose once more through the variegated window and rustled the prints of the French dancers on the wall, children's voices sounded in the street and then fell away to nothing, and Sarah sat still in the armchair with her white hands folded in her lap and her eye fixed on the tea caddy a yard away from her head. Her lips moved and it may have been that she was talking to herself, but if so her speech was soundless and did not contend with the noise of the wind. A ginger cat that Mrs Mayhew sometimes conciliated with scraps of fish came twisting round the door, which had been left an inch or two open, and sat down by the hearth, where it began examining its whiskers and Sarah became dully aware of it. Finding that the spell of her contemplation was broken, she rose up from the chair, stretched her arms above her head and let them fall, took a pair of florins from the pocket of her dress and placed them on the mantelpiece and then busied herself with various utensils that lay in a heap by the side of the grate. Still as she did this, conveying a china plate and a bone-handled knife to the occasional table and then delving into a cupboard for the half of a loaf and a morsel of butter, her mind did not cease to turn on the subject that had occupied her for the past hour.

The encounter with Esther had discomposed her, not merely because it had recalled to her a life that she had thought past, but because it had awakened in her resentments which she imagined that time had begun to soften but which now seemed to jut out from her imagination quite in the old way. At the same time the contrast between the life that Esther now led and her own circumstances could not but fail to strike her and distress her. Why should she not be Esther, she wondered, and live in a villa at Shepherd's Bush and have a servant girl to tyrannise? In this way Sarah waxed very wrathful, assuring herself that she had been ill-used both by providence and those persons about her. And yet, she told herself, she knew things about Esther that Esther herself did not know. She was aware, too, that much could be made of this knowledge, should she so choose, and the thought of the power thereby conferred on her was very pleasant.

Brooding continually on these and other matters, one eye still fixed on the tea caddy as she chewed her fragment of bread, she returned to her chair. Certain scenes in her past life, she now realised, were very vivid to her: an afternoon at Easton Hall when she and William had escaped Mrs Finnie's vigilant eye and gone wandering by the river and grown very confidential; Esther's face as she bent over her work; the rooks in the elms. On her forearm there was a red mark extending beyond the muslin cuff to her wrist, and she remembered the day on which it had been placed there and the passions that had caused it. The thoughts were not pleasant to her and she stood up again with such a start that the ginger cat made off prudently in the direction of the door. It was in her power, she knew, to ameliorate this hurt, to cause pain to others that would be a satisfaction to herself. And yet . . .

The tea caddy was now in her hands. She did not know how it had come there. She could not remember picking it up. The face of the royal personage stared up at her. The red-faced gentleman she had met in the Strand had said that he was a military man and had come within a yard of the royal personage at some review, and she had not known whether to believe him. There she was with her hand inside the tea caddy. How had it come there? She had not wished to place it there, surely? And yet she was shaking the contents out onto the surface of the occasional table. There was not a great deal. A silk handkerchief that she had had from her old mistress as a present five years since. A little jet dog with a partridge stuck in his mouth. A string of buttons looped up and tied in bow knots at the end. Each of them reminded her of some passage in her life without in any way calming her or causing her to reflect on what she did. And now there it was, a scrap of paper which she could not read, but which she knew stated an hour at which she should meet the person who had sent it, signed off with a pair of initials in black ink which she could interpret for she had traced them with her fingers a dozen times.

The paper was a month old, and in ordinary circumstances would have been thrown swiftly away, but for some reason she had kept it and brooded over it in the way that a heathen native broods over his fetish of feathers and straw. A month ago, she recalled, William had given her a five-pound note, but there had been no more largesse from that quarter. The vision of Esther in her villa, with her meek servant, came to her again and she gave a little stamp with her boot upon the bare floorboard. She knew that if she did what her mind now counselled her to do she would injure William as much as Esther, and yet the knowledge of it did not dissuade her. And so she meditated on until the room grew dark and voices sounded on the stairs – men and women together – and the house became animated around her. Finally, when the evening had come, with her mind still calculating, yet feeling that she could stay no longer in the confined space, she rose to her feet, clasped a jacket around her meagre shoulders and ventured out into the street.

It was past six o'clock and the nocturnal life of Newington Butts was at its early peak. Costers' barrows were drawn up by the roadside, their arrays of produce lit by flaring gas-jets. Dull-eyed men leaned out of public-house doorways to converse with children sent to fetch them home. All this Sarah saw as she walked along, silent and solitary in the great crowd of vagrant humanity. There were a couple of soldiers in red coats – a recruiting sergeant and his mate, she thought – marching in tandem on the far side of the street, and she stood and watched them, thinking – though she knew in her heart that it was the merest fancy – that the younger of them resembled her brother. Queerly the thought affected her more powerfully than any of her previous reflections, and she quickened her pace and hastened on. The dark alleys and courts ran away from her and the people seemed to disappear under her gaze. There was a police station on the corner of the Walworth Road, and having stopped for a moment to gather her jacket more tightly around her shoulders, she bowed her head and stepped inside.

XXVIII

Questions and Answers

—. . . Come now, Miss Spalding, there is nothing to fear if you will tell the truth. Where is William Latch?

—I do not know. Indeed I do not.

—What are his habits? Where does he go?

—To the Green Man in Wellington Street, I think. And to Mr Pardew's in Carter Lane.

—Pardew?

—He is Mr Pardew's man. That is what he says.

—Where does his money come from? Is he a warm man?

—Indeed, sir, he seems to do well by his business, for there is always money about the house.

—More money now than there was formerly?

—There has always been money. Perhaps. I do not know (*weeps*).

—There is no need to agitate yourself, indeed there is not. What work did he say that he was engaged upon?

—Only that he was Mr Pardew's man. That he collected his bills and went upon his errands.

—And yet he wished to manufacture leather aprons. Had he experience in such a trade?

—Not to my knowledge.

—Did leather goods of that kind come into the house?

—I think not.

—Were you ever admitted to the room when he and Bob Grace were at work?

—Never. I was told that the fire was so hot that it would be a danger to me.

—How long did this process continue?

—A week. Ten days. Sometimes the house grew so hot that I went

384

out and walked on the Green or among the market stalls.

—Did you not enquire what he and Grace were about?

—I was told that I should mind my business and it was no concern of mine . . .

—. . . How came you by this letter?

—It was given me by Mrs Ireland.

—Yet it is dated six months since. You made no effort to deliver it?

—No.

—Why is that?

—I cannot say.

—Did Latch know of the letter?

—I cannot say.

—Have you any knowledge of its contents?

—. . . (weeps)

—Come, the sergeant shall fetch you water. Have you any knowledge of its contents?

—I have read it, yes.

—Was she who wrote it in her right mind, would you say?

—I cannot say.

—You cannot say?

—No, I cannot (weeps).

*

QUESTIONING OF THE MAN PEARCE

Q: Come now, let us have some account of you.

A: Account of me! You shall hear nothing from me, unless I've a mind. If I was a gentleman you would not cotch me here and you knows it.

Q: On your arrest at Epsom you had twenty pounds in your pocket. How did you come by it?

A: It was honestly earned, that is all I can say.

Q: Well, let us leave that for a while. What is your connection with the man Pardew?

A: None. I never met him before this Derby Day.

Q: A pair of shoes were taken from your lodgings and were found to have fragments of gold embedded in the soles. What do you say to that?

A: I have no knowledge of it.

Q: And leather gauntlets, badly scorched, as if held to a flame. Have you any knowledge of that?

A: The same. Will you keep me here all night?

Q: If I have a mind I shall keep you here all week. Who is Bob Grace?

A: He is a fellow I know.

Q: What sort of a fellow?

A: A very nice fellow. But you had better ask him.

Q: I prefer to ask you. You know that he was employed by Mr Pardew?

A: He may have said so. It was nothing to me.

Q: And yet you were seen in his offices on two occasions by independent witnesses. What have you to say to that?

A: Nothing.

Q: Mrs Sharp, who keeps your lodgings, states that on a day in the summer of this year she came upon forty sovereigns in the cupboard of your room.

A: What was kept in my cupboard was no business of hers.

Q: I must warn you of the peril you are in, indeed I must. Tell us about Pardew.

A: There is nothing to tell.

Q: Were you ever in Suffolk?

A: In my recollection, no.

Q: And this is not yours?

A: It is a pretty toy. But no, I never saw it.

Q: And yet you would know how to use it?

A: You may think what you will. It is no concern of mine.

Q: I would have you flogged if it were in my power.

A: But it is not. I have done nothing. Let me go.

XXIX

The Firm of Pardew & Co. is Wound Up

Mr Pardew sat in the office at Carter Lane with its bleary window and its view of the dome of St Paul's. It was ten o'clock in the morning, an hour at which it might have been supposed that the life of the room would have reached its zenith, that all manner of schemes would be in a state of strenuous advancement. In fact Mr Pardew was alone and silent. Dressed in his customary sober suit, with his stick laid out on the desk before him and with a newspaper unfurled beneath his gaze, his outward demeanour, as he alternately bent his eyes over the black print and glared up at the bleary window, seemed in no way to differ from that of other mornings. And yet his clerk, had he been in the room, might have noticed that Mr Pardew's gaze strayed ever so occasionally to the door and that a sudden noise from the street caused him to jerk up his head with a quite singular expression of interest. He was one of those men who are able to conceal their frets and anxieties, and though all manner of terrors gnawed at his vitals, still he was determined that none but himself should know of their existence.

An hour had elapsed since Mr Pardew had arrived at his office, and that had been spent in ceaseless brooding. A further thirty-six had passed since Pearce had fallen into the hands of Captain McTurk. Mr Pardew did not know the exact circumstances of this falling, but he knew some of them, for he was the kind of man who has confederates even among the ranks of his enemies. Whether it was that Mr Pardew possessed an ally at the court of Captain McTurk I do not know, but it was a fact that on the evening of Pearce's arrest a whisper of it had reached his ears. A less cool-headed man than Mr Pardew would, I think, at this juncture have taken his leave, fled on some boat to the Continent, or to some remote part of the country where he could lie hidden, but Mr Pardew, having considered the situation in his ruminative way, pondered what Pearce might be induced to tell Captain McTurk and what he might not, had decided that a short period of grace was still allowed him and that there were one or two affairs that it required him to settle before his departure.

Putting down the paper, Mr Pardew delved into his desk and emerged with two sheets of writing paper. Taking up his pen, and again pausing to consider a sudden clatter of cartwheels from the street beyond, he scrawled a few lines upon the first sheet, delved in his desk once more for an envelope and addressed the letter to *Jas Dixey Esq., Easton Hall, nr Watton, Norfolk*. The second sheet he brooded over for several minutes. Then, with somewhat more care than he had brought to the first letter, he wrote the following:

I am summoned out of town unexpectedly. I cannot say when I shall return. The enclosed will cover all immediate expenses. It may be that enquiry will be made of you regarding my whereabouts. If so, you may honestly say that you know nothing of them.
 Yrs affnly
  R. Pardew

This Mr Pardew sealed up in a second envelope together with a twenty-pound note and addressed to *Miss J. Tomsett, Laburnam Villas, St John's Wood*. It may be that as he searched for the stamp that was to adorn it his mind returned to the vision of himself and a young woman with a pink-and-white complexion riding in a carriage by the river at Richmond, but if so his face did not betray the fact. Barely had Mr Pardew completed the business of stamping the letters and concealing them in his breast-pocket than there came a determined rattling at the door. Very coolly, but making sure that his stick was well within his line of vision, Mr Pardew returned to his desk, sat down at it and had just completed the manoeuvre when Bob Grace, somewhat dishevelled and with his hat pulled down low over his eyes, tumbled into the room.

It would have been immediately apparent to any impartial observer that the relationship between Mr Pardew and his clerk, whatever its former ambiguities, had now taken on a somewhat different aspect.

'What are you up to then?' Grace demanded, standing in the centre of the room and breathing stertorously. 'Locked up in here like an old spider eh?'

'I could ask the same of you,' Mr Pardew remarked, baring his teeth in a somewhat ghastly smile, while making sure that the stick lay within his reach. 'It is gone ten.'

'Oh yes,' Grace countered. 'And half a dozen bills wanting renewing at six weeks, I suppose? And a p'liceman not waiting outside my house and following me all the way here until I give him the slip at Blackfriars?' His eye, roving fearfully around the room, fell upon a travelling bag placed in a little recess by the door. 'You're a-going to split, ain't you? That's what you're up to, isn't it? Well, I'm not going to stand for it, do you hear?'

'I am not going to split, as you put it,' Mr Pardew observed, a shade less emolliently. 'I have been sitting here going about my business since half past eight.'

But Grace's eyes – very muddy eyes they were, that looked as if their owner had been awake half the night – were still trained upon the travelling bag.

'What business?' he nearly snarled. 'There ain't no business left to do, and you knows it. Only p'licemen waiting outside a fellow's house and the man as knows everything about it sitting there with a travelling bag all neat and packed.' He lowered his voice. 'Perhaps I ought to go and tell that p'liceman something that might interest him. Like who did for a certain gentleman down in Suffolk for one. Like who played that trick on old Mr Fardel for another. No, you *shan't* hit me with your blessed stick!'

For Mr Pardew, rising up from his desk, very red and with his chin bristling up, had lashed out suddenly with his walking-stick, missing the body of his clerk, who skipped nimbly out of the line of his stroke, but smiting the floor so hard that the stick broke in two pieces and fell from his hand.

'You old villain!' Grace sang at him. 'Go on! Hit me and I'll do for you, see if I don't.'

But Mr Pardew's moment of wrath had passed. He knew that no good could come from attempting to strike his clerk again, knew also that only a display of sweet reasonableness would achieve the object he had in mind. Accordingly he picked up the two halves of the stick and placed them carefully on the desk, his mind working all the time over the best means of obtaining this end. Grace, meanwhile, looked haplessly around him, made a nervous little movement in his employer's direction, thought better of it and subsided. As he did so there came another rattle at the door, less forceful than Grace's and suggestive only of a tentative enquiry.

'That'll be Dewar,' Grace confirmed. 'Saw him a-follerin' me up the street as I came by.'

Grace's surmise was correct. Pushing open the door, Dewar came timidly into the room. He was dressed not in the uniform of the railway company but in a nondescript suit of black. As with Grace, there was a vacancy about his eyes indicative of some deep disquiet.

'Why ain't you at work, Dewar?' Mr Pardew wondered.

'Suspended from duty aren't I?' Dewar replied mournfully. 'Got a letter telling me to stay at home while inquiries were being made.' Having spoken the words he seemed overcome with anxiety, sat down heavily in a chair and gazed about him with an air of terrible hopelessness. 'Was a policeman called at the house last night,' he said. 'Saw him coming and managed to slip out, and my wife told him I was away, but what's to be done? What's to be done, eh?'

Seated once more at his desk, hands playing with the fragments of the broken stick, Mr Pardew regarded his lieutenants. He was aware that the game was nearly up, that if an attempt were being made to apprehend Grace and Dewar then his own turn would not be far behind. In his subordinates – Grace, wary and indignant at his side, Dewar silent and reproachful in the chair – he had no interest. They could go to the Devil as far as he was concerned. And yet Mr Pardew knew that men who go to the Devil very often wish to take other men with them. Consequently he softened the set of his features, made a small gesture of appeasement with his hand and smiled in what might have been interpreted as a confidential way.

'There is no need for alarm,' he proposed. 'Indeed there is not. Naturally, Pearce being taken complicates matters.'

'Pearce is in quod?' Grace whistled. 'Then we're done for, you old Jew!'

'Listen to me. There is no need for alarm. Who is to know what Pearce may say and what he won't? As for you, Dewar, you have been questioned half a dozen times and no one any the wiser.'

'That's so,' Dewar conceded. 'But it was a torture to me and you knows it. I've half a mind to tell all I know simply to give myself ease. 'Twould be a relief to me to do so, indeed it would.'

'You've fixed us good and proper, that's what you've done,' Grace announced. 'Where's William Latch if it comes to that? Called at his house yesterday and there's no one there and no maid to answer the door neither. See that bag there on the floor, Dewar, my boy? He's going to split, that's about the strength of it, and leave us behind. What do you say to that, you old villain?'

Mr Pardew continued to smile.

'Nobody is to be left behind,' he observed. 'Come with me if you wish. Only there are no funds to take us. Look! Here is my pocket book. Let me only go out to the bank in Eastcheap and we may be in France by this evening.'

There was a silence as Grace and Dewar considered his words.

'You're an old villain,' Grace said. 'What's to stop you taking your hook? I'll come with you to the bank, that's what I'll do.'

'With policemen looking for you in the streets? You had much better stay here.'

'And have you disappear while I'm waiting? You old villain, you.'

'You shall have charge of my travelling bag while I am gone. Will that satisfy you?'

They continued to wrangle about this until Dewar's voice, mournful but insistent, broke over the argument.

'I won't go.'

'You won't go?' Grace looked at him queerly. 'Why won't you go, eh?'

'My wife's near dying,' Dewar told him. 'I shan't leave her whatever I've done.'

'But say that Pearce goes Queen's Evidence?'

'I don't care,' Dewar repeated sullenly. 'My wife's near dying. I shan't leave her.'

They wrangled a little more, but the gravity of their situation both scared and calmed them. In the end it was decided that Grace and Dewar would remain in the office, together with Mr Pardew's travelling bag, while the latter departed in a closed cab to the bank in Eastcheap, from which he would return in not more than half an hour. Silent and subdued, Grace and Dewar watched him go. Then, as there came no noise from the street and as Mr Pardew had obliged them by locking the door firmly behind him, Grace's spirits revived a little.

'Why don't you want to go when you has the chance?' he enquired curiously of Dewar.

'It's as I said. I can't leave my wife.'

'But you could be took and put into quod and she'd miss you all the same.'

'That's true, I suppose. But where shall you go?' Dewar's face as he asked this showed a wholly naïve interest, as if the idea of anyone quitting their native shore was quite remarkable to him.

'Go? Why, anywhere there's a man to pay for it. But he's a sly one, that Pardew. I shall have to watch him, I daresay.' Grace's tone as he said this was that of some wealthy householder who suspects that his butler may be stealing sherry. 'But I had the measure of him just now, didn't I, Dewar? Makin' him leave his bag here when for two pins he'd have taken it away and gone.' The travelling bag, still lying in the recess near the door and apparently very tightly packed with Mr Pardew's belongings, for whatever was in it seemed to strain against the leather sides, appeared to interest him and he strode towards it and prodded it with the toe of his boot. 'Tell you what, Dewar my boy, let's haul up this item on to the desk and take a look at it. Ain't it heavy though? Ten to one the old villain has the rest of the gold in here. Is it locked? No it ain't. Now that's curious.' His fingers played for a moment over the clasp, where-upon Dewar, standing a yard or two behind him, heard him let out a tremendous shriek, a veritable wail of rage as if the metal of the clasp burned red-hot.

'Whatever's the matter?'

'Don't you see? Look how the old villain has swindled us!'

Dewar followed his gaze. Then he too drew in his breath, for the travelling bag contained nothing but packets of lead shot.

'Why there aren't no clothes at all!'

'The villain!' Grace screamed. 'The old villain! I'll cut his throat before I'm done. I'll tell every tale there is to be told, see if I don't. Do you know that he had his own partner murdered once? And a man down in Suffolk on account of some scheme he was a party to? Why, I'll . . .'

And then he ceased his expostulations, for he became aware of a noise in the street somewhat above the ordinary sounds of passers-by going about their business.

'What's the matter?' Dewar wondered. 'What is it?'

As if by way of an answer there came a fierce rattling at the door-knob, which twisted violently in its groove. A shout, indistinct but unambiguous, sounded from the street. Grace cowered by his desk.

'They're going to break down the door,' he said grimly. 'You'll see.'

To Dewar, standing a short way behind him, his eye, too, fixed on the quivering door-knob and the frame of the door itself, which now began to shake beneath the weight of the repeated blows delivered to it, it seemed as if the situation in which he found himself was not quite real. He discovered that he registered only small things – a little vein in Grace's head that pulsed and bulged like a roving snake, the packets of lead shot lying in the travelling bag, a pen-nib fallen to the floor and resting in a crack between the boards. Not quite knowing why he did it he bent down to retrieve the nib and placed it in the pocket of his coat. On the instant there was an almighty crash and the door flew open with a force sufficient almost to drive the frame from its hinges.

Of what followed he had only a confused recollection. There were policemen in the room, three or four of them at least, who, though they moved in his direction, seemed fascinated by Grace, who, dashing to the door, made a mighty effort to fling them off but was beaten down and hurled into a corner with his hands thrown up to protect himself and his feet kicking out like pistons. Tumbling over a chair and evading the grasp of a man who seemed to trip and fall over the travelling bag as he came, Dewar found himself standing in the doorway, the noise from the ransacked office ringing in his ears, but apparently alone.

Immediately he fled down the street, not pausing to look behind him, reached the corner – he was now almost come to the margin of St Paul's Churchyard – and stopped to catch his breath. There were two officers following him, he realised, but a good way behind and not moving with great speed. Dodging in and out of the knots of passers-by, who regarded him with keen interest, he sped on towards Cannon Street in blind panic, came to a crossing and rushed upon it, heedless of the traffic. Before he could gain the further side the shaft of a cart struck him on the breast and threw him down. A man helped him to his feet and enquired if he were injured.

'Hurt? No, no: it's all right.'

To the man's surprise, and that of other people standing near him, he walked on quickly, hardly feeling any pain. But within a few moments there came a sensation of nausea, an ominous warmth in the back of his throat, and he stopped and vomited up a quantity of blood. Sympathetic passers-by were all about him – he could see no sign of his pursuers – but he threw them off, drops of blood spraying onto his jacket cuffs and his shirt-front. Passing the corner where Cannon Street leads into Watling Street, the memory of an ancient conversation came into his head, of Dunbar standing in the deserted boat-house at the loch-side, giving his address and telling him to look him up. What was the number? 18. He was sure it was 18. He was conscious now of a pain between his ribs, and knew that he was conspicuous to the people through whom he passed. These onlookers shrank from him as he moved desperately along the street. Number 18 was a corn chandler's, with its goods spilling out onto the pavement, but there were rooms above and he seized upon a boy who was standing in the shop doorway and demanded:

'Does Mr Dunbar live here? I must see him. Mr Dunbar.'

Seeing his bloodied clothes and the agonised expression on his face, the boy started back in fright. As luck would have it there was a noise of footsteps on the wooden stair behind him and Dunbar, a brown-paper package under one arm and a newspaper in his hand, moved slowly into view. Seeing Dewar, he set down the brown-paper package and looked at him keenly.

'Who's this? Why it's Dewar, who wondered why men should collect eggs!' Then his eye fell upon Dewar's crimson shirt-front. 'But heavens, you're injured, man. What's the matter with you?'

'It's nothing – truly.' Dewar's mouth was full of blood as he spoke. 'Only I must come inside. Let me come inside!'

A whistle sounded at the end of Watling Street. To the surprise of Dunbar, whose hand still grasped him by the shoulder, Dewar sank to his knees on the pavement amid the corn chandler's spreading paraphernalia. Here the policemen, coming up at a run with their faces very red, found him in a state of insensibility with Dunbar feeling his pulse for signs of life. At first it was proposed that a cab should be fetched, then, when an examination of the prisoner had been conducted, a police doctor and a stretcher. Shortly afterwards, when the crowd of onlookers had dispersed and the police ambulance rolled off through the dust, the corn chandler's boy emerged from the shop with a bucket of water and began silently to wash the blood from the grey stone step.

XXX

Some Destinies

FROM THE DIARY OF THE REV. JOSIAH CRAWLEY,
CURATE OF EASTON

15 November 1866

Aghast, on returning to these pages, to find three years now gone since first I came here. Three years! And what is there to show? And yet there have been passages in my life when I could account for each passing day, so plenteously filled were they with good work done on the Lord's good business. Now the memory of the week past is like a blank page in a book from which the words have ebbed away, quite beyond the power of calling back. Thought of unburdening myself to Margesson, but – as ever – shrank from the candid confession of my woes, from which no good ever came. A month now since I last saw Ely.

17 November 1866

Winter encroaches on every side. White mist, that in these parts hangs over the fields at dawn, still there at dusk; geese abound on the lakes and meres; haw berries ripe on the hedge. My landlady confined to bed with a bronchial ailment, necessitating on my part the perform-ance of many irksome chores. Mrs Forester much gratified by my condescension. 'There's many a gentleman wouldn't stand for such treatment, &c. She is a good woman and I would perforce do my best by her. A curious letter from Cousin Richard. A living in which he has some faint interest at the coast here to fall free this next quarter-day. What would be my opinion? Wrote, as best I could, on my behalf, sending my tutor's commendation, the letter Warden Plender addressed to me when I took my fellowship, but I have suffered too much disappointment to set great store by it.

20 November 1866

Much troubled by conscience, I determined to make a visit to the Hall, to which every species of rumour continues to adhere. Dixey not seen in the parish for a month, a bailiff absolutely heard enquiring of him in Watton High Street, &c. Rain falling incessantly through my journey gave the estate a yet more melancholy aspect than I remembered: the grass grown up a foot high by the driveway; the window panes at the lodge smashed and broken. Approaching the house, in which no sign of life seemed apparent, I found myself visited by the queerest apprehension and misgiving, to the extent that I could scarcely bring myself to belabour the great front door. Receiving no answer to my repeated summonses (which clamour resounded inside the house, I fancied, like the roll of some ghostly drum) I wandered around the side of the house. Here all was fallen into the rankest desuetude: weeds grown up in the kitchen garden; the door of the keeper's cottage swinging from its hinge and a pig peering out from within.

It was by this time perhaps three in the afternoon, the light begin-ning to fade, and I would gladly have taken my leave, thinking that I could do no good, that the place was altogether shut up and deserted, when a face appeared at the window – a queer pale face rising up out of nowhere and, I will confess, giving me such a start as I never before felt in life – and a man, whom I recognised as Randall the butler, came stepping across the grass. Having had much courtesy from him in the past I prepared to greet him civilly, only to detect a look of great anger in his face. I had no business here, he told me before I could speak a word – Mr Dixey would not see me, would not see anyone, and I should do no good. I replied, as coolly as I could in the circumstances. That I regarded Mr Dixey as my friend, that my duty as a Christian and as a minister of God brought me here, not only on behalf of Mr Dixey but another person that I knew rested beneath his roof. At this Randall seemed transformed by an emotion that might either have been fear or solicitude. Mr Dixey would not see me, he repeated. I should go at once, or he could not be held responsible for what might happen. At this, I confess, I began almost to laugh and yet there was something in the man's expression that stifled the laugh in my throat. The great gloomy house, Randall's pale face regarding me in the half-light, the thought of Dixey roaming the empty corridors – for I believe that no servant other than Randall remained – the woman confined in some remote chamber: all this worked on me to such an effect that, to my shame, I stole away through the kitchen garden and on into the woods with the howls of Dixey's dogs in their kennels ringing in my ears, regained the road with my heart pounding and a dreadful sense of there being someone or something almost at my heels. And yet there was nothing, only the mist and the movement of the trees in the wind, and so I made my way home very troubled by what I had seen and the thought of what it might portend.

24 November 1866
So I am to be Vicar of Holkham! A letter from Cousin Richard setting out the terms of my incumbency realising in me the greatest exultation. There is a fine rectory, apparently, and 800*l* a year besides.

27 November 1866
To Ely.

*

In the study, his hand supported by the ferrule of the square desk, the stuffed bear stiff and cumbersome a yard from his elbow, Mr Dixey watches at the high window. The gravel drive that lies beneath it, its inflexions curving away around the rank lawn and the fountain with its dripping caryatid, is quite empty. It is a week now since anyone came along it and that was only the postman – Sam Postman, Mr Dixey thinks he is called – who rapped at the door for two minutes without an answer and then reluctantly departed, leaving the letter propped up against the door. It is a wonder, Mr Dixey thinks, that the servants did not collect it. Then he remembers that the servants are gone, away to Watton, Lynn and Norwich, and that he watched them go. There is a suspicion – a footfall in the distance, a door seeming to close far away – that Randall may still be in the house, but Mr Dixey cannot be sure.

In the end he retrieved the letter himself. It lies now on the desk beside him, flanked by the display cabinets, the specimen cases and the bead-eyed bear. In the grate a coal or two still flickers red-white, and there are other letters stacked on a chair to the right of the hearth, for Mr Dixey has been burning his correspondence. Great dockets and folds of foolscap, many of them crossed over and sealed and recalling the days before envelopes, all gone crackling into the flames. Looking at the piles of ash banked up on either side of the winking coals, Mr Dixey wonders from where in the human heart rises the urge to reconstitute that which has been obliterated. The only trace of a Dodo that endures, apart from a half-dozen pages of contradictory drawings, is the half of a leathery hide kept preserved in the Oxford museum. All that is left of the Moa are a few bones found in the dirt of a New Zealand cave. Perhaps, Mr Dixey thinks, at some future point an anatomist will attempt to reconstruct his life rather as the naturalists attempt to reimagine *Didus ineptus* from the accounts of the Dutch travellers to Mauritius two centuries before. The thought is curiously consoling, but the vision it conjures up of persons unknown to him busily at work here at the centre of his private world is more than he can bear.

Guided by some prompting he cannot quite explain he slides open the lid of the nearest display case, brings out the two marsh harrier eggs that lie within and balances them on his palm. They weigh nothing, so light, he thinks, that they might float. Regretfully he crushes the eggs beneath his fingers, breathing in the faint odour compounded of earth, albumen and decay. There are other things than letters to destroy, he thinks.

The letter, Mr Dixey divines, has destroyed his hopes. Now there are connections to be made. People will no longer see him as himself but as part of a complex chain of incident, collusion and desire. That is the way of things. His hand is on another display case now: an eagle's egg taken from the loch at Strathspey. Again he crunches it between his fingers. Once, as a young man, he shot at a golden eagle high on a hill-top in Sutherland, but at the moment he raised his gun to his shoulder the bird tracked away, lifted by a spiral of wind he could not see, and the bullet went wide. He would have fired again, had not the sun suddenly risen up from behind a cloud to blind him.

A movement beyond the window catches his eye and he stares once more into the pale December light. There is a carriage approaching down the gravel drive. Mr Dixey can see the coachman's grey head bobbing up and down as the transom shifts beneath him. As he looks on the carriage makes a half-turn into the wide space before the front of the house and stops. Watching the people who emerge from it –

a sharp-featured middle-aged man commands them, whom Mr Dixey has never seen – he thinks that if he wished he could throw open the window and fling more of the eggs down upon their heads. He has a sudden vision of the shells, white and papery, slowly descending like snowflakes through the chilly air.

He takes a last look through the window. Curiously the men – there are four of them – seem in no hurry. Conferring, heads angled together above the gravel, they have the air of pleasure-seekers, anxious to inspect their guidebooks before setting forth on their tour of the grand house. Mr Dixey moves rapidly down the great staircase into the hall and thence into the servants' quarters. The kitchen cat, cleaning her paws on the big oak table, watches him as he goes. The kitchen door is half-open, has been so for some time apparently, for there is a little whirl of old leaves, dirt and grass-ends upon the threshold, and Mr Dixey passes through it. In the distance he can hear the dogs howling. He cannot remember when they were last fed, but it is not less than three days since.

The first belt of trees is within reach now and he plunges into it, stands breathing heavily with his gaze fixed upon the house. He wonders how long it will be safe to stay here, concealed in this thicket, and whether there may be other men approaching silently through the grounds to cut off his retreat. As if to confirm this suspicion something stirs in the dense bank of foliage to his left. Instantly he hastens away down the woodland path. It seems to him as he moves that the place is unnaturally still, that there should be birds calling, but that they are gone – the dogs have stopped howling, he registers – and that his breath sounds unusually loud in his ears.

There is another stirring – so faint as to be hardly perceptible but a stirring nonetheless – in the trees and he turns round, more in curiosity than alarm, to inspect what it is that haunts his steps, here in a Norfolk wood on a winter's afternoon in the thirtieth year of the reign of little Victoria of Saxe-Coburg, the niece of the sailor king, whom once he saw on a hot afternoon in Windsor with the brass bands playing and the rooks cawing frenziedly above the distant elms.

The rest you know.

*

'Nothing to be discarded, mind,' Captain McTurk instructed as they came into the house. 'Everything to be kept.'

The lower parts of the house are empty and undisturbed. In the servants' quarters a silence. In the pantry a rat sitting on its hind-quarters eating at a rancid ham. In the drawing room a half-inch of dust upon the lacquer table and the old Dixeys in their frames.

In Mr Dixey's study a great chaos: the windows raised and the curtains billowing in the wind; Bruin cast lengthways upon his paws and a great lump torn out of his ursine head; a litter of broken shells and scattered books; a microscope thrown upon the carpet with its lens smashed in two.

'He has destroyed – everything,' said Captain McTurk.

'Not quite everything, I think,' remarked Mr Masterson. 'See here.'

On the great table, under a dome of glass, a circular plate, spread with moss, on which sit a pair of perfect ruddy-brown eggs and an inscription, printed in elegant italic script on a slip of paper. Captain McTurk bent to examine it.

'*Pandion haliaetus*. What is that?'

But Mr Masterson had read his Latin at Charterhouse School.

'Osprey eggs,' he explained. 'A great rarity, I believe.'

*

All this time, needless to relate, Captain McTurk and his men had been ceaselessly at work on the public's behalf. It is remarkable, is it not, the volume of evidence that will suddenly spring to hand when the perpetrator of a crime has finally been unmasked? Let a man stand charged with stealing a sheep and immediately a parcel of corroborating detail will be found torn open and spilling its contents at his feet. Witness A will allege that he enquired of him the best way of cooking mutton, witness B confirm that he attempted to borrow from him a carving knife and fork, witness C relate that he was seen gathering the materials for a mint sauce, and out of all this testimony and supposition is instantly constructed a vast edifice of guilt. So it was with Captain McTurk's investigation. He had fished sedulously in the turbid lake concealing the affairs of Mr Pardew, Mr Dixey and sundry other persons connected to them, and all kinds of curious things had come up struggling on his hook. He had been to Easton Hall and examined its contents most thoroughly. He had made a visit to Jemima at her villa in St John's Wood, consulted Mr Caraway of St John's College and called upon Mr Dunbar in Watling Street but found the latter gone into the country. The landlord of the Black Dog had wilted beneath his gaze, Mrs Farthing had curtseyed in his presence and it was rumoured that His Grace the Duke of —— had been absolutely compelled to forsake his ducal mansion and spend an exceedingly comfortless hour in the little room behind the stable yard in Northumberland Street.

In this way all manner of confidential remarks had been made into Captain McTurk's ear and all manner of confidential documents reluctantly entrusted to his care. Half a dozen counterfeit cheques drawn on provincial banks by persons unknown; private communications sent by Mr Dixey to his lawyer; a little scrap of paper – heaven knows where it came from – in which a gentleman signing himself 'R.P.' (Mr Pardew's initials, certainly, but no doubt shared by many other persons) conveyed certain immensely suggestive instructions: all these had somehow found their way into Captain McTurk's grasp, and it was felt by those who monitor the achievements of our public servants that the captain had excelled himself.

And yet, flattered as he was by these encomia, Captain McTurk was uneasy. It is one thing to have amassed a quantity of evidence, forensic and circumstantial, which may be of use to a prosecuting counsel. It is quite another to secure a conviction. Captain McTurk had not the slightest doubt that certain crimes, and certain of them very heinous crimes, had been committed. A quantity of fraudulent cheques had been passed through the banking system. An audacious robbery had taken place on the Dover mail train. A gentleman had apparently been bludgeoned to death in Suffolk. That gentleman's wife had been held, apparently against her will, by another gentleman who proposed to marry her and thereby secure the inheritance with which her late husband had entrusted him. That each of these misdeeds was, to a certain degree, connected with the others Captain McTurk was sure. And yet, given that two of the persons he desired most urgently to interview were dead, the second in a manner so dreadful that Captain McTurk shuddered to remember it, and the third unaccountably vanished from sight, the proof might be difficult to obtain. And so, as he sat in his office above the stable yard, with Mr Masterson returning almost daily with the results of some freshly executed commission, Captain McTurk searched for some key that would unlock these mysteries.

For a while he thought he had found it in Mr Crabbe and yet Mr Crabbe, it soon became clear, was quite equal to his stratagems. What p.319 **'Sir William Smith's Dictionary'** *A Dictionary of the Bible* (1860–3) by Sir William Smith (1813–93).

p.319 **'Mrs Brookfield's new novel'** Possibly *Only George*, published in 1866.

XXIII

p.326 ***'Cornhill'*** The most successful monthly periodical of the mid-Victorian age, launched by George Smith in January 1860 with Thackeray as its founding editor.

p.326 ***'Fraser's'*** Founded by James Fraser in 1830, with William Maginn as its first editor, *Fraser's Magazine* was initially known for its riotous High Tory bohemianism. Notable 'Fraserians' included Thackeray, Carlyle and James Hogg. In later years, under the editorship of G. W. Nickisson, it became a more conventional chronicle of Victorian life.

p.330 **'as sober as Father Mathew'** The Irish priest Theobald Mathew (1790–1856), crusader for total abstinence, who having campaigned successfully in his native land arrived in London in 1843. Jane Carlyle, who attended one of his gatherings, described it as 'the only religious meeting I have ever seen in Cockneyland which had not plenty of scoffers at its heels'.

XXX

p.414 **'one of Mr Leighton's Attic paintings'** Frederick Leighton (1830–96), celebrated Victorian classical artist, president of the Royal Academy, 1878, raised to the peerage shortly before his death.